CAMP SLASHER LAKE

VOL. 1

CAMP SLASHER LAKE: VOLUME ONE
Copyright © 2022 Fedowar Press, LLC

www.FedowarPress.com

All rights reserved. No part of this book may be used or reproduced in any manner whatsoever, without written permission, except in the case of brief quotations embedded in articles and reviews. For more information, please contact publisher at info@FedowarPress.com.

ISBN-13 (Digital): 978-1-956492-13-2
ISBN-13 (Paperback): 978-1-956492-15-6
ISBN-13 (Hardcover): 978-1-956492-16-3

Edited by 360 Editing (a division of Uncomfortably Dark Horror).
Editors: Candace Nola. Mort Stone. Darcy Rose.
Cover Design by Don Noble of Rooster Republic Press
Interior Design by D.W. Hitz

Copyright to individual works contained within this anthology are property of their respective authors.

Camp Hell and the Hot Tub Hotties by Patrick C. Harrison III; Bad Party by Brian McNatt; Tall, Dark and Rancid by Gerri R. Gray; The Backwoods Decapitator by John Adam Gosham; The Handyman by Nicholas Stella; The Children of Dagon by Carlton Herzog; The Faith by Derek Austin Johnson; The Deathless by Vincent Wolfram; A Love to Die For by J.D. Kellner; Work Retreat by D.W. Hitz

Camp Slasher Lake: Volume One is a work of fiction. Names, characters, places and incidents are either products of the authors' imaginations, or the authors have used them fictitiously. Any resemblance to actual events or persons, living or dead, is entirely coincidental.

This book is dedicated to the Horror Community at large. Without the help of those involved on social media, websites, and groups dedicated to Indie Horror, this book may not have been possible. You are the best. Thank you for your support.

CONTENTS

FOREWARD   1

CAMP HELL AND THE HOT TUB HOTTIES   3
by *Patrick C. Harrison III*

BAD PARTY by *Brian McNatt*   39

TALL, DARK AND RANCID by *Gerri R. Gray*   69

THE BACKWOODS DECAPITATOR   89
by *John Adam Gosham*

THE HANDYMAN by *Nicholas Stella*   123

THE CHILDREN OF DAGON by *Carlton Herzog*   163

THE FAITH by *Derek Austin Johnson*   195

THE DEATHLESS by *Vincent Wolfram*   219

A LOVE TO DIE FOR by *J.D. Kellner*   269

WORK RETREAT by *D.W. Hitz*   293

ACKNOWLEDGEMENTS   345

ABOUT THE AUTHORS   346

FOREWORD

This whole thing came about as a dream that I wasn't even sure was possible. Surely there weren't as many people interested in old-school slashers as I would have hoped. I mean, I'm usually in the minority, so would there even be interest from other authors? Readers?

When I put out the call for submissions, I was instantly shown that I was not alone, and the feeling was phenomenal. The influx of interest and authors who had stories to tell blew me away, as did their tales. One after another, the quality of work from those wanting to take part only grew and grew. There came so many great pieces, that even after culling down to the best fitting, there were still too many for one book.

So here we are. Volume One of a two-part adventure into blood, tension, and fear. On behalf of all the contributors who have graced these pages with their works, enjoy.

D.W. Hitz
Fedowar Press

Camp Hell and the Hot Tub Hotties

by Patrick C. Harrison III

Owen Returns to Camp Hell

RICK ASTLEY'S BARITONE VOICE BELTING out "Never Gonna Give You Up" through the crackling speakers of a boombox tuned to the max, didn't quite drown out the screams of children.

Day one was always like this, Owen knew. It was his third season at Camp Helton—Camp Hell for short, naturally—and he knew damn well the blended screams of excited kids and those suffering separation anxiety would last most of the day. But these first twenty minutes or so, as children filed from the camp bus and their parent's cars, were the worst. The absolute fucking worst.

"Yo, Owen," Joey said, trotting up to where Owen stood, leaned against the log railing outside the camp's welcome center, the sun beating down on him, "I thought you said you weren't coming back for another season."

Joey was another camp counselor. He was short but stout, muscular, and he kept his black hair permed. He always wore shirts that were way too tight and with the sleeves rolled up,

CAMP HELL AND THE HOT TUB HOTTIES
by PATRICK C. HARRISON III

even the yellow Camp Helton shirt which he currently wore, with its silhouette depiction of woodlands and a wolf howling at the moon.

"Yeah, well, I'm here, ain't I?" Owen said, turning his head away from Joey and looking past the welcome center, into the woods where he could just make out the first few cabins before the lake. He chewed on a toothpick, wishing it was a cigarette. He fished around in his jean shorts for a pack of Camels, knowing damn well his cancer sticks were on his nightstand in the camp counselor cabin, the CCC.

"I knew your ass would be back," Joey said, leaning against the railing beside Owen and crossing his arms, pushing his biceps out more, as if this would impress somebody. "What kinda chicks we working with this summer? Any lookers?"

"Like it matters to you," Owen said, shaking his head and scooting a foot or so away from Joey so no passerby would mistake them for queers. "You porked that Wilma chick last year. Beached whale Wilma, everyone called her. Didn't stop you from diving in headfirst."

"That's a goddamn lie!" Joey said in mock—or perhaps serious—anger, turning his head toward Owen with a glare.

"Did you get lost swimming around in her cooch, Joey? To be honest, I was worried for your life when you bedded down with ol' Wilma. Didn't seem safe without a life preserver."

"I said, that's a goddamn lie!"

"Gentlemen!" came an uneasy shout from behind them, a shout that wanted to be stern but only came off weak and pathetic.

Owen turned his head without moving an inch from the railing, seeing Dorian Proctor, the camp manager standing just outside the welcome center doors. Of course, it was Dorian Proctor. He lived for Camp Helton the way other men lived for baseball or fishing or banging chicks. He was here all summer and much of the rest of the year, hosting campouts and whatnots for the Boy Scouts and Girl Scouts and whatever goddamn religious youth groups he could convince to pay his precious little camp a visit. And he didn't even own the place; some old grandma with the last name Helton did.

"Gentlemen," Proctor said again, a little calmer and steadier this time, "we can't be speaking that way in front of the children."

"Yeah, Joey," Owen said with a smirk, turning back to face the children that were piling out of vehicles and giving hugs to parents, a couple of which were glaring in Owen and Joey's general direction. Owen smiled and waved.

"Sorry about that, Mr. Proctor," Joey huffed. "Owen was telling lies."

"Lies or not, no more of that, please," Proctor said, laughing nervously. Then, walking past Owen and Joey, spreading his arms out wide, he said in a cheerful voice, "Welcome to Camp Helton, children! Welcome to Camp Helton!"

Owen chuckled as Joey punched him lightly in the arm. The last several kids were filing from the bus, most of them between six and ten years old. Some looked grim, others chipper. There was a little blonde girl with eyes so light blue that Owen could see their brilliance from thirty feet away. There was a scrawny kid with glasses, picking his nose as he descended the steps, who was likely to be bullied by half the older kids at camp. There was a fat kid carrying a bag of Cheetos and a black kid with hair styled like Michael Jackson. There were two girls holding hands, singing some New Kids on the Block song. Then, coming off the bus last, were three kids in single file that looked exactly the same—three red-headed boys, sporting the same pale skin and the same green shirts and khaki shorts.

"Look, triplets," Joey said, elbowing Owen. "Identical triplets."

"I'm not blind, dumbass," Owen said, elbowing back.

The triplets smiled identical smiles and waved at Owen and Joey, who each gave a little wave back. Owen was about to comment to Joey on how those three shits were gonna get burnt as fuck in the July sun, when Brooke Fitzgerald entered his field of vision, walking through a horde of children, smiling

CAMP HELL AND THE HOT TUB HOTTIES
by PATRICK C. HARRISON III

her bright smile as she greeted them individually. Brooke had big blonde hair, big tits that pressed against her yellow Camp Helton shirt, and big toned thighs extending from her short white shorts.

"That, Joey," Owen said, "is why I came back for another year."

"God, yes," Joey said, tugging at his crotch. "I'd sell my soul to get with Brooke."

"She's mine this year. You wait and see."

"Remember that pink bikini she wore last year? Christ almighty, I jerked off to that image at least a hundred times over the last year."

Owen turned his head to Joey with a look of disgust. "Jesus, Joey. Don't tell me that shit." Beyond Joey, Owen saw three more camp counselors walking toward the group of children, all three female, all three looking not half bad. Another blonde, an Asian chick, and a black chick, each of them looking well-proportioned and wearing camp uniforms as tight as they could find them. The Asian girl glanced over at Owen and smiled; he smiled back.

"You heard what they installed at the CCC this spring, didn't you?" Joey said, breaking Owen's concentration.

"No, what?" Owen said, annoyed.

"They put in a hot tub out on the deck. It's the back deck too, so ol' Proctor won't be able to see any shenanigans from his cabin."

"Wait, there's a hot tub at the counselors' cabin?" Owen said. "Are you serious? Don't fuck with me, Joey."

"Scout's honor." Joey held up three fingers to show he was telling the truth.

"Jesus Christ, this is going to be a great season."

Oscar Cleans Up

OSCAR MENDEZ HAD BEEN AT Camp Hell (like many of the counselors, Oscar preferred the name Camp Hell over Camp Helton) nearly as many years as Dorian Proctor—going on two decades. It wasn't that he enjoyed his job or liked children or even liked the scenery of mountainous woodlands on a crystal-clear lake; Oscar had worked all these years at the camp because it was perhaps the only prospective employer that hadn't bothered to run a background check.

Oscar was the camp's cook. He was also convicted of a double murder back in '52, then released after nineteen years for good behavior.

He was content at Camp Hell. There were certainly worse jobs. Living in a trailer nestled in the mountains miles away from any major city, he was lucky to have any job at all. Proctor would call him up whenever a Scout troop or church group had plans to visit the camp, and he'd drive his little Datsun pickup the ten miles to the camp and setup shop in the kitchen, cooking stews and chilis and burgers and fried catfish—all for a never-ending line of snot-nosed children.

Summers, naturally, were the worst. Rather than small groups of kids brought to Camp Hell by an adult leader or two, they were dropped off by the dozens, all screaming and whining in various states of excitement or panic. And who was to care for these twerps? Why a bunch of horny teenagers branded as counselors, of course. If there was anything more useless and stupid than a child, it was a horny teenager.

At 56, Oscar wasn't too fond of the stupid or the horny. He just wanted to be left alone. And that's what the evenings were

CAMP HELL AND THE HOT TUB HOTTIES
by PATRICK C. HARRISON III

for, after the kids had stuffed their faces and filled their bellies, and after the counselors had made their way back to the CCC to partake in whatever activities they partook in with the kids asleep and the moon hanging high.

He lit a cigarette in the dim light of the camp kitchen, then ran a damp rag across the stainless countertop for the umpteenth time. Johnny Cash was tuned low on the boombox above the stove, and Oscar sang along as he blew out blue smoke. A dinner of beef stew and cornbread had been served for night one—an easy meal to clean up. Only the cherry cobbler dessert, which crusted the inner rims of the pans with blackened batter, could cause any sort of challenge for Oscar. Thus, he had those pans soaking in the industrial-sized sink overnight.

There was half a pint of tequila in the walk-in freezer, nestled secretly amongst a pile of shrink-wrapped pot roast, and Oscar thought a good, long swig of the stuff would make mopping the kitchen floors a little more pleasurable. A little burn in the throat and buzz in the brains. Tucking the rag into his back pocket, Oscar smiled and inhaled on his cigarette as he moved toward the freezer.

His hand was on the stainless handle, just beginning to give her a turn, when he heard a thump just outside the kitchen.

Not a thump, really, but a thud, like something landing heavily on the tiled floor of the hall outside the kitchen, leading one way into the cafeteria, where all the brats ate their meals, and the other way to the entrance door, where all the brats made their arrival from the campgrounds.

Oscar stopped, listening, trying to hear over the boombox, which was now playing Patsy Cline, low but loud enough that Oscar wasn't sure if he was hearing anymore movement outside the kitchen.

"That you, Dorian?" Oscar called, stepping over to the boombox and flicking it off. "I ain't got no more stew if that's what you're here for. Already tossed it."

He listened for a moment but heard nothing more. Taking a few steps toward the swinging doors leading to the hall, he tried peering out the circular windows, seeing nothing out of the ordinary, only a dim hallway, lit by nothing more than moonlight shining through the hall's windows.

"Got a little cobbler left, though, if you want it," Oscar offered, taking another step forward.

But Dorian Proctor would have answered Oscar's calls, had he been the one visiting the dining hall. Dorian wouldn't stand outside the swinging doors in silence. He was too much of a pussy for pranks, Oscar knew.

"Hey," he called, "you kids need to get your asses out of here! You're supposed to be in your cabins. Go on! *Ándale!*"

Still nothing. Not a sound. No thump or thud. Not a giggle or rustle of movement. Only the constant buzz of kitchen fluorescents and the summer singing of katydids. Oscar edged up to the swinging doors, putting his face to one of the circular windows, his breath causing it to fog.

There was no one in the hall that Oscar could see. But he had heard a thud — he was certain of it!

"Dorian?" Oscar said, feeling uneasy all the sudden. He was sweating in his pits and on his forehead. "That you, *hombre*?"

After several long seconds of silence, Oscar huffed at his own cowardice and pushed the swinging door open, stepping out into the hallway, a scowl on his face, prepared to greet any pranking camper with a hailstorm of profanity-laced shouts. But there was no camper; at least, not an entire camper.

Sitting in the middle of the wood plank floor not far from the door that led outside, was a head — the shaggy-haired head of a ten or eleven-year-old boy, his face spattered with dried blood, his eyes and mouth wide with shock, his neck a mangled mess, spilling the last of his dark, oxygen-deprived blood on the floorboards.

"What in the hell?" Oscar said, taking a nervous step backward, not completely believing what his eyes were seeing.

Just then, a clatter came from the other end of the hallway, in the direction of the cafeteria. Oscar, his heart thumping at a furious pace, whipped his head in that direction, his eyes wide

CAMP HELL AND THE HOT TUB HOTTIES
by PATRICK C. HARRISON III

as they stared into the dark doorway leading into the cafeteria. Slowly, a form emerged from the darkness, filling the doorway.

Oscar gasped. He was on the verge of screaming when his throat was ripped out.

Brooke Looks in the Mirror

BROOKE FITZGERALD LOOKED AT HER nude reflection in the bathroom mirror, frowning.

The haze of her hot shower still hung in the air, and the mirror was foggy but clear enough to see the pimple that had sprung-up on her chin in the last day or so. Sure, Brooke had full breasts that had yet to lose their fight with gravity, and, sure, she had strong legs and a plump bottom, and, sure, she had emerald-colored eyes that mesmerized men and women alike, but…a zit on her chin was un-fucking-acceptable. She'd turned twenty in May; her days as a zit-faced teenager were supposed to be over.

It was little more than a pink bump, so she resisted the urge to squeeze it. Sighing, she looked over the rest of her body, only mildly pleased. Most young ladies would kill to have a body like hers. And *all* men would kill for a night in her bed. But for Brooke, her stomach could be a little more toned, her teeth could be a little whiter, and her bush could be trimmed a little neater. There wouldn't be any stray hairs sticking out from beneath her bikini bottoms—lord, no—but that bush still looked a bit unkempt.

Owen would want those bikini bottoms laying on the floor of his room, which was right across the hall from Brooke's room and only two doors down from the bathroom she was currently in. In the CCC, all six counselors stayed together, each with their own room, one bathroom for the girls and one for the boys.

Brooke had held out on Owen last year. She'd been going steady with Lance at the time. But he'd joined the army in January and was now stationed overseas. Lance couldn't very

CAMP HELL AND THE HOT TUB HOTTIES
by PATRICK C. HARRISON III

well expect her to not have any fun in his absence. No, she wouldn't hold out on Owen this year. She would let loose. She might even play around with one of the female counselors; Brooke was adventurous in that way. And she was pretty sure Akira was a lesbian. It was only their first day of camp, but Brooke had caught Akira looking at her a number of times.

Shrugging at her reflection, Brooke grasped the neon green bikini draped over the towel bar and put it on, giving herself only a momentary glance in the mirror as she opened the door and made her way out of the bathroom, where she nearly bumped into Owen as he made his way toward the stairs that would lead them to the day room, which opened onto the deck with the newly-installed hot tub.

"Watch where you're going, doofus," Brooke said, playfully swatting Owen's arm. He was shirtless and wearing swimming trunks, an unlit cigarette jutting from his mouth. "Those are bad for you, you know." She pointed at the cigarette and scrunched her face.

"Spending a month of my life each year watching a bunch of crazy kids is bad for me," Owen said. Removing the cigarette from his mouth and holding it between the two of them like a relic, he continued: "This, my dear, this is therapeutic."

"Keeps you from going all nutso on the kids, huh?" Brooke said, smirking.

"Keeps me from tossing them all in the middle of the lake without life preservers," Owen said, taking a second to look her up and down. "You're looking good, Brooke. Looking nice. I like the suit. Let's get down to that hot tub. Joey has it bubbling already, and he snuck in some high-quality hooch and even higher quality grass."

"I'm sure he did," she said, rolling her eyes. "I'll be down in a minute. Gonna check in on Akira first."

Proctor Goes Peeping

"YOU'RE DOING A WONDERFUL JOB, Dorian. You're diligent and intelligent and the most trusted camp manager in the Western Hemisphere."

Dorian Proctor said these affirmations aloud to himself beneath the glowing moon, standing just outside his small cabin, a stone's throw from the fishing pier reaching out into the gentle lake waters like a middle finger.

"No one suspects a thing," Proctor added.

He and the counselors would rotate working the night watch, spending the hours between 9pm and 6am walking amongst the cabins with a flashlight in hand, a whistle around one's neck, and a walkie talkie clipped to one's belt. Proctor always took the first night, not only because the new campers could be quite anxious and rowdy after day one, but also because he, himself, was quite excited to have the campers at Camp Helton. Even if he wasn't the night watchman on this first evening, he would undoubtedly lie in bed awake until the wee hours.

"Watchman One to CCC," Proctor said, keying the walkie talkie, "all campers are secure in their cabins, and I am beginning my patrol. Over."

Snowy static was the only return when he released his thumb from the walkie talkie. The other, of course, was in the Camp Counselor's Cabin, presumably on an end table in the day room with the volume turned all the way up. But Proctor was aware of how well counselors in their teens and early twenties listened for the walkie talkie. And Birdie Helton's decision to, for whatever insane reason, install a hot tub at the CCC,

CAMP HELL AND THE HOT TUB HOTTIES
by PATRICK C. HARRISON III

would make it even more difficult to reach the counselors after daylight hours.

"Watchman One to CCC, over," Proctor said, a little more forceful this time.

"This is CCC, Watchman," came the staticky voice of LaKendra, followed by a squeal of laughter, as if she'd been tickled. "Over and out!"

Proctor sighed, wanting to call the girl out on her improper radio etiquette, but decided against it. He had better things to do on this night.

Though the moon was nearly full, providing suitable light for navigating the interior of the camp, Proctor flicked his flashlight on, scanning the area around his cabin. There was a gentle breeze, rustling leaves and pine branches only slightly, and causing lazy waves to lap at the lakeshore. Looking east, away from the lake and toward the woods, he could make out several of the campers' cabins, scattered amongst the trees, a good thirty yards separating each one. Further up was the dining hall and the showers, and beyond that the welcoming center. And if Proctor were to trek far enough northeast from his current position, which he wouldn't, he would come to the CCC, which sat alone about a quarter mile from the last camper cabin, far enough away for their evening antics to be quelled by the trees.

Ascending a gradual incline as he walked away from his cabin, Proctor shined the flashlight from one structure to another. It was still early—just after 10pm—and being it was the first night, many campers would still be awake, chatting amongst themselves or crying for Mommy and Daddy. Proctor would likely spend half the night consoling children.

But first, it was time for a little peek.

Just a quick peek. It was too early for much more.

Proctor made his way over to the twelve to fourteen-year-old boys' cabin, the one that he knew from experience was typically the rowdiest. Making his way to the rear of the structure, his booted feet treading lightly on the ground, he came to a small hole, expelling a tiny beam of light from the bathroom within. The hole was small enough to go largely unnoticed—many wooden planks had flaws, after all—but just large enough for Proctor to see through.

He leaned forward, pressing his face against the wooden wall, his left eye hovering over the hole. The light was momentarily harsh on his eye, but it quickly adjusted.

Proctor's view was that of a single stall, with a toilet and a roll of TP. (To his left would be urinal, but it was too difficult to see anything worthwhile when a kid was up against a urinal, so no hole had been placed near that.) The stall was better anyway, Proctor knew. You never knew what was going to happen. Sometimes they'd do nothing more than take a piss or drop a deuce (which didn't disappoint him, by any means), but other times—other times Proctor might come across a sprout jerking his turkey or a lass rubbing her flesh pocket. Even better, there were times, usually after the kids got to know each other better, that they'd go in stalls together. Then things could get really exciting.

He waited impatiently for several minutes, his eye to the wall, his ears hearing the muffled conversations of young teenage boys beyond the bathroom. Proctor was about to move on to another cabin when the bathroom door opened.

A slender boy wearing a tank-top and shorts walked in front of the stall door and paused. Proctor fished around in his pocket for the spy camera he'd ordered out of a magazine, ready to snap a picture if the scene called for it. But then the kid moved past the stall to the urinal, where Proctor could hear him take a piss.

He moved on, going from one cabin to the next, peeping in holes but also doing his rounds, making sure no *real* predators were lurking about. No one that would actually touch the kids or hurt them. Proctor loved the kids. He wanted no harm done to them; none at all. He just wanted a little looksee from time to time.

The last cabin Proctor came to, before he would start all over again, was the eight and nine-year-old boys' cabin. This

CAMP HELL AND THE HOT TUB HOTTIES
by PATRICK C. HARRISON III

cabin was situated highest on the ridge and furthest from the lake, because history had taught Proctor that boys between those ages were just as likely as teenage boys to sneak out in the night to go for a swim, but much *more* likely to drown or almost drown whilst enjoying their midnight fun.

Having struck out for the most part thus far on his first round of peeping, Proctor started toward the rear of the cabin to where the hole was, when something in his periphery caught his attention. It wasn't that anything moved as he went past the front of the cabin, swinging the flashlight back and forth; it was that something was present in his field of vision that should not have been. At first, it didn't register. But Proctor had walked the campgrounds thousands of times over the years, and he knew darn well when something was out of place.

A human foot was not supposed to be there on the steps leading up to the cabin door.

"What the…" Proctor started, backing up a few steps and turning the flashlight on the four wooden boards that made up the steps to the cabin, further illuminating what the yellow porch light already revealed.

And yep, there it was—a foot. A child's foot, to be more precise. It was sitting on the second step from the ground, like some kid was climbing the stairs and just left his right foot—severed at the ankle—behind as he took the last two steps and went into the cabin.

Except, it couldn't be a real foot, Proctor knew. That would be ridiculous.

There were occasional injuries at Camp Helton, sure. Injuries happen when kids are taking part in a plethora of outdoor activities. There had even been three deaths in Proctor's tenure—two drownings and one Cub Scout thrown from a horse.

But this was a prank, plain and simple. Injuries, no matter how slight or how severe, always caused a lot of noise, especially from eight and nine-year-olds. And the type of injury that would leave a severed foot sitting on a porch would be caused by what, a bear attack or a chainsaw wielding madman? Those would be quite noisy indeed.

Proctor laughed to himself as he approached the steps to the cabin. The boys were clever. They even made his heart speed up a bit for a minute. The spattering of blood on the steps helped. But they could have at least laid the foot over on its side or tossed it in the grass to make it look more realistic.

"Very funny boys," Proctor said, coming upon the bottom step. "You almost had me."

He mounted the first step with one foot, then paused, looking down on the severed foot...*prop?* It had to be a prop. Something made for one of those gore movies that were so popular now. But it looked so damn real. At the ankle, where the foot was severed, it was jagged looking, with morsels of meat and flaps of flesh hanging down the sides, the white of broken bone at the thing's center.

If Proctor didn't know better, he'd say it was real.

Even though he *knew* it couldn't be, he felt a pang of nervousness in his chest. And he took a wide stride as he ascended the remaining steps to the door, avoiding any chance of coming in contact with the foot. On the stoop, Proctor grasped the brass handle of the door, noting specks of red along the wooden frame.

"Very funny, boys," he said uneasily, swallowing hard as he turned the handle, slowly swinging the door inward.

He shown the beam of his flashlight into the cabin's interior, wanting to get a glimpse inside before proceeding down the row of bunks, expecting to see messy-haired boys looking up from their pillows, rubbing their eyes and wondering who was disturbing their slumber at this hour. Instead, everything the light landed on was painted red.

The cabin's interior was covered from floor to ceiling in blood and body parts. The blankets and mattresses were soaked and held puddles of crimson. The body parts littering the area that Proctor could see were largely unidentifiable, due to the fact it looked like they'd been run through a blender. There was a small finger here, an organ of some sort there, an ear lying

CAMP HELL AND THE HOT TUB HOTTIES
by PATRICK C. HARRISON III

at the center of a soaked pillow, a severed tongue just inside the doorstep. Besides that, the room was simply red, decorated with clumps of meat and bits of bone.

It was as if everyone within the cabin had swallowed a stick of dynamite.

"Jesus," Proctor said, beyond terrified, the flashlight falling from his hand.

Without thinking, he stumbled backward and fell down the four steps to the ground, knocking the severed foot into the bushes as he did so, landing with a painful thud on his back. He scrambled to his feet in a panic, looking wide-eyed at the dark doorway to the cabin, mumbling terrified words of incoherence. He turned from the cabin — all thoughts of his peeping tom escapades gone from his brain — and made to run, but immediately came to halt.

"N-no," Proctor said, pissing himself, too frightened to move from what was before him.

Before a sharp, jagged appendage pierced his breastplate and turned his flesh to mush, Dorian Proctor had time to think that someone was going to find all those pictures of kids he had stashed beneath the mattress in his cabin.

Akira Has a Secret

BROOKE PULLED AWAY FROM HER, Akira tugging her bottom lip with her teeth as they parted. Akira smiled slyly at the other girl, the fingers of one hand interlaced with the string of Brooke's green bikini bottoms, the other tucked secretly beneath the pillow at the head of her bed, which she was sitting on as Brooke leaned in from where she stood.

"They're waiting on us downstairs," Brooke whispered, kissing her more delicately this time.

"They can wait a little longer," Akira said, biting her lip, moving her fingers along the seam of the bikini bottoms until she was at the center, at which point she moved downward, rubbing Brooke' s mound gently. Her other hand tightened around the object beneath the pillow. "They can wait."

Brooke gasped and shuddered beneath Akira's touch. She was certain that, while the other girl played-up her boldness, her experience with the same sex was minimal at best. Brooke's heart was likely about to burst with a combination of excitement and anxiety. And her pussy was likely as slick as a mucous-secreting slug. Akira could almost smell her lust.

She knew the second she saw Brooke that she would have her before the month was over — she would have them *all* before the month was over — but she didn't quite expect Brooke to make the first move, coming into Akira's room and running her hand along her body (Akira, too, was in a string bikini; hers solid black) and placing her lips atop hers. She didn't expect it, but she certainly wasn't going to turn it away.

"I think I want a drink first," Brooke said, laughing nervously and stepping away from Akira's touch. "You know, to loosen

CAMP HELL AND THE HOT TUB HOTTIES
by PATRICK C. HARRISON III

up a little."

"Brooke, honey," Akira said, leaning back on the bed and spreading her legs, "you're going to be between my legs before the night is over whether you've had a drink or not."

"Oh, my goodness," Brooke said, flushing red, her hand attempting to shield an embarrassed smile as she took another step backward. "I've got to go."

Akira smirked at her as she left the room, nearly bumping into the doorframe as she went. Alone now, she sighed, sitting up and pulling her hand out from beneath the pillow holding the fixed blade knife with a five-inch Damascus blade and beautiful pearl grips. It was made for her by her father, a swordsmith, before Akira killed him with it.

She'd killed both her parents that night. After the years they'd spent prostituting her, many would say her actions were justified. As for the thirteen she'd killed since then…well, they were just too good in bed. As a rule, anyone who gave Akira an orgasm ended up with their throats slit and their genitals butchered. Such was the price of pleasure.

Joey Takes a Leak

SITTING IN THE HOT TUB, Joey took a conservative swig of the plastic cup filled with moonshine and Coke. He knew all too well what hard hooch would do to a hard dick—make it soft as a gummy worm in the July sun, that's what.

"You wanna drag?" Bridgett said, sitting across the tub from him. She was the only other person in the hot tub, currently. Her body wasn't half bad, in Joey's opinion—full tits that sagged a bit and a decent ass—but her face…Lord Jesus, if she looked any more like a horse, he'd feed her an apple and throw a saddle over her back.

"Sure," Joey said, reaching across and taking the joint from her. He took a drag and held it, coughing it out only when he absolutely had to, then passing it back to Bridgett.

She smiled at him, showing her large, awkward teeth and gums. Joey smiled weakly back and looked back toward the day room as Owen and LaKendra came walking out onto the porch, LaKendra's hand laced inside Owen's arm as if she thought she might fall if she let go. The deck wasn't wet from hot tub water—no one had gotten out after getting in yet—so Joey guessed she just wanted to put her hand on Owen. Lucky bastard. LaKendra had a perfect hourglass figure that included a plump butt, and a beautiful smile to boot. Not to mention, Brooke had been flirting with the guy all damn day.

"How's the water, Shorty?" Owen said, smiling broadly. Joey hated it when he called him Shorty. He only did it in front of the girls.

"It's hot as your mom's loins, you fuck," Joey said, puffing his chest and flexing his shoulder muscles when he noticed

CAMP HELL AND THE HOT TUB HOTTIES
by PATRICK C. HARRISON III

LaKendra looking at him.

"Good one, Joey," Bridgett said, laughing and snorting annoyingly.

Joey rolled his eyes. Owen stepped into the tub, then assisted LaKendra with getting in, holding her hand and placing his other hand on her hip, as if she was in serious danger of taking a nose dive to the bottom and drowning.

"Thank you, Owen," she said, sitting down between him and Bridgett.

"You bet," Owen said, not bothering to hide the fact that he was staring at her tits.

"Where's Brooke and what's-her-name, the Asian chick?" Joey said as Bridgett passed the joint to LaKendra, who inhaled deeply on it and immediately went into a coughing fit.

"They'll be down in a minute, I guess," Owen said, still looking at LaKendra's tits—they jiggled quite nicely as she hacked out marijuana smoke.

"What do you think of that moonshine?"

"I think it tastes like shit if you don't mix it with a gallon of Coke," Owen said, turning back to face Joey. "Tastes like turpentine mixed with diesel mixed with dog piss."

"Yeah, well, it gets the job done," Joey said, taking another swig of his drink.

"It does get the job done," Bridgett echoed, to which no one responded.

LaKendra passed the joint to Owen, who took a drag so long that an inch of ash fell into the water when he was done.

"Geez, smoke it all up, why don't you," Joey said, annoyed. When Owen laughed and took another hit, he said: "I'm going to take a piss."

He lifted himself from the hot tub, flexing as best he could as he did so, and plopped onto the wooden deck. He was making his way to the day room door when LaKendra spoke up.

"White boy, don't go running through the cabin with your wet self. You want me slipping and falling?"

Joey looked down at himself and said, "Um, no. I'll dry off."

CAMP SLASHER LAKE: VOLUME ONE

"Just go piss in the woods," Owen said. "We're far enough away from the kids' cabins."

"Oh, yeah," Joey said. "I'll do that."

"Don't piss in the wind, Shorty."

"Ain't nothing short here," Joey said, grabbing his crotch as he made his way toward the handful of steps from the deck to the ground.

"Not what I heard," Owen said, sliding his arm around LaKendra's shoulder.

Joey, gritting his teeth and seething, trotted down the steps and headed into the darkness barefoot. There was decent moonlight and his eyes adjusted quickly as he made his way past several pines. Once he was a hundred feet or so away from the cabin, he stopped, coming alongside a tree.

Pulling the front of his shorts down, he took his dick out and commenced peeing, frowning as he did so. Owen wasn't wrong: Joey's height wasn't the only thing lacking. But size didn't matter, right? He'd read that in *Playboy* one time. He'd even had a girlfriend that said it once. It was the way you used your prick that mattered. That's what they said, anyhow. Once done, he sighed and tucked the little thing away.

"Christ, give me some kind of luck this summer," he said, looking up through the branches to the stars.

Suddenly there was a snap of twigs, followed by the movement of brush. Joey's head whipped to the left, the direction the sound came from. In the dim light, he saw no movement, only the ghostly pine trees reaching up and up. Joey stood like a statue, cupping one hand around his ear, listening for more movement. Maybe it was a raccoon or a bunny or something. But could something that small snap a twig?

"Surprise!"

Joey yelped and nearly jumped from his skin, his heart suddenly beating so hard and fast that he thought it may soon turn into a medical emergency. He spun around toward the shout, ready to punch whoever scared the bejeezus out of him, when…he realized he was standing face to face with Bridgett.

CAMP HELL AND THE HOT TUB HOTTIES
by PATRICK C. HARRISON III

"Did I scare you?" she said, smiling and showing her gums. She too had sauntered out here barefoot, still wearing her bikini, dripping wet.

"Fuck yes, er, I mean no," Joey stammered. "I just don't like being surprised."

"Oh," Bridgett said, lowering her head, like a dog who'd been yelled at. "Are you mad at me?"

"What? No." Joey ran his palm across his face and groaned silently. Why the hell had Bridgett followed him out here? Was she wanting to make-out out here in the woods? Was she wanting to boink? Jesus, Joey would do Bridgett if she was all he could get, but he planned on giving the other girls—any of them—a try first. "No, I'm not mad, Bridgett. I'm just…what are doing out here? You might've seen me taking a leak or something."

Bridgett giggled at this, though Joey hadn't meant it to be funny. "I don't know. I wanted to get away from the others for a second, I guess. And…I wanted to be alone with you for a sec, Joey. Just me and you."

She looked up at him then with a bashful smile, and Joey realized for the first time that Bridgett was the only counselor this year that was shorter than him. Even the Asian chick, Akira, was taller than he was. He saw her in this moment differently, cute, and curvy, as long as she didn't smile too big. She wasn't so bad. Maybe he could—

Suddenly a burst of warm wetness hit him in the face and chest, and he gasped, sucking in the salty liquid, along with several chewy pieces of something. Joey, temporarily blinded by whatever sprayed him, gagged and hacked the stuff from his mouth. He wiped at his eyes, clearing them as best he could, and looked at his hands. They were covered in what could only be fresh blood.

"What the fu—" he started, then stopped mid-*fuck* when his eyes caught sight of what was before him.

Bridgett stood there with the blank stare of a corpse, and jutting from her chest was a giant, bony claw, as big around at its girthiest as a baseball bat, and twice as long, curved up toward the heavens, dripping with viscera. Behind Bridgett, something massive moved in the dark shadows of the pine tree.

"*No, please!*" he yelled.

But Joey's plea went unheeded.

LaKendra in the Middle

SHE HAD ALL OF THIRTY seconds alone with Owen.
He was the only male at Camp Helton that was worth even a cursory glance. Joey was a short meathead with a dirty mouth and Dorian Proctor was dweeby and creepy as fuck at the same time. Besides a cook that looked like he should be behind bars, Owen was the only other cock of legal age at camp. He wasn't the most handsome guy on the planet, but he was tall and slender and had a good sense of humor. LaKendra intended to lose her virginity this summer, and she intended to have Owen take it.

Except that the second Bridgett went in search of Joey (LaKendra actually asked Bridgett ahead of time if she could find a way to give her and Owen some alone time), Brooke came walking out onto the deck in her bright green bikini, swaying her hips and smiling, her breasts practically spilling out of her top.

"I'm here, I'm here," Brooke said, smiling at Owen then winking at LaKendra.

LaKendra offered a weak smile in return. She wouldn't get anywhere with that bitch Brooke around, thinking she's God's gift to men everywhere. She was openly flirtatious with Owen even when they were doing activities with the kids earlier. And, of course, Owen was readily accepting of whatever advances Brooke dished out, swooning at her every movement. And now here she was getting in the hot tub, spoiling any chance LaKendra had for this night.

Oddly, though, Brooke was getting in next to *her*, rather than next to Owen, putting LaKendra between the two of them.

CAMP SLASHER LAKE: VOLUME ONE

What kind of game was Brooke playing with this move? Was it an intimidation tactic? Was it a way of showing that even if LaKendra was closer to him, Owen would still show Brooke all the attention? This was already becoming the case.

"H-hey, Brooke," Owen said. His arm was still around LaKendra's shoulders but loosely, no longer gripping her left shoulder with his hand.

"Hey, Owen, how's it hanging?" Brooke said, smiling and biting her lip as she lowered herself into the bubbling water. "Might not be hanging at all, I guess. Might be standing on end, right, LaKendra?" She elbowed LaKendra, laughing.

"Um," LaKendra said, unsure how to respond.

Owen laughed nervously and removed his arm from LaKendra's shoulders. She couldn't be certain, but she thought Owen tugged at his bathing suit, probably trying to corral a boner.

"Where's the weed?" Brooke said, directing her question at Owen, of course.

"Oh, um, right behind you there's another joint and the lighter," Owen said. "We already kinda burned one." He chuckled like an idiot after that.

Yep, he definitely had eyes for Brooke and her titties. LaKendra felt stuck between them, even forgotten, which was likely exactly what the bitch wanted. As if she didn't feel invisible enough already, now Brooke had turned around and come halfway out of the hot tub to reach for the joint and lighter situated atop Owen's flip-flops on the deck. Doing this, she bent over, sticking her ass in the air, pointing directly at Owen, her bikini bottoms sliding up her ass crack just the way guys liked.

"Goddamn," Owen said under his breath, his eyes glued to Brooke's backside.

"Are you serious, Brooke?" LaKendra said, rolling her eyes and turning away from her ass, crossing her arms.

"What?" Brooke said, lowering herself back into the water and turning around, the lit joint jutting from her mouth. She inhaled and coughed out the smoke like it was her first time.

"Nobody wants to see your ass in the air," LaKendra said,

CAMP HELL AND THE HOT TUB HOTTIES
by PATRICK C. HARRISON III

knowing it was a complete falsehood.

"Is that right?" Brooke said, raising an eyebrow. "I bet Owen liked it. Isn't that right, Owen? And I bet you liked it too, bitch. I bet you want me as much as he does, you hood dike." She took another drag on the joint and smiled.

"Excuse me?" LaKendra said, glaring back at her.

"You heard me. Akira in there, she wants my pussy. She said so. I guarantee you do too, bitch. Everybody does." She blew smoke into LaKendra's face and laughed.

"Okay, okay, no need to get testy," Owen said, attempting a nervous laugh.

"Bitch," LaKendra said, furious now, jerking the joint from Brooke's fingers and planting it between her lips, "not a damn person wants to look at you with that big ass zit on your chin." She sucked in on the joint, filling her lungs with smoke as Brooke gasped, her mouth dropping open in shock.

"What the fuck did you just say?" Brooke sneered.

"You heard me, slut," LaKendra said, blowing smoke into the girl's face.

"Okay, hold on, hold on," Owen said, placing his hand on LaKendra's shoulder and giving her a slight tug. "Easy, girls. No need for all this."

Brooke's eyes shot from LaKendra to Owen then back again. Her upper lip twitched. She appeared to be slowly calming, her shoulders going from rigid to relaxed. But then something in the depths of her grey matter must have told her she couldn't be bad-mouthed like that by some black chick. Because then she attacked.

Brooke's right hand rose from the steamy, bubbling water and stuck LaKendra in the face with a well-placed slap, knocking the joint from her mouth, sending it searing into the suds. She was yelling profane remarks and almost growling as she rained more slaps down on her, slapping her from each side, connecting with her head, face, and shoulders, hitting her but doing very little real damage.

With her left arm held protectively over her head, LaKendra's right came up out of the water, her hand balled tightly into a fist. The punch connected hard beneath Brooke's chin, causing her teeth to clack together, briefly stunning the girl and bringing a halt to her slaps. But the pause was only momentary.

The two girls went at each other like cats fighting over a filet mignon. Their claws were out, their teeth were bared, and the water from the hot tub was splashing all over the place. Owen attempted to half-heartedly pull them apart but got nowhere with it. Brooke, with one raging swipe of her hand, snagged LaKendra's bikini top and ripped it off. She looked at it, pleased, and tossed it over the side of the deck.

LaKendra gasped but didn't halt her attack. After popping Brooke in the face a second time, she went for the girl's top, which came off easily, and tossed it over the side with her own.

"My goodness, ladies," Akira said, standing at the edge of the tub with her hands on her hips, "y'all decided to get all feisty without me."

Akira Has a Plan

THE KNIFE WAS NOW IN a plastic sheath, secured around her right thigh with a rubber strap. There was no sense in hiding it, Akira figured. The others may question it, but she could easily play it off. She hadn't intended to start killing tonight — the counselor job was a month long, after all — but after getting worked up with Brooke, she figured why the hell not.

Seeing LaKendra and Brooke fighting with their tops off was more than a little exciting. Akira knew from experience that rage was one brief side-step from lust. With just a nudge, she could turn this hot tub brawl into an orgy. And then, after a wealth of orgasms, a massacre. Bridgett and Joey seemed to have momentarily left the party, but when they returned, they would partake in the festivities as well.

"You girls need to kiss and make up," she said, still looking down on them outside the hot tub. The girls had stopped fighting to look at her, but still had their arms tangled around each other. "Make love not war, right? Isn't that like a saying or some shit?"

"I need to get my fucking bikini top," Brooke said, releasing LaKendra and covering her breasts with one arm, while trying to pull herself from the hot tub with the other.

"Oh, don't bother," Akira said, holding up a hand. She pulled a string on her black bikini top, untying it, then pulled it off and tossed it to the deck, exposing her small but perky tits, her nipples sharp with lust. "Now we're all the same."

They were all silent watching her walk sexily to the hot tub and step in beside Owen, then lower herself to a seated position, the bubbling water tickling at her nipples.

CAMP SLASHER LAKE: VOLUME ONE

"Warm and wet," Akira said, splashing water on her neck and face, "just like I like it. So," she looked at LaKendra and Brooke in unison, "what were you two skanks fighting about?"

"Skanks?" LaKendra said, ruffling her brow.

"This bitch wants to talk shit," Brooke said, glaring at LaKendra.

"Mmm," Akira said, nodding but not really caring what either of them said. No matter what started the quarrel, it was over Owen. He was the only male even a smidgen handsome in this camp.

Owen seemed about to say something—perhaps a joke to lighten the mood—but Akira grabbed him behind the neck and pulled him to her, pressing her lips to his, shoving her tongue in his mouth, meeting his. She kissed him long and hard, to the silence of the others, and reached through the water, taking hold of his quickly stiffening cock through his bathing suit. He shivered at her touch, and she strengthened her grip. When she finally pulled away from him, Owen wore an expression of pure shock. Akira looked to LaKendra and Brooke, who appeared equally dumbfounded.

"Don't fight over Owen, girls," she said. "We can all share. We can have a lot of fun this summer, don't you think?"

"You must be crazy," LaKendra said, barely audible over the bubbles.

"Oh, I'm not crazy," Akira said, swimming the short distance to be directly in front of LaKendra, placing her hands atop the girl's knees. "Is it crazy for me to want you most of all, LaKendra? Is it crazy for me to want to pop your cherry?"

LaKendra gasped, pulling her knees away from Akira's touch, clearly uncomfortable.

"I can tell a virgin when I see one. But not for long, my dear."

LaKendra tried to push her away, but Akira caught her wrists and forced herself onto her lap, kissing the woman's full lips with the same desire she showed for Owen. At first, LaKendra struggled, but after only a second or two, her mouth welcomed Akira's tongue into hers, and the tightness in her

CAMP HELL AND THE HOT TUB HOTTIES
by PATRICK C. HARRISON III

arms relaxed, her hands going to Akira's hips, holding her there softly.

"There, see?" Akira said, pulling away.

LaKendra smiled an embarrassed smile and didn't seem the least bit bothered with having the girl in her lap anymore. Akira looked to Brooke, who looked in awe.

"Brooke, I know you're game, right? Do you want to play with us?"

Brooke had begun to nod, a silly grin on her face, when they heard the noise.

Owen's Dream Goes to Shit

OWEN COULDN'T BELIEVE WHAT WAS happening. This was *Penthouse* level shit. Only in porno flicks and guys' wildest fantasies did stuff like this happen, where three top notch-looking chicks were apparently willing to roll in the sheets—or in the hot tub, as it were—with one dude. It was a dream come true.

The sound from the nearby woods—a cracking of a few branches in tandem—barely registered for Owen. His mind was on the three topless ladies before him and nothing more, his cock hard enough to break bricks. Perhaps not even a nearby nuclear blast could pull his attention away from the immediate situation.

"What was that?" LaKendra said, seeming to be the only one to notice.

Akira, coming out of LaKendra's lap, was leaning in to kiss Brooke when more branches broke, closer to the deck this time, along with a rustle of bushes. LaKendra stood, looking in the direction of the noise, and Owen noticed the goosebumps cropping up on her wet flesh, her nipples sharp and dripping water.

"Seriously, you guys, what was that?"

"Probably just Joey and Bridgett," Owen said, looking to Akira and Brooke as they embraced, their lips coming together. "They're probably getting it on out there or something."

LaKendra relaxed for a split second, then tensed again and said, "I don't think so. I think I see something out there."

Only then did Owen pull his gaze away from Brooke and Akira to look into the blackness of the woods. He looked just in time to see an arm flying through the darkness, landing with a

CAMP HELL AND THE HOT TUB HOTTIES
by PATRICK C. HARRISON III

thud on the deck, sliding across the wood and coming to a stop at the edge of the hot tub, a trail of blood left behind from where it was severed at the shoulder.

Owen looked at it dumbly. It was an arm—a human arm—hairy and muscular and…was that *Joey's* arm?

"What the hell?" he said, his brain not registering completely, still fighting with the lust of the moment.

Akira stood, scowling at the arm, and Owen noticed for the first time the knife strapped to her thigh. Brooke too stood, all three of the girls now standing topless and dripping wet. But, Owen knew, the excitement that was present mere seconds ago was lost. He stood, tugging at his bathing suit, allowing his rapidly shrinking cock to fall back into place.

"Is that seriously an arm?" he asked.

"It's an arm," Akira said, still looking at it like it was an algebra equation in need of solving.

"What the fuck is going on?" Brooke said.

But before any of them could respond, the thing pounced from the darkness.

To Owen, there seemed to be no identifiable face to look at. It leapt from the trees, a mass of pale flesh and appendages—numerous tentacles and several multi-elbowed arms without hands, only a single giant hooked claw extending from the wrists of these arms. Eyes dotted the mass in various places, as did ears, with no sign of a coherent design or symmetry. The only aspect of the creature that appeared free of chaotic construct, were the three mouths at the things center, all in a line, and filled with jagged teeth.

The creature landed on the deck before them, an arm's length from Joey's severed arm, the wooden planks beneath it creaking with strain. It towered over the hot tub, at least ten feet tall, standing not on legs but on a mass of slithering, flesh-toned tentacles. It didn't speak or growl or roar; it simply bared its terrible teeth from its three mouths and clicked its claws together, as if sharpening kitchen knives.

In tandem, Brooke and LaKendra climbed out the other side

of the hot tub in a panic, screaming as they got to the deck and prepared to run wildly to God knows where. But they would never get the chance to run. Owen stood like a statue, watching unbelievingly. Akira, he noticed, stood at the center of the hot tub, the water bubbling all around her, with her knife already in hand.

One long clawed arm whipped out at LaKendra, hitting her in the neck as she fled, decapitating her in mid-stride. Her body collapsed instantly, and her head popped into the air, where a second claw's sharp tip caught it by piercing LaKendra's eyeball. Holding her head like an olive on a toothpick, the long arm bent its many elbows and deposited the head into the creature's center mouth.

At the same time, tentacles enwrapped Brooke just as her feet left the deck in an attempt to jump to the ground. She screamed as tentacles by the dozens attacked, wrapping around her legs and arms, covering her breasts and encircling her neck, leaving only her head peeking out of the mass of snake-like appendages. Then they began to squeeze, tightening like a multi-layered vise. Brooke's screams ceased as her trachea collapsed, and her face turned beet red, eyes and veins bulging. Three fingers stuck out between the tentacles on the right side, and they snapped from the pressure. She turned impossibly red in the face. Red, then crimson, then a deep reddish purple that was the color of death by pressure. Then her eyes exploded from their sockets and blood and brain matter burst from her ears. Blood poured from between the tentacles, a waterfall of gore.

Owen was petrified, unable to scream or run or fight. He stood in absolute horror, awaiting his turn, awaiting oblivion. Akira, on the other hand, fought.

As Brooke's lifeless body was being brought back across the hot tub by the mass of tentacles—spilling blood the whole way, turning the bubbling water red—Akira lunged at the beast, climbing the steps out of the water and jumping across the deck, her knife leading the way. She plunged it into a random eye on the thing's side, and its mouth on that side screamed a

CAMP HELL AND THE HOT TUB HOTTIES
by PATRICK C. HARRISON III

hawkish screech.

She didn't stop there.

Akira stabbed and sliced, puncturing every eye she could find, slicing off one ear after another, cutting tentacles as they tried to get at her. Brooke's crushed body was dropped, and the tentacles went after Akira in a flurry. She fought furiously, slicing every appendage that attempted to touch her. But they were many. Tentacles encircled one leg and others wrapped around her waist.

Undeterred, she fought on, moving her attack focus from the tentacles to the thing's midsection, where she plunged the knife repeatedly. Clawed arms swung at her, but she ducked and weaved, helped by the fact that she blinded the fucking thing. She tore at the same spot, ripping into the meat of the creature, creating a hole beneath its three mouths, tearing out vessels and organs of unknown use. Blood poured from the wound with greater copiousness the deeper she went, spraying out of it, drenching Akira and the deck around her. It was teetering now, the fight slipping out of it with its life, the tentacles releasing their grip, the heavy claws falling weakly to the wood. And Akira kept up her attack, burrowing into the thing like a dog digging a hole.

When it finally toppled over, Owen thought Akira was crushed by its heft. But she emerged from beneath, naked except for her bikini bottoms, covered in blood and still holding her knife. She stood looking at it, rage still present on her face, when it began to change.

The mass of flesh and appendages slowly pulled apart into three pieces, shrinking like a slug covered in salt, excreted a putrid viscous goop from its pores as the forms changed. Tentacles and clawed arms retracted and melted away amongst the mutating forms. And then Owen realized what they were.

Now lying amongst the stinking goop and gore, were three red-headed boys. The identical triplets who'd arrived off the bus earlier that day, were now naked and curled into balls on the deck, with stab wounds covering their little bodies, seepage of the damage done pouring from each wound.

"Jesus Christ," Owen said, still standing in the blood red hot tub.

"I don't think Jesus had much to do with that fucking thing," Akira said, looking from one boy to the next to the next.

"Is it some kind of alien or something?" he said.

"How the hell should I know?" Akira said, walking over the gory remains of Brooke and stepping into the hot tub. She pointed the knife at Owen. "Now, I need you to fuck me and fuck me good. You better make me cum, Owen."

Bad Party

by Brian McNatt

> *"Tell me 'bout the Danny Mann*
> *Crouching in the corner*
> *With his bloody, crooked axe*
> *He'll send you to the coroner."*
> —an old schoolyard taunt

ON THE MORNING OF SATURDAY, October 31st, 1987, five mailboxes scattered throughout the small town of Chickasha, Oklahoma were found with a plain, unmarked envelope. No postage, no return address, hand-delivered and each directly addressed to the younger member or members of the household. Inside each envelope, a letter, handwritten, though none of the recipients recognized the writing as belonging to anyone they knew.

Dear Brittany/Dear Jamie/Dear Laurence/Dear Arnold/Dear Stephanie & Steven,
You are cordially invited to the premiere Halloween party of the season, tonight at the remarkable Murder House. You know the one. There is only one. Tonight, will be a night of scares and revelry, a night not to be missed or forgotten. The end of the year will

BAD PARTY by BRIAN McNATT

be here before you know it, and there are so many wants left to be done. Come together, where the pithy adults cannot find us, and make this Halloween night one to remember... for all who make it to daybreak.

Costumes not required. Food will be provided; it is encouraged each attendee bring additional snacks of choice. DO NOT TALK ABOUT HIM.

Happy Halloween.

"Huh." Brittany Sterling flipped the invitation around on the off-chance she found more to read on the back of the letter, and then looked to the front again. She tugged her neon pink-dyed bangs from her eyes and read through the invite again. She grinned, bright as the highlights in her platinum hair, as she turned and started back to her house from the mailbox. The sun shone cool and orange leaves skittered across the road. "Rocking."

Arnold Burton almost didn't notice the letter in his rush to get back to his bedroom. He slammed the front door shut behind him, and tossed the small collection in a haphazard stack on the kitchen table as he stomped through, only barely catching his own name scrawled across the plain white envelope. He snatched it back up before anyone else could see it, even though both the parents were well-distracted by their argument in the backyard, and ran, slamming and locking his bedroom door behind him.

"Those assholes are gonna have the whole neighborhood listening in to their dirty laundry."

He threw on a cassette of Poison, dialed the volume up until the yelling from the parental units only sounded like a part of the song, and then regarded the letter again. He wracked his brain for a moment but could not think of any times he had gotten a letter not from his school, wanting to discuss his poor grades or poorer attendance record. His curiosity spiked like the prom night punch bowl as he tore the envelope open and read the invite. He grinned and read it again, gaze catching on the promise of the Murder House. "Fucking aces!"

"Mom, Mom, Mom!" cried out Jamie, as she ran into the kitchen, letting the door bang shut behind her in her played-up excitement. The trio of dogs in their open-topped crates began barking a frenzy at the loud noise.

From where she sat at the kitchen counter, trying to look through the minutes of the previous evening's school board meeting, Mrs. Manning groaned at the sudden onslaught of noise, the papers falling from her hands as she began rubbing her temples. Jamie, not caring, ignored this and held the letter up in triumph. "Mom, I got a letter! An invite to a Halloween party! May I go, please, oh please, oh please?"

Mrs. Manning took a long, deep drag of her coffee before answering. "Short notice for an invite. You'd think... what time?"

Jamie made a show of checking the letter, free hand tapping the drumbeat her aunt taught her against her hip. "It is... sundown to... oh... I guess it says to daybreak, but I bet that's just whenever we feel like calling it a night. I can't imagine anyone actually wanting to party from dusk 'til dawn. Oh, please let me go, Mom! I have not been to a Halloween party all high school, and who knows what I won't have time for once I get into college!"

At last, Jamie's mom turned a smile her way, tired and distracted as it might have been. "I just count it a lucky thing,

BAD PARTY by BRIAN McNATT

you still bother asking permission, the way you hang around my sister all the time and listen to her... well, never mind. You're a good girl, Jamie. Loud, but good. You expecting any friends of yours at this party?"

"I'm sure all my favorites will be there," Jamie claimed, keeping it to herself how, aside from Brittany Cooper down the block, she didn't particularly HAVE friends to show up. But this hardly mattered. Parties were for finding friends, and the more people she didn't know in the Murder House, she thought, the easier it all would be.

"Do not talk about him. Do not talk about him? Who's him, and why shouldn't we talk about him? Laurence?"

Laurence Graves shrugged at his friend's questions, continuing to push the cart down the grocery store aisle at his usual leisurely pace. An easy smile adorned his lips, one he had spent many an hour in front of the mirror practicing, and to each girl they passed in their shopping venture, he sent off a quick wink and an extra shine. More often than not it got him a sigh or a roll of the eyes in return, but nothing ventured...

"Laurence? Any ideas?"

"I don't know, Gabe," said Laurence, drawing the cart to a stop. Ignoring how his best friend of many years bumped into the cart at the sudden stop, Laurence bent down and grabbed a handful of bags of marshmallows, throwing them in before continuing on. The invite said they were welcome to bring their own snacks along, and he aimed to please. "Probably talking about Danny Mann, though we're not supposed to talk about him, hah. Hey, how do chips and salsa sound? Or no, we might want to avoid anything spicy, don't know the state of the toilets there at the... the place of the party," he concluded more softly as an older gentleman passed them by with a suspicious eye. "Just the place of the party."

CAMP SLASHER LAKE: VOLUME ONE

"Hey, here's an idea," said Gabriel Barnes, hurrying up to walk beside Laurence instead of behind. "Let's pretend for a moment that my family and I only moved to Chickasha a couple of years ago and haven't lived here all our lives. Oh wait, you don't need to pretend, that's actually how things are. WHO is Danny Mann? And why does he sound like someone from a playground rhyme, something you'd find little girls singing while jumping rope or whatever little girls do?"

"There is a playground rhyme about him, good bud," remarked Laurence. The pair of them turned down into another aisle and Laurence began stocking up on all his favorite sodas. "Don't ask me how it goes, though, that sort of thing is kid stuff. Yeah, that's it. You wouldn't know about him or the murders after all, I suppose. But, oh yeah, they were the talk of the town for years and years. An absolute tragedy, or disaster. Whatever you want to call it. Happened in my parents' time. One Halloween, this guy went on a total psychotic rampage and... wait, is it still a rampage if it's confined to one place?"

"I don't think the semantics really matter," mumbled Gabe. He looked a little sick from the conversation already. Laurence dropped in a case of Dad's root beer to cheer him up. "But let me guess. The Murder House?"

"Got it in one," said Laurence, smiling again. They found their way to another aisle. Laurence grabbed a bag of tortilla chips after all. "Yeah, the Murder House. God, I haven't thought about all this in a long spell. Great idea for a Halloween party, should've had it myself. Anyway, so it's Halloween Eve. There's a party going on, everyone is having a grand old time—as much as you can, back in the old days—when suddenly, the guy hosting the party, Daniel Mann, completely loses his shit. Nobody knows why. The lone survivor of the night, name withheld by the authorities 'for their protection' said he began ranting about the moon. Nobody knew what he was on about. Nobody cared either, once he grabbed a big carving knife from the kitchen and began carving people up with it. Seven people murdered right in that house, they say. Throats slit and bellies opened to let their guts all spill out like spaghetti noodles."

Gabe put his hand on the side of the cart, forcing it to stop as he leaned on it for support. His eyes were closed, and for a moment, Laurence worried his insides were on the way out. "Hey, uh, maybe go find the restrooms if you're gonna—"

"Shut up," hissed Gabe, grimacing as if from the sound of his own voice. "Just... really regretting I ever asked. God, please tell me this maniac's at least rotting away in some prison somewhere."

"Oh, I'm sure he's rotting away somewhere," said Laurence. Gabe opened his eyes and looked at Laurence again, and Laurence smiled wider. "He died as well, that very night. That lone survivor I mentioned? According to her own account, they doused Danny Mann in kerosene and set him on fire. Nearly burned the whole house down before the town fire department got everything contained."

"Oh my God."

Laurence nodded in agreement. He pulled the cart over, and stopped at the end of an aisle, beside a large display of Halloween candy. He watched a group of girls he vaguely recognized from high school pass them by, winking to each in turn, and managing to get one wink in return. A clearing throat from Gabe returned him to the topic at hand. "Yeah, yeah. Anyway, I ought to fix something I said earlier. Everyone only THINKS he died as well that night. Nobody actually knows."

Gabe frowned and looked at Laurence with freshly suspicious eyes. "How do you not..."

"Know?" finished Laurence. He shrugged, then turned and began loading the cart up with bags of chocolate and other choice candies. "By not finding the body. Danny Mann stumbled off shrieking in agony, or so the story goes, but the survivor turned tail and fled the house rather than pursue. Probably I'd do the same. I just set the guy on fire and escaped from a burning building; I'm not going to stick around long enough to get myself killed trying to make sure the job was done. That's what the police are for. But when the fires were out, and the police were there... nothing. No body but the bodies of the victims. No sign of him as the days turned into weeks turned into months and years. And so, the legend of Danny Mann was born."

"God," said Gabe. The last thing said by either of them until they were well along the line for checking out. "And you want to go to this party even despite knowing... all of that?"

"Well, sure!" said Laurence, drawing his shades from his sleeveless denim jacket and flipping them on. "That's all ancient history, my dude. Can't let ancient history keep you from partying!"

"And... you think I should come along because..."

"Because you're my best bud," said Laurence, and though the remark seemed glib, he meant it in whole sincerity. "And Halloween is the season for spooks and parties with your best bud, my man. So, let's give the town legend the middle finger and hope somebody remembers to bring the beer!"

"You think they'll want beer?"

"I don't fucking care, just let me... get this... gah!"

The prolonged crack of old wood carried across the forlorn suburb as the Murder House's door at last gave way to Steven's crowbar. The high school senior laughed in victory, slipped the tool back into his duffel bag, pushing the door open the rest of the way before stepping aside and bowing to his sister sitting bored on the porch railing. "Ladies first, madame."

"And fools last." Stephanie hopped to her feet and stretched, grabbing one of the pair of black plastic trash bags they were using to carry their Halloween goods from the splintered deck. She took a step for the door, then paused, the hairs on the back of her neck prickling at the sudden feel of... something. She turned and looked around. The evening sun fell along its westward journey, casting the town in deep oranges, and deeper shadows. Far down the road, past two intersections, she could still dimly make out the white and blue of the town library and the orange brick of the church across the way from it. Nearer at hand, children in costumes, both homemade and store-bought, trundled along the sidewalks from house to house with their traditional cries of "TRICK OR TREAT!," striking Stephanie with an unexpected, wholly unwelcome sense of nostalgia. "God, when did we stop doing that?"

Behind her, Steven followed her gaze, her twin less nostalgic, more bored. "When you caught Halloween III on cable that one time and became convinced your trick or treat mask was going to eat your head off. But if you're going to stand there longing for Hershey bars and Skittles, I guess tonight it's pigs before wine."

The mood died. Stephanie groaned as she turned and marched for the door. She made no attempt NOT to hit her brother with her bag as she went. "It's 'pearls before swine,' you idiot."

"Sorry, sis. I guess all the wine Mom drank just went to my umbilical cord."

Stephanie opened her mouth to protest, then stopped. She stood in the central hall of the Murder House, and a chill ran down her spine at the mere thought of it. To her right, the wall opened almost immediately into a large den with a fireplace and several couches, all centered around a heavy-looking coffee table. To the left, the wall went on a little further before opening into a dining room, the dust-choked wallpaper peeling, the front wall dominated by a large bay window boarded up with thick slabs of wood. Opposite the window, a door into the kitchen. And straight ahead down the hallway, empty picture frames along one wall, and stairs to the second floor along the other.

"God," she said, shuffling along into the den, "J-girl was right. This place is spooky."

"This place is old," said Steven, throwing both his duffel bag and another plastic trash bag onto one of the couches. Plumes of dust rose, and the piece of furniture groaned. Steven grimaced. "Correction. This place is ancient. Might want to do some dusting before the guests arrive, oh sinister sis."

She shot him a look as she set her bag—far more gently—in a free corner of the den. "Dusting with what, my bare hands? Never mind, I'll use your dumbass head. You're clearly not using it and you've got enough hair anyway."

"Oh, ye of little faith—but devastating wit, ow." Steven opened his duffel bag again and drew out a pair of paper towel rolls. "Voila. You can take the den here; I'll handle the kitchen. Just the worst of it so we can set up the décor without sneezing our brains out. Sound fair?"

"Sounds... adequate." Stephanie, not wanting to outright say her brother had surprised her with his forethought, said no more, only marched forward to take one of the rolls.

Separating, they set to work as Steven had suggested. Soon enough, Stephanie became glad she had decided to wear a scarf against the wind, wrapping it tight around her mouth and nose to guard against the worst of the dust that kicked up as she went over the couches, tables, and the fireplace mantelpiece with paper towel after paper towel. The air grew thick and hazy, particles dancing in the slowly fading light coming in through the slats on the great bay window. Twice, Stephanie had to retreat to the kitchen for a moment to wash her hands in the sink, too overcome by the sensation of filth clinging to her to continue working. "Ugh. I don't know if I could do this if we didn't have running water here."

"Why IS there running water here, now've you brought it up?" asked Steven as he cleaned the last edge of the kitchen counter's island. "I thought this house was abandoned and left to rot ages ago, after the—"

"Don't talk about him!" Stephanie snapped, though with the slightest of grins, as she gave up on the den as "good enough" and started helping her brother in the kitchen. All the food would be set out there. It needed a higher standard of cleanliness. "And abandoned for a while, yeah, but left to rot? A house this nice? Nah. A few years ago, Dad says, it was mostly fixed up and put back on the market. Worst of the fire damage, upgrading the electricity, fixing up the plumbing—that reminds me, one moment."

Dropping her latest wad of used paper into the kitchen waste bin sitting where the fridge once had been, Stephanie plodded over and flipped the light switch once, twice, three times. On the last time, the bare bulbs sprouting from the ceiling flickered, then turned on with a hazy yellow glow. "Excellent."

"Better than the lantern backup plan," agreed Steven, mirroring Stephanie in flicking on the living room lights. "Alright, now this is gonna be a party."

The decorations and snacks were easier. Strings of little plastic skulls and bats along the walls. A trio of carved and grinning—those who had felt the sting of Stephanie's words might have called them sneering—jack o' lanterns along the mantelpiece over the fireplace, another center stage on the coffee table and surrounded by bowls of choice Halloween candies. Candles, more for show than a need for light, sat inside the lanterns, and above the fireplace. In another corner of the living room, borrowed from the USAO science lab, stood a human skeleton, a real one to Stephanie's unease and Steven's delight, kept standing by metal pins in the proper joints. A makeshift mask wrapped over its head, the black plastic of a trash bag wound taut, two holes punctured through the front as "eye" holes, even though the skeleton had none.

"God, that's creepy," said Stephanie.

"It's a Halloween party," said Steven. "That's the point. 'sides, it was your idea to have it here, at the literal Murder House, sis. The creepiness was already here."

Stephanie made no answer at first. She left the living room to idle down the central hallway, looking with curiosity where she had never gone before but had always heard so much about. "Dad's had the place on the market for years. Nobody's buying it, not after what happened. Somebody had to use it for something. You think we should've gotten beer for this?"

"Yes, absolutely. Great, heaping cases of it." Steven joined her in the hallway, first setting a cackling pumpkin on the stairway banister, then running up the stairs to the first landing. From there, he tied one end of a rope to the railing, the other end around the neck of a child-sized dummy in a witch's outfit and flung the macabre decoration over to dangle in the center of the hallway. "Fortunately," he called down, grinning as Stephanie looked up at him, "I've got a deal made! Pizza delivery guy's gonna have more beer than we could ever drink when he shows up!"

Stephanie grimaced. It sounded expensive. It sounded like... "Kevin? You invited Kevin to my party? Ugh. How are you even paying him?"

"With a date!" Steven proclaimed, still grinning.

Deciding she didn't at all want to know WHO the date would be with, Stephanie returned her attention to her explorations. She found a door—most likely to the basement—beneath the stairs and gave the doorknob a tug. Nothing. She tried to turn it and found it wouldn't budge. Locked. "Damn it all, we don't have the keys to any of this. Broken enough... ugh."

Only then, standing at the far end of the hallway in thought, she noticed the smell. An old, dry, thoroughly dead and rotting smell, ashen and cloying. Though, weak, blessedly weak. She might not have registered the smell at all if she hadn't smelled it before. Once, years before, Steven had been sick, forcing their father to take her on the yearly hunting trip to the family land. The second day, late in the morning when the sun had been up and cooking the world for hours, she found a dead deer. Thoroughly dead, and with good portions of it eaten, the rest left burning out beneath the endless Oklahoma sky. Tanned jerky, all natural, eat at your own risk.

"St-Steven..."

"Yeah, I smell it too," he said, coming down the stairs in a clatter and rush. He stood a moment in the hall, face wrinkled in a messy mix of thought and disgust, and then he nodded to the wall, opposite the door Stephanie had tried, and failed at. "It's in there, I think. Like a hundred fat rats decided to have their own little suicide pact at once. Ughh. Hold on, there."

He hurried to the den. Stephanie remained, forearm pressed against her nose in a vain attempt at shielding against the stench, wondering if she might vomit, if elsewhere in the house smelled even worse, if this might ruin the party before it could start.

Distracted by her worries, she didn't notice Steven return until he stood right beside her. Not until he raised the crowbar over his head, a manic gleam awake in his eyes. By then she could only watch, his body already in motion. "Steven, WAIT—"

He didn't wait, battering a deep gouge into the brittle wood and plaster before the shout registered with him. He looked to her, brow creased, crowbar remaining half-buried into the wall. "Huh?"

For a moment, Stephanie couldn't speak, mouth working but no words coming out. Her hands found her head, combed her frizzy hair back. She stared at the damage and fought to process the catastrophe before them. "Oh, God. Ohhhh, God, no... God, when I make my remarks about you being an idiot, this is what I'm talking about. This is what I'm talking about! Oh, God!"

"I still don't get it," said Steven, giving an absentminded tug on the crowbar as he did. "The smell was bothering you, I tried to find—"

"Dad's going to freak out when he sees this!" cried Stephanie, heart warring between the horror of the vandalism and anger at her twin brother for getting them in this mess. "You idiot! Doors get broken all the time; you replace them as easy as you replace a flat tire! This is damage INSIDE the house! He's going to want to know how it happened! Steven, you bastard, stop messing around with that crowbar, just pull it out!"

"I'm trying," he grunted, both hands now gripping the length of metal and pulling. Stephanie could see his arms trembling, the muscles in his neck straining, as he began to struggle with the crowbar in earnest. One of his boots pressed against the ancient wallpaper, and he grunted, putting his full weight into the task. "It's stuck on something, or... almost feels like... something pulling..."

Stephanie moved to help her brother, horror, and anger both cooled by concern, when at last, he stumbled back with a cry of victory, more of the wall giving out in a sudden plume of dust. Stephanie hurriedly covered her mouth with the top of her shirt and backed away, eyes still stinging at the fresh rush of the horrid stench. Even as she gagged, Steven cheered. "Hah! I beat you, stupid wall! I beat you! Dad ought to thank me for finding whatever..."

The sense of accomplishment withered as the cloud of dust and broken plaster settled. The pair saw the unobstructed top half of a man hanging out from the wall, the unmistakable source of the wretched odor. Stomach already weak from the smell, Stephanie nearly vomited at the sight of the man. Dead, long dead, long enough to be withered and dry, blackened skin drawn tight and cracked over his bones until the burnt remnants of his clothes hung off him like the rags of a peasant mummy. Though he hung from the wall at the waist, his head sat twisted around on his shoulders, hideously broken, allowing slack jawbone and empty eye sockets to gape up at Stephanie and Steven with what seemed a silent maniac's laugh. One arm hung limp, the other forward, bony fingers caught on the hooked end of the crowbar.

"Oh, God," whispered Stephanie, the words slipping out unnoticed, a habit desperately and thoughtlessly clung to. "Ste... Steven?"

"Ye, yeah?"

"Is that..." Stephanie tried to wet her lips, tasted, and felt bits of dust settle on them, and hurriedly spat in disgust. "D-Da-Danny Mann?"

"I... yeah, I think it is. Who else could it be?"

The pair drew closer in lock-step, breaths held in unspoken anticipation. Stephanie's thoughts whirled. She marveled at the discovery, at once sickened, and exhilarated. Far better than any dumb Halloween party, the close to one of the great

BAD PARTY by BRIAN McNATT

mysteries of town history, adding a new chapter to an urban legend grown—

The bony fingers, not caught on the crowbar's hook but clutching it, tightened their grip. Stephanie lost her words at the sight, lost her breath, her balance, stumbling away in terror until her back struck the far wall, driving a scream out of her.

Steven startled at her scream and turned to look aghast at her, not having seen the movement from the long-dead man. "Steph? What—"

The sound of the wall further crumbling as Danny Mann clambered his way free drew Steven's attention back to the dead man, getting only a brief second to gape at the corpse looming over him before the crowbar's sharpened edge drove in through his stomach and out through his lower back. Stephanie screamed again, eyes burning with her brother's blood splattered across her face. Steven screamed with her, shrieked utter agony, writhing, and heaving like a bug pinned to corkboard. Danny Mann wrenched the crowbar up, through Steven's belly into his chest, gouts of frothy blood vomiting from both his gaping mouth and split-open middle, then—

Steven fell silent, a lifeless puppet collapsing into its own spilled innards as Danny Mann drew the crowbar free. He turned to her, and Stephanie found the sense at last to push herself off the wall and run. Sandals slipped in the spreading pool of her brother's blood, and she fell, still screaming, tips of her outstretched fingers glancing off the front door's knob.

Danny Mann stomped a heavy boot down on one ankle to pin her and raised the crowbar high.

The screams echoed unheeded into the evening air. The shadows crept on. The sun fell. The crowds of children, with parents and without, slowed to a trickle. As night began in earnest, five found their way to stand at the fence to the Murder

CAMP SLASHER LAKE: VOLUME ONE

House, acknowledging each other with quiet greeting, before regarding the decrepit building. The lights were all on and the front door stood ajar, casting a heavy yellow light across the grassy, pumpkin-riddled yard like a long, rancid tongue waiting to scoop them in.

"I don't like it," said Jamie, the first to speak among them to even her own surprise. "It looks like it wants to eat us."

"Houses don't eat people, girl," said Laurence, tone both playful and scornful. "PEOPLE eat people."

"No, no," said Arnold, looking to join in on the fun. "People don't eat people, MONSTERS eat people. Monsters like the Danny Mann!"

"Shhh!" hissed Jamie, turning to look at Arnold with wide eyes, only half-faking her fear. "You're not supposed to talk about him! The letter said so!"

Arnold scoffed and straightened his leather jacket. "Only letter I care about is A, for ass! Come on, you sissies, I ain't standing around out here all night. It's supposed to be a party!"

"Yeah!" cheered Brittany, jumping high enough in her — technically festive — pink and teal cheerleader costume to give the group a spritely glimpse of bright white beneath the skirt before starting at a skip for the open door. Laurence loosed an answering cheer and raced after, a stereotypical cowboy in dress hauling a number of plastic shopping bags.

Once the pair had raced on, Arnold shifted his boombox from one broad shoulder to another and leaned over to where Jamie and Gabe still watched on, uncertain. "I lied, anyway. I also care about the letter E, for expendables." And then, laughing, he hit PLAY on his loaded cassette, filling the evening street with the blaring sounds of Dokken as he strolled up to the house as well.

Left alone now on the sidewalk, Jamie and Gabe shared a look, Jamie smiling and adjusting her black witch's hat, Gabe swallowing and feeling increasingly dumb in his half-hearted try at a police officer. He said to her "I guess... safety in numbers, if you're scared?"

BAD PARTY by BRIAN McNATT

"I'm not scared," protested Jamie, looking back up at the house. A shadow, perhaps the party-hardy Arnold, moved past one of the upstairs windows. "I just like to follow the rules."

"Right, yeah, me too," said Gabe, following her gaze to the house. "Rules are... usually rules for a reason. Good stuff. But still, probably better to follow the rule AT the party, with the rest. Yeah?"

"Yeah," agreed Jamie. "At the party."

"Cool, you two can help me carry all this."

Jamie didn't scream at the new voice from behind them, but she did jump. She had not noticed the pizza delivery guy drive up and park behind them until he spoke, equal parts bored and impatient, as he opened the passenger-side front door. "Pizza delivery to, I quote, 'The Best Damn Halloween Party Ever.' End quote. Pizza and sundry."

Despite her embarrassment, Jamie noticed the "sundry" quickly enough. Alongside the several boxes of pizza were cases of beer. She fought against the urge to laugh at how the others almost seemed to be asking for murder and death and opened her mouth to protest, but Gabe had already ducked into the car to start grabbing what he could. "Kevin, my man! Ohhh, there's only one ass dumb enough to get you to deliver beer—"

"—Steven, you maniac!" called out Arnold, leading the way into the main den with a case of beer under each arm. "You're a goddamn hero and your decorations are tight!"

Following after the rest with a box of brownies in hand, Jamie paused in the front hall and regarded the bloodied-up figure of a woman hanging from the stairs in distaste. Clothes torn, sodden with the red dripping down from beneath a black plastic trash bag wrapped tight around the head. An impressive but macabre decoration, Jamie thought. Certainly tasteless, but then, she wasn't the one in charge of decorations...

CAMP SLASHER LAKE: VOLUME ONE

Cheers rang from the den. Jamie followed them to find the party in full swing. Brittany danced around to the ear-shredding music from the latter's boombox in front of the fireplace, spilling beer all about, while Laurence lounged on one of the couches, eating pizza while eyeing Brittany with rapt attention. Arnold stood on the sidelines, cheering the bouncing girl on between deep gulps of his own beer.

"Have you seen Steven or Stephanie?" asked Gabe from Jamie's side, unnoticed until he spoke up. Startled, Jamie turned and stumbled away, knocking into the prop skeleton. It wobbled, tipped over against Arnold. He squawked in alarm at the sudden thrust of bones into his face, spurring laughs at his expense from Brittany and Laurence.

"Oh my gosh!" said Jamie, yanking the prop off Arnold, then wilting away as he turned a glare on her. "It was an accident, I didn't mean to—I was startled, I—"

"You!" huffed Arnold, jabbing a finger down at her "are harshing my punk groove!"

"Your face is harshing everybody's groove," Gabe snapped back at him, moving to stand a little way between Arnold and Jamie. "You and your girly screams. Just chill, have another beer, and enjoy this nice Halloween party Stephanie and Steven set up for us."

Arnold looked like he wanted to argue more, perhaps something along the lines of punks not taking orders from cowboys. But before he could manage another word, Laurence turned the music volume down and asked from the couch "What makes you think this is their party, man?"

Gabe jerked a thumb over to Kevin, the delivery guy helping himself to a bowl of mixed Halloween candy left on the coffee table. "Because they ordered the pizza—and the beer—from him. Though, you know, if Steven doesn't pop up to pay, I reckon that job falls to whoever's had the most pizza... or beer."

"It wasn't cheap," added Kevin through a mouthful of Hershey's chocolate.

Laurence started at this, glanced down at his pizza-greased

BAD PARTY by BRIAN McNATT

hands, then shared a look with Arnold and his depleted beer. The punk rocker raised a hand, fingerless leather glove crinkling as it tightened into a fist. Watching the exchange, Jamie had to stifle a laugh as Laurence immediately stood from the couch, almost tripping over it in his haste. "Oh hey, yeah, now that you mentioned it! We heard some moving around upstairs just before y'all came in! Probably Steven just setting up a big scare while we get comfy down here. Tis the season for that sort of thing, yeah? I'll just go up there with ya and... make sure he pays you all you're owed. Somebody save me a beer, nobody take my seat. Gabe, buddy, I'm looking at you."

"Yeah, whatever," mumbled Kevin with a shuffle toward the main hall and stairs, at the same instant as Gabe glibly answered "Don't count on it!"

"Come on, Arnie!" shouted Brittany. "Dance with me!"

"Man, that is an uncomfortably realistic fake corpse," remarked Laurence as the pair trudged up the stairs to the second floor.

Beside and two steps ahead, Kevin glanced at the hanging body in question, then shrugged. "Eh. I haven't seen enough dead bodies to really know real from fake."

Laurence's pace slowed. "That... sounds a little like you have seen SOME dead bodies."

"I'm a pizza delivery guy. How many corpses do you think I've seen?"

"I don't want to answer that."

On the second floor, even more dusty and decrepit than the first, they found three doors along a dark hall. Only one stood open, light spilling out to meet them. They went to it and found a barren room, none of the Halloween spooks and contraptions Laurence had been expecting to greet them, decorated only to the sparsest degree with an old desk and solitary chair and closed closet door, the undraped window gaping stupidly out onto the front yard. In the chair, facing away from the pair, sat Steven.

"Alright," said Kevin after a long moment of quiet staring, the lazy tone of disrespect in his voice sounding far more forced than it had downstairs. "I'll admit—grudgingly—that's pretty creepy. Congratulate yourself on a job well done, I actually jumped a little."

"I wasn't in on this," said Laurence, words trailing away as he continued to stare at the man in the chair. He shared a few classes with the other boy over in the town high school, hung out on occasion at the drive-in theater. Not the best of friends, but friends enough Laurence thought he knew the sort of scares Steven went for. The blatant stuff, the gross-out stuff, the machetes chopping heads in half and skeletons glistening with the chewed-up viscera still clinging to them popping out of closets. Nothing so subtle as...

"Kev, wait a minute," Laurence began.

"Stevey, my man!" shouted Kevin, ignoring or not catching the warning as he crossed the room for the chair. A hand reached out to take Steven's shoulder. "Nice spook job, but I've got other deliveries to make tonight and that beer was not easy to get away with! Come on, the game's up—"

"Kev," Laurence tried again. But words failed him as Kevin grabbed the seated man's shoulder and gave it a shake, and with a wet squelch of meat against meat, the head toppled from its neck and onto the floor.

Sudden unreality settled over the scene. From downstairs drifted the faint music of the party, and fainter, the high tones of voices raised in laughter. Laurence looked down at the head on the floor, found Steven staring up at him with eyes glazed and unblinking, the skin carved with horrid precision from his face. A coldness against which no heavy blanket or roaring fire could hold sway struck Laurence and he stumbled aside to lean against the wall beside the closet door. He looked up from the carved head to the sounds of Kevin babbling, found him staring at a hand now red and sticky with the corpse's blood, staring and shaking and babbling nonsense words.

"Kev... Kevin, we, we need to—"

The closet door burst off its hinges and knocked Laurence off his feet, a rupture of dizzying pain exploded as the back of his head struck the dusty hardwood floor. For untold seconds, all above, and around him, whirled a confusion of screams and moving bodies, a wet THUNK, a tearing, a wetter gasp of pain. His vision regained its sense and Laurence stared up at a living corpse of a man dressed in the rags of the long-dead, the skin of Steven's face draped over his head like a mask. The monster—the Danny Mann, some crouched, terrified on the playground child in Laurence's head whispered—held a crowbar before him, the hooked end of the tool embedded deep into Kevin's belly.

"Oh God!" wailed the delivery driver, the bright blood pouring from his mouth as tears ran from his eyes. An arm reached out toward Laurence on the floor, a fresh scream tearing from him, as the Danny Mann lifted him from his twitching feet by the crowbar and carried him across the room. "Please, God, please! God, help—"

A sudden thrust, like shoveling coal into a fire or scraping snow from a driveway, and the Danny Mann threw Kevin through the window, his begging lost in the crash of wood and shattering glass. Moments later, a distant thud of body hitting ground outside, and then nothing. The metal music played on downstairs.

Laurence, numbed in his fright, got to his feet slowly. He should have shouted for the others downstairs, screamed at the top of his lungs until they heard him. More, he should have turned and run for his life, the odds seeming in his favor as the Danny Mann stood a moment at the window and regarded his latest kill before turning almost leisurely to Laurence. But these thoughts never occurred to him. The world had tilted at an angle when he saw the dead walking and killing again, hardly anything occurred to Laurence except for the same reaction that comes to the deer standing in the road when a car races with full headlights towards it.

The Danny Mann strode forward, crowbar raised.

"Anyone know any good, scary stories? I want to hear a scary story!"

Jamie cast a wary glance toward where Brittany sat on the other couch, having long expected the demand from her lone friend at the party. Brittany was someone used to making commands and having others satisfy them. In the bare half an hour—no, Jamie found with a glance at her wristwatch, closer to forty minutes—since the party started, Brittany wanted to dance until Arnold all but threw himself to the mercy of the couch. She wanted the most topping-laden slices of pizza and each of her favorite pieces of candy from the various Halloween bowls scattered around. She wanted to talk, dominating the flow of conversation in the den through sheer force of will and sheer quantity of what she had to say about school, about the dance competitions she participated in, about the house, about the holiday, about the boys at the party and what must be taking Laurence and the rest to come back down, for Steven and Stephanie to show themselves.

Another day, another social situation, Jamie found the attitude inspiring, even likable—she saw nothing malicious about Brittany, only an overabundance of self. There and then, among relative strangers and friends-of-friends, the party girl only existed.

"Come on," continued Brittany, glancing around with a smile as she unwrapped another Tootsie Roll and popped it in her pink-lipstick mouth. "Scary stories are the best, everyone knows this, I can't be the only one here with some rattling around like bats in my belfry. Arnold! Big rocker dude! What have you got?"

The "big rocker dude" mumbled something under his

BAD PARTY by BRIAN McNATT

breath, then stood, shrugging off his leather jacket and tossing it where he'd been sitting. "I've 'got' to go find someplace to take a leak around here. That cheap beer's going through me faster than I went through the school cheerleader team."

"There's a bathroom with a working toilet upstairs and down the hall," said Jamie, jerking a thumb over her shoulder for emphasis.

At nearly the exact same time, "You did no such thing," said Gabe, who had consumed far more moderate amounts of everything on offer that evening. "My sister's on the high school cheerleading team, and she never said a word about you."

Brittany rolled her eyes. "Not exactly something you go bragging about to family. Whatever. Arnold, come on, you can't leave me alone with these two nerds!"

"There's just no helping it, Brit Babe," said Arnold, not unkindly as he squeezed past the couch and back to the central hallway. "But a man's got to do what a man's got to do, and right now this man's shaping up to do Number 2."

"Nobody needed to know that," remarked Gabe to Arnold's retreating back. And then, looking to the two girls remaining with him, a note of embarrassment to his tone, "I'm not... a nerd. I mean, I run track, you know."

Brittany gave him a look. "You've spent half the evening trying to convince your girlfriend here that Ralph Bakshi's Lord of the Whatever movie is better than the book. For all I care, you just said you participate in the school's math triathlon. God damn it..."

"She's... not my girlfriend," mumbled Gabe, with the same embarrassed tone.

"I have a story I could tell," said Jamie once Arnold's heavy-booted steps disappeared into the deeps of the house. "A story about this house. About the Danny Mann."

"Aw, jeez," said Gabe, not looking half as disappointed as he sounded. "Laurence told me that one earlier today. House party, guy went murder-crazy, only one survivor. He made it sound like it's something everyone in town is just expected to know."

"He made it sound right," remarked Brittany, sighing softly as she leaned back into the couch, lollipop hanging from her mouth. "Where did that loser get off to, anyway..."

"I'm sure they're all hanging around somewhere," said Jamie, thinking again of the macabre decoration in the front hall. She smiled. "Besides, that's just what the town knows, and the town doesn't know half of what it thinks it does. I've got family who was involved in the case, she knows all the details of how that night really went down. Only, it was so horrible, the cops and everyone hushed it up quiet, didn't let a squeak out. But my family knows. I know."

Brittany sat straight again on the couch, speculative gaze toward Jamie, smile sweet as the candies she'd been gorging on during the party. "You are making some big promises here, little witch. I'll be disappointed if you don't manage to keep them."

Jamie blushed and adjusted the wide-brimmed hat on her head. She had almost forgotten about her costume.

Gabe made one last, valiant effort to stave off the inevitable. "The rule! Come on, girls. In the invitation, we were told not talk about... you know..."

"The Danny Mann," said Jamie, putting on a smile to match Brittany's. "I reckon plenty of rules have already been broken tonight, one more can't hurt. And 'sides, Stephanie's hanging around here, somewhere. She can stop us talking if it's really that important to her. It's her party, after all."

The three of them waited for a moment around the coffee table, in quiet and unspoken but mutually felt expectation. Brittany stood and walked over to the fireplace mantel to switch off Arnold's boombox, and they listened, and still there came nothing. Jamie heard the faint sounds of many footsteps on the second floor and paid them no mind. In the central hallway, the body decoration creaked on its taut rope, its red dripping onto the hardwood floor.

"The story known to town has a thing or two right," began

BAD PARTY by BRIAN McNATT

Jamie, bringing her focus back to her small audience. "It was Danny Mann, in this house, one Halloween night a decade ago, but it being a party, according to the lone survivor, was just a cover story. Danny Mann and the others with him that night were Devil worshippers. WITCHES. It was a cult thing."

"Like Dungeons & Dragons?" asked Brittany.

"Oh, for God's sake," groaned Gabe, "that is not—"

"Danny Mann was the muscle of the group, the butcher," continued Jamie, roughshod over this interruption. "Or so the survivor said. The one who split the meat and spilt the blood, when the blood work needed doing. Butcher of Baphomet."

"Or so the survivor said?" asked Brittany.

Jamie nodded. "That night was supposed to be a special night. They were a young cult, I guess as far as those things go, and it would be their first ritual try on the old Samhain night. Danny Mann had kidnapped a young woman for the occasion, they would try to make contact with the Devil himself. And according to the survivor, they did."

The creak of the rope in the entrance hall stopped. The wind rose to a hungering gale outside, rattling the glass of the windows in their panes, and then fell away. Wood groaned at the top of the staircase.

"I think I like the public story better," said Brittany.

"There's really no such thing as the Devil," said Gabe. In a floundering act of defiance against the chilling mood of the house, he grabbed one of the last slices of pizza and took a mouth-filling bite, asking as he chewed, "and if they summoned the Devil, why'd the Danny Mann start killing everyone? Sounds like they were the most successful cult of Devil worshippers this country's ever seen."

Jamie shrugged. "Who knows? Maybe it was a religious schism, for lack of any better term on my part. Maybe there was a disagreement over who among them exactly was being favored. Maybe the Devil isn't at all like any of us think he is, and all we can imagine is only a poor shade of the truth. Whatever it happened for, the survivor says, the demon they had summoned went into Danny Mann and he began killing both the sacrifices and the other cultists, he wouldn't or couldn't stop until the ritual artifacts were scattered from their table. Then, the house 'ate' Danny Mann, and—"

Four lumbering knocks sounded from the front door, startling Jamie from her story. She stood and looked toward the doorway to the central hall, a hand clutching at the front of her witch's dress. Gabe and Brittany stood beside her, their gazes following. After a few seconds, three more knocks sounded, weaker than the first four.

"It's the cops," whispered Brittany, all the party girl pop gone from her voice at the threat of arrest—or worse, parental disappointment. "This is private property, oh God, we're not supposed to be here! We're trespassing!"

"It's not the cops," Gabe whispered back, steps light as he slowly edged around the couch. "The cops would bang harder, and they'd be shouting for us to open the door. Is the door even locked?"

"Just ignore it!" hissed Jamie, standing and following after Gabe despite her own warning, Brittany coming along at her heels. "It's probably just pranksters. This is the Murder House and it's Halloween, I'm surprised we've managed this long without any trouble. Let's just ignore them, or better yet, go upstairs to see what's taking everyone else so—"

A solitary knock sounded against the door, loud and hard. The three jumped from it. Then, Gabe squared his shoulders and quickened his pace. "I'm seeing who has a mind to break the damn door down!"

As startled as she felt by this sudden turn of events, Jamie reached her hand out to grab at Gabe's shoulder too late, fingertips only grazing his tee before he took the handle and wrenched the door open. A sharp inhale of breath. Brittany screamed, Jamie barely keeping herself from making it a duet. The pizza delivery driver, Kevin, stood crooked on the front porch, hands plastered to his gut and thick sheets of red ran down his lower half, a horrid twist to his back and a smashed-in droop to his left eye. Bits of glass peppered him, lending further rivulets of blood to drip onto the rotten wood below.

"Guh-gotta get out," he wheezed, stumbling forward a step and forcing Gabe to scramble backward. A harsh noise of grating bone sounded from him. "Go... God... you gotta—"

A wizened shadow dropped to the ground behind Kevin with a heavy THUD, loomed tall with a blood-soaked crowbar held even higher. For one heartbeat, it might have been a holiday prank gone too far. Then the crowbar fell, and the dying man's head burst apart, wet, and chunky like a watermelon. Blood, bits of bone, and meat splattered across Gabe's front, and he shrieked, stumbling back further until he tripped and fell onto the stairs. Brittany screamed with him but darted forward, grabbing the door, and slamming it shut, even as the death-minded dead man strode over the warm corpse toward them.

"Danny Mann," whispered Jamie, feet nailed to the floor by the rush of everything happening, something warm and horrid trailing down her legs at the first-hand look at death. No thought, only animal knowing. "Danny Mann!"

The hooked end of the crowbar stabbed through the front door. Brittany flinched back from her efforts to drag a hallway lampstand against the door handle, instead turned and hauled Gabe back to his feet. "Party's over! Go! Now!"

The front door shuddered beneath the Danny Mann's blows, the hook tearing loose great chunks of wood, the hinges pulling free of the wall. Yielding to Brittany's shoving hands, Gabe wheeled around the stairwell banister for the back of the house, stopping as he nearly ran face-first into the dangling body's legs. He backed up, hands grabbing at his hair as a sharp keen of horror rose from him. "Oh God, it's a re-ru-real—"

"Gabe, damn you!" shouted Brittany, still shoving at him rather than running for her own life. "Jamie, help me with this idiot!"

"... no," said Jamie, grabbing one of the other girl's hands and pulling her away from Gabe and back to the door, instead up the stairs. "No no, we gotta go find the others! Arnold just went up there, he could still be—we can't just leave him—"

Wood crashed behind them, peppering their backs. Both turned, Brittany blanching as the Danny Mann marched back into the house over the front door's shattered remains. With a snarl of mixed terror and frustration, she yanked her hand from Jamie's hold, gave up her efforts to push Gabe past Stephanie's hanging corpse, and dove past it herself, ignoring the other girl's screams chasing after her. Gabe's scream rose over it, cut off with sudden ferocity by the wet THWACK of metal striking flesh.

The other end of the house, the back end, lay dark except for the lonely rays slipping from the well-lit den and kitchen. The door to the backyard stood locked. Brittany rammed herself against it once, twice, three times before she caught the heavy tread of the Danny Mann slowly coming her way. She tried another door to the side and found a broom cupboard full of cobwebs and dust. She whimpered and slammed the door shut, spun, and tried a door opposite it. In the dark, she caught a dim impression of a narrow hall, white-walled, the floor dangerous with discarded drapes and broken shoes. Brittany closed this door quietly behind herself and crept down the hallway, one hand extended to each wall in the dying hope of feeling another door, another turn to put between herself and the killer.

Somewhere behind her, distant but deafening, someone— Jamie, she thought—wailed in sudden terror, then fell silent. Brittany clapped one hand over her mouth to stifle her own answering scream and pushed forward as quickly as she dared. Twice, she tripped over things she could not see, things which squelched in the dark and smelled sweetly pungent. Once, her hand found a doorknob on the wall, but it would not turn even when she put her whole body into it.

Behind her, farther down the hall than she expected, there came the creak of a door opening. Brittany paused, jerked her head around to stare behind her. The back hallway swelled as dark as she remembered it... but in there with her walked a deeper darkness, a heavy black shape, slowly striding her way with something long, and heavy, and sharp grasped tight in its unseen hands.

Brittany bit against the whimper wanting to slip free and turned around, almost breaking her nose against the door at the far end of the hallway. At this she did cry, half in relief, grabbing for the handle. For half a second, she panicked, certain it would not turn, and the last thing she would hear before the sudden burst of pain and death would be her own hammering heart and rushing blood.

The doorknob turned. She threw herself through the door and slammed it shut behind her with a click of the lock. In the same breath, something huge slammed against the door from the other side, huge and angry. Brittany stared; breath held. The door, too, held.

"Go away," hissed Brittany. She did not wait for an answer, turning and looking around for anything of use. A small window looking out onto the house's side yard let in enough from the streetlights to show her she'd made it to the garage, a small wall of old and rusting tools mounted beneath the window. She saw, scattered around her, forgotten bags of ancient trash, a dust-heaped lawnmower of great antiquity, bundles of garden hose, stacks of newspaper wrapped together with twine, a corner of the garage dominated with shovels, hoes, and rakes. In another corner, old tarps and fishing rods, the sad remains of camping equipment lost to the past.

Brittany looked back and forth between the tools at her disposal, and the garage door out onto the front driveway for several seconds, then went and grabbed the longest of the shovels. She hurried to the garage door and jammed the head in under it, then when she realized she needed a fulcrum, she ran and grabbed the metal tackle box from the fishing supplies, dragging a heavy sack of gardening soil with her as well. Her eyes burned with tears. They ran unheeded as she put the box down, set the shaft of the shovel over it, and with a deep breath, pushed.

The old hinges screeched. Her arms trembled. The door rose two inches, three, five. She sobbed with the sudden flood of relief and grabbed for the bag of gardening soil. Teeth clenched and sweat dripping, she slung it over her end of the shovel to keep the garage door levered open, at least long enough for her to—

"B-Brittany?"

At her name she froze, dropped already to one knee. She looked from the door back into the house, heard the soft voice call out to her, again. She swallowed and slowly stood, barely daring to hope. "Jamie?"

"Oh God, Brittany!" the other girl's voice wailed, someone tugging on the doorknob. "I-I hid up the stairs as he killed Gabe. I th-thought he killed you when he c-came back, but I had t-to had to know. Let me in, please! God, Brittany, before he comes back this way! I don't wa-wanna die!"

Brittany was already moving. She unlocked the garage door and threw it open, grabbed Jamie's hand the same as the other girl had grabbed hers before and dragged her in, toward the escape route. "I've got you, I've got you! This way, hurry, we can—"

But Jamie planted her feet halfway there, grip on Brittany's hand becoming like iron. Brittany looked to her, mouth opening to ask why, but then the Danny Mann loomed into the doorway behind Jamie, shoulders slowly rising and falling in sick mimicry of breathing. Brittany gasped and yanked her hand free with enough force she thought for a moment she'd dislocated the wrist, falling hard on her rear to stare up at the both of them. She sat there for a long moment, not comprehending. "I don't... I don't..."

"Doing the dumb blonde cheerleader routine proud," remarked Jamie with a smile. "I said I had family involved in the original case."

Brittany floundered. "I... we all thought... the police—"

Jamie's smile grew wider. "Did I say the family involved was a cop?"

BAD PARTY by BRIAN McNATT

Without a word, Brittany twisted around and crawled for the gap beneath the garage door. The Danny Mann stormed after her. She got herself almost halfway under when the wood and metal creaked, shrieked, slammed down into the middle of her back.

SNAP.

Jamie watched unblinking as the Danny Mann brought the door down five, six, seven times, the cheerleader's screams muffled through the wood, but sharp enough as bone was crushed, and meat torn. The other girl's legs kicked blindly, nothing but spasms, and it seemed like the whole house shook from the force of the blows, until finally the Danny Mann slammed the garage door a final time, a thick and dark fluid spurting out from Brittany's organs and her screaming outside reaching a crescendo. The Danny Mann backed away, only enough to squat and grab his final victim's legs by the ankles.

"Oh, darkest god, yes," hissed Jamie.

The Danny Mann stood back to his full height and turned, yanking. Whatever connective tissues remained ripped and Brittany's lower half, from her belly button down, came away from the rest of her, tossed to the other side of the garage. Outside on the driveway, her screams fell into blood-frothing gurgles, and then to silence.

For a minute, the Danny Mann stood motionless and took in his work. Then he looked to Jamie, black pits staring out through the gaps of his face mask. Jamie adjusted her witch's hat once more, out of habit as she looked to him with adoration. "Uncle Daniel..."

Tall, Dark and Rancid

by Gerri R. Gray

THE SPICY AROMA OF APPLE-CINNAMON permeated the inside of Lenore Finch's house as she made her daily rounds with her eight-ounce can of air freshener. It mingled with the other sweet fragrances unleashed by the numerous scented candles and jars of potpourri positioned throughout the residence. The smell produced an overwhelming, almost intoxicating, perfume that hung heavy in the air.

She paused in front of the hall mirror and gazed at her reflection. *Howard loved when I wore my hair up like this,* she thought. *He always said it reminded him of Audrey Hepburn.* Fighting a twinge of sadness, she did a careful inspection of her lipstick and eye make-up to make sure nothing was smudged. She wanted to look her best for the man who was coming to call on her. His name was Terry Robards, and he lived in the next town over. She had never met him in person before but had heard a slew of wonderful things about him from her best friend, Carole, who had arranged the blind date. According to Carole, he was "very charming, for a pharmacist," and could be a tad on the shy side at first.

Lenore checked her wristwatch for the time. In less than an hour, she would be on her first date since the untimely death of

TALL, DARK AND RANCID by GERRI R. GRAY

her husband from sudden cardiac arrest. She headed downstairs to the kitchen to make herself a drink, hoping a gin and tonic would help to calm the butterflies in her stomach. *Nothing must go wrong tonight*, she told herself as she pulled open the door to the well-stocked liquor cabinet. *Everything has to be perfect.* But no sooner had she wrapped her fingers around a bottle of Beefeater than the chiming of the doorbell echoed melodiously throughout the house, startling her out of her thoughts.

She looked down again at her wristwatch. *It couldn't be Terry*, she thought. *I'm not expecting him to arrive this soon.* She shut the cabinet door and headed to the foyer. The doorbell rang again, and the butterflies in her stomach fluttered wildly. She took a deep breath to steady her nerves and then opened the door.

Outside on the stoop stood a denim-clad man holding a single red rose. He was tall and dark-haired, just as Carole had described him over the phone. And, despite his eyes being obscured by a pair of dark aviator sunglasses, he appeared to be much younger than Lenore had expected. Not that that was a bad thing in her book by any means.

Behind him, the early-November sky, the color of granite tombstones, formed a bleak backdrop. Windborne leaves, their brilliant autumn colors now faded, swirled around his snake-skin cowboy boots like dancing rats. Spots of raindrops began to speckle the flagstone pathway leading from the front door to the street, where, oddly, no vehicle was parked.

"Hello. Are you Terry?" Lenore asked the stranger. "Terry Robards?" Goosebumps were beginning to spring up on her exposed arms as she stood in the open doorway, giving her ivory skin the less-than-alluring appearance of a plucked goose. As she attempted to rub them away, she wondered if the chill that hung heavy in the air was to blame, or was it her date night jitters, a feeling she hadn't experienced since her very first date with Howard, decades ago.

The man responded to Lenore's query with a nod of his head and extended the rose to her. He remained cloaked in silence as if waiting for her to make the next move. A muscle flinched in

his cheek, causing one side of his bushy mustache to twitch.
 Lenore remembered Carole mentioning Terry's shyness. Truth be told, she found it a rather endearing quality. However, the shaggy walrus mustache drooping over her date's upper lip was an entirely different matter. No heads up had been given on that particular attribute, which she found less than appealing. Dearly departed Howard had always kept his face clean-shaven. Facial hair would never do. Lenore made a mental note to recharge his old electric shaver to use later.
 Hoping that her date wouldn't notice her goosebumps, she reached out to accept the rose. As she held it below her nose and inhaled its fragrance, the man took her other hand in his rough, manly paw and raised it to his mouth. He then gazed into her eyes through his tinted lenses and placed a kiss upon the back of her hand, which seemed to make his breathing quicken. Lenore found his reaction a trifle odd, but flattering, nonetheless. She couldn't remember the last time a gentleman had kissed her hand.
 "I'm Lenore," she said, smiling as she introduced herself. "It's a pleasure to finally meet you, Terry. Carole's told me so much about you—all good, I might add." A nervous giggle escaped her lips. "Do come in and make yourself comfortable."
 She ushered him inside her home and led him into a dark-paneled parlor bathed in the dim glow of a Spanish wrought iron chandelier dangling above. She paused to poke the fire in her stone fireplace back to life. She then looked up at her reflection in the large baroque mirror that hung over a mantel flanked by intricately carved gargoyles with the most menacing of faces. Relieved to find her hair and make-up still in place, she proceeded to place the red rose into a cut-crystal bud vase that sat on the mantel next to an Edwardian clock. She offered her guest a drink, which he declined with a shake of his head. *Damn it*, she thought. *A teetotaler.* She motioned for him to sit down next to her on a tufted, leather Chesterfield of oxblood red, which he did.
 A low growl of thunder sounded off in the darkening

TALL, DARK AND RANCID by GERRI R. GRAY

distance as the man sat down and removed his sunglasses. He smiled as his eyes connected with Lenore's, and she smiled back at him. Despite the overgrown mustache, he wasn't a bad looking fellow, albeit not nearly as handsome as Howard.

Dear, dead Howard. On his deathbed, just before his untimely demise, he had told his distraught wife that he didn't wish for her to spend the rest of her life a lonely widow. He said it was — her *duty* — to find someone new after he died. She wondered if he would approve of her choice.

"Nice place you have here," he commented, his eyes scanning the room. Their gaze locked upon a large mahogany curio cabinet. It was brimming with grotesque statues of horned anthropomorphic creatures, nightmarish death masks, and bizarre primitive fetishes. His nose wrinkled in bewilderment as he stared at the macabre menagerie.

"I can tell by the expression on your face that you possess an appreciation for fine art," Lenore commented. "My husband, I mean my *late* husband, had a passion for… the unusual. He collected these little oddities during his many travels abroad. He was particularly fond of occult artifacts from Africa and the Middle East."

The man shifted his gaze back to Lenore. "You don't say." He offered up another smile. "Occult artifacts…that's different. Some people might even call it weird. But, hey, everybody collects something, right? Some people collect antiques, some collect trophies. Either way, it's the thrill of the hunt that makes collecting all worthwhile."

Lenore nodded her head. "Truer words were never spoken." Her eyes suddenly brightened. "The artifacts in that curio are just a small part of the collection. There's more upstairs. Much more. And some very special pieces that I think you might find interesting. I'd be happy to show you if — "

Before she could finish her sentence, the ringing of the old, black rotary telephone in the other room interrupted her. *Damn it! Someone's got bad timing.* Rising from the sofa, she politely excused herself and hurried to the den to answer the phone, which sat atop an antique writing desk.

"Hello?" she said into the mouthpiece, trying her utmost not to sound irritated.

"Hi," said a man's voice. "Is this Lenore?"

"Yes. Who is this?" Lenore enquired. She didn't recognize the voice in her ear.

"It's Terry. Terry Robards."

Terry Robards? "Is this some sort of a joke?"

"No joke. But I do have some bad news. I'm afraid I'm having a bit of trouble with the old Caddy. Can't seem to get her started. So, it's looking like I won't be able to keep our date tonight."

Horror and disbelief pummeled Lenore like a brutal fist, rendering her stunned, almost to the point of speechlessness. "Terry?" she squeaked.

"I can't begin to tell you how truly sorry I am, Lenore. You have no idea how much I was looking forward to meeting you. I even had something very special planned. If you're not busy tomorrow evening, perhaps we can reschedule our date for then?"

A shiver descended upon Lenore's spine. Her hands turned to ice, and she felt the phone slipping from her grasp. "Oh, no…"

At that moment, a startling boom of thunder vibrated the house. The connection crackled and then the line went dead with a buzz. As she returned the handset to the cradle, her thoughts quickly flashed to the stranger she had left in the parlor. *If he isn't Terry, then who the hell is he?* She felt a shiver of dread run through her body and thought it best to arm herself with a weapon of some sort in the event that his intentions were unsavory. Her mind recalled Howard's old bronze ritual dagger with the dragon-shaped handle—a souvenir he had brought home from a Tibetan excursion many decades ago. He always kept it in the top drawer of the desk, and frequently used it as a letter open, right up until the day that he departed this world. She pulled the drawer towards her and took the dagger in her

TALL, DARK AND RANCID by GERRI R. GRAY

right hand, the metallic dragon leaving its impression in her palm as she tightened her grip on it.

Concealing the dagger behind her back, she returned to the parlor to confront the imposter, only to find him nowhere in sight.

"Terry?" she called out, even though she now knew that wasn't his true name.

Her call was answered only by dead silence, save for the ticking of the clock on the fireplace mantel.

Lenore exited the parlor and cautiously made her way down the hall to the foyer, where she found the front door standing wide open. Dead leaves tumbled across the checkerboard marble floor, as a bone-chilling gust of wind came sweeping in with a ghostly moan, making the flames of Lenore's scented candles flicker wildly. Above, the tinkling prisms of a glittering chandelier stirred in the rush of air like tiny skeletons performing a danse macabre.

Lenore peered from the doorway as another gust of wind stormed in, prickling her exposed flesh. Outside, monstrous clouds of mordant black were amassing. Her eyes scanned the front area of her house as the bare branches of trees waved at her like scolding fingers. But there was no trace of the mysterious man. Surmising that he took flight after overhearing her conversation with the real Terry, Lenore let out a sigh of relief. She shut the door and locked it securely. *Weirdo*, she thought.

She returned to the parlor, plucked the red rose from the vase, and tossed it onto the crackling logs in the stone fireplace. Its petals curled and shriveled, and it emitted what sounded like a tiny whimper as the flames consumed its beauty.

Lenore headed into the kitchen for a broom and dustpan with which to clean up the leaves in the foyer. She laid the dagger upon the kitchen table, next to a can of air freshener — one of many that she kept throughout the house, ready for employment in the event that any foul odor should rear its ugly head.

She let out a scream as the door of the utility closet suddenly burst open and the man in the snakeskin boots lunged at her, his teeth bared, his eyes wild. Within seconds, she found his rough, meaty hands clamped around her throat, stopping her breath. A wave of horror swept over her. She could scarcely believe what was happening. It was like a horrible dream. She dug her fingernails into his wrists, drawing small rivulets of blood. She kicked and struggled to pull his hands away from her neck, but to no avail. His strength overpowered her.

"Women are the most beautiful," the man grunted, "when death dances in their eyes."

Lenore's ears were ringing and she felt a small trickle of blood emanate from one of her ear canals. She began to feel lightheaded and detached from her body. She knew if she blacked out that would mean certain death at the hands of her assailant. As long as she clung to consciousness, she had a fighting chance to save her life. Mustering every ounce of her remaining strength, she drove her knee up into the man's groin as hard as she could. It had no effect. Refusing to give up, she rammed her knee into his testicles again, and again, and again until he finally released his death grip on her throat and doubled over, howling in pain.

A rush of oxygen filled Lenore's deprived lungs. Gasping, she turned to flee from the kitchen, but her escape was thwarted when the man seized her by the hair and slammed her into the kitchen table, toppling the can of air freshener, which rolled off the table and onto the floor with a loud clunk.

"You let the devil into your house when you invited me in!" he yelled.

Without hesitation, Lenore grabbed the dagger from the table. Once again, the bronze dragon imprinted its ancient image into the palm of her hand. A struggle ensued and the blade bit into the man's upper arm. Blood blossomed like a dark red rose, staining the lacerated sleeve of his denim shirt.

"You rotten whore!" he snarled as he caught Lenore by the wrist and wrestled the dagger away from her. He backhanded her across the face, a monstrous grin twisting his lips. The force of the blow sent her crashing onto the cold, tiled floor. Her head swam in a daze.

When her fog cleared and her eyes could focus again, Lenore found the man kneeling over her, holding Howard's dagger against her bruised throat. She felt death was imminent and wondered if she would actually see her life flash before her eyes as she drew her final breath. Or was that simply an old wives' tale?

"Look what you did to my arm!" the man yelled. His warm breath was like an ill breeze violating Lenore's face. His tone became mocking. "That's no way for you to behave on our first date, Lenore." He shook his head, indicating his disapproval. "No way at all." He grinned, but then his face became somber. "And we were having such a fun time too…before you stabbed me."

"Who are you, and why are you doing this?" Lenore sobbed, tears glistening in her eyes, black trails of eyeliner and mascara running down the sides of her face. "What is it that you want from me? Money? Is that what you want? My husband left me with lots of money. We can go to the bank in the morning, and I'll withdraw all of it and give it to you. I promise. Please, just don't kill me!"

"Shut up! Shut up! Shut up!" the man bellowed with rage. He pressed the blade of the dagger harder against Lenore's trembling throat. "I didn't come here for your filthy money! Do I look like a goddamn robber to you? Or some kind of Skid Row loser?" Madness gleamed in his dark eyes. "Answer me, or I'll slit your throat right now!"

A cold sweat was forming on Lenore's forehead. "No, no, of course not," she nervously tried to assure him, hoping to diffuse his sudden swell of anger. "I'm sorry. I didn't mean to offend you. I don't think you're a bad person. But you're hurting me. Please. Put down the dagger. You don't have to do this. I can help you if you let me."

"You must think you're something pretty special, don't you? Well, you aren't!" the man growled through a spray of spittle. "You're no different than all the others I've hunted and gutted. You're nothing but a meat trophy!" His breathing became heavy as he slithered a finger lightly across the contours of Lenore's face. His voice softened. "I can smell your fear, Lenore. It smells, oh, so sweet," he whispered into her ear.

Wincing, Lenore turned away in a feeble attempt to escape his touch. Her eyes spied the fallen can of air freshener on the floor. It was within arm's reach.

"It makes me hungry," he continued, his arousal increasing. "It makes me want to rip you apart and devour you. And I will. I'm going to do things that you've never, in your worst nightmares, imagined." His breathing became frenzied. His head tilted back, and his eyes rolled up as if in rapture.

Seizing her opportunity, Lenore grabbed the can of air freshener, and before the man could react, she blasted his eyes with a blinding burst of the aerosol. He pulled the dagger away from her throat and instinctively covered his eyes with his hands in a fruitless attempt to suppress the burning sensation that assaulted them. Lenore struck the side of his head with the can. The blow was hard enough to put a dent in the metal. With one sudden, hard shove, she pushed his body off of hers and ran from the kitchen as fast as she could.

Cursing all women of the world, the man staggered in a besotted fashion to the kitchen sink and proceeded to splash copious amounts of cold water into his bleary, burning eyes. When enough of the chemical irritant had been flushed out, enabling a return of vision, he picked up the bloodstained dagger and set out to find Lenore…and to finish her off.

With stealthy footsteps, he moved through the house like an animal hunting prey. He searched the first floor in its entirety, and then made his way upstairs to the bedrooms, looking in closets, behind chairs and under beds.

There was only one bedroom remaining in which to look. It was at the end of the hall, hidden behind a white six-panel door. The man licked his lips in anticipation of the orgy of slaughter he was planning for his victim. As he crept towards the room, he deliberately scraped the point of the dagger along the wall. It produced an ominous sound, like the tearing of flesh, as it ripped a long gash in the floral wallpaper.

He turned the knob and gave the door a shove. It swung open with a slight creak. Without warning, the malodorous smell of something musty came rushing into his nostrils. Ignoring the odor, he stepped inside, dagger poised to strike.

It was a capacious, high-ceilinged room, decorated, like much of the rest of the house, with dark antique furniture. A massive canopy bed, draped on all sides in heavy scarlet linens, stood at one side of the room, facing a pair of tall French doors leading to a small balcony overlooking the front of the property. Large oil paintings depicting fiendish-looking, winged creatures that were not of this world adorned the brocade walls, giving the room a weird vibe. But even weirder were the two open coffins sitting side-by-side on the floor in the center of the room.

"What the hell?" the killer muttered to himself as he slowly advanced toward the coffins. The nearer he drew to them, the more phenomenal in its foulness the musty odor became.

He found one coffin to be empty, but the other was occupied. Inside it lay what appeared to be the mummified remains of a man dressed in formal attire, a black bow tie around its desiccated neck. The skin on the corpse's gaunt face clung like a hideous leather mask over its skull, and its ears, nose and eyelids were a blackish color. Hanging loosely on its withered ring finger was a gold band set with a large black onyx, the stone engraved with mysterious symbols—runes or perhaps hieroglyphs. It looked to be a relic from a time long past.

He slowly laid the dagger at the edge of the coffin and stared at the ring for several moments, as if mesmerized. Then he tugged it from the mummified man's digit and slid it onto the fourth finger of his left hand. It was a perfect fit.

As his eyes remained transfixed on the ring, Lenore emerged from her hiding spot behind one of the floor-length drapery panels flanking the French doors. In her right hand, she held a gun with a silencer on the end of its barrel. She raised it and aimed it at her assailant's heart, which she concluded was as black as the depths of Hades.

"I see you've met my husband," she remarked. "Unlike you, Howard is a *true* gentleman." With her gun still pointed at the man who intended to murder her, she turned to the musty corpse in the coffin and spoke to it as if it were still alive. "Howard, sweetie, I hope you can hear me. Tonight is the night, just as I promised. This man here is going to be your new vessel. I do hope you approve of him."

The man snapped out of his trance. "New vessel? What the hell is that supposed to mean?"

"It means I'm going to help you, just like I said I would. You're a sick man, a rabid animal, but I'm going to fix all that. I'm going to give you a brand-new lease on life. I know it's hard for you to believe, but I swear it's true. I have the knowledge… the ability to do that."

"What the hell are you babbling about?"

Lenore smiled. "Let me enlighten you. You see, I'm going to perform a soul transfer, right here in this very room. It's an ancient ritual. Extremely powerful. It will enable Howard's soul to take possession of your physical body, essentially rebirthing him. And you'll be…"

"Like two peas in a pod?" he interrupted, flippantly.

"Not exactly," Lenore explained. "You see, all workings of black magic require a sacrifice of some sort as payment to the old gods—the dark ones who have roamed the earth for eons before the birth of Christ. That malignant thing within you that passes for a soul will be offered up to them in accordance with the ancient laws of sacrifice. They will devour it, and then, that part of you will simply cease to exist. But there's no reason for you to worry. It'll be quick and painless, unlike the torture you like to put your female victims through. Now, kindly get into the empty coffin."

Lenore could tell by the man's roar of laughter that he discredited her words.

TALL, DARK AND RANCID by GERRI R. GRAY

"You can't be serious, lady," the man snickered. "No hocus pocus or ancient gods are going to bring that stiff over there back to life. If you actually believe you can resurrect the dead by transferring souls or whatever, you belong in a nut house."

Lenore grinned with amusement. "Do I? If you ask me, I'd say that was the pot, or the *crack*pot in your case, calling the kettle black. Now, do as I tell you and get into that damn coffin before I lose what little patience I have left."

The man began to inch his way towards Lenore. "You aren't going to shoot me. You don't have the guts to pull that trigger. You and I both know that." He wrinkled up his nose. "All that blood and guts everywhere…"

Lenore cocked the gun and shouted, "I'll shoot you if I have to! I swear it! Don't make me do it. I prefer not to put holes in Howard's body-to-be."

The man stopped in his tracks and threw his hands up in the air. "Okay, okay. Take it easy, Lenore. I'll play your whacked-out little game…for now." He took a step back, turned and stepped into the coffin. He stared blankly at Lenore, his hands still raised. "Now what?"

"Now lie down," Lenore instructed. "Do it!"

The man did as he was told. Lenore walked over to the coffin, reached into her pocket with her free hand and extracted a handful of strange black powder, which she blew into his face as though she were blowing him a kiss. He began coughing furiously. His eyeballs rolled up into his head, and soon, an acrid, black fluid began dribbling from his nostrils and the corners of his mouth. Lenore slammed the lid shut and locked it to prevent the man from escaping before the somniferous properties of the powder took their full effect.

The sound of her captive's fists pounding frantically against the inside of the burial container that enveloped his body was a sweet melody to Lenore's ears. It brought a smile to her lips and inspired within her a sense of euphoria.

And then the melody ceased and there was only silence, save for the low moaning of the wind about the velvet-draped

CAMP SLASHER LAKE: VOLUME ONE

windows.

"It won't be long now, sweetie," she whispered to her husband's corpse. "Soon, very soon, we will be together again."

After giving the room another blast of apple-cinnamon and drawing the drapes on the French doors, Lenore began preparing for the long-awaited ritual that she believed would reunite her with Howard. She dabbed her forehead with a drop of perfumed anointing oil she'd obtained from an occult apothecary shop. Its aroma was heavy and almost intoxicating. She then cloaked herself in a black ritual robe edged with mystical gold symbols. She drew a large magic circle on the floor around the two coffins, marking each of the four cardinal direction points with black pillar candles. Her heart thumped with excitement as she opened a black, leather-bound grimoire and began reciting an evocation written in an ancient tongue. The words from her book of magic spells reverberated on her lips, waking the old gods from their deep, dark slumber.

Lightning set the sky ablaze, followed by a peal of thunder that rattled the heavens. The French doors blew open and the velvet drapes danced wildly in the wind that howled through the room like a pack of wolves—or, as Howard was fond of saying, a choir of sinners.

Having completed the final step of the ritual, Lenore closed the grimoire and set it upon her ornately carved dresser, next to the gun. Butterflies were aflutter again in the pit of her stomach as she eagerly unlocked the coffin containing the body that now served as the living vessel for Howard's disembodied soul.

"Wake up, Howard," she cooed. "The ritual is over. It's time for you live again!"

She waited for a response but received none. Not even the faintest sign of revival. After a few restive moments, she tried once again to rouse Howard's soul from its sleep. But still the

TALL, DARK AND RANCID by GERRI R. GRAY

vessel's eyes remained shut, his mouth wide open, frozen in a silent scream. He didn't appear to be breathing, which prompted Lenore to press her ear to his chest and listen for a heartbeat. There was none.

She grabbed one of the hands that had tried to brutally strangle the life from her earlier. It had a waxen pallor and felt like a chunk of refrigerated meat. She screamed, "Howard! I implore you to wake up! Take possession of this man's body now, before it's too late! It's your new vessel!"

Then she took notice of the onyx ring. She attempted to slide it from the man's lifeless finger but was unable to budge it more than a fraction of an inch. The finger was swollen and refused to give up its talismanic treasure. Determined to retrieve the ring and return it to its rightful place on her husband's hand, even if it meant resorting to the use of gardening shears to sever the finger, she wiggled and twisted and yanked it until, at last, she was able to pull it off.

"I don't know what went wrong," she lamented, as she slid the ring back onto Howard's finger. "I followed the ritual to a tee. I don't understand why it didn't…"

She lapsed into speechlessness as she observed in wonderment Howard's hollow chest suddenly rise and fall as he heaved in a breath and released it. A morsel of dust spilled from his nostrils. It was an unearthly sight, but one that set Lenore's heart reeling. After all this time, her beloved was at last returning from beyond the grave, albeit not in the intended body.

"The magic worked!" Lenore cheered. "And just as I was beginning to lose all hope. Howard, sweetie…can you hear me? It's Lenore. Rise and shine. Your sleep of death is over!"

Lenore's delight quickly turned into horror as Howard's cadaverous eyelids unfolded before her, revealing two spider-infested holes where his eyes should have been. To her shock, he suddenly sprang up. His horrendous hands, with greenish skin stretched tight like parchment over its bones, latched onto her wrists like a pair of vise grips. A terror-filled scream rose from her lungs as he attempted to pull her into the coffin with him.

Struggling to free herself from the corpse's clutches, she found it possessed great strength despite its wizened state. Howard's decayed mouth opened and the voice that resounded was not that of Howard, but rather of the killer in cowboy boots, whose body lay exanimate in the other coffin, ripe with the smell of death.

"You twisted witch!" he bellowed with a puff of musty dust. "You put me in the body of your dead husband! I should have slit your stinkin' throat when I had the chance!"

Lenore belted out another scream and wrested herself free. She ran for the gun on the dresser, her heart pounding wildly in her chest. She wondered if a bullet would suffice to kill something that was already dead… something that, by all laws of nature, was not even supposed to exist. She tripped over one of the black pillar candles and fell face-first to the hardwood parquet floor. As she scrambled to her feet, she saw that the corpse had climbed out of its coffin and was stumbling toward her. She made it to the dresser and took the gun in her hand, took aim at the thing that was once her husband, and pulled the trigger.

The gun jammed.

She pulled the trigger a second time.

Again, the gun jammed.

The advancing monstrosity was but inches away from being within arm's reach of Lenore. She threw the inoperative gun at it. It struck the corpse in the chest but did not faze it. She lifted the heavy grimoire from the top of the dresser with both her hands, and with a grunt, swung the book with all her might at the side of the corpse's head. It made impact with a loud thud that made Howard's teeth rattle. The head tore away from its neck and sailed across the room, striking one of the demonic paintings on the wall and sending it crashing to the floor. From the stump of its neck, hundreds of tiny spiders emerged. But even sans head, Howard's possessed corpse remained animated.

Its hands were wrapping around Lenore's throat when she

rammed the grimoire into the corpse's chest, sending it staggering backwards. She gave it a furious shove with her foot, causing it to topple back into the confines of its coffin. Wasting no time, she retrieved Howard's head and tossed it into the coffin as well. *This isn't exactly what I had planned for the evening*, she thought as she secured the lid.

Riddled with exhaustion and shaken to the core, Lenore changed out of her ritual attire and cleaned herself up. Afterwards, she settled down in her Rococo style tufted chair, where she soothed her frazzled nerves with a much-needed gin and tonic and pondered the strange events of the day. She scolded herself for letting that deranged man into her home. How could she have been so careless? After several close brushes with death, she felt fortunate to still be alive, although crushed by the failure of the ritual. What could have gone wrong? She was sure she'd followed all the instructions outlined in the grimoire... and then she realized Howard's onyx ring was on the other man's finger during the ritual.

His wearing of the ring must have somehow affected the ritual, transferring the wrong soul into the wrong body, she surmised. *I'll have to make sure nothing like that happens next time.*

The chiming of the doorbell derailed her train of thought.

Who on earth could be at the door? she wondered. An unsettling thought caused a wave of dread to rise inside her, and she sprung from her comfortable chair. *Could it be that someone — perhaps a neighbor or some passerby — heard screaming coming from the house and phoned the police?*

She opened the French doors and, with a sense of foreboding, stepped out onto the small, windswept balcony, which afforded her a view of the front door below. Looking down, she observed a well-dressed man standing on the stoop. He was tall with dark, wavy hair. In one hand he held a flat, white box tied with a red bow, in the other a bouquet of purple dahlias. He turned and began walking towards an older model Cadillac parked on the street in front of the house.

"Hello!" Lenore called down to the man. He turned and

looked up at her. "Can I help you?"

A smile appeared on his face. "Hello there!" he replied, as he started back for the house. "I'm Terry Robards. And you must be the lovely Lenore."

Lenore nodded her head. After everything she had just been through, she wasn't sure if his words were truthful.

"I finally got the Caddy to turn over," he explained, pointing at the car. "She can be a bit temperamental at times. Anyway, I tried calling you to tell you I was coming, but the phone lines were down. I hope it's not too late for us to have our date…if you haven't had a change of heart, that is."

Lenore began to tingle with excitement. *A second chance to perform the soul transfer*, she thought. *This time, I'll make sure nothing goes wrong.*

"No change of heart," she gleefully assured Terry. "Give me a minute or two and I'll be right down."

He smiled and nodded his head.

Lenore quickly checked her hair and make-up in the mirror, then took a long fashion scarf from one of the drawers in the ornate dresser and wrapped it around her neck to conceal the bruises. She also made sure to refill her pocket with the black sleeping powder in case she couldn't make Terry pass out with alcohol or a roofie. As she headed out of the bedroom, a banging sounded from the inside of Howard's coffin. His decapitated corpse was trying to get out.

Ignoring the noise, Lenore hurried down the stairs, spritzing the air with more apple-cinnamon scented spray as she went. She hoped it would mask the musty odor of her mummified husband, as well as the death stench of the other man, who needed to be dragged down to the cellar, dismembered with Howard's power tools, and shoveled into the incinerator. But that was a task that needed to wait until morning. This night was reserved for something far more important.

Lenore turned on the stereo in an effort to drown out the banging before opening the front door and greeting her date. His brown eyes twinkled at her. His face was clean-shaven and

TALL, DARK AND RANCID by GERRI R. GRAY

blessed with handsome features, although not as handsome as Howard, of course. His cheeks took on a rosy blush as he presented Lenore with heart-shaped chocolates and flowers. *Carole was right about him. He is very charming...for a pharmacist.*

"I hope you like chocolates," he said in a bashful manner. "I hope you like dahlias too. I would have brought you a dozen red roses, but I didn't want you to think I was the Red Rose Killer."

"The Red Rose Killer?"

"You haven't heard? He's a modern-day Jack the Ripper who likes to butcher women. His last victim was a retired schoolteacher from the next town over. I'll spare you all the gory details of the murders, but this psycho likes to leave behind a red rose dipped in blood at his crime scenes. The cops haven't caught him yet, so you need to keep your doors and windows locked and be very careful who you let into your home."

A chill ran through Lenore's body. "How horrible!" she remarked, as another ripple of goosebumps began to break out across her arms. "There certainly are a lot of sick people running around loose in this world."

Terry nodded his head in agreement, and then Lenore led him into the dark-paneled parlor and offered him a drink.

"I'll have whatever you're drinking," he said, politely.

"Okay then. Two gin and tonics coming right up! Just as soon as I find a vase for these beautiful flowers."

The banging was growing louder. No longer could the music conceal it.

Terry gave Lenore a puzzled look. "What's that noise?"

Lenore's mind raced to find an answer—one that would sound convincing. "That? Oh, it's nothing to worry about. Just a loose shutter on one of the upstairs windows. It bangs like that every time the wind blows. One of these days I'll have to get a handyman to fix it."

"I'd be more than happy to take a look at it sometime tomorrow, if you have a tall ladder," Terry offered. "I might be a pharmacist by trade, but I've been known to be pretty handy around the house."

The banging came to an abrupt stop and the house went eerily silent.

Lenore thanked Terry, and then with bouquet in hand, headed to the kitchen for a vase and two glasses of gin and tonic, one of which would be spiked with a pulverized sleeping tablet. Halfway down the hall, she hesitated. *Was that a creak on the stairs?* She listened for a few moments, barely breathing, her heart in her throat. The noise did not repeat. Dismissing it as her imagination or the wind blowing outside, she continued on her way.

She had just placed the dahlias in a hand-painted, ceramic vase and was filling it with cold water from the kitchen tap when she suddenly felt a pricking sensation, like the jab of a hypodermic needle, in her buttocks. Before she could comprehend what was happening, she lapsed into unconsciousness and slumped to the floor, where she lay surrounded by purple dahlias and pieces of the broken vase.

When Lenore regained consciousness, she found herself in a candlelit basement, her body attired in a wedding gown of white lace and strapped securely to a gurney. She struggled to free herself but could do little more than wiggle her fingers and toes and turn her head a bit in either direction. A rancid smell of rotting meat permeated her olfactory senses, and she soon realized its source was the putrefying body of a dead woman that was sitting upright in a chair beside her.

Both eyes of the corpse were black and blue, and its forehead appeared to be split right across, practically from one ear to the other. The head was missing patches of hair from its scalp, and slivers of ivory-colored bone peeked through spots on the discolored arms and legs where the flesh had rotted off. Flies and gnats buzzed about the lifeless horror that had, at one time, been a living, breathing woman. From one of the nostrils of its broken nose, a wriggling maggot came forth, and dropped into its lap.

Lenore heard the sound of approaching footsteps. She didn't

know if someone was coming to rescue or to murder her. She felt trapped in a nightmare. Nothing made sense. Her anxiety intensified as the footsteps grew louder. She prayed it wasn't the Red Rose Killer. And then Terry appeared in her field of vision.

"Terry!" Lenore cried out. "Thank God it's you! Where are we? Why am I strapped to this gurney?"

"Shhh. There's no need for you to panic," Terry answered. He gently caressed Lenore's cheek with the back of his fingers and offered her a comforting smile. "You're okay now, and everything will be all right. I promise."

"Why is there a dead woman sitting in that chair? Did you… did you kill her?"

A slight smile pulled at Terry's lips, and he looked upon the corpse with a loving gaze.

"That's my wife, Katherine…or, rather, what's left of her. She was killed in a car accident just over a month ago. A drunk driver t-boned her at an intersection downtown. She died instantly." He turned back to Lenore. "I've kept her down here in our basement because I can't bear to let her go."

It was then that Lenore's eyes glimpsed the black leather-bound book in Terry's hand, and she began to realize her fate. Struggling harder against the leather straps pinning her down, she beseeched the widowed man to free her, promising him the moon in exchange for her release. But her tear-filled pleading proved to be in vain. She begged him not to hurt her.

"I have no intention of harming you, Lenore." Terry began lighting black candles and placing them at the four quarters of a circle inscribed on the floor. "You're the perfect vessel for Katherine's soul." He opened the black book and started reciting an evocation written in an ancient tongue.

Lenore's scream was muted by the deafening rumble of thunder that shook the very foundation of the house as the old gods once again awakened from their deep, dark slumber.

The Backwoods Decapitator

by John Adam Gosham

SYLVIE AWOKE TO A GRINDING sound, almost like breathing. Shadows shifted against the tent canvas. She reached over for Jesse. His sleeping bag was empty. She could hear the gentle swirl and churn of water down by the shore.

She wriggled out of her sleeping bag and looked out onto the lake. In the moonlight, Jesse stood hip-deep in the water.

"Sylv!" he called out. "Come on in."

"You're crazy!" she called back. "It's too cold!"

"Come find out!"

She threw on her jacket and crawled out of the tent. Pine needles and pebbles scraped at her hands and knees. She made her way barefoot down the incline to the lake. They'd found the spot at twilight, the dense underbrush opening onto a narrow stretch of water, the pines thick and primeval on the opposite shore. It wasn't quite as pretty at night. And now it was cold, too.

But still, Sylvie went down to the lake. Jesse was always doing spontaneous things like this, and she couldn't help but follow. It was the reason she'd let him take her this deep into the woods.

"Isn't the water, like, gross?" she asked as she approached.

THE BACKWOODS DECAPITATOR
by JOHN ADAM GOSHAM

"Feels fine to me," Jesse said. "It's less gross in the dark. Are you coming in or not?"

"I didn't bring a suit."

"You know you don't need it. Now, get in here."

She shrugged off her jacket and went in. The water was bone-hollowing cold. But then, Jesse had her in his embrace and the numbness gave way to a familiar warmth. They circled as they kissed, as if dancing to a slow song. Then, Sylvie pulled back, covering herself.

"Jess," she hissed in a whisper.

"What is it?"

"Look up at the shoreline."

There was someone standing beside their tent.

"Hey!" Jesse yelled.

The shadow man stood motionless, save for the heaving breaths.

"We're just camping here tonight!" Jesse said. "We'll be gone in the morning."

The man was massive. Next to his silhouette, their Coleman looked like a pup tent.

"But right now, we'd like some privacy, if you don't mind."

The silhouette seemed to unlimber, then it was brandishing something long enough to be another limb. Before Jesse could say anything, the shadow man swung around in the direction of their tent. Metal caught moonlight. An edged weapon large as a fan blade sliced through the canvas and guy ropes, and the tent wobbled as if wind-swept.

"HEY!"

Jesse waded toward the shore, fists clenched.

"Big mistake, asshole!"

But as the massive man turned and started down the incline, Sylvie saw that it was Jesse who'd made the mistake. The intruder eliminated the distance between himself and Jesse in two steps. In a beam of moonlight, Sylvie saw a flash of blade and tattered sleeves, and then, Jesse stopped in his tracks. The machete swung around and cut through Jesse's neck. Jesse's head tumbled into the water with a splash. Spurts of blood pattered onto the shore.

The scream lodged itself in Sylvie's throat, choking her. She let out convulsive gasps, pitching forward at the waist with each one. The hooded hulk was sloshing into the water now, eyes ablaze with moonlight, and fury spiraling out of the ragged eye-holes in his hood.

"No!" she rasped. "*No! Please!*"

But Sylvie couldn't hear her last words as the masked man crashed through the lake water and reared back with the machete.

"Camp," Fiona said, "just isn't me."

"You really think so?" Talia asked, elbow on the crest of the steering wheel, road coursing along the lenses of her shades. "Cuz I can leave you off right here, if that's what you want. You can hitchhike back."

"That's nice of you to offer," Fiona said dryly, eyeing the ragged pine on either side of the road. They hadn't seen another car for the last half-hour. "I guess there's no turning back. What's that sign say up there?"

"That's the road we want," Talia said, gearing down. "Next left."

"Fantastic," Fiona murmured.

They turned onto gravel. Talia accelerated and rocks kicked up against the undercarriage of the hatchback.

"Surely," Talia said, "you can drum up a little more enthusiasm than that. Didn't you ever go to camp when you were a kid?"

"No. Never."

"Well, didn't your—" Talia caught herself. "Didn't you at least go camping?"

"Did my parents ever take me, you mean? Yes. They did.

THE BACKWOODS DECAPITATOR
by JOHN ADAM GOSHAM

And that was a total mess."

"Sorry," Talia said. She began to nod. "But you know what? This is going to be totally different. There's bound to be a few decent, chill people up here. It'll be good to get away from the city, get some air off the lake. You're probably going to love it. You bivouac a camp, you portage a canoe or two, and you find things out about yourself. You'll feel better, I guarantee."

"I sure hope so," Fiona said.

"At least until the kids show up. Now, keep your eyes peeled for the Manitou Lake sign. It's supposed to be a right."

All Fiona could see was dense forest, overgrown with underbrush. The pine was much thicker now, and it rushed by in a blur of deep green.

"I had no idea it was this far off the road. Now, what the hell is this?" Talia said.

As they made their way around a rightward curve, a vehicle came into view beside the ditch. It was a matte-black pickup with big wheels, the rims also black. It had been left parked across a break in the treeline. Talia geared down and started to brake.

"What are you doing?" Fiona asked.

Talia eased off the gravel and onto the grassy shoulder of the road.

"I think," Talia said, "this is the place."

"But there's no one here—"

As Fiona said it, people emerged from the treeline.

Leading the trio was a blonde girl in cuffed dungarees. She pulled along with her a wavy-haired guy who offered an aw-shucks smile. Trailing behind them was a brooding dude who went no further than the truck box, resting a sinewy forearm on the tailgate.

"Are you looking for the camp, too?" the blonde girl asked

as Fiona rolled down the passenger's window.

"That we are," Talia said.

"You've found it," said the wavy-haired guy, pointing across the road to the opposite ditch. A tiny, weather-beaten sign teetered there. CAMP MANITOU LAKE, it read in barely discernible letters.

"That's the good news," the blonde girl said. "The bad news is, we can't really get the truck in, and now, we're blocking your way. I'm Shauna, by the way. This is Ethan. And back there is Dirk."

Ethan tipped an imaginary cap. Dirk curled his lip and turned to face the break in the treeline.

"We're counselors," Shauna said.

"So are we. I'm Talia, and this is Fiona. So, what exactly happened with the truck?"

"The goddamn trail's too narrow," Dirk called back.

Talia frowned. "Your truck looks like it could handle a little off-road."

"You'd think," Ethan said. "But Dirk doesn't want it to get scratched."

"Hey," Dirk said, "I just got this thing painted. Those branches could wreak havoc."

"We tried to call the supervisor," Shauna said. "But there's no cell service. At least not any we can get."

"I can probably make it through," Talia said. "We've got room in the hatch if you want to throw your stuff in there. The backseat fits three, not necessarily comfortably. Back the truck up and we can make this happen."

"And just leave my truck out here?" Dirk asked, lip still curled.

"It's not exactly rush hour," Talia said.

"Fine," Dirk said. "Whatever."

He got in the truck and backed up so that Talia had room to get through. Shauna, Ethan, and Dirk put their luggage in the hatch, and then the three of them crammed into the backseat. Talia guided the weighted-down hatchback toward the fissure

THE BACKWOODS DECAPITATOR
by JOHN ADAM GOSHAM

in the trees. There was a trail there, but it looked more like two bike paths — twin ruts with a grassy rise in-between.

"You weren't kidding," Talia said. "This *is* narrow."

"And getting narrower," Ethan said. Branches screeched against the exterior of the car. Leaves reached through the passenger's side window, and Fiona rolled it up.

"I'm actually really glad," Dirk said, hand splayed on the roof to keep his balance as they bounded along the rough road, "we took you girls' car."

"Jeez," Shauna said. "Maybe we shouldn't go any further. Maybe there's another way in. If you want to turn back—"

The trees on the right side of the trail relented, and all at once the hatchback entered into an open area. Log buildings hid behind very tall grass. The sun receded behind a cloud bank. A few hundred yards up ahead, the ebbing light played upon lake water.

Talia smiled, brow furrowed. "This must be... it?"

"Are we early?" Shauna asked. "Are we too late? It feels like we're the only ones here."

But they weren't. The door to the nearest building slammed open on rusty hinges and someone lumbered down the steps toward them.

"Salutations!" the man hollered as he approached the car, hand outstretched in a wave. "You must be the counselors! I've been expecting you."

"Mr. Alexander?" Talia said out the open window.

"Not Mr. Alexander," the man said, swinging around the side of the car. "Call me Niles, please. Let me be the first to welcome you to the new Camp Manitou Lake. Now, if you'll just follow me, you can park up here."

Niles directed Talia to pull up in front of a squat, shabby cabin, and then gave a thumbs up. Fiona vaguely recognized

CAMP SLASHER LAKE: VOLUME ONE

Niles as the man she'd Zoomed with for her job interview. The lighting must have been more favorable on Zoom. In the natural light, Niles looked peaked. He wore his eel-black hair combed back. He appeared to be around thirty, maybe even older. He was tall and rangy, broad-shouldered but with a bit of a slouch.

"Talia, Shauna, Dirk, and Ethan," Niles announced as they got out of the car. "Fiona. It's good to see you all made it here in one piece. In one car, no less."

"Barely," Talia said. "That trail back there was a challenge."

"Yeah," Dirk said. "I had to leave my truck out on the road."

"It'll be safe there," Niles said, with a dismissive wrist-flip. "That's an old logging road, and no one logs out here anymore."

"But can we log in?" Ethan asked, palming his iPhone. "I haven't been able to get any signal out here whatsoever."

Niles looked momentarily pained. "Worry not," he said with a sudden smirk. "The Wi-Fi will be up in a few days. It's one among the tasks we have to deal with before the children arrive. We'll get to those in time."

Shauna closed one eye. "And the kids are due here on—"

"Monday," Niles said. "If you absolutely must get a hold of someone in the meantime, there's a landline in the main cabin where I am. But right now, you probably want to dispense with your luggage."

Niles pointed to the squat, shabby cabin.

"This cabin directly in front of us," Niles said, "is the 'ladies' cabin' for the female counselors." He made air quotes with his fingers. "The 'gents' cabin' is on the other side of the children's lodgings, over by the water. But don't worry so much about gender assignments. Sleep wherever you see fit. Should you need a shower, the bathrooms are behind the main cabin. I'll see to it they'll be ready by tonight, though I still have some tinkering to do with the cistern. In the meantime, if nature calls, please do use the outhouses."

Fiona looked to Talia. Talia looked away.

"But right now," Niles continued, "your initiation to Camp Manitou Lake will not be complete until you change into your

THE BACKWOODS DECAPITATOR
by JOHN ADAM GOSHAM

uniforms. You'll find those in your cabins. I'll leave you to that. Then we'll reconvene out here and allocate the tasks."

Dirk and Ethan headed over to their cabin and the girls walked up the steps to theirs. Fiona trailed behind.

"Rustic," Talia said as she regarded the high grass reaching up to the top step. She pushed open the door. Shauna wrinkled her nose as the moldering smell wafted over them.

"To put it gently," Shauna said.

Talia flipped on the light switch. A fluorescent light flickered on... and on... and kept flickering.

The cabin's interior was a single room with cots pressed up against every wall. In the very center sat a circular table bearing a coal-oil lamp and a layer of dust. Everything seemed at least fifty years old, save for the pristine t-shirts laid out on the plaid flannel bedspreads. The light flickered away.

Talia tossed her keys on the table and headed for the cot in the northeast corner. Here, she dropped her bags and wrestled into the shirt. It was raglan style, black on the sleeves.

"Fits a little snug," Talia said.

"At least they're clean," Shauna added, sitting down gingerly on the cot against the west wall, wincing as it squawked. "This place really needs a dusting. And these cots aren't going to be comfortable at all. I think I'm going to sleep in Ethan's cabin tonight. It can't be much worse."

"Good thinking," Talia said. "Maybe I'll find a way into the gents' cabin, too."

Fiona remained stock still in the doorway under the persistent flicker of the light. "I think," she said, flipping off the switch, "I'd like to go home."

"Don't say that." Talia said.

"This place is a shithole," Fiona said delicately, her eyes following the motes of dust in the light from the small picture window.

"And it's up to us to make it *our* shithole," Talia said. "Now, come on. Put on your skimpy top like Shauna and me, and let's get this place cleaned up."

CAMP SLASHER LAKE: VOLUME ONE

Once they'd divided up the chores, Niles went on his way to the cistern, and the counselors went about their assigned tasks. Shauna volunteered to clean the shower room. Ethan went down to the beach to set up the swimming area. Dirk got tasked with the grass and was hacking down rudimentary trails with the noisy motorized whip. That left Talia and Fiona with cobweb duty.

Talia found herself de-cobwebbing the outside of the girl campers' cabin with an ancient straw broom. Every so often, she'd see Fiona, twirling away at the cobwebs on the boys' cabin, and they'd pause to exchange wan smiles. Fiona looked wistful, which was a bit of an improvement.

Talia used a stepladder to get at the peak in the roof. She had to do a balancing act to reach the dense cobwebs at the very top. As she fully extended from the top rung of the ladder, the whir of the motorized grass whip cut out. She heard footsteps. Dirk sidled up to the stepladder, eyeing her form.

"You're very graceful," he said.

"And you're pretty handy with the weed whacker," Talia said, stepping down to the bottom rung.

"What we need is a goddamn swather," Dirk said. "The grass is waist high in places."

"Isn't there a lawnmower?" Talia asked.

"Apparently," Dirk said, "but this guy Niles says it's in the shop. He says he's gonna try to fix it for tomorrow."

"Well," Talia said, uninterested, "too bad you're not getting paid by the hour."

Fiona stepped back into view, and Talia waved at her. Fiona stilled her broom and waved back. Dirk surveyed their exchange.

"So," Dirk said, as Fiona resumed her task. "What's the deal with your friend there?"

THE BACKWOODS DECAPITATOR
by JOHN ADAM GOSHAM

"Fiona?"

"Yeah."

"She's a little... shy."

"No, I mean, is she single?"

"She is," Talia said, lowering her voice. "But you wouldn't want anything to do with her, nor she with you. Her parents just went through a really bad divorce."

"A lot of people get divorced," Dirk said. "How bad could it be?"

"Mutual-restraining-order bad. She's probably not looking for a relationship."

"Who said anything about a relationship?"

"I'm saying this," Talia said, swinging the broom's cobweb-covered head under Dirk's chin. "Leave her be."

Dirk drew back. Spiders crawled amid the twined web and straw. "And what about you?" he asked. "Any recent break-ups?"

"None worth remembering."

"So, what does that mean?" Dirk asked. "You're open for—"

Niles was approaching. Talia took an unconscious step up the ladder. Dirk raised the grass whip, hand readied on the starter. Niles stopped, staked his hands on his hips, and appraised them. He wore a quivering smirk.

"Sorry, boss," Dirk said. "We'll get back to work."

"No, no," Niles said. "Fraternize away. Don't mind me. I was just marveling at what strides you've made. As I see it, everything's progressing just fine."

"Thanks," Talia said, and it sounded like a question.

"Oh, and you'll be glad to know," Niles said, "the showers should be fully functional as of now."

With that, he gave a wave and moved on.

"You didn't answer my question," Dirk said, turning back to Talia.

"You wanted to know if I was single," Talia said, climbing up to the top rung of the stepladder. "And I am. So, with that settled, you can go back to whacking it."

CAMP SLASHER LAKE: VOLUME ONE

In the heat of the day, the counselors took a break. Ethan urged them to come down to the lake to cool off. He'd mopped the dock and put out new buoys. He couldn't do much about the algae, though, and the water bore an uninviting green scum. Only Dirk and Ethan braved it by diving in. Talia sunned herself on the wooden walkway in a bikini. Shauna and Fiona sat on the edge of the dock, shoes off. Fiona dipped her toes in the water, and they came out green.

"It won't hurt you," Dirk said, watching from the water with a jagged grin. "You ladies should give it a try."

"I'm comfortable here," Talia said, the clouds moving across the lenses of her shades. "I'm just glad to get out of that counselor's uniform."

"Tell me about it," Shauna said. "It doesn't leave very much to the imagination."

"I'm not complaining," Dirk said.

"Shut up, Dirk," said Talia.

"You think that was by design?" Shauna asked.

"Do I think Niles made the uniforms too small by design?" Talia said. "No. Take a look at this place. I don't think anything's by design."

"You don't think he's perving on you?" Dirk asked, tilting his head toward the camp where Niles was moving back and forth, hauling around kindling. When Niles saw them looking, he lowered his load and waved. The counselors waved back, and Niles continued on his way with the wood, temporarily relieved of his slouch.

"There's only one perv here," Talia said, lowering her shades to eyeball Dirk, "and he's scummier than the water."

"Fuck you," Dirk said, and then side-stroked away toward the buoys.

"It's really not that bad once you get in," Ethan said, climb-

THE BACKWOODS DECAPITATOR
by JOHN ADAM GOSHAM

ing out of the water and onto the dock via one of the pilings.

"I'll wait 'til the kids are here," Talia said.

"Who'd let their kids swim in that?" Shauna asked.

"Not me," Talia said. "But these aren't my kids."

"I wouldn't worry about it," Ethan said, toweling himself off. "Niles said he's bringing in a machine to clear the algae and the weeds."

"Tomorrow, right?" Talia said. "It's always tomorrow with this guy. He doesn't seem to be in any hurry to fix this place up. There's no way we're going to be ready for Monday. We haven't even been inside the kids' cabins."

"You should see the shower-rooms," Shauna said. "The grime in there is, like, generational. I'm still not finished."

"I can help you with that this afternoon, Shauna," Fiona said.

"Would you?" Shauna said, shading her eyes with her hand. "That's sweet of you."

Fiona looked away. "It's no problem. I mean why should the burden fall on one—"

"Fiona? Is something wrong?"

Something moved in the treeline down the shore—something scintillating in the sun—or so Fiona thought. As soon as she'd picked it up, she lost it.

"Nothing," Fiona said. "I just thought—"

A hulking figure vaulted out of the water, sending spray up into the air. Talia shrieked as brawny arms enwrapped her, pulling her off the dock and into the water.

She thrashed to the surface and Dirk's grinning face followed after her.

"I told you it wouldn't hurt!" Dirk said.

"Fuck you," Talia said, pulling away. "Disgusting! Now, I'm going to look like the fucking She-Hulk. Thanks a lot."

Shauna and Ethan laughed. Clearly, Talia wasn't as offended as she claimed to be. Fiona smiled, too, but she was still staring at the treeline that ran unbroken down the lake.

CAMP SLASHER LAKE: VOLUME ONE

The counselors worked on the camp until dusk. Niles commandeered Ethan and Dirk and had them build a fire. There was a fire pit located in the common area in front of the cabins, and once the fire got going, the counselors gathered on the log benches arranged around it. They roasted wieners over the open fire, supplementing them with potato salad. Talia shared a log with Dirk, apparently already forgiving him for pulling her into the lake. Fiona had a log all to herself.

After they'd eaten, Niles produced a guitar. He urged Ethan to play some songs. Ethan was shy, but Shauna gave him some encouragement, and eventually, he threw the strap over his shoulder. He made a few halting attempts to get through 'Brown-Eyed Girl' for Shauna's benefit. It became clear that Ethan only knew a few chords, so he set the guitar aside.

An awkward silence mounted, offset by the crackle of the fire. Niles broke up the lull.

"So," he said, "I don't want to beat around the bush about Caleb."

"Who?" Dirk asked.

"Caleb Graves," Niles said, only his wattled profile visible against the black.

Talia looked to Fiona. Fiona shrugged. Ethan and Shauna wore the same mystified expression.

"Should we know who this person is?" Talia asked.

"You haven't heard the stories?" Niles said. "The legend? It's fairly well-known around these parts, even if no one wants to tell it anymore."

He paused for dramatic effect, perhaps a beat too long.

"And now, you're going to tell us?" Talia asked.

"I will," Niles said, eyes flickering with the campfire light. "I will, but only because I must. It's the responsible thing to do. Caleb Graves grew up just a few miles from here on the other

THE BACKWOODS DECAPITATOR
by JOHN ADAM GOSHAM

side of the lake, but 'grew up' is a bit of a misrepresentation. He never really was small. He stood as tall as a grown man by the time he was ten. He didn't last long in school. He didn't mix well with others. He didn't talk, and it's not clear how much he understood. He didn't have much of an IQ, but he wasn't stupid. He could see things, perceive things no one else could. He seemed very well-acquainted with pain, and he had much to teach his fellow pupils on the subject. He'd stand in the shade, gimlet-eyed, waiting like a python. Sometimes he'd lash out, but mostly he'd just wait. What was he waiting for? The teachers and the principals couldn't answer that. Neither could the counselors and the psychiatrists. But then, one fateful day in the early summer, the question was answered. Caleb Graves took an axe to his mother. He took an axe to his sisters. He took an axe to all their male suitors, too. They found the heads floating in the lake. The sheriff's office sent a whole squadron of officers to apprehend Caleb, but they never got a chance to try. No one could find him. He'd just disappeared into these woods. They had a manhunt for him, but Caleb Graves was never found. Everyone just assumed he drowned in the lake or perished due to the elements. But every now and again, someone would claim to see him. Every year or two, someone had a Caleb Graves sighting. The Backwoods Decapitator, as they called him. Some thought he'd survived, living on deer, and rabbits, and roots, and whatever else he could find, wearing a mask to hide his ugliness. People go missing here every year, hikers, and campers, and hunters—hell, even loggers. Just last month, a couple went missing trying to camp off the grid on the north end of the lake. Most never get found. But some do. Only their bodies, though. The heads are cut clean off. And every once in a while, a head washes up on the shore."

"Oh, God," Talia said, rolling her eyes.

"It all began in these woods forty years ago in June," Niles said, "right around the time this camp closed for good. No one wanted to send their kids to a camp near where a lunatic was on the loose. Some say they still see him, and that he's still alive—

bigger, keener, even more feral. Maybe the Backwoods Decapitator is still out there... When you don't know where he is, well, then he might as well be everywhere, no?"

Ethan took his arm from around Shauna's shoulder and applauded. Shauna joined in.

"Bravo!" Ethan said. "The kids are going to love it."

"For sure," Shauna said. "It's pretty spooky."

"I don't know," Talia said. "You've got to give these kids a little more credit. By the time they're eight or nine, they've probably heard a few hundred stories based on that exact template."

"No," Niles said. "They won't have. Because this one is true."

"Okay, Niles," Dirk said. "You can drop the crap theatrics. We're not eight years old."

Niles drew back, smirking. "I thought I'd at least give you fair warning."

"Ha-ha," Shauna said, letting her palms clap down on her knees. "I've got to say, this was a lot of fun. But I'm exhausted. I think I'm ready to hit the hay."

"Me too," Ethan said. "Goodnight, everybody. Have fun out here."

Talia got up. "I've had enough fun for one day. I think I'm going to brave the showers. I need to get all this algae and fire stank off of me."

"I'll go with you," Dirk said. "Who knows what's hiding in that grass?"

"I don't need an escort," Talia said. "But another set of eyes won't hurt. Good night."

"Good night."

The pairs went their separate ways. From the opposite side of the fire, Niles eyed Fiona.

"It appears that you're the odd one out," Niles said.

Fiona murmured, hugging herself tighter against the cold.

"Strange though it may seem," Niles continued, "I can appreciate your situation. Everyone's pairing off and you're just there, an island unto yourself. It's rather awkward, isn't it?"

THE BACKWOODS DECAPITATOR
by JOHN ADAM GOSHAM

"Yes," Fiona said, "it is awkward."

Niles smirked, firelight dancing on his ashen face. "Don't worry. I'm here with you. Not that I'm propositioning you or anything. That would be grossly inappropriate as your employer. What I mean is that I'm with you *in spirit*. Believe it or not, I myself have gotten rather accustomed to being the odd one out."

"Really?" Fiona asked.

"Yes," Niles said. "In fact, I've made peace with it. I've resigned myself to never finding someone."

"I'm sure you'll find someone," Fiona said, not entirely believing it.

"That's nice of you to say," Niles said. "Although sometimes it's not a person but rather a place that we need. And I think I've found my true calling with this camp."

"That's really lovely to hear," Fiona said, manufacturing a smile. "I hope you don't mind if I turn in, too. Do you need help putting out the fire?"

"No, no," Niles said. "I can manage it myself. You go off to bed. I'll see you very early tomorrow. And in the meantime, be careful not to walk in on anyone *in flagrante*."

"Don't worry," Fiona said. "It's nothing I haven't seen before."

Niles snorted a laugh. "Of course," he said. "Of course."

"Good night, Niles."

The gents' cabin was a carbon copy of the ladies,' though the fluorescent light didn't flicker. It cast a steady pall over Shauna and Ethan as they prepared for bed.

"E," Shauna said, hanging up her jacket, "do you think there was anything to that story of Niles's?"

Ethan let out a sharp snort. "Not for a second."

"There's not even a grain of truth in there?"

"No way," Ethan said, peeling off his counselor shirt. "I went to junior high in the town just north of here. I think I would have heard something about this, this Caleb Graves character. Clearly, that's a made-up name. It's just one of those yarns you tell kids, so they don't wander away from camp. If only Niles had put as much effort into getting this camp ready as he did into cobbling together that story."

"Yeah, I think you're right twice-over," Shauna said. "It was pretty rough out there today. That shower room was more than a two-person job. Fiona was talking about leaving. Now, I'm thinking the same way. If it doesn't get any better tomorrow, I might want to go home."

Even in the dim yellow light, Shauna could see Ethan's expression change. He took her by the waist, and his frown turned into a half-smile.

"I need the money," Ethan said. "But I'll tell you what. If it doesn't get any better tomorrow, we'll find a way to get out of here."

"Thanks, E," Shauna said, and kissed Ethan on the nose. "Now, let's get to bed. It's freezing in here."

Ethan grabbed the sleeping bags. He laid Shauna's out on the cot in the northwest corner. He tossed his own sleeping bag onto the floor.

"What are you doing?" Shauna asked.

"I'm giving you the cot. You don't want it?"

"I'm not going to let you sleep on the floor."

"You think that cot will hold us both?"

"I'm thinking about staying warm," Shauna said, palming her shoulders.

"Alright," Ethan said, throwing open the sleeping bag. "We'll see if we both fit."

Once he was inside, Shauna climbed in after him in her clothes. He zipped them up.

"We did it!" Shauna said in the cylinder of cottony darkness they now inhabited together.

"Huzzah," Ethan said, his voice even more crisp and husky

THE BACKWOODS DECAPITATOR
by JOHN ADAM GOSHAM

in the confined space.

"We should celebrate," Shauna said. "Do you want to fool around?"

"Maybe I'll take a rain check," Ethan said. "There's not a lot of room to maneuver in here."

"Yeah," Shauna said. "I only asked because I thought it might generate some more warmth. And I guess it's not worth the risk of Dirk walking in on us."

"I'm not sure Dirk's going to be coming back here tonight," Ethan said. "Now, let's get some sleep."

Ethan fell asleep quickly. The evenness of his breathing soothed Shauna. His breath warmed her. She held him tight and, smiling in the dark, drifted off toward sleep.

She was awakened by the sound of the cabin door. It hit the interior wall but didn't come closed.

"It's okay, Dirk," Shauna said, her voice muffled. "We're decent."

No reply came, apart from Ethan's brief stirring. Shauna unzipped the zipper, poking her head out. A man's shadow blotted the open doorway, moonlight spilling in from behind.

"Really, Dirk," Shauna said. "It's okay. You can come in and turn on the light."

The shadow did not move.

"Come in, Dirk," Shauna said, about as petulant as she could sound. "And close the door. You're letting in the cold. Jeez."

She tucked herself back into the warmth of the sleeping bag and her boyfriend and zipped up again. Finally, he was coming in. Shauna heard what were clearly boot-steps before the sledgehammer hit her in the head.

The impact hollowed out her ears, and then the hammer came down onto her body and she could feel her ribs break. Ethan jolted awake with a howl as the hammerhead smashed down into his spine. Shauna tried to scream but it came out as a muted rasp, and then the hammer slammed into her neck. Every gasp died in her throat as the hammer fell indiscrimi-

CAMP SLASHER LAKE: VOLUME ONE

nately, battering their bodies. Kicking at the blankets, not so much kicks but spasms, actually, Ethan was now on top of her, taking blow after blow to his spinal column and occiput in short succession. Blood was smearing the interior fabric, and its coppery musk hung heavy in the humid sleeping-bag air. Then, the hammerhead hit Shauna square in the temple and it was like she'd been cast off, set afloat and sinking down, shrinking deeper, away from the sultry, bloody air and the wet sounds of her lover getting bludgeoned, aware only of the vibrations of each downward swing, like a drum beat diminishing into the distance. And then the beat stopped, and she was plummeting again, landing with a thumping squelch on the cabin floor. And there was Ethan juddering atop her, his bone fractures prodding into her, and then, the last of his life shook out of him. There was only one beat now, high up in her pummeled torso, and it, too, was fading.

Talia closed her eyes, turned the faucet, and braced herself for an invigorating pulse of hot water. What she got instead was bracing cold. She doubled back, letting out a yelp. She snaked her arms around the jets of ice water streaming from the shower head and gripped both faucets. Maybe hot and cold were ass-backwards. She played with the faucets, twisting one way and the other. The stream of water only seemed to get colder. At last, Talia gave up on a hot shower and settled for splashing the cold water onto her body. She wound up damp with freezing hands.

The door to the shower-room banged open. Talia turned off the faucet. Over the protesting metal, she heard the scrape of footsteps.

"Fiona?" she asked.

No answer.

"Shauna?"

THE BACKWOODS DECAPITATOR
by JOHN ADAM GOSHAM

Talia threw on her towel and poked her head out of the shower curtain. She could see no one. She stepped out of the shower, padding along the cruddy concrete floor. On the other side of the room, the toilet stalls were all closed, except for the one at the end.

"Fiona, if that's you, I have shampoo you can use, but the water's—"

A stall burst open behind her, and a hand clamped over her mouth, muffling her shriek. Talia kicked against her captor's grip and then whirled around to see Dirk.

"Shh, shh," Dirk said. "Easy now!"

Dirk took his hand from her mouth. He wore only a towel around his waist.

"What the fuck was that?" Talia wanted to know. "What's wrong with you, you fucking creep?"

"Relax," Dirk said. "I'm not perving on you."

"Then, why are you in the girls' shower butt-ass naked grabbing people?"

"I didn't want to startle you."

"Oh, okay. And how did that go?"

"Look," Dirk said. "I just wanted to try the showers in here to see if I could get some more hot water. The showers in the boys' went cold."

"You had hot water? Be thankful. All I could get was liquid ice in here."

"Maybe it's cuz we were both running hot at the same time."

"Yeah, no shit."

Dirk shrugged. "Well, maybe if we gave it a few minutes and got in there together—"

"Whoa!" Talia said. "Nice try. And you said you're not perving."

"You want to get clean, don't you?"

Talia smiled. "You're very right. I do want to get clean. So, you know what? I'll call your bluff."

Dirk perked up.

"We'll do a business shower," Talia said.

"A business shower?"

"As in, no funny business. We go in there, and we keep things strictly professional. No prolonged eye contact, no touching, and at least a foot between us at all times, or as much as the shower space allows."

"Seriously?"

"Dead serious. Come on. Maybe it's warmed up again. Now you go in first."

Dirk looked at her cock-eyed as he made his way into the shower.

"You gonna lose the towel?" Talia asked.

Dirk unwrapped his towel and tossed it out of the shower. Talia hung up her towel and stepped in. She maneuvered the faucets, and cold water coursed out. She stood with her back against her side of the shower, and Dirk followed suit on his side. Meanwhile, cold water formed a conical veil between them.

"Here we go," Talia said. "Warmth!"

She stepped into the stream, wetting her hair. Dirk took a step forward.

"Too close?" he asked.

"I'll let you know," Talia said, spurting a dollop of shampoo onto her palm. "You want some?"

"Sure, thanks," he said, taking the shampoo bottle.

Water splashed off Talia's shoulders and clavicle and onto Dirk as she lathered her hair. Dirk turned away.

"What's up?"

"Nothing," Dirk said, lathering his hair furiously, staring straight ahead into the wall.

"Turn around."

"No, it's okay, really."

"Turn around!"

Dirk turned halfway.

"Of course," Talia said. "Someone's gone into business for himself."

"Sorry," Dirk muttered.

THE BACKWOODS DECAPITATOR
by JOHN ADAM GOSHAM

"Nothing to be sorry about," Talia said, leaning in under the shower head and rinsing the shampoo out of her hair. "Looks like you've got a fine, upstanding junior partner there."

She tossed back her hair, eyeing Dirk.

"But let's face it. I just don't think he'd fit in in this kind of corporate environment."

Talia gave her hair another turn under the shower head and then stepped away, reaching for the curtain. The water had turned cold again.

"But don't worry," she said, gathering her hair into a rope and giving it a squeeze. "Maybe there'll be an opening soon."

She leaned in and brushed a kiss on Dirk's wet cheek.

"I'll leave it running," Talia said. "I think you two could use a cold shower after all. Good night, D."

Talia toweled herself off and changed into her clothes as the shower hissed on. Then, she headed back out into the night, pausing for a moment outside the shower-room door to allow her eyes to adjust to the over-saturated black. She started onto the freshly whacked path back to the ladies' cabin. A breeze swept through the tall grass on either side of the trail. Her eyes were taking their time adjusting, so Talia guided herself by the dim light of the generator behind the little girls' cabin. The breeze picked up and she heard something like footsteps, but against the swish of the grass, she couldn't tell where from. Talia pulled up to a stop.

"Okay, Dirk," Talia said. "One jump scare's enough for tonight."

Something moved in the shadows around the generator.

"Hello?"

The massive, gloved hand shot out of the dark and gripped Talia by the hair. With one decisive yank, it twisted her around in a frenzied pirouette. She tried to scream, but then the cold blade was at her throat, and then the sensation ran hot across her skin. Blood spurted out in gouts as the hunting knife sawed down into her trachea. Talia struggled bug-eyed, gurgling blood, and dropped to her knees, left to die in the uncut grass.

Dirk clenched up and bore down and the cold shower ended up doing him some good. It had cut through the sexual tension, at the very least. As he dried himself off, his teeth chattered like a little kid's, but no one was watching, so what did it matter? He slipped back into his jeans and shoes but opted against the jacket and the skin-tight counselor shirt. Beads of water still clung to the hair on his chest and arms, and he didn't want to risk getting his outerwear wet. He stepped outside bare-chested, letting the breeze dry him out as he made his way back to the gents' cabin. In the fire pit, coals still smoldered, and Dirk appreciated the pocket of warmth they offered him as he passed. He thumped up the steps of his cabin and found the door ajar.

"Hello?"

He heard a low, croupy moan, faint against the breeze.

"Am I... interrupting?" Dirk asked.

The weak, warbling sobs continued. It was Shauna.

"Cuz I can come back in ten minutes if you—"

There were tiny little words to be heard. Dirk pushed open the door and stepped into the cabin.

"—*help m-m-me... help uh-uh-us...*"

"What the fuck?" Dirk snorted. "I'm gonna turn on the light!"

And when he did, Dirk's larynx bobbed savagely in his throat.

On the floor lay a sleeping bag soaked with blood. Ripples moved through it as someone wriggled vainly inside. The cabin stank of pulverized flesh.

"Everybody okay?" Dirk whispered.

He inched closer to the sleeping bag, reaching for the zipper. He pulled it down. In the narrow, triangular window that opened into the sleeping bag, he saw a single brown eye rolling and darting and searching behind a tangle of blood-soaked hair

THE BACKWOODS DECAPITATOR
by JOHN ADAM GOSHAM

and bruised skin.

"Shauna," Dirk whispered. "W-what the fuck?"

A colossal heaviness moved through Dirk's limbs and his hand dragged the zipper down further. He glimpsed another eye—Ethan's—hanging limply from its crushed socket.

Dirk screamed and scrambled backward through the door. He clambered down the steps, hollering at full throat. He sprinted around the fire pit and past the ladies' cabin, shrieking. He veered at an angle in the direction of the supervisor's cabin and set his course for the narrow opening to the trail. When he got there, he'd have a mile through the bush and then he'd be home free.

Against his hysterical shrieks and the wind-tunnel rushing past his ears as he ran, Dirk did not hear the weed whacker whirring to life. He saw only a flash as the spinning blades swung out from the shadows and intercepted him in mid-stride, burrowing into his solar plexus. Blood bubbled out of his abdomen and then his mouth as he tried to fight free. And as he struggled, his attacker pulled out from the shadows, the massive man holding the weed whacker. Dirk saw a hooded face, a blank slate save for two eyeholes that projected a black so dark it was almost glossy, actually spiraling out and boring into him like the weed whacker currently pureeing his internal organs.

Sleep had not come quickly for Fiona. In the undifferentiated black and utter silence of the cabin, all the old episodes came flickering back in snippets. She'd tossed and turned in her cot to elude them, but then the whole production was playing in full.

Her mother, glassy-eyed, grabbing the knife, hefting it, saying matter-of-factly that she didn't know whether to cut her wrists or to cut his throat. Her father, half-drunk, telling her that, either way, she should go ahead and try it. Fiona, the interminable audience, feeling almost disappointed when her mother let the knife clatter to the floor, wanting more than anything else to scream.

Someone was screaming, and this was neither dream nor memory. Fiona shot up, instantly wide awake. The blubbering shrieks came from in front of the cabin. There was a loud whir, as if someone was cutting grass again but at night. Fiona threw off the blankets and rushed to the picture window. She'd hadn't undressed before bed, but even in her jacket, what she saw froze her in a tableau.

It had to be a performance. It had to be a joke.

There was Dirk, on his back, every limb spasming as a hooded figure towered over him, holding what looked and sounded like a weed whacker against his torso. Gore geysered up into the air.

Fiona could not parse what she was seeing. Her mind's eye emptied out. Her stream of consciousness stopped, and only one thought remained.

Fuck this.

Fiona came unfrozen. She darted toward the table and her hand swept across its surface involuntarily, collecting up Talia's car keys. Fiona barged out the door and pounded down the steps toward the hatchback. The hooded man seemed too preoccupied with whatever he was doing with Dirk to look over. Fiona reached for the door handle, only now articulating the plan she'd charted out on autopilot.

I'm going to get in the car, and I'm getting the fuck out of here. But first, I'm going to honk the horn and take whoever wants to go with —

Talia collapsed into Fiona, pushing her off stride.

"Talia, what the —"

Fiona interrupted herself with a glottal gasp as she looked into the open wound hacked out of Talia's throat, and as she felt the gentle jets of blood spouting out onto her. On the strength of her revulsion, Fiona pushed Talia's dying weight away. Talia teetered on her feet, air soughing out of her throat, her head tipping obscenely far back on her neck. With jaw unhinged,

THE BACKWOODS DECAPITATOR
by JOHN ADAM GOSHAM

it was almost as if Talia had two mouths now. She fell to the ground, dead. Feeling the heat of her best friend's blood on her hands and face, Fiona finally gave voice to her scream.

The scream echoed off the trees and across the lake. The weed whacker stopped. Fiona caught sight of the hooded maniac turning toward her.

Fiona yanked open the car door and threw herself behind the wheel. As she struggled to slot the key into the ignition, she mashed the horn with her palm.

The maniac tossed aside his grass whip and reached across his back for something else as he made his way toward the hatchback.

Fiona jammed the key into the ignition and turned it over. The hatchback started, the lights coming up on the girls' cabin. In the reflection from the picture window, Fiona could see the maniac raising an axe. She wrenched the gearshift into drive and—

THWACK! The maniac swung the axe head down into the rear passenger-side tire and hit his mark. Air soughed out of the wheel, making a sound like Talia's throat. The car sank.

"No! No! No!" Fiona hollered, struggling in vain with the gearshift.

The axe rose again, and the maniac swung it into the front tire on the passenger's side. It landed true.

"*Goddammit!*" Fiona brayed.

But this time, the maniac had gone too deep into the tire. The axe head was wedged in the wheel, and he struggled to withdraw it. The car sagged now on the passenger's side. Fiona's only hope was the main cabin and the phone.

She kicked open the car door and sprinted over to the steps leading up to the main cabin's entrance.

"Niles!" she screamed, pounding on the door. "Niles! Open the fucking door!"

The maniac had freed the axe from the wheel, and now he was taking heavy, measured steps toward the main cabin. Fiona charged into the door with all her weight, and it came open part way. As she shouldered her way through the door, the maniac made the first step up, and for a fleeting instant, Fiona's eyes locked onto his—or at least where his eyes should have been. Her pursuer wore goggles underneath the mask, and the goggles dripped blood.

Inside the cabin, Fiona threw the door closed behind her and locked it. In the dim light, she saw chairs pulled up to a counter and she grabbed one instinctively, slamming it up under the doorknob.

"Niles, is this some kind of fucking joke?"

In the dim light, the place didn't look like a camp supervisor's cabin. It didn't look like much of anything. There were some horror movie posters on the wall and several discarded cans of Monster. There wasn't much else, but there was a phone on the counter. Even if it all turned out to be a joke, the man in the hood had vandalized Talia's car, so calling the cops was well in order.

"Niles!" Fiona yelled, yanking the phone off the receiver, her voice almost unrecognizable, coming straight from her heaving stomach. "Wake up! We've got to do something! Things are getting—"

There was no dial tone.

"*Niles!*" she screamed, hammering on the numbers, "what's wrong with the fucking ph—"

The doorknob rattled manically as if possessed. Then came the shotgun blasts of the madman slamming shoulder-first into the door. The chair held. Then the axe-head split the door in two.

Fiona backpedaled down the hall, keeping her eye on the door as it disintegrated before her. As the hooded hulk kicked through the door, standing tall in the threshold, Fiona twisted around and stumbled sidelong to the back bedroom, keeping her pursuer in her peripheral view.

There was a window in the bedroom. She'd have to go through it. She waited until her pursuer started to gain speed down the hall, and then she sprinted for the window, lunging,

THE BACKWOODS DECAPITATOR
by JOHN ADAM GOSHAM

and smashing her way out into the night.

Fiona hit the ground hard on her side, glass shards smarting in her arms and face. She staggered to her feet, looking back to see the hooded man regarding her from the shattered window, tilting his head quizzically as she limped away.

"Fuck you!" Fiona hollered.

Biting her lip to fight through the mounting pain in her hip, Fiona started into a limping run. She had to beat him around to the front of the house. She set her sights on Dirk, lying face-up in a wet crimson mess. She fought hard to ignore Talia, face-down, and definitely not faking. As Fiona came parallel with the main cabin, she heard the maniac pounding down the stairs, and then he materialized from the shadows, tackling her in his arms.

Fiona fought hard to get away, but the maniac had too much mass. He gripped her by her sleeve and yanked her into the air, stripping off the jacket and bringing her down to the ground with force. Then, he stood over her, holding the axe perpendicular to his body, contemplating her. Her sprawled-out body appeared in stereo in his bloody goggles.

"W-who are you?" Fiona sputtered. She didn't struggle. She just wanted to know this much before she was butchered or whatever else was going to happen. "What do you want?"

The hooded man began to nod. He nodded for a long time. He hefted the axe again, releasing his upper hand from the handle. Taking it by the head, he held the axe out to her, handle first.

"Wh-what?"

"Take it," came the maniac's voice, deadened by the hood.

The axe-handle quivered in mid-air. Fiona pulled herself back. Sitting up, she reached for the axe.

"What?" she asked again as she took the axe in her hand.

The maniac took off his hood and, with it, his goggles.

"I said, take it," Niles said, dropping to his knees, looking her in the eye. "And now I'm going to tell you what to do with it."

"Stand up."

Fiona did as commanded. The axe felt heavy as an anchor, and she labored to get to her feet. "What's going on here, Niles? What do you want with me?"

"I want you to kill me," Niles said. "I want you to take that axe and bury it deep in my skull. That's what I want."

"N-no."

"Yes. Or you could cut off my head. It's not as easy as it might seem, but you could try. It's what I've always wanted, I've come to realize. And I know you can do it."

"Why?" Fiona asked. "Why me? Why any of this? Why don't you just kill yourself?"

Niles smirked. "I considered it, at one point. You can only be the odd man out for so many years before you realize you don't want to live anymore, if you've ever really been alive to begin with. You can only console yourself with so many video games and bad movies on the strength of your trust fund, after all. I could've hanged myself. I could've cut my wrists. But there are better ways to die than suicide. I thought I might at least have some fun with it. Might as well go out in style. But it's harder and harder to get a gun, and mass shootings are so impersonal. So, I decided to invest in something more... *involved*. A legacy project, you might call this camp. I get to live my dream, and live a little bit of the local history, too. Become a part of the lore. Things went better than I ever could have expected. And now, it's up to you to deliver the *coup de grace*. Put that axe in my head, Fiona."

"But *why*?"

"Because you're the innocent one, Fiona. You're the one who survives. As soon as I interviewed you, I knew. You're not like the others. You didn't just pair off with reckless abandon. You're so... pure. Virginal. And in some ways, we're not so

THE BACKWOODS DECAPITATOR
by JOHN ADAM GOSHAM

different, guys like me and girls like you. While the others pair off, we go it alone. Of course, the guys like me, we end up terminally alone and ignoble in our parents' basements. But the girls like you, you have the nice kids, the nice lives, the admirable jobs, the immaculate families. I love girls like that. And if I can't have any of what you have in life, then I can at least have you in my death. I can at least die at the hand of someone who will one day have it all. It's the best of all possible deaths, at least from my perspective. And in the lead-up, I got the chance to make those people who aren't at all like us get acquainted with some pain they might actually understand. In the end, I could make you into everything you're supposed to be, Fiona."

Fiona shook her head. Chewing violently at her lip, she tasted her own blood.

"Now, do it!" Niles hollered. "Pick up the axe!"

Fiona lifted the axe.

"Yes, that's it! Higher! Yes! Now bring it down!"

The axe trembled in Fiona's hands.

"Do it now! In the head, Fiona! *Right in the head*!"

Fiona kicked Niles in the chest and sent him onto this back.

"Yes!" Niles yelled. "That's right! Now we're getting somewhere! Do what you will!"

Fiona stepped on Niles' right arm, holding it down with her sneaker.

"You don't know me," Fiona snarled, then brought down the axe into Niles' hand.

He shrieked with pain and joy and surprise as the axe lopped off his index and middle fingers.

"*Argh!* What are you doing?!" he keened.

"We're getting to know each other," Fiona said. She picked up the severed fingers and tossed them into the grass. They parted ways in mid-air, blood arcing behind them.

"No!" he huffed. "In the head!"

Fiona swung the axe like a golf club into Niles' knee. He bawled as the axe-head cut through cartilage and hit bone.

"No!" he wailed. "No, no, *no*! In the head! *Oof*!"

~ 118 ~

Fiona speared Niles in his gut with the top of the axe-head. As he doubled up, hitching, she reached for the knife holstered on his hip. She pinned down his left hand under her knee and stabbed him through the palm. Niles screamed, and his fingers splayed out as if by reflex. Fiona stood and held the axe aloft again and came down aiming for the pinkie. It came off in one blow.

"*Arrrrgh!*"

Niles screamed so hard, it sounded as if he was laughing. Tears poured down his face.

Fiona cut off the rest of the fingers on Niles' left hand one by one. Some took more strokes than others. The thumb was the hardest. She hacked away at his collateral ligaments, harder and harder, each blow bringing back those nights in her room with any given boyfriend—so many boyfriends—turning up the music as her parents' bickering gained in pitch downstairs, waiting for the thrown glass to shatter.

Finally, the bloody thumb came free, quivering like a slug in the dirt.

"Okay," Niles puffed, staring at the sky, voice reedy as he hyperventilated. "*Okay.* We've had our fun. Now just kill me. Fiona?"

She was already up on her feet and trudging away, knife in one hand, axe in the other.

"Fiona!"

She found her stride in spite of the pain.

"Fiona! Don't leave me like this!"

He was sobbing.

"FIONA! FINISH YOUR JOB!"

Dirk was dead. Fiona knelt by his side and sorted through the gore, a foamy churn of blood on his flayed torso and jeans. In his hip pocket, she found his keys.

"WHORE!"

Niles' voice was getting lost in the breeze. By the time Fiona made it to the trail out, the screaming had stopped. Niles had given up on his fantasy.

THE BACKWOODS DECAPITATOR
by JOHN ADAM GOSHAM

For a half-second, Fiona felt a little better.

Fiona made a steady trudge through the woods, her head on a swivel, her knife and axe at the ready. The woods went on forever, and Fiona came to feel heavy with exhaustion as the adrenaline faded. She reached the road as dawn was breaking.

Dirk's truck sat where he'd left it. Fiona unlocked the door and pulled herself into the cab. She turned over the ignition and the engine roared to life.

She shifted into gear and put her foot on the gas, easing the speedometer up to 30 miles-per-hour on the gravel. Her head sagged, her forehead seeking the crest of the steering wheel. She started around the curve in the road. And as she came around the bend, she screamed.

There was a giant man standing in the road. His clothes were ragged and moldering. He wore a gnarled hood, and even from a hundred yards away, she could see the naked eyes beneath, pin-wheeling with rage. He gripped a rusted machete.

Fiona swerved off the road and went into the ditch on two wheels. The treeline rushed out to meet her and then came the deafening crash and everything went black.

Fiona opened her eyes onto the hospital room. The nurse watched over her with a half-kindly, half-pitying look on her face. The attending physician stood at the foot of the bed. He made a brief note on his clipboard and turned to the two police officers standing in the doorway.

"Good," the doctor said. "She's regained consciousness now and she's stable. You may come in, officers."

The doctor paced out of the room and the officers stepped

in. The younger one, Brady, glanced back at Murphy, the senior officer. Murphy nodded, and Brady cleared his throat.

"Ms. Harrington," Officer Brady said, "we'd like to ask you some questions about what happened to you."

"Are they dead?" Fiona asked.

Officer Brady pursed his lips. "Yes, ma'am. I'm afraid they are. We found no survivors."

"And you took him away?"

The officers looked at each other. Brady blinked rapidly. "Took who away, ma'am? We found no survivors."

"Niles," Fiona said, spitting out the name. "The camp supervisor. He's the one who did this. I fought him off... I, I—"

"Ma'am," said the older officer. "I'm very sorry to inform you, we found Mr. Alexander deceased, too."

"No..." Fiona whispered. "No!"

"Ma'am?"

"That can't be. That just can't be! I left him alive, I purposely left him lying and—"

Fiona cut herself off. Officer Brady took a step toward the bed.

"What is it, ma'am?"

Fiona's eyes widened. She stared past the officers. "Then it was..."

"Do you have any idea who might have done this?"

"Caleb Graves," Fiona whispered.

"Who?" asked Officer Brady.

Officer Murphy's face elongated. He shut his eyes. He nodded, then opened them again. The nurse was staring at the floor.

"I, I think we've heard enough for now," Murphy said. "Thank you for your time, Ms. Harrington. We'll be in touch with you again very soon."

Fiona said nothing. She gazed at the shape of her feet underneath the blankets, catatonic.

In the hospital hall, Officer Brady kneaded his cap in his hands.

THE BACKWOODS DECAPITATOR
by JOHN ADAM GOSHAM

"I hate to say it," he called back to Murphy, who was trailing behind him. "But she might even be a suspect at this point. She had a lot of weaponry in that truck with her, that's for sure. Murph? You okay?"

"I'm fine," Murphy croaked. "I'm not sure it's her."

"You got any idea what she was whispering there at the end?"

"No clue," Murphy muttered. "I didn't really hear."

But he had heard. The name was Caleb Graves, the Backwoods Decapitator, a name he'd been trying to forget for 40 years. It was Murphy's first week on the job, and they'd sent him out there with everybody else the day it had happened. He'd never been on a scene so grisly ever since; praise be to Jesus. Not until today. Back then, he wouldn't have been able to imagine a head could be cut so cleanly off a neck, and so many times over. Murphy had to see it not to believe. And then, this morning they found that camp owner in among all the rest of the mangled dead kids, and Murphy had to see it all over again. The state forensics boys had found all his fingers, but they were still out there fishing around for that poor bastard's head.

Their best bet, Murphy knew, was to look in the lake.

The Handyman

by Nicholas Stella

Brock

BROCK BROUGHT HIS JEEP TO a gentle halt on the gravel outside Bernie's Bait and Tackle, a small, run-down shack slumped on the side of the road like a dying dog. "Stretch your legs, people," he announced, turning to Holly in the passenger seat, favouring her with a white-toothed smile. "I'll get some directions."

"...about ...direction," came a muffled voice from the back seat.

"What was that?" Brock looked into the back seat, at Wizard, Randall and Daisy, each with a smile on their face.

"Randall was just talking about directions," Daisy said, as the rear doors were flung open, and the back seaters leapt from the cabin.

"Did you hear them?" Brock asked Holly.

"Just something about getting directions," she replied, putting her handbag over her shoulder.

Brock huffed and climbed out, suddenly smiling as his pectorals, biceps and triceps strained against the fabric of his shirt. He jogged around the front of the Jeep and caught up with Holly, taking her by the hand.

"Too hot, Brock," she said, removing her hand from his.

"It *is* kind of sticky," he said, looking around at the sound of laughter, at the three idiots who had managed to spoil what was supposed to be a two-person trip. "Supposed to be a storm later."

"I might just go and lie on the grass with Wiz…"

"Stay with me," he pleaded. "Let's chat with some of the local wildlife."

He bounded up the creaking steps of the bait shop and opened the rickety door, allowing Holly to enter first. He followed her inside, a drip of perspiration tracing its way down the side of his face.

"Sending me in first to face the danger?" she asked.

"Just trying to be a gentleman," he replied.

The counter was unattended, and a quick scan of the shop showed that no one was present. A refrigerator full of bait whirred in the corner and one of the ceiling lights was buzzing and flickering in the rear of the shop.

"What's that smell?" Holly complained, wrinkling her nose, making her way to the back of the store.

"It is a bait shop, Hol Hol," Brock said. "Not a perfumery."

"Hello?" Holly called.

Brock rung the rusty bell sitting on the counter, its ring instantly stillborn. He nosed around a dusty magazine rack before wandering over to a fridge, looking down through the glass at bags of shrimp packed in beside one another, spindly legs entwined, black eyes glassy.

He looked up at Holly who was peeking behind a curtain covering a doorway at the rear of the shop.

"Hey," he called out. "Don't go in there. That's probably where someone lives."

"I thought there might have been a bathroom back there," she said, flicking the curtain back into place. "Just to freshen up a bit."

CAMP SLASHER LAKE: VOLUME ONE

"Oo thouldn't uthe the toilet back there."

Brock turned to the front door, finding a skinny man in dirty overalls standing on the threshold.

"Sorry," Brock said. "We couldn't find anyone."

A string of saliva hung from the man's mouth, and he wiped it away with a dirty hand.

"Thath fine," he said, looking at them each in turn, then limping into the store. "But oo thouldn't be thtaying 'round here."

"We just…wanted some directions," Holly said.

"Directhons, oo thay," he said, wincing as he limped. "Where ith it oo want to go?"

"The Crags," Brock said. "We heard there's a swimming hole…"

"You don't want to be goin' to no Cragth," he said, hobbling at Brock. "Crathed lunaticth on the looth 'round theeth part'th."

"Lunatic alright." Holly said. "I'll be outside."

"Lunaticth!" he said, limping behind the counter and sitting on a stool. "On the looth!" He wiped more saliva from his mouth, adding it to his stained overalls. "Apolageeth if I'm hard to underth'tand. My mouth ith all numb from the dentith't."

"Tough morning?"

"Tough couple of dayth," he added. "Hurt my back nailing boardth over the windowth yeth'terday. Got me thith limp."

"Why are you boarding up the windows?" Brock asked.

"To keep him out," he replied. "The Athfixiator ith a local boy. He ethcaped and now people thayin' he ith coming home."

"Did you say The Asphyxiator?"

"Yeth," he replied. "Stuffth hith victimth moutheth with anything he can find. Mud. Paper. Thand. Cloth. Holdth 'em down till they t'thoke right in front of him."

"You don't think we should go to the Crags?"

"Hell, no," he shot back. "I'm here fortithying my houth and bithneth, getting' all grubby, and my overallth filthy. You think I normally live like thith? And you want to go thwimming with him out in the woodth thomewhere?"

THE HANDYMAN by NICHOLAS STELLA

"Any ideas where else we could go?" Brock asked. "We've driven all this way."

"Creature Comfort'th Inn ith back down the road apieth."

"Are we good to go?" Holly was outside on the steps.

"On account of this asylum breakout, it might be best if we stayed indoors," Brock said. "What do you think, Hol Hol?"

"I'm not camping outside with a madman about."

Holly

"HELLO?" HOLLY WHISPERED AS SHE made her way to the rear of the store where a dark curtain hung over a doorway.

An overhead light flashed and buzzed, casting a harsh brightness one moment, before a gloom settled the next. She reached out with a hand, a musty odour rising as she drew nearer to the curtain. Her trembling fingers brushed the heavy material as she drew it back just a little, listening to her heartbeat thump in her ears, her breath held.

She jumped at the dull ring of a bell, drawing her hand back, looking around at Brock and clenching her jaw as he nosed around the counter.

With the moment broken, she reached forward and drew the curtain aside, peering into the dark room beyond. The windows were all boarded up and the room was full of dark shapes.

"Hey," he called out. "Don't go in there. That's probably where someone lives."

"I thought there might have been a bathroom back there," she said, flicking the curtain back into place. "Just to freshen up a bit."

"Oo thouldn't uthe the toilet back there."

Holly looked to the front door. A man wearing a dusty cap with a hammer in his hand stood in the doorway.

"Sorry," Brock said. "We couldn't find anyone."

Holly looked around the store, searching for another way out. Apart from the front door which had a local yokel holding a hammer, the only other exit was through the heavy curtain and into a room with boarded windows.

~ 127 ~

THE HANDYMAN by NICHOLAS STELLA

"Thath fine," he said, limping into the store. "But oo thouldn't be thtaying 'round here."

"We just… wanted some directions," Holly said with a small stammer.

"Directhons, oo thay," he said, wincing as he limped further into the store. "Where ith it oo want to go?"

"The Crags," Brock said. "We heard there's a swimming hole…"

Holly entered the aisle closest to the windows and edged her way towards the recently vacated doorway.

"You don't want to be goin' to no Cragth," he said, hobbling at Brock. "Crathed lunaticth on the looth 'round theeth part'th."

"Lunatic alright." Holly said, and with a quick skip, was at the threshold. "I'll be outside."

She jumped the three steps to the ground, glad to be out in the afternoon sunshine. Wizard, Randall, and Daisy were still lying on the grass under the tree.

"We didn't think you'd make it out of that place alive," Randall said, sitting up. "I bet it's full of animal bone mobiles and framed faded pictures of old people."

"You're not far off the mark," she said. "The guy who runs the place has a speech impediment, walks with a limp, and dribbles all over his dirty overalls."

"We saw him limping past," Wizard said in his slow drawl, not bothering to get up or open his eyes. "The limp and the dirty overalls were enough for us, but the drooling and the speech impediment cement this guy as a classic local in his native environment."

"Did you get directions?" Daisy asked.

"Well, the guy inside said there's a lunatic on the loose."

"In addition to himself?" Wizard asked, opening an eye.

"Seriously?" Randall asked.

Daisy got to her feet.

"That's what he said," Holly replied. "Escaped from an asylum around here."

"I don't want to go camping if that's true," Daisy said.

~ 128 ~

"We've come all this way," Randall said. "Are we going to ruin the weekend on what some drooling idiot says?"

"I'm not going to chance it," she continued, before turning to Holly. "Are you happy to be sleeping in a tent, knowing this?"

"Not at all."

"Come on, Hol Hol," Wizard said with a smile. He stood, smoothed his long hair, and flexed his skinny arms. "I can look after my Hol Hol."

Holly scooped a handful of leaves from the ground and threw them at her brother. "Stop it with the Hol Hol!"

"If you don't want to camp, we don't have to," Randall said, making a tentative step towards her.

"I'll go and tell Brock that we're not going to camp," she said, turning away as Randall approached, keeping her distance, trying to be subtle.

She jogged back to the bait shop and gingerly trod the steps, looking into the gloom.

"Are we good to go?"

"On account of this asylum breakout, it might be best if we stayed indoors," Brock said. "What do you think, Hol Hol?"

"I'm not camping outside with a madman about," she replied, her jaw tensed.

Randall

"**IF YOU DON'T WANT TO** camp, we don't have to." Randall took half a step towards Holly, stopped, and then continued in her direction.

She turned from him and made a few quick steps on her way back to the bait shop. Randall remained where he was, his eyes torn between her bouncing brown ponytail and exquisitely formed calves.

"Give it up, Randy," Wizard said. "My sister only goes for the athletes."

"But she can't stand this guy," Randall said, turning to his friend. "I don't even know why he's here. It used to be just the four of us."

"She told me this weekend is make or break," Daisy said.

"It's already broken." Randall left his two friends on the grass and walked back to the Jeep as Brock and Holly exited the bait shop.

He quickly climbed into the vehicle, making sure he sat in the middle on the rear seat, where he could easily chat and make Holly laugh with one of his occasional zingers.

With everyone on board, the Jeep roared to life with a throaty rumble.

"First time, every time, Brocko," Randall said, elbowing Wizard.

"Of course," Brock said, turning around and pointing the Jeep back the way they had come. "Recently serviced and a new battery."

"Do you know how to get to this place?" Randall asked.

"Just back along this road, as far as I know."

CAMP SLASHER LAKE: VOLUME ONE

"I remember seeing a sign on the way here," Holly said.

"You... you've always been very observant," Randall said, sitting forward.

Holly didn't respond, so he sat back in his seat, not knowing what to follow that compliment up with.

"Real smooth," Wizard whispered to him.

Randall kept to himself, not joining the banter of the others as the afternoon waned, as the sunshine gave way to gloom, and the first spots of rain hit the windshield in fat drops. The wind chased fallen leaves across the road and branches reaching over the asphalt swayed under its rising influence.

They followed a sign pointing them off the main road and onto a gravel track that meandered under the thick foliage of the woods, light rain pattering the windscreen.

Brock parked the Jeep in front of a building crouched amongst the trees, signposted as the Creature Comforts Inn.

"This is Two-Star Accommodation," Randall said, reading from the Inn's website. "Enjoy a magical stay at the cosy Creature Comforts Inn nestled deep in the Waru Woods on the banks of Luderick Lake."

"You have reception here?" Daisy asked.

"Four bars of it," Randall replied. "They have a games room with a vending machine and a..."

"How about a pillow menu?" Wizard said. "I don't stay anywhere that doesn't have a pillow menu."

"I hope so," Randall fired back. "That would give me a whole range of smothering options for when you start snoring."

"We might still be able to get a swim in, Hol Hol," Brock said, climbing from the car.

"Up for a swim, Hol Hol?" Randall whispered, before following Wizard from the Jeep.

Hidden behind foliage and cloud, the late afternoon was unable to penetrate the gloom at ground level as the friends removed their packs from the Jeep and made their way to the building.

"Welcome travellers!" A bald man, with a greying handle-

THE HANDYMAN by NICHOLAS STELLA

bar moustache, stood behind a desk. "I'm glad you've found your way to the Creature Comforts Inn!"

Brock greeted the man in return. "I'm glad we've found our way here too," he said, dropping his pack. "Even with my Jeep, I didn't fancy driving in these stormy…"

Randall turned right around and went back outside, sitting on the top step, his pack on the ground in front of him. The rain had stopped but he could hear water dripping in the trees, weeping its way from leaf to leaf.

"Are you alright?" Daisy sat down beside him.

"I can't stand that guy." Randall dropped his voice, doing his best Brock impersonation. "I'm so glad to be here at the Creature Blah Blah Inn. Did I mention I drove here in my super turbo SUV with my biceps popping out?"

"Don't let him get to you," she said. "He's just a big buffoon and even Holly is realizing it."

"Even if she dumps him, she's never going to go out with me."

"Then you need to quit pining for her and look further afield."

"You probably think I'm a buffoon as well," he said, turning to Daisy, drawn to the smattering of light freckles dotted across her cheeks.

"All men are buffoons," she said. "That's why I stay away from them."

Wizard

"WELCOME TRAVELLERS!" THE MAN BEHIND the desk was wearing a bright yellow shirt with a black fish printed on it. "I'm glad you've found your way to the Creature Comforts Inn!"

"I'm glad we've found our way here too," Brock replied. "Even with my Jeep, I didn't fancy driving in these stormy conditions."

"How many cabins do you need?"

"Holly and I, Wizard and Randy can share, and Daisy will have her own."

"*You* look like a Wizard," the attendant said, throwing him a key. "The path outside leads to the cabins. Trail on the other side of the car park leads to the games room. Beers in the fridge are a buck a piece."

"You got it."

Wizard left the office with the key to Cabin One in his hand and gave Randall a gentle kick as he went past. "You and me," he said. "But not you, Daisy."

"Thank Goddess for that," she shot back.

With Randall behind him, Wizard followed a leaf-strewn path, turning onto a narrow trail signposted for Cabin One. It was quiet except for their footsteps, the sound of raindrops in the trees, and the occasional bird call.

"That's no cabin," Wizard said as they came to a stop outside their lodgings. "That's just some mass-produced demountable."

"You were expecting something made of logs cut by flannel shirt wearing lumberjacks?"

"That's what a cabin is and that guy in the office shouldn't have said we have *Cabin* One," he said, running his eyes over the fibreboard disappointment in front of him. "He should have said we have… I don't know… Prefabricated Demountable One."

"I suppose it wasn't what I was expecting either."

"And the beers in the games room are a buck," Wizard said, continuing his cynical roll.

"A dollar for a beer is pretty good." Randall snatched the key from his friend and unlocked the door.

"I know, but I just wanted to keep dumping on the place."

Wizard nosed around inside for a moment, then lay down on one of the beds. The interior of their lodgings was basic but comfortable enough for a single night stay. He dozed in the half-light filtering in through the curtains, listening to the sound of a gentle scratching on the roof.

"You going to get up any time soon?"

Wizard opened his eyes to a dark room, save for a small splash of light shed from Randall's phone on the other bed.

"Did I go to sleep?"

"Yep." Randall stood, putting his phone in his pocket. "You wanna go to the games room? Maybe get something to eat?"

Using the flashlights on their phones, Wizard and Randall walked along the dark path and across the car park. They followed a rough track until they came across a cabin with the door open and the lights and television on.

"What sort of games do you think they have?" Randall asked as they entered.

"Food first," Wizard said, making a bee line for the vending machine. "Cheese puffs and a Choc-o-mate, washed down with a cold bottle of Electro-Clown Energy Boost will be my dining experience this evening." He fed the machine a handful of monetary nutrition, pressed a few buttons, and dinner was served via a quick tumble into a tarnished chute that was sticky to his touch.

"I thought we were gonna smash some suds," Randall said, pointing to a fridge full of beer cans. "Only a dollar."

"I'm on antibiotics for my ear infection," Wizard said. "The doc said it wasn't wise to mix my medication with alcohol."

"Well, I'm not going to drink alone," Randall replied, fishing through his pockets. "I'll just get some dinner."

With his stomach full of cheese cultures, emulsifiers, and glucuronolactone, Wizard turned his attention to the selection of games on offer. A bookcase was stocked with a good array of board games ranging from favourites like *Monopoly* and *Scrabble* to more niche and lesser-known selections like *Foolish Deaths* and *Llamas in Underpants*.

Wizard removed *Scrabble* from the bookcase and began setting up on the table they had dined upon, looking up at the blaring television with distaste. "Where's the remote, Randy?" he asked. "I can't concentrate on Scrabble if that thing is on."

"Hang on," Randall replied. "They're talking about that escaped loony on the news."

"... *was arrested at a popular swimming hole, The Crags, earlier this evening. Ivan Knewby, also known as the Asphyxiator is currently in the custody of police ...*"

Randall clicked the remote and the screen went dark. "All's well that ends well."

Daisy

"**YOU PROBABLY THINK I'M A** buffoon as well," Randall said.

"All men are buffoons," Daisy said, turning away from his stare. "That's why I stay away from them."

"You and me." Wizard exited the office, dangling the key above Randall's head. "But not you, Daisy."

"Thank Goddess for that." The thought of spending the night in the same room as her childhood friends no longer held the same charm that it once had.

She stood as the two teenagers disappeared down a path into the woods. A man with a satchel over his shoulder and some sort of tool in his hand was standing on the other side of the car park. He looked at her from the shadows, tilting his head back, and to the side as if in appraisal.

Daisy raised her arm and gave him a tentative wave, giving her fingers a little wiggle.

The man remained where he was for a moment longer, before he turned and disappeared into the woods.

Daisy rubbed her goose-pimpled arms, feeling a prickle creep up her spine.

She stood in the silence and the growing dark, looking into the woods where the man had gone.

"Cabin Three, Daisy," Holly said, jingling multiple keys next to her ear.

"Holy shit!" Daisy turned and stumbled backwards down the steps, managing to remain on her feet.

"Sorry," Holly said, clapping her hands across her mouth. "I didn't mean to…"

"Don't worry," Daisy replied, turning away from them, looking back at the woods. "I just saw a man out there."

"Probably hiking," Brock said.

"He had a tool in his hand for some reason. What sort of hiker carries tools about?"

"Maybe he's the caretaker," he said. "Come on. Let's check out the digs."

Daisy followed Brock and Holly down the path to the cabins, looking out into the woods at the darkness that had descended.

"We're down here," Brock said, pointing to a small trail. "You're probably just a little further along."

"Do you want to come back later?" Holly asked.

"No, it's okay. I'm just going to eat some biscuits, do some reading, and then hit the sack."

"But what about the weekend? We had plans to do things."

"I was looking forward to bouldering up at the Crags, but now that's off, I'm just feeling a bit flat."

"Feel free to come visit," Holly said.

"Knock first!" Brock called out as he walked down the trail to the cabin.

"He *wishes*," Holly whispered.

Daisy continued alone along the path, quickening her pace, looking around her, key in hand and positioned ready to slide into the lock. A bird called as she stopped in front of the door, but holding her key firm, it slid into the lock as sweetly as you please and, with a manoeuvre that involved swinging the door open, removing the key, skipping inside and slamming the door closed, she shut the night outside.

She lay on the bed with a plate of cheese, crackers, and dried apricots at hand. The ceiling lights, bedside lamp, and TV were all on, filling the room with bright light and televised conversation. The window was right beside her, but it showed only darkness.

She picked up her book, eager to be transported somewhere else, preferably to a place where it was daytime, when her bookmark slipped out.

THE HANDYMAN by NICHOLAS STELLA

It was a photo of Riley.

They had been at the beach that day, and Riley had been complaining about having water in her ear when Daisy had taken the photo. She had a finger in her ear and a half-smile had crept onto her face.

She slotted the photo back into the book, placed it on the bed, and closed her eyes.

She sat up at the sound of someone on the path outside. She crept to the window, looking out into the darkness, watching as Brock and Holly disappeared into the woods.

Brock

"KNOCK FIRST!" BROCK DIDN'T WANT that stick-in-the mud turning up unannounced, spoiling their evening. He knew Holly had been distant lately and this was his chance to try and remedy things.

He unlocked the door, holding it open for her. "My lady," he said, standing on the threshold, giving his arm a theatrical sweep, showcasing everything that the lodgings of the Creature Comforts Inn had to offer. "Paradise awaits."

"I just need to freshen up," she said, heading straight for the bathroom.

The room was nothing more than he expected but perhaps a little less. The wall paint was yellowing, and the mattress looked a little downtrodden. It was impeccably clean but just a little tired, with a few wrinkles around the edges.

"Take your time," Brock called out once the bathroom door had been closed. He rummaged through his pack and removed a small blanket along with a freezer bag. He unzipped it and checked on the condition of the contents. The punnet of strawberries sitting amongst the ice packs was undamaged and still cold. The bottles of fruit nectar were beaded with moisture, but like the punnetised strawberries, still cold to the touch.

As the bathroom door opened, he threw a blanket over his shoulder and tucked the freezer bag under an arm, highlighting his biceps; a bit of a tease that had been a sure-fire winner for the ladies over the years.

"What's all that?" Holly asked.

"Picnic by the lake," he said with a smile, revealing his pearly whites in much the same way as his arms were on display. "Even if we can't go to the Crags, we can at least do something."

"I don't know," Holly said, looking around the room. "We don't even know how to get there."

"I'm sure it's signposted." Brock made a move towards the door. "Do you really want to spend the night in here?"

"As long as we don't have to trudge too far to find it."

"It'll be a cinch," Brock said, opening the door. He led her down the small trail and onto the main path.

"Are you sure it's this way?" she asked, as they passed Daisy's cabin.

"Positive," Brock said, as he stumbled in the dark, rescuing the freezer bag before it hit the ground.

A light came on behind him and he turned to see Holly using the flashlight on her phone to illuminate the way.

"There," he said, spying a sign that read Luderick Lake with an arrow conveniently pointing in its supposed direction. He followed the narrow path, brushing past wet branches and leaves.

"Are you *sure* it's down this way?" Holly asked.

"The sign said so." He looked back, momentarily blinded by Holly's light.

"Crap," she said.

"What?"

"I've just soaked a shoe in a puddle," she said. "I'm not going to trudge any further along this path. Come and get me when you've found it."

"Are you sure you want to stay here?"

"Yes."

"Alone?"

"Yes."

"In the woods?"

"Yes."

"With a lunatic on the loose?"

"You have two minutes to find the lake and come back and get me."

"Easily done," he said, handing her the blanket and turning on the flashlight on his phone. "You won't even get the chance to miss me."

Brock hurried off further down the path, the spread of his light managing to push back the darkness a little way in front of him, illuminating the dripping branches that encroached on either side. The light caught the eyes of a small animal just off the path, but it scampered away before he could see what it was.

He pushed through a veil of hanging leaves and found himself on the shore of Luderick Lake. The water was laid out smooth and placid from the sandy shore; the light of the moon cast upon it like a shimmering sheet.

"Beautiful," he said, placing the freezer bag on the ground.

He hurried back along the path, his clothes wet from the rain-sodden foliage, suddenly coming across Holly stopped in the path, covering her eyes.

"I found it just like I said I would."

Holly

WITH BROCK OFF LOOKING FOR his lake, Holly felt very small in the woods, and very alone in the darkness with only a meagre beam of light for company.
Alone.
Something scurried through the undergrowth off the path, and she turned her light in the direction of the noise.
In the woods.
A branch snapped behind her and she turned, pointing the weak light at where she thought it was.
With a lunatic on the loose.
She stepped backwards, the tip of a single wet leaf brushing its gentle self over the back of her neck, and she took off, throwing the blanket aside.
Running without heed, she stumbled along the path, drenched in rainwater and nervous perspiration, the light jumping erratically in her shaking hand.
She covered her eyes, blinded by a light coming from the opposite direction.
"I found it just like I said I would."
"Well done, Magellan," she said, brushing leaves from her hair.
"What happened to you?"
"Nothing. Where's this lake?"
She stepped off the path and onto the shore, looking at a grim expanse of dark water leading away from a beach covered in fallen sticks and sharp rocks. An eerie mist lay above the surface, lit almost yellow by the cloud-covered moon.
"Beautiful, isn't it?" Brock said.

"It's more like a swamp than a lake."

"Oh..." Brock paused. "I have chilled strawberries and drinks. We can put the blanket... Where's the blanket?"

"I dropped it."

"I could find a log for us to sit on," he said, looking along the shore. "And we could just... look at the lake."

"As depressing as it sounds, I'd rather sit on that old bed in our cabin and watch infomercials." She looked down at her wet clothes, picking leaves off her shirt.

"I have an idea," Brock said. "As our clothes are soaking wet, maybe we should take them off and go for a skinny dip."

Holly looked at the swamp-like body of water in front of her and then back at her boyfriend. "I think I'll spend the night in Daisy's cabin."

"What's wrong?"

"You've dragged me out in the dark, through the woods, to some sort of disgusting pond and you suggest that I swim naked in it." She crossed her arms. "I don't think we're on the same page."

"I knew that I was struggling to hold onto you," he said, picking up the freezer bag.

She followed her ex-boyfriend along the path, stopping for a moment as he picked the blanket up out of the leaves and mud. They retraced their footsteps along the path until they came upon Daisy's cabin.

"Aren't you going to Daisy's?"

"I think I can do things without you," she said, leaving Brock and Daisy's cabin behind, her shoes crushing sodden leaf litter as she went.

Upon coming across the car park, Holly used her phone to illuminate the map of the area, taking in the position of the games room. If she was going to turn up at Daisy's, then she couldn't turn up empty-handed, but at the same time, traipsing through the dark along a path until she came across the games room with its beer fridge was not something she relished.

She looked back down the way she had come and saw a

figure standing on the path.

"Go to bed, Brock," she called out, crossing the car park, and starting up the path in the direction of the games room.

The path headed uphill and was harder going than the way she had taken to the lake. The light from her phone showed the path to be pocked with holes. Vines and partially hidden roots crept across the way making footing tricky and navigation difficult.

She could see a lit cabin up ahead but what she thought was the main path was heading away in another direction. With a small trail opening up in front of her, Holly decided to follow it, staggering along the rough terrain and fending off hanging vines and foliage.

Brushing a cobweb from her face, her foot caught under something on the trail, and she fell, her phone flying from her hand and going dark.

Randall

"THAT'S NOT A WORD," RANDALL said, casting a suspicious eye over the most recent addition of nonsensical words on the Scrabble board.

"Bibble is indeed a word," Wizard replied, sitting back in his chair, looking pleased with himself.

"I've been placing good words like *portal* and *broken*," he continued, "but I've never heard of *quimp*, *pookle* or…" Randall stopped, cocking his head at the sound of something outside. "Did you hear that?"

"All I hear is the sound of your Scrabble campaign coming crashing to the ground."

"No, I'm serious." Randall walked to the window and put his nose to the glass, cupping his hands around his face to see outside. "Maybe we should go out to see what it is."

"You want…" he paused. "You want the two of us to go outside into the woods on a rainy night with a lunatic on the loose to investigate a noise?"

"That guy was caught." Randall turned to find that Wizard was now lying down on a tatty sofa next to the beer fridge.

"Right, he was," Wizard continued. "But we'll go outside and then you'll decide that we should split up…"

"I'm not an idiot," Randall said, glancing across at Wizard as he walked to the front door.

"Says the guy who cops a machete in the head."

Standing just outside the door, the woods before him were a confusion of trees and shrubs. He took a step further as his eyes adjusted to the morass before him. He could hear someone moving through the woods, could hear the breaking of twigs

THE HANDYMAN by NICHOLAS STELLA

and brushing of foliage and suddenly, a dark shape was bursting from the woods and rushing up at him where he stood on the top step.

"I'm glad you're nice, and dry, and clean sitting up here in your cosy games room!" Holly pushed past him and went inside.

"I didn't know that…"

"And my phone is flickering on and off." Holly, with leaves in her hair and mud on her shirt, tapped forcefully on her phone with a grubby finger.

"What happened to you?" Wizard asked from the sofa. "I thought you and lover boy were going to be romantically entangled this evening."

"I need a beer," she said, stampeding over to the fridge, removing a can, and opening it with all the grace of a long-haul truck driver. She put it to her lips and guzzled half the can before continuing. "My *ex*-boyfriend dragged me to the lake which was more like a swamp and then suggested we swim naked in it!" She attacked the can again in another display of aggressive imbibition.

"You two are over?" Wizard turned and performed a rapid double-eyebrow raise in Randall's direction.

Randall felt his pulse race.

"You bet we are!"

Randall felt is cheeks grow warm.

"So, you're on the lookout for a new beau?"

Randall hurried across the room and sat down, looking with feigned interest at the Scrabble board.

"Nope." Holly finished the beer and dropped it into the rubbish bin. "I'm staying with Daisy tonight."

"I think the beers cost a dollar each," Randall said in a small and hollow voice. He pointed to an ice-cream bucket on a table next to the fridge.

"Well," Holly said, removing a number of cans from the fridge. "The Creature Comforts Inn can sue me!" She stomped across the room in her wet shoes and strode out into the night.

CAMP SLASHER LAKE: VOLUME ONE

"I think *Bibble* won me the game," Wizard said, getting up from the sofa, and following his sister out the door.

Randall sighed and tidied up the Scrabble set. On his way out, he dropped six dollars in coins into the ice-cream bucket.

Wizard

"YOU TWO ARE OVER?" WIZARD asked his sister. He raised and lowered his eyebrows a few times, looking directly at Randall, knowing his friend would be embarrassed.

"You bet we are!"

"So, you're on the lookout for a new beau?" He smiled, watching Randall scurry across to the Scrabble board.

"Nope." Holly drained her beer and dropped the can into the trash. "I'm staying with Daisy tonight."

"I think the beers cost a dollar each." Randall sounded defeated.

"Well," Holly said, grabbing beer cans from the fridge. "The Creature Comforts Inn can sue me!" She flicked her blonde hair with comic arrogance and made her exit.

"I think *Bibble* won me the game." Wizard smiled at Randall and hurried after his sister.

He followed the dodgy path away from the games room, his sister's darting shape obscured by the heavy growth of trees. She had dated fools in the past, their arrogance brought on by a mixture of good genetics, access to money and parental validation. But all in all, Brock had been one of the better ones, his respect and enthusiasm for her all too apparent in his needy lovesick behaviour.

"Are you off men for good?" Wizard asked, catching up to his sister as they crossed the car park.

"Of course not," Holly said. "But stop letting Randall think he has a chance."

"He's loved you since primary school."

"Take some of these," she said, handing a couple of cold

cans to him.

They stopped in their tracks at the sound of a scream that slit the silence like a slice of lightning in a dark sky. He looked at his sister, her eyes wide and staring.

"Where did that come from?" A shiver ran down his spine as he looked up and down the path.

"I couldn't tell."

Wizard's feet were rooted to the ground and his bladder felt uncomfortably full, as the sound of running footsteps drew near.

"What the hell was that?" Randall whispered as he emerged from the darkness.

"We should check on Daisy." Holly dropped the beer and ran.

Wizard ran after her, the cans falling from his arms as he followed the trail.

"What's going on?" Brock called out from his doorway.

Wizard ignored him and kept running, easily outdistanced by his sister, until he came to Daisy's cabin. The front door was open, and the lights were on. Holly was standing on the stoop looking in.

"What is it?" he asked, stopping behind her, looking into the cabin beyond.

An open satchel lay on the floor with its contents spilling free.

"What the hell are they?" Wizard asked, unable to make out the small pile of things on the floor.

"Hands," Holly said.

Daisy

AFTER SEEING HOLLY AND BROCK disappear down the path, Daisy climbed back onto the bed and turned on the television.

"In breaking news, an escaped inmate from the Epworth Psychiatric Hospital was arrested at popular swimming hole, The Crags, earlier this evening. Ivan Knewby, also known as the Asphyxiator is currently in the custody of police. Still at large however, is Martin Clover, also known as The Handyman for his habit of severing the…"

"Now is not the time," Daisy said, clicking the television off.

She lay back, removing the photograph of Riley from her book, a smile crossing her lips as she thought of that day at the beach. Placing the photo on her stomach and covering it with her interlocked hands, she closed her eyes.

There was a gentle rapping at the door.

"Who is it?" she called out.

"Handyman," came the soft reply.

"I don't think there's anything wrong in here," Daisy said, climbing from the bed and making her way to the door.

"The previous guest complained of…"

"I can't hear you," Daisy said, pulling the door open, recoiling first at the smell and then the sight of the small figure on the stoop.

She tried to slam the door, but the man was across the threshold as nimble as a hare, causing Daisy to retreat into the room. She grabbed her phone from the bedside table, along with the lamp, the cord coming free of the socket.

He wore a stained tracksuit and had a dirty satchel looped over a shoulder, looking at her with pale blue eyes, smiling with a mouthful of small yellow teeth. "Into my satchel you will go," he whispered, dropping the bag onto the floor in front of him.

Daisy stared aghast at the severed hands tumbling free like rubber novelties. She dry retched, bending over, unable to take her eyes off five nails painted bright pink.

The man reached into the bag with one hand that was his and a smaller one that had been stitched clumsily onto the stump of his other arm, fumbling around, and spilling more of the five-digit mementos onto the floor. As he pulled a rusted cleaver from the satchel, Daisy screamed loud and long, throwing the lamp at the man, the heavy base striking him on the top of the head.

With the phone in her hand, she jumped his sprawled body and was out the door, into the night, running through the trees.

Brock

AT THE SOUND OF THE scream, Brock's urine stopped mid-stream. He bolted from the bathroom and ran to the open doorway. He looked up at the main path and saw several figures running past.

"What's going on?" he shouted.

Not getting a response, he ran after the runners along the main path until he saw Daisy's cabin. Holly, Wizard and Randall were crowded around the door, looking in.

"What are you looking at?" he asked, standing beside them, and looking over into the cabin.

Randall pushed past him and vomited into the garden.

"Chopped off hands," Wizard said, entering the room.

"What?" Brock stepped inside, looking for a moment at the hands strewn across the floor and then at the photo of Riley lying a little further away. "Where's Daisy?" The bathroom door was open, and the room was empty.

"She could be anywhere," Holly said, running a little way down the path. "We need to find her."

"I think we should split up," Brock said, exiting the cabin. "With more of us looking…"

"No. No. No." Wizard was approaching him, waving his arms around. "Under no circumstances do we split up."

"I agree," Randall said as he spat into the garden. "We stay together."

"I'm calling the police," Holly said, tapping on her flickering phone.

Brock looked at Randall, who was pale as a sheet with his shirt covered in vomit. "You're with me, Wizard. We're going to see the guy in the office," he said, before turning to Holly. "You and Randall lock yourselves in the cabin in case Daisy comes back here."

Holly

"PLEASE STATE YOUR EMERGENCY."

"My friend is missing and there are chopped off hands in a bag on the floor!"

"Are you currently in any danger?"

"I'm in a cabin staring at severed hands on the floor!"

"Is the door locked?"

"Yes."

"Is anyone there with you?"

"Randall."

"Are either you or Randall hurt?"

"No."

"Can you give me your location?"

"The comforts… comforts…" she hesitated, looking at Randall.

"Creature Comforts Inn."

"The Creature Comforts Inn," she said.

"I'm contacting local law enforcement as we speak," the operator said. *"Is there somewhere that you could meet them when they arrive?"*

"The car park, I guess."

"Okay. Make your way to the car park, but only if it is safe to do so."

"She wants us to go to the car park to wait for the police." She looked at Randall who was fixated on the bag of hands.

"Go outside?" Randall's eyes widened. "There's someone out there chopping people's hands off!"

"And Daisy is out there!" She looked at Randall standing there, his chest sunken, shoulders hunched forward. "I'm not going to cower in here with you while she could be in trouble."

She stomped across the room and entered the kitchenette, opening drawers until she found cutlery. Removing a kitchen knife for herself, she also grabbed a handful of forks for Randall.

"Take these," she said, handing the tined dining instruments to Randall. "It's better than a poke in the eye with a sharp stick."

"I'd feel safer with a sharp stick," he said. "What am I supposed to do with these?"

"Bundle them together and stab the bad man," she said, heading out the door, knowing that like always, he would follow.

Randall

RANDALL HESITATED FOR A MOMENT before going outside after Holly. The bundle of forks was awkward in his grasp, but he thought they could do some damage if he needed them as a last resort.

He hurried until he caught up with her on the trail. "Do you think the police will be here soon?"

"I don't know."

Randall looked from side to side at the dark woods that bordered both sides of the narrow trail. "So... I guess I can just stab this guy if I need to?"

"If your life is in danger, go to town on him."

"I just haven't stabbed anyone before," he said, repositioning the forks. "Will I get into trouble?"

"Look," Holly whisper-shouted, stopping in the path and turning to face him. "You'll be in a hell of a lot more trouble if you don't stab him."

"Right," he said, back on the move, jogging to catch back up.

He shuddered at the thought of plunging a handful of forks into someone's body, feeling the tines initially face resistance before plunging into soft tissue or hitting bone and glancing off. He wasn't sure if he could do it.

Looking at Holly striding in front of him with the knife in her hand, he knew she meant business.

And for the first time in all the years he had spent adoring her, this would be his chance to prove himself worthy. He was useless on the football field or in the swimming pool, but in the dark woods with a killer on the loose, he was going to be an all-star.

If this hand-chopping madman was to appear, then he would be there, all forks blazing.

He was snapped out of his dreams of playing the hero by a shouted voice behind him.

"Run! Run! Run!"

Wizard

WIZARD WAITED ON THE MAIN trail while Brock ducked into his cabin to get the keys to the Jeep.

He looked about, his skin prickling, the moon hidden above by canopy and thick cloud.

He let loose a long shuddering breath he didn't know he had been holding when Brock came out, jingling the keys and hurrying down the path.

"We should go and see the manager," Brock said, pointing up at the office as they ran into the car park.

Despite the danger of the situation, Wizard was quite happy with the way everything was panning out. Good decisions were being made. He was paired up with a six-and-a-half-foot athlete capable of beating the life out of most people on the planet, Holly was calling the police, and he was on the way to see the Manager of the Creature Comforts Inn who would certainly know what to do.

"Do you think he's even there?" Wizard asked, noticing that the lights were off.

"Let's find out," Brock replied as they climbed the stairs.

They opened the door and a bell jingled softly.

"Hello?" Wizard said.

The front office was deserted.

"I'm going to check the next room," he said, noticing an open doorway leading out of the office.

He crept over, looking around the corner into a dim room. He could make out a table and chairs along with a sofa, behind which was a gentle source of light.

"Hello?' he said, creeping towards the sofa.

He stopped when he saw a pair of legs lying on the floor.

"Get in here Brock," he said, continuing further, seeing a little more of the body, afraid for what he might find.

The body sat up. "Can I help you?"

Wizard screamed and recoiled, backing away into Brock and screaming again.

"What are you doing on the bloody floor?" Wizard shouted. "I thought you were dead!"

"Why would you think I was dead?" The manager got to his feet, revealing the phone in his hand, and pulling the pods from his ears. "I was just listening to a podcast."

"There's a madman on the loose," he said. "He's chopping people's hands off!"

"I'll call the sheriff," the manager said, tapping a number into his phone. "I've got his private number."

"You believe me? Just like that?"

"Of course," the manager replied.

At the sound of screaming and shouting, Wizard and Brock bundled out of the room, through the office and out into the car park.

Daisy

DAISY CURLED UP INTO A ball underneath a shrub, remaining still. She switched her phone to silent and slid it into a pocket.

Footsteps approached, leaves crinkling under each step.

"I noticed that you have such a slender wrist," a voice whispered.

She tensed, closing her eyes as something crawled across her foot with prickly little legs.

"One quick snick of my cleaver and that beautiful hand would be off as quick as you please."

The sound of the footsteps receded as her pursuer headed in another direction.

"What's going on?" She opened her eyes at the sound of Brock's voice.

She listened intently, hoping to catch something else, but for a while she just lay with only silence around her.

"She could be anywhere." That was Holly. "We need to find her."

Daisy wanted to run but terror had wrapped its cold arms around her, its frigid fingers sending prickles of anxiety up and down her spine.

"No. No. No. Under no circumstances do we split up."

She lifted her head a little at the sound of Wizard's raised voice, listening for the crinkling leaves or the whispering voice.

She lay still for a while longer, wriggling her fingers and toes, moving her arms and legs just a little, preparing for flight.

With no evidence of a crinkle or a whisper, she was on her feet and running through the woods and onto the trail.

She heard movement on the far side of the cabin and looked back. The slight man was after her, one hand holding the cleaver, the other swinging awkwardly from the broken stitching holding onto the stump of his forearm.

She turned back and saw figures on the path ahead. "Run! Run! Run!" she shouted.

She was shouting and screaming nonsense by the time she caught up with Holly and Randall in the car park. Brock and Wizard were descending the steps from the office.

She looked back down the path and saw him coming, running silently.

"He's coming!" she shouted, running to the Jeep, and trying the passenger side door.

The vehicle beeped, the lights flashed, and the door sprung open. She jumped inside and was soon joined by the others. Brock was in the front beside her, slotting the key into the ignition as she watched the Handyman slam the cleaver on the bonnet. The stitching on his newly acquired hand tore free, causing it to bounce up and hit the windshield.

She cackled as the engine roared to life and the Jeep leapt forward with the Handyman clinging to the bonnet like a deranged hood ornament. He looked at her with a sparkle in his eyes and in that moment of madness, she decided that she would call Riley when it was all over.

The Jeep hit the office steps and Daisy hit the airbag.

The Handyman

THE HANDYMAN SLAMMED THE CLEAVER down onto the bonnet of the car. He hit it with his new hand as well, the one from the blonde girl outside the gym. The stitching broke and it came away, this beautiful new hand of his. The engine was loud in his ears, but he looked at the curly haired girl on the other side of the windscreen. She had such fine hands and she had freckles on her cheeks.

The car came to a sudden halt, and he was pinned against the stairs. The car reversed and he managed to lift his head, looking down at his caved chest and hips that were bent back the wrong way.

The girl with the nice hands and freckles stumbled from the car and looked at him, swaying on her feet.

"Hit him again!" he heard her shout, and he closed his eyes, waiting for the end.

The Children of Dagon
by Carlton Herzog

BLIND FROG LAKE GOT ITS name from the freakish absence of eyeballs in the local amphibian population. That grim defect aroused considerable speculation both as to its source and how the frog population flourished without the benefit of sight. The more superstitious locals attributed the optical blight to supernatural forces. Specifically, the shipwreck of the *Mercy*, a vessel carrying refugees from the remote south pacific around Cape Horn to Innsmouth, Massachusetts. The ill-fated *Mercy* had fallen victim to a hurricane off the Florida coast.

When the Floridians of Old Hickory, a beachfront village, spotted the wreck, the entire fishing fleet joined in the rescue but when the fishermen got a closer look at the survivors, they found them to have queer, narrow heads, flat noses, and bulging eyes that never shut. They called themselves the Children of Dagon, a god they claimed resided in deepest, darkest primordial depths of the ocean. The fishermen were simple, Old Testament folk. They did not take kindly to the castaways' heathenish array of monstrous clubs and spears littered about the sinking ship. The glittering saws were still tufted with bits of human hair, and their sickles were still stained red from their last bloody harvest at sea. So, the villagers did what Moses did to the pagan city of Midian: they "butchered the shrunken head-peddling, purple rascals." They started with the babies, forty-six in all, and then moved onto the adults. When they were finished, their chum buckets overflowed with arms, legs, torsos, and heads. The Old Hickory fishing fleet had an exceptionally productive fishing season that year.

The more fleet-footed cannibals got away and headed inland. The rumor is they settled in the forest around what was then the cabin resort at Crystal Lake. Soon thereafter, cabin guests claimed the area was haunted by corpses carrying their own heads, human limbs inching along the trails looking for a body, and walking grave clothes filled with nothing but clusters of long black hair. Then the guests began disappearing without a trace, and the ones that didn't disappear went murderously insane, either at the cabins or upon their return to the town of Hickory.

Year after year, the rental season turned into an orgy of blood. One noteworthy example was the woman found with an axe protruding from her forehead. Another time, a tourist found a pile of torsos next to a pile of heads as if they were LEGOS waiting to be assembled. Then there were the charred remains of unidentified unfortunates burned alive at the stake. But it wasn't until the frogs proliferated and went blind that Ezekiel Harmon, the property owner, shut down the cabins and the lake in 1976. Harmon justified his decision by stressing that, "Them damn frogs are a sure sign the devil done taken hold up there and ain't letting go." In 1988, he sold the property to a real estate consortium that was singularly unimpressed with the "hysteria" over specters, disappearances, and blind frogs. So much so, it changed the lake's name from Crystal to Blind Frog. The company's official response to the claims of a mass demonic invasion consisted of the simple declaration that "We ain't afraid of no ghosts."

In 1989, Big Hair and the Bongos — a Portland based punk band — rented Cabin Number One for the summer. The Bongos did not entirely fit the 80's hairband mode of Def Leppard,

CAMP SLASHER LAKE: VOLUME ONE

Motley Crue, and Twisted Sister. With their big beehive hairdos and thrift store clothes, the female band members emulated the B-52s. That accounted for the band's unapologetically campy performances with such genre defying songs such as *Wacky Crappy People*, *Private Dildo*, and *Cock Lobster*.

When Ace, the band's drummer, heard about the tall tales about Blind Frog Lake, he was intrigued. He loved the *Dead by Dawn Cabin* series. It was a role-playing game that paid homage to slasher films such as *Friday The 13th* and *Halloween*. The game asked players to survive a slasher villain that's hunting them down. Cults, demons, and eldritch gods were all part of *Dead by Dawn Cabin*'s story, helping to build an incredibly eerie tone that evoked classic 80s horror films.

Ace suggested the group spend Halloween at Blind Frog Lake. After all, Florida autumns were as warm as a New England summer, and so, eminently suitable for a beach holiday. He did not, however, disclose Blind Frog's sordid history. After the group agreed the vacation spot was sterling, Ace called in a reservation with Blind Frog leasing. Two weeks later, they drove to Old Hickory in their crystal blue chevy conversion van. At the leasing office, they met with Constantine Roshenko, a Russian transplant with an accent thick as molasses. He was a stout, barrel-chested fellow, with grey hair, and teeth that could bite an apple through a fence.

"Come in, my Comrade Bongos. Welcome to Old Hickory."

Nick, the band's bass guitarist, did the talking for the band.

"Did you turn on the juice so we can watch the telly? I can't miss *Cheers*, *Married with Children* and *The A-Team*. And can you provide us with the backup generator, gas, and lanterns like I asked?"

"Da, Comrade Nick. Iz all there. Vood for the fireplace, some iron pots, pokers."

"Jolly good then. Here's the check. Now, where do I sign?"

THE CHILDREN OF DAGON by CARLTON HERZOG

After they closed on their summer lease, Big Hair and the Bongos stopped for a drink at the Blind Frog Café. The women's exaggerated bouffant hairdos provoked snickers and stares. When their waiter overheard that they were heading to the lake, he borrowed a line from *The Fly* and cautioned them to 'Be afraid. Be very afraid.'

"And why's that?" asked Nick.

"When people come back from there, they come back wrong. Not Stephen King's book, *Pet Sematary* wrong, because they're still alive, but generally crazy and homicidal."

"Could you be more specific?"

"*Texas Chainsaw Massacre* wrong. Organs stuffed in glass jars wrong. Last year, one nut job chopped up four people, switched their body parts around, stitched them back together and then hung them between two poles like a hammock. One had the arms of a black man, the legs of a woman, the genitals of a man, and the breasts of a woman. He stuck a mannequin's head on upside down. When the cops found him, he had a leg in his mouth and was sucking out the bone marrow."

Meatball, the band's lead male vocalist laughed. "'Creepy. But we've heard all the stories about people disappearing and becoming homicidal. Do we look like people who are afraid of weird shit?"

The waiter frowned, "Suit yourself, tough guy. But just last week, a married couple came back from the lake. The wife promptly chopped off her husband's head and tossed it into a bucket. She then played with the cadaver for 'two to three hours' after his death, using several knives to dismember the body. She said a bread knife 'worked the best,' because of the 'serrated blade.'"

Nobody said a word.

"Then, there's all those disappearances. They stopped when the cabins were shut down, and then started up again once they were reopened. I shudder to think what nameless things might be crawling around up there."

Nick retorted, "Look pal, I appreciate the advice. But I am a stud, not a poser. If there is something evil up there, it 'will not like me when I'm angry' any more than it would like Lou Ferrigno's Hulk. So, if we wont to 'dance with the devil in the pale moonlight,' that's our concern, not yours. Bring us the check so we can be on our way."

The waiter said, "It's your funeral," and handed him the check.

After the Big Hairs unpacked and settled in, they broke out the Coors, coke, and weed. As was their want, they sprawled out on the wicker and bean bag chairs and proceeded to needle Roxy, who was crazier than a bag of rats in a burning meth lab. She was a drug burnout who sold and distributed the drugs of the day. Consequently, she had an extensive lexicon of contemporary narcotics that the band members liked to plumb.

Nick asked, "So, Roxy, you are something of an expert when it comes to mind-altering substances. Rumor has it you have a sandwich named after you at the Betty Ford Clinic."

"Keep it up, douchebag, and I'll pull those leotards so far up, you'll be wearing your balls as a bolo tie."

"Always gotta' bring a gun to a knife fight. Should I have asked if this is your home planet?"

"Okay. I'll just cut out your balls and use the sack as a purse."

"Calm down. I just want to know how many names there are for normal powdered coke?"

"Classic, ching, charles, charlie, pedro, bolivian marching powder, nose candy, blow, white, dust, and snow. For crack cocaine; glass, rock, gravel, grit, hail, and black."

"Most impressive. Now, professor, how many names are there for pot?"

"Hash, Maryjane, Weed, Gear, Dope, resin, grass, pot, ganja, Chronic, Herb, and Bud."

THE CHILDREN OF DAGON by CARLTON HERZOG

"Too bad there isn't a drug Jeopardy or Wheel of Fortune. You could make a fortune."

The conversation eventually meandered around to the paranormal and settled on past lives.

Mia, aka Big Hair, the lead female vocalist, was a staunch believer in reincarnation. She said, "I have watched hypnotherapists do past life regression with adults. While in a trance their subjects writhe as they remember agonizing deaths, weep copiously at the death of loved ones, or burst into foreign languages they have never even heard of. I majored in psychology and studied Jung. He argued that we all have access in dreams, meditation, or hypnosis to a stratum of the unconscious mind which is universal. Rightly prepared, anyone of us can dip into the great collective memory bank of mankind. "

"You're saying neither time nor place exists for the soul? By that logic, a soul could see all human history in an instant," Ace said.

"Yes. Man is a plural being. There is no one 'I' in us, but hundreds, thousands in every one of us," said Mia.

"In some quarters, they call that schizophrenia. In others, multiple personality disorder. However, you slice it, all this crazy talk is making my head spin more than usual."

"I think it's all the hits you took off the bong, Ace. I'm burnt. I think I'll turn in for the night," Roxy replied.

The others followed suit. That night, Big Hair and the Bongos slept fitfully in their new digs. They would learn that when we sleep, we lie in the shadow of other worlds. Things grotesque and supernatural come to us at their fullest. They do everything they can to seep inside our heads, and burrow into our hearts, so we may become their beacons of darkness in the light.

Roxy shrieked as she sprang from the bed. She ran around the cabin waking her companions. When she had everyone's attention, she recounted her vivid nightmare.

"I was on a boat that shipwrecked. But I wasn't me. I was a native in a sarong holding a baby. I was covered in tattoos as was everyone else. American fishermen came on board to rescue us. They looked at us funny. I understood when I looked around. The people I was with had frog like-faces with big, bulging eyes.

"One of our rescuers said, 'Why they ain't even human. They be freaks of nature. And they be bringing their baby freaks with them. I for one ain't letting 'em on my boat.' Other fishermen pointed to a bunch of shrunken heads dangling from a line across the tilted deck. One picked up a toothed sickle with fresh blood on it.

"'These fuckers be cannibals and head shrinkers. We can't take them ashore and let them practice their devil ways. And we can't take a chance some will swim to shore. We got to kill them where they stand. Get me one of them axes. You three, take the babies and bash their brains, chop them up and dump them in buckets. We can use them for chum. Same for the adults.'

"I cowered in a corner as I watched the men murder the men, women, and children on the ship. I remember people asking for mercy. Or was that the name of the ship. I can't say for sure because they weren't speaking English. It was some weird language of barks and chirps. But I could understand them. When one fisherman came to me, he grabbed my baby by his legs and smashed him into the ship's side, again, and again. Then, he took out a knife, cut off his arms and legs, then threw it all into a large, wooden bucket.

"He came at me with his knife. I was screaming. I picked up a lance and drove it into his eye. I pushed him back and over the side with the barb still in his eye. I felt a sharp pain my back as another man stabbed me. I fell over. When he bent down to finish the job, I grabbed his beard, pulled him to me, and bit down on his nose. He tried to wriggle free, but I wouldn't let

THE CHILDREN OF DAGON by CARLTON HERZOG

go. I could taste his blood in my mouth. I smelled pee. He had wet himself. As the fight went out of him, I pushed him aside. I took his knife and straddled him. I stabbed his face, then again, and again, and again until it was nothing but blood and pulp.

"By now, the ship had pitched forward, and it was hard for anyone to maintain secure footing on the slick deck. I saw several islanders dive over the side. I wanted to join them in the swim to shore. But two fishermen grabbed me and slammed my head into the bulkhead.

"'Aye, she's too ugly to fuck. I wouldn't want them big, bulgy eyes staring at me as I put it to her.'

"'If you ask me, she's got a bit of frog in her.'

"One of them took a native spear and plunged it through my gut, into the bulkhead. As I tried with my last bit of strength to free myself, one of them took a machete and severed my left arm. I watched as the blood jetted from the stump that was my shoulder. He did the same to my right arm. Then, I felt myself drift above my body. The ship and all its carnage faded from view as I soared higher and higher. I could see others soaring with me toward a great light. A resonant chorus filled the air. It was the music of the graveyard, and its notes vibrated within me.

"My nightmare became an uncanny flux of sound and pageantry. I was moving toward orders of existence beyond all definition. I was no longer frustrated by the limitations of body and had achieved a purely informational existence. Unmoored from the reliance on my own body, I could move about and inhabit and control others. But I had an overriding impulse to experience the fecundity of blood, as if the slaughter and the gallons of blood spilled around me, had repurposed me into a floating abattoir."

The Bongos focused on calming Roxy down with liquor and weed. But she was so spooked by the nightmare that her eyes rolled back in her head, horse like. She had gone completely around the bend and wasn't coming back any time soon.

Ace snuck up on her with a syringe full of heroin. He thought to himself, "If this doesn't calm her down, nothing will."

He had the others hold her down while Mia put a tourniquet on Roxy's arm. Ace jammed the needle in and plunged the calmative into her bloodstream. Roxy went quiet for a moment, then broke free from her caregivers. She smashed a lamp over Ace's head, kicked Candy a solid one in the shin, and threw up—as heroin users do after the initial injection—on Trudy. She shed her clothes and charged out of the cabin. The rest of the band was too stunned to chase after her.

"She'll be back when she wants another fix or gets hungry. I don't think she'll go far buck-naked. It's still early. Let's have some breakfast and we'll go from there.'

Blind Frog Lake was one of those places where the dawn chorus echoes through the forest, and the mist lingers well into the day. After Roxy's berserker rage, Big Hair Mia had felt a strong pull toward the water, and it was more than just idle curiosity. She left the cabin as the sun began to move up and across the sky. It cast a silver bridge across Blind Frog Lake that soon glittered like the pieces of a broken mirror. Mia looked down to the far end of the lake where the marsh rolled wide with thickets of gently swaying cattails. Full throated melodies called to her from the adjacent woods of muscular oaks and maples.

Mia was struck by the immensity of Blind Frog Lake's placid waters. She imagined herself touching its perfect bottom and experiencing the stillness of its invisible life below. It occurred to her that she'd lived a life entirely in New York City, a rotten Gotham sliding down the behavioral sink of ubiquitous graffiti, the stench of uncollected garbage, and two murders a day.

But now she was free. Outfitted in a neon-colored, high-rise bikini, she strolled along the beach to a bouquet of pleasant fragrances. She had left her blue jelly sandals home because she loved the feel of wet sand between her toes as she walked.

THE CHILDREN OF DAGON by CARLTON HERZOG

Listening to A Flock of Seagulls' *I Ran* on her Walkman, she laughed to herself at the singer's signature hairstyle of two airfoils on either side of his head with a downward swoop covering one eye.

Her musing was interrupted by a curious vibration in the air and ground. She turned to see a small army of green croaking frogs hopping behind her. It filled her with inestimable joy.

"What's up, little hoppers? Am I your new god? I must ask. How can you see where you are going without eyes? Really, how do you know where to shoot your tongues, and how do you avoid the bigger things that want to eat you?"

She smirked and kept walking, lost in euphoria. But as she continued, the beach ahead of her was no longer a stretch of white sand. It had become a spectral place of terrible cypress woods with ugly roots and malignant hanging nooses of Spanish mosses. She heard the muffled beat of tom-toms accentuated at intervals with blood-curdling shrieks. Just ahead, she saw a horde of human abnormality, void of clothing, braying around a ring-shaped bonfire. In the center of which could be seen a grotesque statute whenever the curtain of flames parted. It was a pestilential thing with a single bulging, fire-red eye, dozens of tentacles, and an enormous maw filled with intestinal teeth.

Trembling with fear, she wondered if the scene was all in her head or a dreaded glimpse of ghostly residue from the distant past. She got her answer when a leering cultist covered in tattoos suddenly materialized before her and sliced off her right hand. Hypnotized by the horror, she dropped to her knees. As she tried to staunch the jetting blood from her artery, a second blade appeared out of thin air and chopped off her other hand. She fell face first into the sand. The phantom blade struck again, first severing her left foot, then her right. She tried to scream for help but could make no sound other than a low rasp. She felt the sand rise and swell as if it were alive. Then, it opened itself and swallowed her.

CAMP SLASHER LAKE: VOLUME ONE

Mia's boyfriend Nick had remained in the cabin with the rest of the band. With his pink and yellow speedo, heavily tattooed chest, and high, blown-out, metal hair, he had remained staunchly committed to the 80s rocker look, despite his current affiliation. When Mia didn't return for breakfast, Nick went looking for her. Like her, he sported a Sony Walkman but opted for Quiet Riot's *Bang Your Head* while toking on a Columbian. He found her footprints as they moved along the beach. They stopped. He kept walking until he reached an intersecting set of footprints: one set beginning at the waters edge, the other coming from the direction he was walking. Perplexed, he looked up and down the beach, then into the water.

As he turned, he found himself leading a procession of blind frogs.

"Don't you little shits know we eat your kind. Deep-fried frog legs are my thing. I didn't believe the stories, but since you have been gracious enough to show yourselves, I'll be back with a sack to collect your slimy little asses." They stopped and faced him with empty eye sockets.

Strange cries and the shivery tinkle of raucous little bells caught his attention. He saw a set of footprints coming toward him. Every now and then, a naked goat-faced man would flash above them, then vanish. Where the phantasms dark body wasn't covered in arcane tattoos, it festered with pustules that leaked a black ooze.

"What the fuck are you supposed to be, the Invisible Asshole?"

The wraith vanished and reappeared wielding a curved machete-like blade. The apparition, now solid, slashed Nick across his chest. Nick staggered back. Before he could scream, the blade cut off his arms at the shoulders with surgical precision. Nick dropped to his knees. Some invisible force kept him

THE CHILDREN OF DAGON by CARLTON HERZOG

from falling face forward. The ghost drove the blade into Nick's head with such supernatural force, the head split in two and hung like testicles from this neck. The gushing blood woke the hungry sand. It heaved and undulated, then opened wide and swallowed Nick's mangled body.

At first, none of the other band members gave much thought to the missing Mia and Nick. The four of them sat around playing Trivial Pursuit. An old, brown plastic radio topped with a Rubik's Cube provided background:

"It's black cat day on Blind Frog Lake. Don't forget the big drawing today to see who gets our Monster Surprise: either a man's digital continuous readout watch, or a Panasonic color television set."

Trudy, a hefty singer known for her robust vocals, teased her spiraling cone of product saturated golden hair. Her bodacious, creamy white breasts spilled from the top of her bikini, as she pulled a card and asked, "In what movie does a crazy hobo pop out from between two parked cars holding two dead rats in his mouth?"

Candy, a skeletal girl with flaming red hair worked into a great expanding starburst on her head, shouted, "That's easy. *Friday the Thirteenth*!"

Prematurely bald, Ace, who sported a silver mullet wig, asked, "Are you sure? Sounds more like *Halloween*."

Meatball fumbled for his *Rabbit in Red Lounge* matches and lit a camel. He sighed then said, "It's easy to confuse the two movies since they both had killers with big kitchen knives and masks. Like all slasher flicks they had the unstoppable killer, the claustrophobic sense of no escape, and of course, the blood."

"True, but the whole unstoppable killer and claustrophobia schtick are also common to *Alien, Aliens, Predator* and *Terminator*. Slashers in space, slasher from space, and slasher from the future."

CAMP SLASHER LAKE: VOLUME ONE

"Okay, but what about John Carpenter's *The Thing*?"

"Shape-shifting slasher from space. That motherfucker killed dogs and people."

"What about Freddy Krueger?"

"Slasher from sleep."

"I think he was supernatural, like Michael Meyers and Jason."

"Does a slasher's origin really matter when he or she is carving you up like a rump roast."

"Well, what if the slasher were gay? Let's face it, the gay genie has popped out of the bottle, and into the streets."

"I don't think a gay killer would wield a blade. He could do his job just by infecting people with AIDS."

"That's stupid. He or she would use a blade. If you ask me, then he or she would have a legitimate motive. After all, Ronald and Nancy Reagan withheld funds in the hope AIDS would kill all the gay men. There was the U.S. Court of Appeals which ruled that there is no fundamental right to be gay. That's the Dredd Scott decision repackaged to fuck gays. Then you have douche bag, Pope Paul II, labeling gays as 'evil' and Margret Thatcher making homosexual relationships illegal. Sure, you've got anti-discrimination laws here and there. And you have the US Army conceding gay recruits could kick ass as well as anybody. But if I were gay, I would have plenty of reasons to hack straight motherfuckers to death."

"I don't agree with that take. You have singers like Boy George and Queen, all living high profile queer lives. They don't radiate a slasher vibe."

"Why should they? They've made it to the big time. Queer entertainers are socially acceptable in the same way black athletes — think Magic Johnson — are accepted while the rest of the black community gets shit on."

THE CHILDREN OF DAGON by CARLTON HERZOG

The back and forth on slashers in cinema and the marginalization of the queer community gradually lost steam. For all their high blown rhetoric, these were stoners with the attention span of a monkey chewing on a fly swatter.

Ace suggested they have a movie night.

"I've brought a ton of slasher flicks. Lifted them from Blockbuster. I say we break out the Jiffy Pop and have us a marathon."

Meatball voiced a qualified acceptance of the proposal.

"I like films that really speak to the primal fear that we, as human beings, have about the unknown. The ones that deal with the inner fear: the unknown realms and the mysticisms that are scary, like *The Shining*."

"Then it's settled. Movie night in the cabin. By the way, have any of you seen Mia or Nick?"

"I thought they went for a beach stroll. A northeaster is coming our way, so I'm sure they'll be back soon. Let's roll some fatties and kick back until they return."

They all kicked back and smoked. The weed inspired Ace to give the others a brief history lesson on the shipwreck and its doomed crew.

"You guys know I'm super curious about occult, weird stuff, right? It turns out that the *Mercy* crew were West Indians or Brava Portuguese from the Cape Verde Islands. Supposedly, they practiced human sacrifice, feeding their victims to their gods who lived inside the earth. They would whip themselves into an animalistic fury, howling, and squawking like lunatics. The legend is that their spirits continue to haunt Blind Frog Lake. Something like twenty people turned up missing over the years. Folks around here believe the ghosts of the murdered natives are to blame. That's why the original owner of this fine lake property got rid of it. And that's why I just had to see the place for myself and pushed for us to spend the Halloween weekend here."

"When were you going to tell us all this?" Trudy asked. "We've already paid for this place. They're not going to give us a refund based on a ghost story."

CAMP SLASHER LAKE: VOLUME ONE

"Weren't you paying attention in the Blue Frog Café? Not that it matters. There are no such things as ghosts. Or did one of you spot Beetlejuice and forgot to tell us?"

"Those murders are nothing to sneeze at. Something ain't right. This place could be the hunting ground for some Jeffrey Dahmer or Richard Ramirez type."

"Where is this sudden concern coming from? If the local cops thought something wasn't right, they would have shut this place down."

"Just the same," Meatball said, "I'm going to find Mia and Nick. The last thing they need is to be out there alone and run into a family of axe-wielding, cannibalistic, Wes Craven fucks."

"Man, you are a total space cadet. Shit like that doesn't happen in real life. This is the 80s — Michael Jackson, Billy Idol, Pac-Man, and IBM. A totally tubular modern era — bitchin', and gnarly — I kid you not," Ace said.

"I'm going. Candy, are you coming? Good. I'm taking my baseball bat. Candy, grab that iron poker from the fireplace."

Meatball and Candy made for the beach while Trudy and Ace made for the upstairs bedroom.

The armed rockers walked up and down the beach searching for their friends, to no avail.

They stopped to rest, sitting hunched on the sand.

"Where could they be? In those woods?"

Before Candy could say anything, she noticed what she thought were footprints advancing toward them.

"Check that out. I think we've found a ghost, or it's found us."

They both stood up and stared at the invisible person walking toward them. They didn't hesitate but turned tail and ran. They had not gone far when Candy heard Meatball let out a bloodcurdling scream. She turned to see a blade flashing in and out of existence as it struck Meatball again, and again. It was swung by a spectral figure that also came and went, a naked figure adorned with cryptic inks, and wearing a diabolical ceremonial mask.

THE CHILDREN OF DAGON by CARLTON HERZOG

Despite her girly name, Candy had grit. She did not quiver or shake. She swung the iron bar at the phantom. It passed through its ephemeral essence, generating a flash and cloud of black smoke. Then, it disappeared altogether.

Fading in and out of consciousness, Meatball was bleeding heavily. But he had seen the iron strike the phantom.

"He vanished because ghosts are repelled by iron. Salt too. You don't have much time. Leave me and ward the house. Grab the iron chess set from the van. Throw the pieces at them to buy yourself some time."

"I'm not leaving you, dude. If that motherfucker or any others like him come back, they'll get more of the same."

"You can't save me. My guts are pouring out of me. I can barely hold in my stomach and intestines. My curiosity got us into this mess. I deserve this. But you and the others need to run for it.

Before Meatball could finish, the sand began to percolate and hum. An instant later, it opened and sucked him down into the earth. For her part, Candy had jumped back. Otherwise, she would have joined him in that silicate abyss.

She turned and ran back to the house. When she got there, she found Ace and Trudy lounging in the living room drinking Heinekens.

"Where are the rest of you?" Ace asked.

"We were attacked. Meatball is dead. Mia and Nick probably are too. We need to protect ourselves." She ran to the kitchen looking for salt.

She came back and began spreading it around the door and windows.

Ace and Trudy looked at her as if she had three heads.

"What are you doing?"

"I am protecting us against the ghost that just hacked Meatball to death on the beach. It's mainly invisible and uses a machete. No, scratch that. It's a ceremonial blade with crazy writing up and down its length. I used an iron bar to repel it. The salt will do the same. You guys need to arm yourselves with the other iron fireplace tools."

"You sound like you're a couple fries short of a Happy Meal."

"I know what I saw. That thing filleted Meatball in front of me. I nearly barfed. Then, the sand swallowed him up. I would say go see the red sand for yourself. But that would not be a smart thing to do. We need to call the cops."

"And tell them what exactly? That we're being chased by angry spirits? Or that it's all in your head because of all the crank and PCP you did with Roxy"? Trudy asked.

"Fuck you, bitch. I know what I saw. If you don't want to help, then I'll go at it alone."

"Come on, Ace, let's go see for ourselves."

"Okay, whatever, lead the way."

The two of them walked along the beach. They were high as kites and laughed at the prospect of running into a bloodthirsty spirit.

"You know, if we're wrong and she's right, this was a really stupid thing to do."

"Well, it is the eighties. And if the slasher movies are a reliable indicator of what will happen next, then…."

The specter materialized behind them. This time it worked more efficiently, striking Ace across the back of his neck and then did the same to Trudy. The specter sliced open Ace's belly left to right, reached, and pulled out his intestines. They lay in a bloody, coiled pile at his feet. He staggered back, then fell forward, face first into his own viscera.

Trudy, halfway between the living and the dead, raised her head, and turned long enough to see a degraded half-human face leering down at her. The next moment, the blade cut into her skull. And as before, when the spirit had accomplished its mission, the red beach sand having had its appetizer, opened, and swallowed whole the main course.

Back at the house, Candy finished warding the points of entry against any phantom incursions. She had tried calling the police on the landline, but all she got was static. When she tried

THE CHILDREN OF DAGON by CARLTON HERZOG

to start the van, it wouldn't turn over. She did however retrieve the chess pieces and stick them in her front pouch.

She ransacked her memory for a clue as to how to survive. In her mind, she revisited *The Shining, Ghostbusters, Beetlejuice, Poltergeist, The Fog,* and *Ghost Story.* None of them offered a glimmer of a real-world solution. She tried to recall ghost stories she had read as a child. They too proved useless.

She would settle for arming herself with an iron poker in each hand, then making her way on foot to town. By now, it was late in the day. She had to choose between fighting ghosts in the near dark, or hunkering down, and leaving in the morning.

Candy opted for staying the night and striking out in the morning. She didn't sleep but sat in a ring of salt, staring at the fire, and clutching the iron poker. Every now and then, she would snort a line of crank to stay awake.

At sunrise, she sucked down a pot of coffee, checked her pouch arsenal, grabbed an iron poker in each hand and headed for town. She kept waiting for her potential pursuers to make a move. But the walk began uneventfully. After a mile or so, she stopped to rest and collect her thoughts. That's when she sensed something was wrong. She looked behind her and, sure enough, there were several sets of footprints moving toward her on the dirt road. She considered running but as she turned back around, she saw more footprints advancing from the opposite direction.

"This is it, Candy baby. Remember the best defense is a good offense," she muttered to herself. She moved toward the ones in front of her. She put the iron rods in her left hand, reached into the pouch and hurled iron chest pieces at her invisible attackers. Bright bursts of light and black smoke swirled around semi-solid figures. Having a visible target, Candy charged forward swinging the iron rods.

She remembered the pursuers behind her. She turned and threw more iron bits, causing half-formed figures appearing in bursts of light and swirling smoke. Then she did as she had done with the wave in front of her. She charged forward like a berserker swinging every which way. It was like the fourth of July on that deserted strip of road.

She spun around and began running toward town. The smoke swirling in the air made her assailants partially visible. That edge allowed her to dodge their strikes and land hers with accuracy. On that leveled playing field, she had no trouble seeing and dispatching the fiends.

She fast walked toward town, pausing every now and then to see or hear some sign of pursuit. Two miles down the road, she was met by a pickup truck. It carried an odd assortment of people, canine faced, and, judging from their lack of thumbs and unibrows, inbred. They did not seem to be from any ethnic group, but rather genetic anomalies, deformed and grotesque.

The man driving the truck stopped and looked at her. He rolled down the window and asked, "Where ya be goin,'? Out for a morning stroll are ya?"

Candy's hackles immediately went up at the sound of that rasping voice saturated with archaisms, together with his bulging right eye and drooping left.

"Yes, out for a walk. I like the fresh air."

"We could give ya a ride. Jump in and we'll take ya wherever ya wants to go. Move over, Ma."

The thing called Ma had a cephalopod shaped head covered in warts. She took a long, loving lick of her thick lips and grinned at Candy with her one good tooth. Candy balked in disgust and turned her gaze back to the driver. She noticed the ink on the man's arm as it dangled lazily out the window. They were the same sort of sigils she had seen on the specter's blade and handle.

"Nope, I'm good, thank you. Please excuse me. I need to be on my way."

"No, ye be coming with us."

The man's son and daughter jumped from the truck and ran at Candy. They came at her with hysterical shrieks and half-ape savagery. Grotesque parodies of people, they had squamous skin like a snake and nearly triangular heads under their wild hair. They grabbed for her with four-fingered stubs ending in long sickle like fingernails.

Candy, who by now, was running on pure adrenalin, did as she did with the ghosts. She furiously swung her iron bars and cracked them both in the jaw. When they dropped, she pounced, smashing their faces again, and again with the pokers, reducing their heads to hair, bone, and pulp.

The road beneath their bodies heaved and roiled as the beach had earlier. Then, it cracked open and swallowed the bodies.

As his children were disappearing into the maw of some eldritch force, the father grabbed Candy by the arms and shook the bars from her hands. He pulled her face close to his and she nearly fainted from the stench of his breath. It smelled of a thousand open graves.

They struggled while the crone he had called Ma leered. Every now and then, she would let out a war whoop or bark like a dog.

Candy managed to wriggle free from the man's grip. But instead of running, she picked up the two iron bars and beat him across his head. He stumbled back, bleeding, and moaning. Undaunted, Candy charged forward and beat him to the ground, then stomped on his head until he stopped moving. With fire in her eyes, she went around the other side of the truck. Ma had locked the door so Candy could not get to her. Candy was not to be deterred. She jumped on the truck's hood and smashed in the windshield. Once that obstruction had been cleared, she beat the crone until she slumped over in her seat.

Candy knew what had to be done. She dragged the hag out of the truck and placed her next to the man. The road began to shift and vibrate, then cracked open, swallowing the bodies. She tried to start the truck but like the van it wouldn't turn over. Everything, it seemed, was at the mercy of some controlling force of demonic temperament. Nightmares sculpted out of the atoms of the local earth.

Candy grabbed the gasoline can from the truck bed and

thoroughly doused the cab. She put the truck in neutral and pushed it as close to the woods as she could. Then she set the whole thing ablaze. Fire might cleanse the place, she thought, and if not cleanse, provide enough smoke to reveal the phantoms arrayed against her. Gathering her iron bars, she watched the fire burn for a moment, then resumed her trip to town.

As she walked down the road, she heard a babel of barked and bleated words. She felt a sentient loathsomeness watching her from the forest, hissing and croaking. She stopped and delivered a speech.

"I don't know what you motherfuckers are. And I don't care. Come at me again. I dare you! So, I can send you back to whatever hell you crawled out of. Let's go, motherfuckers. I'm right here, are you going to talk me to death?"

Silence—pure and crystalline as the driven snow in Norway—followed. Whatever devil that lived in the earth and brought the ghosts out of the shadow realm had been sated. First, with the bodies of her friends and now, with those of the mongrel family.

She considered going back and torching the house to prevent anyone else experiencing the horrors that she had. But after some reflection, she decided the most prudent course of action was to get as far away as possible. And that is exactly what she tried to do.

In all the commotion, she had forgotten about the elusive Roxy. Making her way back to town, she wondered what had become of her.

"Odds are one or more of the monsters had chopped her up, or the ground had swallowed her. Then again, maybe she's flitting about as a madwoman of the forest, eating small game alive and reliving the hellish nightmare that drove her to be a creature of the woods. I better be ready just in case she goes apeshit on me. I didn't come this far to get sliced up by some crackhead extraordinaire."

A bit farther along, she heard a crashing sound in the brush coming toward her. The cracking, snapping sounds became louder and louder. A wild pig ran squealing past her. For a moment, she thought the matter was closed.

But on its heels, Roxy, the insane human juggernaut, most likely possessed by one or more of the demonic spirits that haunted the lake, came into view. She had been hunting the pig. Her only weapon, a rusty machete. When she saw Candy, she let out a bloodcurdling scream, followed by, "I'll kill you, bitch! You butchered my baby!"

As she got closer, Candy saw that Roxy had two sunken, black craters where her eyes should have been. Candy asked herself, "How the fuck can she see where she is going?" Candy also saw and heard the horde of blind frogs hopping behind Roxy. Only these frogs were as black and as big as dogs. Candy debated whether she should run away, run toward her, or just hold her ground. She opted for the last.

When Roxy exploded from the green, Candy, who at one time had been a capable softball hitter, swung her iron poker straight into Roxy's face. There was a loud crack as it connected. Roxy's momentum was diverted sideways. She slammed face first into the dirt road and slid on that same face for a solid three feet. Roxy lay still, letting out a groan.

Candy cautiously walked toward her.

"Girlfriend, I'm sorry. But you were going to take me out. Are you okay? Can you get up?"

With that last question, she hopped to her feet like a crazed jackrabbit on steroids. The left side of her face was now sharing space with the right side. A makeshift, fiendish deformity that only added to Candy's horror and Roxy's rage.

Roxy stopped for a moment and felt her face. She spit out blood and teeth.

"You've made me prettier than before. How thoughtful. Now I can have my own Late Nite Show. 'Here's Johnny!' bitch."

CAMP SLASHER LAKE: VOLUME ONE

She charged at Candy again. Candy caught her on the side of the head, but not before Roxy struck a glancing blow down Candy's chest. Roxy lay on the ground cursing Candy, who sprinted bloody and scared into the woods. Somewhere in the escape, she dropped her iron pokers. She came to an abandoned cabin, ran inside, and threw the wooden bolt over the door. Next, she closed the wooden shutters and looked around the dark cabin for anything that might give her an edge. She found a claw hammer and screwdriver, both made of steel and tin alloys. She waited for the inevitable attack.

Twenty minutes went by. She heard a light rapping on the door.

"'Little pigs, little pigs, let me come in. Not by the hair of your chiny-chin-chins? Then I'll huff, and I'll puff, and I'll blow your house in.'"

Candy could hear Roxy kicking at the door, then banging on the windows. But she seemed to be making no real attempt to enter. It struck Candy that all the banging was meant as a distraction for something else. "That lunatic has something else up her sleeve. But what?" she asked herself.

The smell of burning woods and leaves gradually suffused into the cabin. Candy realized that Roxy intended one of two things: drive her out of the cabin by setting it ablaze, or if Candy chose to stay, burn her alive. The cabin had no indoor water source, so she had no way to fight the fire. She remembered seeing a hand driven well pump just off the steps but that would do her no good.

In a moment of clarity, she said, "Salt." So, she hunted around the cabin and found a mildewed box of salt. Her plan was simple. Throw salt on Roxy and see what happened. If the possessing spirit took a permanent powder, she could get Roxy medical help in town. If not, then she had the hammer and screwdrivers in her belt.

She put salt in her mouth to prevent any ghost from taking possession of her.

"I'm coming out, Roxy. I want to join your murder club and

THE CHILDREN OF DAGON by CARLTON HERZOG

kill with reckless abandon."

There was dead silence.

"Didn't you hear me, Roxy, I want to switch teams and play for the criminally insane. Come on, girlfriend, throw me a bone. Let's kiss and make up."

The silence remained unbroken. Candy debated her next move.

"Logic tells me these ghosts aren't stupid. Probably suspect I'm up to something. Well, those flames aren't getting any smaller, so it's now or never."

Candy yanked open the door and stepped aside. Roxy came barreling in like a locomotive. Roxy's momentum carried her straight into a rickety table that splintered on impact. Candy threw salt on her. The nebulous form of a native woman emerged from her and wafted toward Candy. More salt and the ghastly apparition disappeared.

"Sister, are you alright?"

"I need a snort."

"Later, we need to get to town. Everybody else is probably dead."

"Oh no, we must go back. I have a pound of uncut coke at the cabin. The street value is $160,000 after it's been cut five or six times. Somebody's coming to buy it tomorrow."

"After what's been happening. Are you out of your mind?"

"I've got another five grand in bills in my purse. And that's my van."

"The van is dead."

"I'll give you an eighth if you come with me. That's 20,000 after it's been cut. And a one thousand dollar retainer."

"Done. First, we go to town. We need iron poles, salt, a shotgun, and a bottle of Jack. Then we rent a car and drive back to the cabin. Maybe we can jumpstart the van."

The two headed into town. They could hear the croaking from the forest paralleling them as they went. The madness of the lake was on the move towards town. Vectors for the lethal insanity the two women would soon encounter.

~ 186 ~

CAMP SLASHER LAKE: VOLUME ONE

They walked into town just past noon. The rolling avenues of Old Hickory were in readiness for Halloween. There were Jack-O-Lanterns, cardboard witches, and plastic skeletons everywhere. The sidewalks were jammed with lively pedestrians. There was a vitality attributable to the festivities later that evening.

Candy saw disturbing things as well. An eerie emerald haze permeated the streets. The people's faces looked slightly frog-like. Every now and then, an enormous eyeless bullfrog could be seen making its way in the gutters. The most disturbing thing were the clowns. Their clothes were shabby and non-descript. They had thin, smooth, pale, oval-shaped heads with wide, bulging eyes. Things that seemed more properly under the earth than above it.

The two women soldiered on until they found Handy Andy's Gun and Tackle.

There was a pile of rusted iron rebar on the curb awaiting pickup. Candy picked up four bars.

"Take these two. I'll get us a shotgun. You find rock salt."

As they entered, Andy Temple greeted them with a "What can I do for you two ladies today?"

"I need a Mossberg Twelve gauge and three boxes of cartridges."

"Mossberg holds 11 shells. That's a lot of tactical firepower for a little lady. Going to a riot?"

"Nope. Just killing ghosts. Here's my credit card. Put whatever my friend brings over onto the bill as well."

After they left the shop, the two found a bench and switched the rock salt for the cartridge's pellets.

"Let's rent a car. I saw a place down the street."

As they were walking, a sea of thin, bloodless faces began following them.

Roxy turned to survey the odd assortment of humanity trailing them. They were a congregation of stiff-legged, dead-eyed townsfolk frozen in a trance.

"We seem to have attracted a following, and not the good

kind. And believe it or not, they've got an army of frogs tagging along."

Candy didn't answer. She turned on her heels and fired two shots into the crowd. There was a collective groan as the black parade stopped dead in its tracks. She fired a second round at the frogs at the head of the procession. The rock salt bits exploded their slimy green bodies, and as they did, Candy swore she heard tiny, tiny screams.

They ran down an alley and then into the first available house. It had an ominously skewed, angular design. If they had time to consider the matter, they might have noticed that peculiarity. Or the unsettling fact that it seemed as if it had been constructed from dreams and vapor posing as solid material.

Candy and Roxy ran up the staircase to the second floor. Here room upon room followed through a maze of interconnecting doors. They found one and ducked inside, locking the door behind them. When they walked to the window to cautiously observe the street below, they found the town of Old Hickory had been replaced with a jungle teeming with beastlike forms. That landscape thronged with plants that changed shapes and colors before their fascinated eyes. As for the sky, it was dominated by a large planet and its moon, as well as a red sun.

"We're not in Kansas anymore."

Candy noticed there were cadaverous generations of giant insects that had sunken and merged into coral. A sculpture of abdomens, legs, and thoraxes heaped without order.

"No, but look over there beyond that pile of fossilized bugs. That's Blind Frog Lake, but not the one we left."

"How can that be?"

"It's Halloween, or Samhain if you prefer. Supposedly the walls between worlds are at their thinnest on this day. Between the living and the dead, and other realities."

"Man, I need me a snort," Roxy exclaimed.

"Me too. But I think if we lay low until morning, whatever is going on out there will be gone once Samhain is over and the sun rises again."

So, they waited and watched through the window. The strange world outside gave way to others that refused to articulate their exact nature or milieu. Nor did the house remain static but began manifesting unusual properties. The beams and boards took on the cast of bones and its walls and floors that of petrified flesh.

What had begun as misty-eyed wonder and bafflement turned into a sense of impending doom.

"Candy, just look at this place. It's not a house. It's an abomination. The next thing you know it will swallow us whole. We have got to get out of Dodge before it's too late."

Even as she spoke, contorted rainbows, and twisted auras lit up the room, indicating the world outside had changed again.

"If we leave now, who knows what kind of world we'll find out there?"

"Or" Roxy said, "it's all an illusion. Some kind of hypnosis to keep us in a fantasy funhouse of bizarre worlds, so we stay put. I don't deny there's spooky shit afoot, but even spooky shit has limits. I've done enough shrooms and acid to know that just because you see something doesn't mean it's real. Think about it: the cuttlefish strobes in different colors to mesmerize its prey. I say we stick our head out the door and decide for ourselves whether what we're seeing is genuine or not. If not, we steal a car, head back to the cabin, grab my shit, then blow this backwater burg for Orlando."

Weapons at the ready, the two crept down the stairs. Candy cracked the door and saw the town of Old Hickory glowing around the full moon. No one was in sight.

Like two hungry raccoons, they slunk along side streets and back alleys. As they circumnavigated main street, blood-curdling screams filled the air.

"Sounds like the nuthouse opened its doors and let all the wackos run free," laughed Roxy.

"Free range crazies, no doubt. Come on, I want to peek."

They crept along the edge of the five and dime. When they reached main street, their jaws dropped at the nightmarish spectacle before them. It was Hieronymus Bosch's phantasmagoria on steroids and a Viking Berserker attack all rolled into one horrible vision of Hell. Hundreds of townsfolk were tearing at one another. Some wielded pipes, tire irons and bats, others used bricks, machetes, pitchforks, and shovels. The unarmed relied on strangulation, and in extreme cases, biting into throats and chewing on faces. A great holiday genocide of which the two women wanted no part.

"Back up, back up. Since they're all busy killing each other, we stand a chance of hotwiring a car," Roxy said.

"Where did you learn to do that?"

"It's a prerequisite at the Miskatonic Drug Dealer Academy."

They came upon a red chevy pickup.

"Before you start pulling wires, let me see if Goober left the keys under the sun visor. Yep, here they be."

The two of them made a beeline out of town. Along the way, they drove through a bloodied, screaming mob. Their Ride of the Valkyries did not have the gravitas of a Wagnerian score. Instead, it consisted of dull thuds, metallic crunches, and 'Look out!' Every now and then they would hit a madman or madwoman at such a sharp angle, the body would fly up onto the hood. Most were removed by non-linear driving moves. A few managed to hang on long enough to shatter the windshield, only to have their heads blown off by rock salt shot.

Once outside the town, they stopped long enough to pack more cartridges with salt. Then they began the cautious drive back to the lake and the pharmacological treasure waiting for them. Candy expected a sightless amphibian committee croaking its message of "Welcome back." But there were no insect, bird, or animal sounds to be heard. An acoustic ambience of pure nothingness, a vacuum, and a void, save for the two women's breathing and the truck's motor.

"I'll keep the truck running. You grab what you need, and we'll go."

Roxy ducked into the cabin. A moment later, the truck died. Candy grabbed the shotgun and other implements of war and got out of the truck. When Roxy failed to reappear, Candy called her name. There was no response. She deliberated whether she should go inside the cabin or simply begin walking back to town. She opted to stick her head inside the cabin.

Roxy smashed Candy with a chair. As Candy fell and lay bleeding from her scalp, Roxy reprised her role as a host for a vengeful spirit.

"Bitch, you killed my baby. Now I'm gonna kill you."

Roxy, chair held high above her own head, advanced menacingly toward her supine friend. Still dazed, Candy could not get herself up. She began crawling away, looking for anything to defend herself with. Before she could do anything, Roxy brought the chair down. She missed the small of Candy's back, cracking the buttocks instead. She put the chair down and proceeded to air her spectral grievances, giving Candy a moment to collect herself.

"I'm a gonna' kill ya slowly, I am. Show ya the same mercy ya showed us aboard the *Mercy*. How's that for a name? Compassion! Forbearance! We'll have none of that here tonight. Ya see, we be the Children of Dagon. We cannot die, though our fleshy bodies rot and decay. I see you shudder at my words. 'Tis well you should. Even now Dagon's legions are crawling along the slimy ocean beds waiting for the signal to rise above the billows and take this world from ya. What a glorious day that will be, the prophesy on our submarine obelisks made manifest."

Candy spotted the two pieces of rebar Roxy must have put aside as she'd claimed her dope and loot. She staggered forward and grabbed them.

"Not today, if I have anything to do with it."

Candy made an awkward lunge toward Roxy, swinging iron as she moved. A glancing blow made Roxy shriek, and for a moment, the angry spirit inside her became visible amid a cloud of orange and black smoke.

"Twill' do ya no good, that iron, I've sunk my hooks deep into this one's soul. I'll not be leaving any time soon."

"I've got time," a bloodied Candy noted. Then she lunged

again and caught Roxy square on a blocking forearm. More smoke and another spectral appearance that subsided. Initially, Candy recognized that there was only one of two ways this could go. Either beat Roxy to within an inch of her life, driving the ghost away, or bludgeon Roxy to death. But then she remembered the shotgun. It had been knocked out of her hands during Roxy's initial assault. Now it lay just outside the cabin. If she could hit Roxy with enough rock salt, then surely, Candy thought, ghost bitch would take a powder.

Candy tried her best impression of Bruce Lee to overwhelm Roxy with a continuous barrage of strikes from her left and right hands. Roxy, however, did not move back. While the strikes wreaked havoc on Roxy's body, the iron was having no effect on the specter inside her.

Candy switched from striking Roxy's arms and shoulders to her face and head. The blows to the right side of Roxy's jaw crushed the bones and muscles, pushing the entirety of the jaw to the left. More strikes and the right side of Roxy's face joined it. Roxy's labored attempts to defend herself kept her in the line of fire, so much so the right side of her head was nothing more than a bleeding cavity filled with broken bone and brain and blood.

When Roxy could no longer keep her balance, she began lurching awkwardly about. As she turned her back, Candy grabbed her hair and, with the other hand, attacked Roxy's spine. There were a series of distinct cracks as Roxy's vertebrae were crushed. Satisfied that Roxy was no longer an ambulatory threat, Candy released her hold. Roxy collapsed into a deformed pile of blood and broken bones.

"Sorry, sister, but it had to be this way. It was either you or me," said an exhausted Candy to the pulpified body of her friend.

After Candy composed herself, she remembered the dope and loot. She rummaged through the destroyed cabin and found both. Her plan was to make it to the next town on foot. There she would make out a police report. Her story would be that all her friends had been killed by the Blind Bullfrog Lake

Slasher and that she had barely escaped with her life. A solid plan if ever there were one.

But it was not to be. As Candy strolled from the cabin, loot and shotgun in hand, she felt a curious vibration all around her. She could hear the music of the graveyards as a resonant chorus filled the air, drowning out the voices of the living. It was a ubiquitous singing that electrified the currents of her own blood.

She began to perceive an otherwise unseen order with signposts to another realm and spectral things of strange suggestion. She felt something coiling up inside her as if some monstrous organism had infiltrated her valves and arteries. Unseen arms and legs had become entangled with her own. She was becoming a part of an invisible tribe in a labyrinthine layering of souls.

A devil approached from out of the rolling mist blanketing the lake and forest. It had a single eye filled with clusters of little eyes. Where one might have expected hands, there were massive talons attached to large bulging pouches. A thousand sightless, croaking frogs hopped in its wake like some great amphibian procession. The devil had an incorporeal grandeur despite its gruesome visage, a god worshipped on some remote island with its own temple of sacred horrors.

It said nothing. With one hand, it offered her a blood-soaked ceremonial machete. With the other, the shrunken heads of all her friends. In her rational mind, Candy knew she should have been repulsed at such a hideous gesture of commonality. But her rational mind was not in control. It was merely an observer peeking through the windows of her now distended eyes. Her other mind did not hesitate to accept the offering. As it did, Candy could see her arms were covered in arcane tattoos. She could also see she was surrounded by thousands, upon thousands of blind frogs, their glistening skin strobing their approval in venomous colors. Rational, still human Candy knew with irreducible certainty that she was a prisoner in a nightmare made real, a nightmare from which there would be no waking, no escape.

THE CHILDREN OF DAGON by CARLTON HERZOG

She watched herself get in the Chevy and start it. In the gloaming, she could see the ghosts of the murdered islanders. Some played the role of cephalophore carrying their own heads. Others assembled themselves as living torsos and inching arms and legs. It was a send-off of sorts for her grisly mission. The miasma of Blind Frog Lake had taken the town of Old Hickory into its bosom that night. In the coming days, Candy would spread that plague to other towns where still others would pick up her mantle and do the same themselves. Soon, the entire world would fall before Candy's wild and staring gaze, and once under her spell, it would carve itself up to the sounds of ironic jeers of ungraspable phantoms from the beyond.

The Faith

by Derek Austin Johnson

A MONTH AFTER KATHY STARTED her senior year, her father announced they were moving. Initially, she expressed apprehension. Part of her wanted to graduate from Mills with her friends–the ones that were left, anyway–instead of having to learn the names of new teachers and the hallways of a new, much larger building. Eventually, anger was replaced by relief. Going back to Mills had been harder than she'd anticipated. Students avoided or taunted her. Teachers stared at her either in pity, or contempt, with her World History teacher Mrs. Seale saying in the middle of class that she was going to Hell. During the parent-teacher conference after Mrs. Seale's "gross and inappropriate behavior" (as her father christened it), the principal suggested the events of last year's Sadie Hawkins dance still weighed on the school.

So, they were leaving.

The news didn't stop Kathy's nightmares.

Often, she lay awake seeing the faces of her friends. Anna, whose blonde hair she always envied. Anna's boyfriend Parker, whose Adonis-like physique belied his desire to study astronomy when they graduated. Tina, bookish but adventurous, with a voice already rasping from a pack-a-day cigarette habit, and possessing a love of insane trivia, like how you could sharpen

THE FAITH by DEREK AUSTIN JOHNSON

a coin by hammering it. Clayton, so methodical, so in love with argument, that Kathy was certain he'd go to law school.

All dead now.

Because of Samuel Crais.

Yes, he was dead, too. But even as they packed and began the process of transferring to her new school, she continued to see him. When she went to the mall with her friends, he lurked in the shadowed spaces between Orange Julius and Camelot Music. He appeared in the arcade section of Godfather's Pizza, green and blue video game lights flashing on his ugly pink doll's mask, then disappeared. She wanted to scream when she and her parents stopped for gas one night, where he towered over the oblivious cashier behind the Stop-N-Go's plate-glass window, each ding of the gas bell punctuating the smooth swings of his hollow-edged butcher knife as the black sockets of his mask bore into her.

She saw him less on moving day, as shopping malls became strip malls, then an occasional restaurant. By the time the only things on either side of the freeway were grass and rice fields, he had disappeared.

Kathy squeezed her notebook to her chest as the English teacher, Mr. Landis, introduced her. She met twenty sets of eyes before hers dropped to the empty desk in the front row, next to a young man with feathered brown hair curling over his jacket collar. *They know everything already*, she thought. Her father had brought them as far away as possible, but somehow, through the collective unconscious or whatever that crazy German psychiatrist called it, the past followed her.

The still moment only lasted a second. Whispers increased to a cacophony as the class lost interest in her.

"You can sit there, Miss Durham," Mr. Landis said, gesturing to the empty desk. "I'll assign a textbook before the next bell."

Kathy slipped her backpack beneath her desk and opened a brand-new spiral notebook. As Mr. Landis began calling roll, she wrote the date in the upper right-hand corner.

"Hey."

She faced the boy next to her. His chin rose in greeting.

"I'm Malcolm. Fowler. Welcome to Shadow Hills, where crazy is just a state of being." When she did not respond, he squirmed. "Where did you come from?"

She considered. His face seemed open and curious, not malevolent. "Northern Houston."

"Oh. Okay. Did you go to Phillips High? Because I'd read about–"

"Fowler," Mr. Landis called out. "Malcolm."

Malcolm straightened and faced his teacher. "Oh. Um, here."

"Very good," Mr. Landis said. "Miss Durham will need some time to acclimate herself to our classroom and curriculum, so let's save our appreciation until after school, shall we?"

The day ended with Kathy's backpack weighted down with books, and threatening to topple her backward, as she stood on the school's front steps waiting for her mother. Crowds of other students passed and hopped into waiting cars with friends or parents. When she began the year at Mills, her mother picked her up every day, either to make sure she got home safely or for visits with her psychiatrist, Dr. Decker. Her mother had said she'd pick her up during the first week at the new school. But school had been out for fifteen minutes, and her mother's aging Volvo never turned into the driveway.

I'll call, she thought. *See if she's held up at the new house waiting for the cable guy. Or drunk and collapsed on the bed, as usual.*

She turned to go inside but ran into someone who had been

behind her.

"Hey. Again."

It was the boy who'd sat next to her this morning. His nose crinkled as he smiled. "Malcolm. We met in Mr. Landis's class, remember?"

A student bumped against her shoulder. She wobbled and fell, her hands taking enough of the fall to keep from bruising her tailbone, as one of her backpack's straps ripped and leapt over her shoulder. Immediately, Malcolm knelt and offered her his hand, while glaring at the boy who'd sent her sprawling.

"You're a real asshole, you know that, Shawn?" Malcolm said as he helped Kathy up.

The boy, Shawn, coolly regarded them. "Sorry, new girl. Kind of ready to get out of here, you know? 'Just another manic Monday,'" he sang and ran across the street, a car horn blaring as he passed.

Malcolm rolled his eyes. "Dumb fuck doesn't even know that it's Thursday. Time is an illusion to him." He pointed to her hands. "Are you okay?"

The heels of her palms were scraped and bloody. She unshouldered her backpack and pulled a small packet of tissues from the front pocket. "It's just a flesh wound," she said in an over-enunciated British accent, then shrugged at Malcolm's look of incomprehension. "Yeah, I'm fine." She pressed a tissue against each palm until blood spotted it, then coiled a padded shoulder strap around her hand.

A gust of wind ruffled Malcolm's hair but did little to cool the unseasonably warm afternoon. On the street, a station wagon passed them, Kathy's eye catching the "Jesus Saves" sticker on its rear bumper, a blood-red cross separating the black letters. Its brake lights blinked before the car sped on. Kathy shuddered.

"Have you been in town long?" Malcolm asked.

"Couple of days," Kathy said. "We got into town Monday. I enrolled here yesterday but it took a while. The principal's office had to contact my old school for paperwork. They couldn't believe my class only had twenty-four students." *Probably dropping*, she thought. She had no idea how many students had been pulled out since Sadie Hawkins.

"That few in a big city? So, it was like a private school or something?" When she nodded, he said, "Which one?"

Kathy's throat squeezed shut as if blocking her reply. "Mills."

"Did you like it there?"

"I guess. My best friend transferred to an all-girls' Catholic school when I started high school. I wanted to go too, but my parents couldn't afford it."

"Yeah," Malcolm said. "I'd leave here in a heartbeat if I could. Seriously, you'd be amazed how this place redefines tedium. We don't even have a decent movie theater, so Shawn and I just cruise the mall because we don't have anything else to do." He jerked his thumb in the direction Shawn had disappeared. "Are you waiting for your mom? Do you need a ride?"

"I am. Or I was. We were supposed to go shopping. We moved before I could buy a new sweater or a jacket."

"I've got a car," Malcolm said. "It's not much, just an old Dodge. But I can drive you if you'd like."

Kathy gave Malcolm a dubious look. "That's okay. I can walk."

"I'm sure you can. It's not far. But your bag feels like you've been assigned half the school library. You'll develop scoliosis lugging it around. If I drive you, I can show you a little of the town, then take you to the mall."

"My mom was going to pay for my clothes. I could just walk home."

"They have a record store, too. And a bookstore. Video arcade and a decent food court. I mean, it probably wouldn't have the same things as what you'd find in Houston, but…"

The backpack felt heavy on her shoulders. Malcolm's eyes were wide and without guile.

She opened her mouth to say no, only to say yes.

THE FAITH by DEREK AUSTIN JOHNSON

The town square wasn't much. A courthouse sat in the center, pink sandstone reddening in the afternoon sun. Stores and restaurants surrounded it, gilt lettering fading on yellowing windows. On one corner sat what looked like rental space for a church, based on the cross stenciled on the glass door. Malcolm pointed out sites of interest, but Kathy found herself concentrating on the shadows beneath the covered store fronts.

While not the size of what she was used to, the mall easily was larger than the town square. The inside was cool, brightly lit, and crowded with more shoppers than Kathy expected, given the sparse number of cars in the expansive parking lot. Skylights illuminated the food court at the mall's center, where Malcolm purchased soft drinks. They walked past a row of posters next to the movie theater's box office–all stuff that was popular last year–then Malcolm led her to the bookstore, where Kathy went to the true crime section and didn't find what she was looking for. At Strawberry's Music, she perused the cassettes but only saw things that were equally outdated: Dire Straits, Bryan Adams, Howard Jones, Van Halen before David Lee Roth left. *Thanks for bringing us here, Dad*, she thought, then told herself it was only a year. Only a year before she could apply to college and go somewhere, anywhere, else.

As a clerk tapped at a cash register to ring up a Howard Jones tape, Kathy glanced at Malcolm. He stood in a corner of the store, carefully flipping through an aisle of vinyl albums. She wondered if he'd wig out if he knew what happened. It was a small town, but the Doll Man's killing spree made national news. Surely, he'd find out. Once he did, it would only be a matter of time before the entire town did, too.

The mall didn't have a Sears or Foley's, and the clothing store they visited didn't stock any jackets Kathy liked. When they left, Malcolm said, "Give me a sec. Nature calls," and disappeared into the men's room.

Kathy leaned against the wall and waited, glancing at the other store fronts. Low music echoed down the hall toward the restroom: Madonna's "Like a Prayer." It surprised her that the mall would play something that recent and controversial. Not even her school allowed it at their dance. She wondered if her Jackie, the friend who'd transferred to Catholic school, was allowed to listen to it.

The crowd thickened on both sides of the mall. Kathy's throat tightened in anxiety as she wondered what was taking Malcolm so long.

She looked at the restroom door, then past it, down a stretch of hallway leading to a door with tinted glass.

At the end of the hallway stood Samuel Crais.

He seemed massive, taut muscle hidden beneath a denim jacket, buttoned all the way to the top. Powerful legs were hugged by frayed, faded blue jeans splattered with dried dark blood and tucked into large brown work boots. A black leather cap with crisp gray rabbit fur covered his head, and on his face was a dirty pink mask that resembled a baby's face.

His chest expanded as he drew a breath, then he approached, footsteps silent. Fluorescent light gleamed on the hollow-edged butcher knife in his gloved hand.

Kathy tried to force a scream out of her mouth, but it wouldn't come. As Crais stepped closer, she glanced over her shoulder.

The crowd parted.

Another step. She wasn't close enough to smell him, but Kathy gagged at the memory of burned meat.

The men's room door opened.

Kathy cried out. She threw the pink Strawberry's Music bag at Crais and ran, a scream erupting from her throat. People got out of her way, their shocked faces blurring from her speed. She pushed through the mall doors and into the parking lot. Brakes screeched and horns honked. Frantically, she looked for Malcolm's car. She didn't stop, even as someone called her name.

THE FAITH by DEREK AUSTIN JOHNSON

A hand grabbed her shoulder and she stumbled, slamming into the trunk of a beige Toyota. She wailed as she turned and raised her hand to punch Crais, only to see Malcolm, panting and red-faced.

"Jesus," he said when he caught his breath, "you're fast. Even in a bag padded with a receipt, cassettes can be dangerous." He pushed the hair away from his forehead, exposing a red welt. "You aren't Nolan Ryan, but you have a solid throwing arm." He handed her the bag from Strawberry's Music, but she refused to take it. "I'm sorry. Are you okay?" He chuckled. "I'm making a habit of asking that, aren't I? But seriously, that wasn't normal. What happened?"

Someone else answered, their voice like a clap of thunder.

"You saw him again, didn't you?"

A man stood at the tail of the Toyota. He was older, with black hair shiny from pomade and sculpted like Elvis, but the lines next to his mouth were deeper, his skin coarser. His gray seersucker suit hugged his lean body like a sausage casing. Behind him were three others, two men and a woman. They held leather books close to their chest, and the woman had a thick, gray paperback with yellow-edged pages. All three wore white, short-sleeved dress shirts and black polyester pants.

All three fixed their eyes on Kathy.

"Miss Durham," he said, his voice smooth as cheap aftershave mixed with venom. "I see you've managed to get away from the dark Satanic Mills." His eyes fell on Malcolm. They were amber, like a snake's. "And hello, good sir. Has this demon-worshipping harlot sucked you into her web of lies?"

Color drained from Kathy's face.

Malcolm's mouth puckered, as if he'd tasted lemonade without sugar. "I think you're bothering Kathy, mister…"

The man laughed again. "Brother, sir. Brother Douglas Coupland. Ms. Durham and I go way back to Memorial City. Don't we, Kathy?" At Malcolm's incomprehension, Coupland's smile widened. "Surely, she told you about the Sadie Hawkins dance at her school. The one where her friends were killed." He pointed. "Deaths she is responsible for."

Tears welled in Kathy's eyes.

"A shame," Coupland said. "You really should think about the people with whom you keep company, young man. Patricia." He held out his hand. The woman placed the gray paperback in his hand, and he offered it to Malcolm. "The writer was a debauched heathen but was able to learn much about the sinner behind you."

On the book's cover was a photo of Kathy, the one that had been run by the newspaper covering what they called the Sadie Hawkins Massacre. She smiled amid splotches of blood and large black lettering. DARK SATANIC MILLS, it read. HOW HIGH SCHOOL STUDENTS SUMMONED A DEMONIC KILLER.

"Read it," Coupland told Malcolm. "You will see for yourself."

Malcolm waved it away. "It looks like trash," he said. "Probably like the person who wrote it. Definitely like the person trying to give it to me."

Coupland smirked and handed the paperback back to Patricia. "Don't get smart with me, boy. Your little friend is a monster. She and her friends brought forth a demon that possessed one of my parishioners. Made him mad with desire. Mad enough to kill people." His head shook in pity. "Poor Samuel. He'd done nothing but treat people with kindness. Then, that slut and her friends held a séance and commanded a demon to take over his body. All because he thought she needed to be saved." He snorted. "You're beyond saving, though, aren't you, Miss Durham?" A quick look back brought the two men behind him closer. "Doug, Graham, don't you believe she's beyond saving?" The disciples beamed.

The tears in Kathy's eyes fell down her cheeks. Malcolm tightened his hands into fists.

"You need to leave her alone."

Coupland stepped closer to Malcolm. "Son, you're not an adult, so you should know better than to take that tone with me. You should know something about the way the world works.

THE FAITH by DEREK AUSTIN JOHNSON

About what some people are capable of." With a forefinger he dabbed at a bead of perspiration on his temple.

"Problem?"

A security guard approached. If Coupland was as lean as a cobra, he was as bulky as a bull, all muscle. A name plate identified him as Ted.

Coupland grinned and waved. "None whatsoever, sir. I was just talking to the young man about his young lady."

Ted assessed the scene. "Based on what I see, an old man is harassing a pair of high school students, one of whom is set to be this year's valedictorian." He nodded to Malcolm. "How's it going, Mal? Senior year been treating you well?"

"Today could be better, Ted."

"You try out for the football team like I recommended?"

Malcolm chuffed. "You know I don't play sports, Ted."

"Oh, you're friends," Coupland said. "Isn't that nice? Maybe you'd like to join our little discussion. I think you'd find it quite fascinating."

Ted sized Coupland up with an air of contempt. "I don't think I have much to discuss with second-rate evangelicals. You and your flock need to leave the premises."

Coupland raised his eyebrows in surprise and chuckled mirthlessly. "Oh? And by what right do you ask us that? Do you know who I am?"

"I know. You're that television preacher from Houston, the one who was caught with that seventeen-year-old prostitute, I hear. I'm amazed you aren't preaching in Huntsville." Coupland blanched. The parishioners behind him looked confused. "And my right? You aren't here to purchase anything, so you're loitering and soliciting. If I ask my friend Malcolm if he feels intimidated, when I contact the police, I'll add suspicion of battery." He raised his hands again. "Your choice. But I imagine your friends in Houston don't have much power to get you out of trouble in this county, do they?"

Coupland sucked his teeth and stared at Ted for several moments, then looked at Malcolm. "Remember what I have said, son. Be careful with her." He gestured for the three disciples to follow him. They got into a nearby car and drove off. On its rear bumper was a sticker that read "Jesus Saves," a blood-red cross between the words.

Malcolm led Kathy to his car and put her Strawberry's Music purchase in the trunk next to an overstuffed Adidas gym bag.

It took a while for Kathy to regain her composure. When she did, Malcolm started the car and drove, and Kathy told him about Samuel Crais, who frequently visited her neighborhood and knocked on doors to talk about the Faith. About how he'd begun following her, finally cornering her in a Baskin Robbins parking lot and tried to feel her up one afternoon. How her father had gone to the police to file an order against him. How Samuel had followed her to the Sadie Hawkins dance, wearing a ridiculous mask and carrying a heavy butcher's knife, killed her friends. How he'd trapped her in a janitor's closet, and how she'd splashed him with turpentine and set him on fire with her friend Tina's lighter, which she'd grabbed as Samuel's knife severed Tina's throat. How Samuel flailed as flames engulfed him, making him and the mask inseparable.

And then there was the fallout. The press, both local and national. The alienation she and her family faced at school and work. They weren't religious, but even their Methodist church shunned them. Dad tried to laugh it off–"You know shit got real when the Methodists don't want anything to do with you"– but it didn't shield the challenges they were having. Even at work, dad became a pariah. People still needed accountants, just not him.

Then there was the true crime book by the former Houston Post reporter. It touched on Coupland's weird cult, but focused on Kathy and her friends, and one detail that seemed timely. When the reporter interviewed Anna's family, he saw a Parker

THE FAITH by DEREK AUSTIN JOHNSON

Brothers Ouija board tucked away on her bookshelf with a copy of V. C. Andrews's *Flowers in the Attic*. Kathy couldn't conceal the anger in her voice as she spoke. "He made things up. Suggested–never said it outright, just put forth the possibility–that Anna was into devil worship based on those two things, and that we put a spell on Samuel that made him go on a killing spree. And people believed it, of course. Everyone we knew abandoned us."

That was when Coupland's church started tormenting them. The Faith first said Kathy's soul needed to be saved. When her family demanded they be left alone, the Faith grew more insistent and dangerous. "Dad tried to sue that writer for defamation, but because he didn't make any direct accusation, our lawyers couldn't do anything. He got a restraining order on the Faith, but they have friends on the city council. And they're all paranoids. When the moron who looked for that gangster's vault said there are a hundred million Satanists in the United States, people's brains just short circuited."

Malcolm turned down the volume of the Mike and the Mechanics song playing on the radio. "So, you moved out here." He chuckled. "Cut off from the rest of the world. Or at least cut off from any part of the city."

She slumped in the passenger seat. "That was Dad's plan, at least." Her breath caught. "I need to tell him about this. About Coupland."

Malcolm nodded in understanding. "Sure, but I wouldn't be too worried. Coupland doesn't have many friends out here. Like Ted, that security guard. He hates people like that. When he was on the debate team, he loved ripping their arguments apart. He graduated last year but I bet he still does that for fun. I can't say much for the cops, but especially when you're…well, a girl…" He shrugged. "Let's just say they don't have a lot of sympathy for guys like Coupland."

At her house, he sat with her in his car. Soft light seeped through white curtains and spilled over the rose bushes in front of the living room windows. It had been the primary reason her mother agreed to move to this house. That, and it was close to a liquor store, Kathy often mused.

Malcolm fidgeted before speaking. "If you need me to talk to your parents, I can. That way they don't have to hear anything from you."

Kathy shook her head. "It'll be easier for me to tell them. They don't know who you are, so they might think…" She grasped for words. "They might think you know all about what happened. At least what's been reported, anyway. That's why I ran to the true crime section in that bookstore. I wanted to see if the book made it here already."

"Please," Malcolm said with a chuckle. "Unless we listen to the radio, we don't get much that's new. Besides, my parents don't pay much attention to the news. Guys like Ted and Shawn don't bother with current events, either."

Kathy tightened her lips and nodded. She opened the car door. Malcolm followed her to the trunk and retrieved her cassette. A streetlamp deepened shadows on the gym bag, making whatever pressed against the black nylon resemble a face.

She opened her mouth to thank him, but Malcolm spoke first.

"Listen, you saw the theater. It isn't much, and they don't get much that's current, but would you like to see something there tomorrow? They're getting that Molly Ringwald movie, the one from last year. I was planning on going and wondered if you'd like to come with me. I can get your ticket. And popcorn," he added. "We can go after you have dinner, too."

Kathy thought. Her father's car wasn't in the driveway. "I have to ask my dad. He's probably not going to be home until later so I couldn't say until tomorrow morning."

Malcolm nodded. "Even if you have to wait until half an hour before show time, that's okay, too."

She gave him a quick hug and the briefest smile. "Thanks for showing me the mall, and for standing up to Coupland." Then Kathy turned and disappeared into the house, watching from the living room window as Malcolm drove away.

THE FAITH by DEREK AUSTIN JOHNSON

Her parents said yes, surprisingly. While they expressed concern at Coupland's appearance, they seemed less so than in Memorial City, and reminded her what to do if there was any issue: find a police officer, or a pay phone, and keep running. Don't stay still, keep away from the shadows. Kathy and her parents had gone over this after the Mills Sadie Hawkins Massacre. "Even though this town seems a lot more sedate, be careful," her father said. "Bring a quarter and call us if you need us to pick you up someplace." Her mother nodded in agreement, a glass of bourbon in her hand. It made Kathy angry that, while her father had become hyper vigilant, her mother retreated into bottles of alcohol.

Malcolm's joy at the news was more effusive than she expected, but made her smile, even as Mr. Landis raised his voice telling other students to settle down once the bell rang, and class began. He offered to give her a ride after school, but she told him her mother had promised she wouldn't forget (be too drunk) to pick her up.

She spent little time preparing for her date because she still hadn't unpacked most of her clothes. At least the jeans and cowl neck sweater were readily available and clean.

Malcolm met her at the door and appeared deferential to her father, who told Malcolm she needed to be back by ten at the latest. Malcolm nodded, and even opened the car door for her.

As the sun settled toward the horizon, Malcolm circled the parking lot, full on a Friday night. Kathy recommended they park near one of the tall streetlamps. A shadow crossed his face as he pulled into a free space, but his eyes registered understanding. *If he asks about what happened*, she thought, *I'll tell him about my friends. I'll tell him what they were like. And if he wants to know more, I can suggest a second date.*

"I want to tell you something," he said as they walked to the mall entrance, "and I hope you don't get mad."

Kathy slowed her pace, allowing him to gain a few steps. Her eyes were wide with wariness.

He offered her a tight-lipped, guilty smile. "I, um, I'd read that book. 'The Dark Satanic Mills.' It came to the bookstore a couple of months ago."

She stared at him in disbelief.

"Don't be angry. Please. It was on the new releases, and I picked it up because, well, it was new. You have no idea how seldom new stuff comes to this town. It just looked like a cool book. I seriously didn't realize the person on the cover was you until I saw Coupland. Please believe me."

Despite his pleas, anger surged through her body. She stormed past him and forcefully pushed open the mall entrance. An OUT OF ORDER sign hung on the pay phone next to the door. Malcolm called her name, but she didn't look back. Instead, she headed toward the theater. She figured she could use their pay phone and call her parents.

Shoppers flooded her path to the theater. They overwhelmed her, but she focused on her destination.

And ran into a woman in a white shirt and black pants. The same woman who was with Coupland yesterday. Patricia. Scowling

"Your friend left you, didn't he? Realized what you really are."

Kathy searched for a security guard. None seemed nearby. She tried to walk around Patricia but was blocked.

"Did he try to break up with you gently, or did he run? That mask of yours slipped and he beheld the demon beneath. Or maybe you came clean, but he couldn't take it. That's right, isn't it? You confessed to murdering an innocent man whose only sin was that he saw you were damned and needing redemption. That boy saw the soullessness in your eyes, the craven evil…"

Kathy hit her. She didn't realize what she had done until blood gushed from the woman's nose, and she felt the sudden sting in her knuckles. Guilt flooded Kathy's body, but also

THE FAITH by DEREK AUSTIN JOHNSON

vindication. She'd hurt this person, actually hurt one of Brother Coupland's disciples, and felt elation rather than grief. She stepped toward Patricia again, but the disciple backed away, her face a mix of surprise, fear, and her own satisfaction. Onlookers stared open-mouthed and parted as Kathy walked to the theater, rubbing her knuckles with her other hand.

"We'll find you!" Patricia shouted, as she opened the mall entrance. "You laid hands on one of the Faith. You will not escape Brother Coupland's judgment, or his wrath." She rubbed the blood from her nose as the glass door silenced her.

The clerk at the movie theater let Kathy use the phone to call her parents. Busy. Worried that Malcolm might try to find her in the theater, Kathy walked through the mall, hyper-alert for any sign of either Malcolm or a security guard–especially the one Malcolm knew. While he might not like Coupland, Kathy was certain he'd call the police for clocking a member of the Faith. Maybe she could claim harassment, but she was sure they'd detain her for assault, at least until her parents picked her up. And her parents…even if they understood, they'd blame Kathy. Just like they'd blamed her for the Sadie Hawkins Massacre.

She checked a clock in the middle of the food court, then window-shopped, her peripheral vision as wide as she could make it. No sign of Malcolm. Or Ted. Or the police. That was odd. Surely somebody would have called 911. Even the police in her old neighborhood responded to calls more quickly than this. Maybe the woman, Patricia, just went straight to Coupland. More reason to call the police, throw herself at their mercy and ask for protection. Reaching into her pocket, she squeezed her hand around a quarter. The theater, she told herself. Go back and try her parents again. She turned around.

And froze.

A doll's face stared back at her from the window of a toy

store. Splotchy pink from overhead lights mottled its milky porcelain skin, the pattern almost identical to Crais's doll mask.

The din of the mall's crowd dimmed, as if someone had turned a volume control to near zero.

The doll's face moved, separated, and crawled across the glass to coalesce into a face Kathy knew all too well.

Standing behind her, on the opposite side of the mall's concourse, was Crais.

Around them both, mall shoppers passed, oblivious of the danger.

Slowly Kathy drifted away from the toy store, then ran toward the movie theater. She'd hide there. It had multiple screens, and if she was in a crowd, Crais wouldn't try anything.

Almost running, she watched Crais's reflection blur and recede. By the time she got to the theater, he was gone. She choked back a sob. *I'm crazy*, she thought. *Or I somehow conjured him back.* Then, she shook the thought away. No, to go down that path was insanity.

The clerk allowed her to try phoning her parents again. No answer.

She hung up the phone, then dialed 911 and told the dispatcher she was being followed. The dispatcher advised her officers were on their way and would meet her in the food court. "Stay visible and around people," the dispatcher told her. "Whoever is following you, they won't do anything in a crowd."

After the call, Kathy went to the food court, bought a Coke, and sat at a table. To convince herself no one was staring at her, she forced herself to concentrate on the people around her as she sipped her drink and suddenly felt anger at Malcolm again. *Of course, he seemed nice*, she told herself. *Because he thought you were pitiful.* She wondered how much he would have pressed her for details about the dance. She thought of Patricia and her bloody nose and felt bad again. And then realized how badly she missed her friends. All four, now gone. And she was forced to come here so her family could get away. She never would,

THE FAITH by DEREK AUSTIN JOHNSON

she realized. If it wasn't Coupland and his church hounding her, then it would be Crais's ghost. Unless he'd escaped...

No. She saw the police around the body. She heard the squelching as a paramedic lifted Crais's mask, and smelled Crais's burned flesh and the paramedic's acidic vomit. Either it was a flashback, her own private Vietnam, as Dad called it, or she was haunted.

The clock read eight o'clock, a bell toning softly. One. Two. Three.

At five, a bloody handkerchief plopped onto her table.

Brother Coupland glared down at her. Two of his disciples stood behind him.

"Where is she?" His voice was calm, and Kathy had to fight to hear him over the crowd. Malice danced in his eyes.

Kathy glared back. "You should know. She's your disciple. Maybe she felt the taste of life without you and your flock and got a makeover." She surprised herself with her boldness.

Coupland chuckled. "Well, look who's developed some spunk," he said as he pulled a handkerchief from his jacket pocket and cupped it as he pushed the bloody cloth toward her.

"Don't touch me with your AIDS rag."

"Quiet, child. Do you see the initials? It's hers. I know because I knew her parents. They gave it to her, one of the few gifts she ever received. I know she was looking for you. It stands to reason she found you. Who's to say you didn't do something?"

"Go fuck yourself, you two-bit Jim Bakker."

As she stood, Kathy threw the drink into his face and pushed the table against his legs, then shoved past the two surprised disciples. People jumped out of her way as she ran toward the mall entrance, pushing at the door.

It wouldn't open.

She pushed harder as the sound of Coupland's voice echoed through the mall, commanding her to stop.

She tried the door one more time, then read the eye-level stenciling. ENTER it read in backwards lettering.

CAMP SLASHER LAKE: VOLUME ONE

 Kathy slammed open the EXIT door. Behind her came the footsteps of leather slapping concrete, then the smell of the sugary soft drink as an arm encircled her and a hand clasped over her mouth, the palm covered in cloth, and she struggled and saw light, then darkness, and as she fell limp, she saw nothing at all.

Kathy woke to dust in her nose and her cheek against cold, dirty linoleum. She was in a windowless room, the only light coming from beneath a heavy door with a large metal knob. There was enough illumination to see a dark cross painted on one of the walls. Though she couldn't tell in the minuscule light, Kathy was certain the cross was red, and guessed she was in that church across the street from the town square's courthouse.
 Sitting up, Kathy bumped her leg against a folding chair which was pushed against a metal table in the center of the room. She shivered and rubbed her arms. Someone had taken off her jacket.
 Muffled footsteps and voices came through the door. Kathy flattened herself on the floor and tried to peer beneath the door, but only discerned vague shadows. She stood and pressed her ear against the door but couldn't make out what anybody was saying.
 More footsteps. Panicked, Kathy backed away from the door and bumped against the chair. They were going to kill her, she knew that much, and she had no way to fight back. Her purse was gone–not that she'd had anything she could have used, anyway. A frantic visual search of the room yielded nothing she could use as a weapon. She squeezed the top of the chair's metal back and thought. She could throw the chair, but it would only buy her a second, maybe two at the most. And then what? Coupland probably had his two disciples beyond the door. Pacing the room, she shoved her hands in her pockets,

THE FAITH by DEREK AUSTIN JOHNSON

fingers brushing against the ridge of the quarter still there.
She stopped, then regarded the chair.
And the table.
She knelt and examined the table's leg. It was metal, with a rubber foot. Standing, she lifted the table edge; heavy, but she could work with it. Kathy pressed her foot against the cap and lifted the table repeatedly until it popped free. Then she kicked the cap away and pushed the edge of the quarter beneath the leg. As she stood, her mind raced with what could go wrong. She remembered Tina saying that sharpening a coin usually required five minutes of hammering. Kathy didn't have the time. She'd have to be exact.
Or the disciples could come through the door before she completed her makeshift weapon. Or even when she let the table drop.
On cue, she heard the doorknob rattle.
Kathy held her breath, lifted the table, and brought the leg down hard on the edge of the quarter.
The doorknob turned. Kathy grabbed the quarter and squeezed it between her middle and ring finger, not knowing if it was sharp enough, as the door swung open and the silhouette of one of Coupland's disciples motioned for her to follow. When she stood her ground, the man darted toward her, grabbed her arm, and marched her into the light, momentarily blinding her.
They were in a plain nave, folding chairs facing a large wooden cross adorned with lit candles whose own light was overpowered by the overhead fluorescents. Behind the chairs, heavy white curtains were drawn over the front window, and a shade was drawn over the door. Next to the cross was a pulpit where Coupland stood, jacket removed, and sleeves rolled over his arms. Next to him was the other disciple, his face a mixture of ecstasy and apprehension.
Coupland pointed to a patch of wine-red carpet. "Bring her right there, Douglas. Graham, bring me the athame. We need to end this now. Before anyone else is killed because of this woman's actions."

CAMP SLASHER LAKE: VOLUME ONE

Kathy struggled, but Douglas's grip was too strong. "Killed? Who's dead?"

Her ears rung from Coupland's barked laugh. "Patricia. Who do you think?" He stepped toward her as Graham placed a leather case on the pulpit and snapped the fasteners. Coupland continued. "Douglas found her body in a dumpster of the mall parking lot. More than that, he saw Crais drag her there. Heard her scream as she was gutted like a fish. You should know what blood smells like, especially mixed with garbage." He snapped his fingers and pointed down. Doug forced her to her knees and shoved her forward, the floor knocking the air from Kathy's lungs. She squeezed her fists tightly, desperate not to let go of the coin. Roughly, Douglas grabbed her shoulder and flipped her over. Pain ran through her back and neck as Douglas straddled her pelvis and seized her wrists.

"It seems your parents paid for your sins as well, Ms. Durham. We visited. Tried to make them see the Faith." He chuckled. "You have no idea how your father begged as I opened your mother like an old wineskin."

Coupland knelt in front of her and opened his hand. Graham placed a double-edged ceremonial silver blade in his hand. The handle was shiny, as if made of onyx. He ran the tip of the blade over Kathy's forehead and nose, hard enough so she could feel it, not so hard that it broke the skin. He trailed it down her lips and chin, and down her torso, pausing at her breasts. "A shame," he said. "If you had not been led down the path of evil, you might have made a good wife."

Kathy swallowed and closed her eyes and agonized about her family and her friends.

The blade pierced her skin over her heart as Coupland mumbled gibberish. Kathy tried to force her hands up, but Douglas's grip was too strong.

"The hell?" Coupland said.

Kathy opened her eyes. It was dark save for the glow of the candles.

"Check the circuit breaker. Maybe something popped."

THE FAITH by DEREK AUSTIN JOHNSON

Graham nodded and disappeared through a door next to the cross. Coupland focused his attention back on Kathy and pressed the blade's point against her chest again.

Two sounds interrupted him: a loud banging against the glass front door, and a scream from the hallway where Graham had gone.

Coupland stood on his knees, looking from the door to the hallway.

Another bang on the door, and a crack as if the glass was breaking.

From the hallway, the erratic thudding of footsteps.

Graham stumbled to the pulpit, his shirt drenched with blood, the handle of a large butcher's knife jutting from the front of his throat.

"Oh, Jesus," Douglas said, loosening his grip on Kathy.

She moved fast. She rose and swiped her fist at Coupland, the flattened edge of the coin between her thumb and forefinger, opening his cheek from his eye all the way to his chin. Kathy slammed into him, and they both fell. Screaming, Coupland dropped the ceremonial knife and clutched at his face, blood welling between his fingers. Kathy grabbed the athame and ran toward the door.

Another loud bang.

The door shattered, glass shards flying.

And through the door came Crais, his hulking physique filling the frame and blocking her way. He cocked his head as if trying to discern who she was.

Kathy's first impulse was to scream. As she did, she rushed Crais and ran the blade of the athame into his chest. Crais made a sound like he was trying to ask a question, then stumbled away. Kathy held onto the athame as it slid from his chest. Blood flowed from the wound, and he collapsed.

Another scream from behind her. Kathy spun around, weapon ready, and tried to make sense of what she was seeing.

Crais was on the floor at her feet. But simultaneously, he stood before Coupland, gloved hand clutching his ear, while in his other a claw hammer turned Coupland's head to shards of bone and lumps of brain. And another was on top of the prone Douglas, bringing a cleaver up and down into his skull until it was wide open.

She looked between the Doll Men.

They weren't the same.

The jackets were similar, but their shades were different. So were their boots.

And the masks were different.

This wasn't Simon Crais's ghost. He hadn't been brought back to life.

Had these people been tormenting her?

She screamed at them, a warrior's sound, and rushed the one with the hammer. He looked up long enough for Kathy to drive the athame into his eye. He bolted upright, staggered and fell backward.

The remaining Crais jumped off Douglas, threw the cleaver aside, and raised his hands. He shouted something like "wait!" as Kathy approached.

Kathy paused, athame poised.

He pulled the mask from his face.

It took everything Kathy had not to kill him immediately.

"You have to understand," Malcolm said. "The accounts we read. What we all realized. Me. Ted." He gestured to the Doll man lying atop Coupland's half-headless body. "Shawn." Pointing to the body covered in glass at the door. "We knew you were strong. You and your friends could summon a demon, and you could kill it. That made you powerful. This–" He touched his mask. "–all this was in celebration of your power. That's what that true crime book proved. We wanted to show our loyalty to you." His eyes fell to Coupland and snarled. "Think about it. Have you ever seen Coupland's god? Of course, you haven't. Because he doesn't exist. But you." He knelt in front of her. "You are Faith personified. And we are your disciples. We wear the garments for you. We even made a pilgrimage to your school to honor you." He reached toward her and touched the

THE FAITH by DEREK AUSTIN JOHNSON

hand with the blade, then brought it to his neck. "And we are prepared to sacrifice ourselves for you."

Kathy's mind raced. Feeling faint, she sucked as much air into her lungs as she could. Her legs felt like rubber, but she kept from collapsing.

"Patricia?"

Malcolm's eyes motioned to the dead body with the blood flowing from its eye. "That was Shawn. He thought she'd try to ambush you in the parking lot. He had to move fast."

She felt like crying. "My parents," she whispered.

Malcolm swallowed. "I'm sorry. Ted followed Coupland and the other two. Thought they might visit your parents." His face softened in pity. "He got there too late."

She slipped from Malcolm's touch and slowly backed away.

"You can't go," Malcolm pleaded. "Look at what we've done for you. Look at how we're prepared to die for you. Our Mother of the Faith."

She stepped outside. On the corner of the street was a payphone.

"You have to bless me!" Malcolm shouted. "You must give me a baptism in my own blood! You're our savior."

Kathy shook her head. "I'm not anything like that," she said, throwing the athame in the street. It clattered on the asphalt. "You read that book, but you don't understand anything. That's not a bible, and I'm not a savior. I didn't want to be a demon like that fucking book said, but I didn't want to be a messiah, either. It's not worth it. I had to watch my friends die because of what some lunatic thought of me. I'd rather have them alive than have some bored morons revere me as a scream queen."

"But we're your disciples!"

"You're not a disciple. You aren't a goddamn thing."

As Malcolm cried, Kathy dialed the number to the police.

The Deathless
by Vincent Wolfram

I

Sea of Japan – Hokkaido – October 8th, 1986

THE CITY OF SAPPORO GLOWED, an orange crescent shining over black waters. Petty Officers Franklin Stuart and George Baxter stood hunched together with their fellow crew. Stuart faced the sea, and Baxter watched the men around him before gazing into the darkness. Mist blew in dancing curls and twists over the surf. It stung like hell when it whipped into their faces.

Stuart was grateful. The air was sharp with cold and bitter with brine. The wind kept him awake. Normally, he was on day watch. He never worked this late.

The men warmed themselves with talk of hot sake and warm springs. Baxter grumbled about missing shore leave. Fujita, their American contact from the Satsebo base, stood at the helm of the fishing boat, grinning at their petty complaints.

The crew stood and watched, rolling with the anxious sea. The USS Goliad waited on the other side of Hokkaido. Russia loomed at their backs.

When he heard the splash of paddles, Stuart eased his hand

THE DEATHLESS by VINCENT WOLFRAM

on the trigger of his rifle. Baxter's gun shook lightly in his grip.

"Girls?" Baxter blurted out in confusion.

"Women," a deadly gentle voice responded.

A skiff glided from the mist. Two women sat at the front, and a large man slumped over in the back, his face in shadows. The two women rowed in concert, but he was struggling to keep an even pace. His shoulders trembled with each unsteady dip of the paddles.

Baxter raised his weapon. "Captain said we were to rendezvous with two people. One of you shouldn't be here."

The other submariners drew their guns, but Chief Petty Officer Boulet shouted at them. "Hold your fire! We're taking all three."

"But sir..."

"Shut it, Mr. Baxter. The passenger list is on a need-to-know basis. Lower your gun."

Baxter lowered it slowly, keeping his eyes trained on the two women. The man in the back was the POW.

Stuart, and another crewmate, Burt, each helped a woman aboard. Stuart took the crushing grip of the petite Latina woman. She lifted herself once she could grab the railing. The younger woman was tall and slight. Burt had to catch her when she lost her footing.

"Clara," the Latina said, by way of introduction, nodding curtly.

"Uh, Yelena. Yelena Tereshkova," the other woman hesitated over the syllables as she spoke. She had a Russian accent. Baxter glared at Yelena.

When the POW reached out for assistance, Stuart, and Baxter both offered their hand. They had to plant their feet to pull the man up.

"Help me out, boy scout," Baxter grunted to Stuart.

The POW was built like a linebacker, an all-American man with a sterling gaze and a strong jaw. Despite his ratty fatigues and the dive knife strapped to his belt, he looked noble and well-kempt. Stuart didn't know what the Russkies had done to him, but they hadn't ruined his good looks.

"Lieutenant Hardy." The CPO greeted him with a salute.

"Maximilian, er, Max," the hunched man demurred. He tried to straighten his back, but the joints popped, and he winced, doubling back down. "Been in prison too long," he offered as an apology.

"No worries, Lieutenant. Let's just get you back to the Goliad and then we're headed home."

"Home?"

"Next stop's Hawaii," Burt interrupted with a smile, reaching out for a handshake.

Max Hardy had to study his hand for an uncomfortable moment before figuring out what to do with it. He offered a weak handshake to each of the crewmen.

"So glad to finally shake your hand, Lt. Hardy," Stuart said, his eyes grave.

"Yeah, me too. Me too." Baxter grinned like a kid.

"Thank you all." Max Hardy's smile was broad and white and winning. His eyes were troubled.

Boulet shut down conversation quickly. He wanted the three rescues debriefed before they spoke with the crew. The bullet-headed Boulet crossed his arms and scanned them. No one met his gaze or spoke. Though Stuart kept his mouth shut, he knew life aboard a submarine; secrets are hard to keep in close quarters. He clocked Clara as a spy. She wouldn't talk, but Yelena would probably be desperate to bond with the crew. She had just escaped from the USSR. Yelena was free for the first time.

Max Hardy could go either way. Stuart figured Hardy was a SEAL, based on the worn fatigues he was wearing. Stuart knew SEALS to be brash types, but after suffering in a Russian prison, undergoing KGB torture, Max might be tight-lipped.

THE DEATHLESS by VINCENT WOLFRAM

Under the merciless gaze of the senior enlisted officer, the three kept silent. Stuart hoped they'd open up over breakfast.

The stars shone in a moonless sky, and the ocean was a rippling sheet of infinite darkness. The fishing boat raced to the rendezvous point on the other side of the island. Even with his understanding of the Global Positioning System, which the captain still called Navstar, Stuart found it miraculous when the sub slid out of the depths only a dozen meters away.

Water streamed away from its gray back. The periscope scanned the horizon.

The Goliad was a new Los Angeles class fast attack sub. Stuart didn't know how important Lt. Hardy was, but the Navy was returning him home in a nuclear sub with enough firepower to start WWIII. No man left behind, indeed.

The rescue crew boarded the sub, leaving the fishing boat in the care of Fujita. He waved as they climbed down the hatch.

Stuart touched down after the last rung, breathing in the familiar funk of amine and diesel that permeated the ship. The ship hummed with CO_2 scrubbers, the engine, the generator, and miles of piping. The deck rocked gently beneath his feet. Once the others had climbed down the ladder, he looked up one last time to see the hatch close on the stars.

Captain Hopkins met them in the hatch room, fore of the reactor, and aft of the control room. Hopkins wore a white dress uniform but an untrimmed black beard, testament to the two months spent offshore.

"Welcome, Clara Cruz,. Lt. Hardy," the captain said.

Hardy tried to straighten again, this time succeeding with a grimace. He stood at attention and saluted, not allowing himself to show weakness in front of the captain. Stuart wondered what agony that was going to cost him tonight when he tried to sleep on his crooked back.

"And your friend?" Hopkins looked at the young woman expectantly.

Baxter twitched at the word *friend*.

The Russian introduced herself. "Yelena Tereshkova,

biochemical engineer," and, as an afterthought, "...defecting to the US of A."

If she intended the line to put the crew at ease, it didn't work on Baxter.

"We're letting a fucking–"

"Petty Officer Baxter," Boulet interrupted, enunciating the words carefully. "Do not. Interrupt. The captain."

Hopkins smirked but did not comment. "Beg your pardon, missus–"

"Doctor."

The captain smiled genially. "–Doctor Tereshkova. You are welcome aboard the USS Goliad. Though, I will ask you to confine yourself to the lower decks in the bunks and the mess." The smiled faded. "And absolutely refrain from entering the reactor room. And then we won't have a problem, will we?" His smile returned as abruptly as it had receded.

"Mr. Stuart, will you escort the ladies to their bunks. Your bunks. Lt. Hardy, you're with me."

"What about their debriefing?" the CPO asked.

"A matter for tomorrow," Captain Hopkins replied. "Besides, Ms. Cruz has her orders already. She won't divulge anything. Dismissed."

Stuart and Baxter saluted as the captain exited, heading forward to the wardroom. Hardy hobbled after, passing neatly under the door while still hunched over.

Baxter laughed, "Heh. Landies usually bang their head ducking through the first time. Hardy got lucky."

"He is hunched over, because he is in great pain," Yelena replied with a sniff.

Baxter sneered. "Yeah, I bet you care a lot, doll."

Stuart shook his head. "C'mon. Quarters are this way."

Baxter called after, "Get it? Doll. Russian. Eh, forget you."

Stuart led Ms. Cruz and Dr. Tereshkova forward past the control room.

"Your friend's an idiot, yes?" Clara asked when they were out of earshot of Baxter.

THE DEATHLESS by VINCENT WOLFRAM

Stuart snorted with laughter. Clara allowed a smile.

The sub shuddered, and the hull creaked around them. The Goliad dove. The deck ceased rocking beneath them as they left the surface waves.

The control room was lit by electronic equipment, the outlines of crewmen traced in green and white by computer monitors and instrument panels. The Officer of the Deck was taking a last look through the viewfinder of the periscope, quietly addressing the helmsman.

The crew members spared the women a glance and no more. An Alfa class Soviet sub had been spotted in the Sea of Japan earlier. The Goliad couldn't outrun an Alfa. It could fight, if need be, but Captain Hopkins didn't want to risk an international incident. Or a war.

Between the control room and Stuart's home, the sonar room, a ladder descended to the lower deck. The aluminum rungs clanged with each of their footfalls.

The berth was full of snoring and muted whispers. At full capacity, the Goliad wouldn't have enough beds for new guests, but it was currently manned by a skeleton crew; the mission was too secretive for more than the bare minimum needed to run the sub. Stuart didn't have bunkmates, so the room was empty. The bunks were stacked to the ceiling–one, two, three– with a narrow gap between them, neat as a catacomb.

"Take the top. I'll be in the middle," Clara ordered Yelena. The scientist complied, slipping off her shoes.

"No pajamas?" Yelena asked, the Slavic pronunciation bleeding through.

"Only Naval uniforms. And all men's," Stuart said, sympathetic to her plight. She was only wearing a blouse and long skirt. Despite the internal heating system, the sub was cold when it dove into deeper waters. The metal walls sapped the heat away.

Yelena pleaded with her eyes. Clara opened her mouth to say no and closed it.

"Fine. Grab us both some clothes." She eyed Stuart warily.

He pulled his own spare clothes out of the storage compartment under his bed for Yelena, but he had to go hunting for Clara. He needed to find a man short enough to match her.

Lou's compartment was down the hall. Stuart ended up waking three of the six sleeping men. There were harsh whispers and shoes were thrown, but Stuart was allowed to borrow Lou's clothes.

When he returned, Stuart was made to stand in the hall until the women finished dressing. He waited so long, he thought they might leave him there overnight. Lou's spare clothes fit Clara well, but the outfit lent to Yelena draped off her narrow shoulders. Stuart pretended not to notice. The look on Clara's face was warning enough.

He drifted off to dreams of sunlit Japanese shores and plum wine, but his doze ended with the heavy footsteps of a large man. The door filled with the shape of Max Hardy, who lurched in making pained grunts. He muttered to himself; the content unclear but suggestive of curses. Stuart wondered if the words were Russian, or if the weary lieutenant had simply lapsed into gibberish.

Max walked to the opposite stack of beds and slotted himself into the bottom bunk, laying on his side. In the gloom, Stuart couldn't see the man's face. For a long time, Stuart wondered whether his eyes were closed, or whether Hardy was staring at him, unseeing in the darkness. Sleep came after an eternity.

Stuart rose at 0600, ready for his watch. Hardy was fast asleep, snoring loudly, and Yelena softly snoozed. Clara was awake, one eye peeking through a fan of long black hair.

"Coming to breakfast?"

She brushed the hair from her face, frowning. "No. I stick with the scientist at all times."

"Want some eggs? Oatmeal?"

THE DEATHLESS by VINCENT WOLFRAM

Clara shook her head. "Coffee. Splash of milk. Actually, make it a big splash. Bet your coffee is awful. Can't stand it black unless it's... Colombian."

"You're from..."

"America, Mr. Stuart. I was born in Miami."

"I wasn't implying–"

"Sailors are always implying." She turned to the wall.

Stuart wasn't ready to piss her off again, so he tightened his lips and walked down the hallway to the mess. The day watch, fresh from their showers, passed the sweaty, irritable night watch.

Without sunlight, meals seem like arbitrary markers in the unvariegated twilight of a submarine. Still, the body knows roughly when it should and should not be awake. The night watch was rough.

Stuart grabbed a plastic tray with eggs, hash, and toast. He sat down with Lou, Burt, and Baxter at an aluminum table. Lou was a short man who spoke with his broad hands and waggling eyebrows. Burt was a sleepy-looking lug with drooping shoulders. They chatted conspiratorially until Stuart joined them.

"So, I heard our visitors stayed with you," Burt said.

"Which one shared your–"

"Don't start, Lou," Stuart said over a cup of coffee.

"What? It's not like you have a girl back home. Nothing wrong with a little female companionship."

"Be sleeping with the enemy if you did," Baxter started. The other men groaned. "No, I'm serious. A Russian scientist on a nuclear sub? That seem safe to you guys? Cap was right to tell her to steer clear of the reactor. Who knows what she could do in there? And the other woman, Clara. Cruz." He emphasized each name.

"Baxter," Stuart warned.

"I'm just saying, Latina woman in this corner of the world. Kinda obvious in Russia. Seems like it would be hard to be a spy... unless she's Cuban."

Stuart scoffed. "She's from Colombia."

"That what she tell you?"

"But she's an American spy," Burt cut in. "And the captain trusted her enough to bring her on the ship. You think he did something stupid like let two commies on board?"

Baxter backpedaled. "Hey now, let's not put words in my mouth. Captain Hopkins is a smart man. But I'm just saying, if there's going to be a double agent aboard..." He shrugged his shoulders.

Stuart wanted to reach over and shake the man. All Stuart knew about the spy was that she had helped Max Hardy escape from the hell that was Russian prison. The lieutenant was going to safely return to his family, and home, thanks to her heroic efforts. He didn't appreciate his friend's xenophobia.

Stuart excused himself from the table and grabbed a coffee for Clara. He was generous with the milk. When he returned to his bunk room, he found Clara propped up on her elbow.

She stole it from his hand, sipping the still scalding drink. There were rings under her eyes. He wondered if she had stayed up to keep an eye on Yelena last night. Or on Hardy.

"Sleep well?"

"Shut up." The words were sharp, but she looked grateful.

Max Hardy continued to snore. Stuart studied the SEAL. From what he'd heard, the Russians fed prisoners bread and water, letting them slowly starve. Max hardly looked like he'd withered in prison. His arms were thick and his chest broad.

"How'd you rescue him?" Stuart whispered.

Clara stared. "You know that information is classified. It's ridiculous we're even in this situation. We should have smuggled him on a plane out of Japan, but the brass wanted to bring him home with pomp and circumstance. I would have preferred more discretion. And speed."

"Wait, why the rush? The Goliad isn't exactly slow. For a submarine, it's basically–"

"Not the point, Mr. Stuart," Clara said flatly. She looked over to Hardy to make sure he was sleeping. "I can tell you this much, since it'll be revealed to the public once Hardy is safely back on American soil. The lieutenant was the subject of human experimentation. That's why we brought along Yel... Dr. Tereshkova. He looks a little worse for wear on the outside, but on the inside he's... well, he's going to need a good doctor."

Stuart frowned. He had expected to see pity in Clara's eyes. All he saw was dim fear.

"Is he going to make it? Can Yelena, pardon, Dr. Tereshkova, fix him?"

"Better pray she can."

Stuart wanted to know more, but the spy ended the conversation. She and Yelena were due for a debriefing soon, and he had to start his shift. He whispered goodbye, and when he left, he thought he heard her say thank you.

The morning passed quickly. The sonar room buzzed with chatter about the new passengers. Stuart kept his headphones on, listening to sonar pings spreading through empty sea, but he couldn't resist checking in on the conversation. As he watched the pixelated rise and fall of the sea floor on the monitor, Stuart listened to speculation about the rescue. "A nuclear sub sent out for one man. I mean, he's a war hero, but still."

Maybe Max had intel on how to bring down the USSR. Maybe the mission was a political favor for a sailor with connections. Maybe the rescue would be made public, a real middle finger to Ivan for all the world to see. Stuart kept quiet. He wouldn't reveal what Clara had told him.

When the men started discussing Dr. Tereshkova and Ms. Cruz, Stuart had to speak up. He called them out for vulgar and xenophobic comments. The men gave him dirty looks, but no one argued with him. They knew Stuart liked to keep things professional.

Mercifully, the lunch break came soon, and Stuart went below decks to the galley. He found Yelena and Clara alone at a table. The other sailors were keeping their distance, so Stuart guessed an officer must have handed down orders to keep them separate. Meanwhile, Hardy sat amid a throng, scarfing down a sloppy joe. Baxter was at his side, slapping him on the back like they were old friends.

Stuart presumed the SEAL had enough company. He sat at the table with Clara and Yelena.

"Hey, can I get another sloppy joe?" Hardy asked through a mouthful.

"Sure, boss," said Charlie Gordon, hurrying off to grab another tray. He should have been in the kitchen with the other culinary specialists, but the kid had been lured out by the promise of meeting the POW.

The two women were quiet. Stuart wouldn't press them to talk. He ate in comfortable silence.

A round of guffaws came from the crowded table. Max Hardy smiled wearily.

"Laying it on a little thick, hmm?" Stuart smirked.

Yelena looked to Clara; her brows knitted.

Clara translated, "He means the other men are trying to earn his favor by laughing harder."

"What?"

Clara explained, "Dr. Tereshkova isn't exactly a native English speaker. You used an idiom. 'Laying it on thick' doesn't translate."

"Why would they want to earn his favor?" Yelena cut in. "He's a very good man, but..."

"Cause he'll be a celebrity when he gets back home," Stuart answered. Another round of laughter came from behind them. "Each one of those sailors will get to say they were part of the rescue mission. That *they* rescued Max."

"A celebrity?" Yelena repeated, bemused.

"Yeah, for being imprisoned by the Communists. And... tortured." Stuart frowned. It sounded strange when he said it aloud.

"Mr. Stuart means that he will be celebrated for the sacrifices he made for his country," Clara said. She said the cynical part more quietly. "And because Americans love a hero who suffers."

"The only thing that still bugs me," Hardy said, "is how long it took to get rescued. Two years going on three?" The

THE DEATHLESS by VINCENT WOLFRAM

SEAL's winning smile faltered. "I mean, they could have gotten me sooner, right? Right?!" He slammed his fist on the table, knocking over his glass. The flash of anger disappeared, and his smile returned. "Oh, whoops. Aha. Of course, I'm grateful for all the trouble you boys went to..."

Stuart knew it would be impolitic to ask, but he wanted more information about Hardy's time in Russia.

"Still classified," Clara replied.

"He was at my lab in Vladivostok," Yelena started. Clara shook her head, stopping the scientist from saying anything further. Stuart locked eyes with the scientist. Max hadn't been locked in prison. Had Dr. Tereshkova experimented on the lieutenant?

Yelena pursued another course, "I am very anxious, Mr. Stuart, to get to America. I love my *Rodina*, the motherland, but I do not love the KGB. Max, that is, Lt. Hardy, was hurt very badly by their agents. I am worried for him. I only hope we escaped in time to..."

Stuart saw the incident in his peripheral vision. There was a splash, an apology, and a blur of motion. A head bent backward. Max Hardy stood up, just over six feet tall, a wet stain down the front of his fatigues. A mug rolled, tracing a line in a puddle of coffee. A man lay on the ground.

Hardy, who'd seemed calm a few minutes ago, was red in the face, cords in his neck taut, muscles straining in his arms. The cafeteria grew quiet, buzzing with nervous chatter. It could have been a reflex. Sailors had fought among themselves before.

But the electrician's mate on the ground, Burt Halloway, wasn't moving. His neck was twisted at an odd angle. His eyes were glassy. The chatter died.

The men were sailors. Many had witnessed death. But nothing like this, not in the mess hall. Not in their own home.

Hardy's body relaxed, the fury leaching away. "I..."

No mob descended on him. No one threw a punch. The hospital corpsman was fetched, and so was the Executive Officer, Lieutenant Commander Jones. Burt Halloway was pronounced dead. The lanky XO pulled witnesses aside and forced the rest to leave the mess hall. Stuart hung in awkward balance between the XO's order and courtesy to Clara and Yelena. He didn't want to abandon them.

The women were as dumbstruck as the rest, but Stuart saw the awful light of recognition in their eyes. He didn't know if Hardy had lashed out before, but he knew they were afraid it would happen again.

Clara and Yelena stood apart from Hardy. They wouldn't leave him, and they didn't dare come near.

Lt. Cdr. Jones interviewed Stuart, Yelena, and Clara next, since they hesitated to leave. Stuart admitted he hadn't seen the incident, but Yelena had full view of it.

"The other man spilled the coffee on Lt. Hardy. It looked like it must have hurt, because my friend, uh, the lieutenant, he punched the other man. I think it was an accident."

The scientist was lying. The XO didn't seem to notice, but Stuart could tell. Her eyes flicked to Hardy. Why would she protect him if she was afraid of him?

Jones dismissed Stuart, Cruz, and Tereshkova with a wave of his hand. Hardy now sat at the table alone, staring at his skinned knuckles. He wasn't handcuffed, nor did he protest leaving. Since there are no brigs aboard a submarine, Hardy was confined to the quarters he was sharing with Stuart.

Hardy went quietly. He seemed lost, a faraway look in his eyes.

By the time Stuart had returned to his post, word had already spread. The crewmen were in shock. Burt Halloway was well loved aboard the USS Goliad. Even as the men tried to soothe themselves with the thought that Burt's death was an accident, there were whispers of what this would mean for Hardy.

The SEAL had just been freed from a Soviet prison. He was supposed to return home in triumph. What would Halloway's death say about the mission? What would the military police say when they returned to American shores?

THE DEATHLESS by VINCENT WOLFRAM

The days that followed were quiet, mournful. Hardy didn't stay confined to quarters at all times, but he only left during off hours, taking his meals in the mess when no one but the cooks would be there. A submarine is tight, but the other sailors did their best to ignore Hardy, never greeting or looking at him as they passed him in the hall.

As the days passed, Hardy looked simultaneously better and worse. His back must have healed, because he was able to stand up straight; he looked a few inches taller. Stuart knew Hardy was stress eating–he had seen the stacks of empty cafeteria trays–but the lieutenant wasn't getting any fatter. His arms were ready to tear the fabric of his sleeves. Hardy must have spent all his spare time exercising. Still, he looked sickly. In spite of the extra weight and muscle, his face looked skeletal, and his joints were too thick in his fingers and elbows and knees.

Dr. Tereshkova was often with him. Though she wasn't a medical doctor, Stuart saw her administering ointments and bandages to him, tending to wounds he had suffered while in the hands of the KGB.

Yelena and Clara were pariahs on board too, guilty by association with Hardy. And Baxter wasn't helping.

"They have to be enemy agents," Baxter said over dinner one night. Stuart sat down with Baxter and his clique, as they huddled over their meatloaf. "They never talk with the rest of the crew."

"Isn't that by orders, chief?"

"Not on your life. You think Clara would be that quiet if she wasn't up to something. If she was a real American, one of us, she wouldn't leave us in the dark about what's going on with the lieutenant. I think they're hiding something. They're always chatting it up with Hardy. You can hear 'em whispering down the hall in the berth. Hardy is a good old American boy. But what have they been telling him, hmm? We may be outside of Russian waters, but maybe we're not outside of Russian influence."

A man screamed from down the hall. Stuart threw down his napkin and ran. Other sailors, including Baxter, came up behind him. Charlie Gordon was standing in front of one of the bunk rooms, tears streaming down his face, hands clasped over his mouth. He whimpered into his fingers. Stuart stepped beside him to see what the cause of commotion was.

The bunk room was red. The gray walls and white sheets were stained with a spray of fresh blood. Seaman Recruit Fitzgerald lay sprawled on the ground, a deep gash in his throat. If the cut was much deeper, he would have been decapitated. Submariners typically deal in explosions, in drowning. The crime scene was harrowing.

Charlie Gordon was too stricken with grief and horror for his bunkmate to move. His wire-framed glasses fogged. Stuart backed away, seeing that there was a trail of blood out the door of the room. It led down the hallway. Down to Stuart's bunks. He rushed, followed by a group of sailors.

Clara was trying to coax Yelena away from Hardy, who sat at the edge of his bunk, blood smeared across his face. The dive knife was jammed in his belt; the blade was crusted over with dried blood. Yelena was tending to a small abrasion on his hand.

"He made me do it. He made me do it," Hardy repeated, his voice hollow.

The sailors crowded behind Stuart. He pushed back. If he wasn't careful, the mob would take Hardy out and kill him. Hardy was a murderer.

"He's sick." Yelena looked to Stuart, pleading.

"You're goddamned right he's sick," someone shouted.

"What'd you do to him, you Red harpy?" Baxter added, trying to muscle his way in.

Stuart noticed that there were cracks in Hardy's face. At first, he thought the man had been clawed by his victim, but upon closer inspection, it looked like the SEAL's skull split through his skin with ridges of bone.

"I didn't mean to do it, I think," he said, a hoarse titter escaping his lips. He was incoherent. "I was just so angry. So hungry. They left me in Vladivostok. Abandoned me. I just wanted a little bite."

"What's going on?" Stuart asked, wary.

"We never should have left my lab," Dr. Tereshkova said.

"Shut up, Yelena."

"Don't you yell at her!" Hardy roared, standing up. Yelena fell to the side, and Clara was quick to pick her up from the parquet floor.

"My bones hurt. I hurt! God, I'm so hungry. I just need a little to eat. What are you all looking at?!"

Charlie Gordon pushed through the crowd. When he saw Hardy covered in blood, Charlie screamed and leaped at the murderer.

"I'll kill you, you son of a bitch!"

Hardy caught his left wrist.

"You're going to do what to me?" Hardy's voice was deep, growling. He lifted the man off the ground. There was a loud crack from Charlie's shoulder, the arm threatening to pop from the socket.

"Just like the KGB. Are you going to shock me with cables? Are you going to pull off my fingernails? I should have stayed to pay them back. I should have skinned them like deer!" Hardy drew his knife and plunged it into the Charlie's chest. He ripped down to the belly button. An arc of blood flowed from the wound, and Gordon's ribs peeked through torn flesh.

Charlie screamed, kicking and thrashing, unable to reach the ground, unable to push away from Hardy. Stomach acid and half-digested food spilled down his shirt and pants.

Hardy ended the scream by biting out Charlie's throat and tossing the corpse at the crowd. There was pandemonium. Yelena scrambled out of the room, closely followed by Clara. Stuart tried to close the door, but Charlie's foot caught in the doorway. Hardy leaned close.

"You think this door will stop me?" he growled through the crack.

Stuart frantically kicked Gordon's foot in and closed the door, leaning against it. Hardy pounded with his fist. "Let me out. Let me out! LET ME OUT!"

Baxter fetched a chair and jammed it against the doorknob. The room was sealed. Hardy was trapped.

II

*Pacific Ocean – Crossing the International Dateline
October 12th, 1986*

TWO OFFICERS STOOD GUARD BEFORE the door. The below decks watch cleared the hallway, sending sailors back to their assigned duties. Stuart was ordered up the ladder with Yelena and Clara. CPO Boulet led the three of them to the wardroom located amidships, off the control room. They wound past the electronic equipment, past glaring men to the small office.

Captain Hopkins sat at a plain oak desk, waiting for them. A circle of senior officers muttered among themselves, growing quiet after the three entered. The captain stared at them until Yelena began to shift uncomfortably in place. Stuart remained standing at attention. Clara stared back.

"Petty Officer Stuart, I need a report."

Stuart gave a summary of what he'd seen but didn't spare the gruesome details. He would not lie by omission.

"Bloody business," the captain said, shaking his head. "We skirted the Russians to avoid a diplomatic incident... now we're dealing with something much worse. You assured me you had this under control, Ms. Cruz."

She protested, "Yelena doesn't have the equipment she needs. She had a full lab in Vladivostok."

"Do not scold, Ms. Cruz. This was my miscalculation. It was not supposed to happen this quickly," Yelena said.

"What wasn't supposed to happen?" one of the senior officers chimed in.

CAMP SLASHER LAKE: VOLUME ONE

Before Stuart could be removed from the room, Yelena was revealing classified information. "Lt. Hardy was one of the test subjects as part of... I guess in English, Project Koschei."

"Project what now?"

"Eh, Koschei the Deathless. He iss a villain in Russian folklore. He is strong. Huge. And he cannot die. The focus of Project Koschei was to study how to stimulate the pituitary gland and testes to produce growth hormone and testosterone, thereby..."

"Can we get that translated into English?" an officer deadpanned.

"It was a super soldier project, sir," Clara said. "They were trying make soldiers who could grow bigger, stronger... Lt. Hardy was a test subject. Since he was an American, he was disposable if the experiment went awry."

"It was purposefully induced acromegaly. It was supposed to be controlled. And I thought we had removed him from the drug regimen soon enough. I did not know that *he* had taken it this far." Tears streamed down Yelena's face.

"Whoa, now. Why are you crying? Who took what too far?" Captain Hopkins asked.

"Head Doctor Alexei Bogdanova," Tereshkova choked. "We were just supposed to experiment with the drug I developed. It was supposed to be reversible. But Dr. Bogdanova must have performed surgery and inserted the glandular inducer into his brain. It's like a pacemaker, except it uses electrical pulses to stimulate the glands. Hardy will experience continuous production of the growth hormone and testosterone. He will grow bigger, angrier. Hungrier. Hardy must undergo surgery to remove the device. But to reverse this process..." She threw up her hands.

Captain Hopkins sighed in relief. "Is that all? We'll just put him under and have the corpsmen work on him."

"You think you can sedate him?" Yelena asked.

"I don't think you understand the situation, sir," Clara said.

A distant scream echoed through the ship. Footsteps beat towards the door. Someone pounded furiously on the door.

THE DEATHLESS by VINCENT WOLFRAM

"Enter."

Baxter burst in, panting.

"Why aren't you at your station in the Attack Room, PO Baxter?" Captain Hopkins glared at the interloper.

"Escaped," Baxter huffed, hands on his knees. "Lt. Hardy escaped. Both guards are dead. Stabbed to death. One had part of his face chewed off. The Chief of the Boat grabbed me and sent me as an errand boy. You and the Cuban are fucked now." He pointed from the Russian scientist to the spy.

"What?"

"The Russian and the Cuban, sir. Hardy told us down in the caf about the weird stuff they did to him. He was supposed to be a Manchurian candidate, pumped up with steroids, and propaganda and whatnot."

Some officers snickered. Others looked unsettled.

"He told you they were going to make him a Manchurian candidate. Like from the book?"

Baxter shifted. "Well, no, not in those words. But it's exactly what it sounded like. And I think you mean the movie. It was a movie."

"Shut up, Mr. Baxter," the captain sighed.

"But you gotta arrest them. They're the ones who did it to him."

"I've heard their testimony, Baxter. Besides, Ms. Cruz is not Cuban."

"That's a Cuban name—"

"And, what's more," Hopkins interrupted, "I believe Dr. Tereshkova is not responsible for this incident. She may, indeed, be the one to rectify this mess. Thank you for reporting, you may go back to your post."

"But—"

The captain dismissed him. "Thank you."

Baxter glowered, the bottom row of his teeth showing, but he didn't disobey. He left without another word.

Captain Hopkins addressed the two women. "Clara Cruz and Yelena Tereshkova. I absolutely believe that you are not

CAMP SLASHER LAKE: VOLUME ONE

responsible for Lt. Hardy's present... derangement. However, in the interests of safety, you are to remain confined to this wardroom until Hardy is safely apprehended. No, don't argue. Just tell us what we need to know to capture him."

Yelena didn't meet the captain's eyes. She paced the room on long graceful legs, speaking to the ceiling. "Well, we never had a test subject develop this far, but he is growing by the hour. In order to feed the muscular and bone growth, he will have to eat often. Search the cafeteria. I think there you will capture him."

"Captain Hopkins." Clara stood at attention. "I'm not a soldier, but I'm proficient in unarmed combat. I know Lt. Hardy. He is, was, a good man. I can assist in tracking him down. I owe it to the crew of the USS Goliad. And to him."

"Permission..." Hopkins chewed it over. "...reluctantly granted. Four are dead, Ms. Cruz. I know you mean well, but you were half his size before he started growing. Don't punch above your weight class. I understand that Hardy is part of your mission. Render assistance as you best see fit. Now, Stuart, Jones, Boulet, with me." The CPO and XO armed themselves with batons, which had only been used in intrusion defense drills; they were better than nothing.

Captain Hopkins stood and nodded to the scientist, who was left under guard in the wardroom. Stuart, Jones, Cruz, and Boulet traveled in his wake. Just outside the room, Hopkins said, "Grab three more men and go down to the mess hall. We should follow Dr. Tereshkova's hunch. Subdue him. He must be taken alive. This is already way out of hand, but I'll be in traction with the White House if he doesn't return to the United States."

"Was this a rescue mission?" The words were out before Stuart could stop himself. He resisted the urge to clap his hands over his mouth. It was too honest. He had voiced the fear that Hardy wasn't just an American in need of rescue. He was intel to be collected by the United States government at all costs.

THE DEATHLESS by VINCENT WOLFRAM

The captain looked at the sonar technician levelly. He stared just long enough to put the fear of God into the man, before saying, "We're going to try our best to ensure it is. So don't screw this up. As you were gentlemen."

Hopkins stalked off to check on the progress of the Goliad with the men in the control room.

Jones and Boulet glared at Stuart and then moved forward.

"Hey, can I join you guys?"

Baxter was skulking by the doorway. He heard they needed volunteers.

Jones shrugged and invited Baxter along. Two more men were pulled from the control room, since they were close at hand. Seaman Recruits Doocy and Ramirez followed. They were both gangly youths with a hint of scruff on their face; Doocy had red wisps on his chin; Ramirez had a black, speckled mustache. They leaned over the ladder leading down to the lower deck.

"What if he's not in the galley?" Jones asked, peering down.

Boulet scoffed. "What's he going to do, hide? It's a sub, sir. There's nowhere for him to escape."

They descended the ladder, and walked down the corridor past the sleeping quarters, stepping gingerly over the clotted pool of blood. Someone had covered Charlie in a sheet. His corpse sat propped up in the bunk room, peering out into the hall.

"Can't believe the captain isn't going to arrest those two," Baxter muttered.

Jones glared at Baxter. "You disrespecting the captain?" The senior officer didn't break eye contact until Baxter muttered no.

"What's that, Baxter?"

"I said, 'No, sir.'"

The recruits knew better than to laugh at Baxter, but Stuart saw them exchange grins. Clara suppressed a smile.

When they arrived in the mess hall, the air was dead. The tables were empty. No one waited in line for mid rations.

"Hey Louis?" Stuart called out for one of the culinary

specialists, a friend of his who worked this watch. "You back there?"

A scuffling sound came from the kitchen. The two senior officers held their batons at the ready. Baxter looked like he was about to open his big mouth until Boulet elbowed him.

They crept around the counter to the kitchen entrance. There was the smell of fresh chopped vegetables and roast chicken. Steam wafted from the pots. At first glance, no one appeared to be in the kitchen. The center island was piled with used utensils and ingredients prepped for the next meal. A cooked chicken cooled on the chopping block.

There was a feeble squeak of rubber on linoleum.

The group rounded the island to find Hardy hunched over PO Louis Brown, his legs kicking out weakly, trying to back away. Hardy sat up, revealing that his hand was wrist-deep in Brown's guts. He pulled out a handful of entrails and took a bite, dabbing his lips and chin with blood.

"Want some?" He offered. His front teeth looked like chisels, his eyeteeth like daggers.

"Help," Louis pleaded, his eyes fluttering.

Red striations ran up and down Hardy's face. Stuart thought they were streaks of blood, but they were stretch marks. His skull was growing.

The officers were so shaken, they didn't have time to react.

Hardy got to his feet, snatched a cleaver from the center island, and swung. SR Doocy was too close. The blade cut through his forehead, drenching his face in a sheet of blood. He was blinded. Doocy stumbled backward, falling to the hard parquet floor. SR Ramirez retreated, scanning for a weapon. Stuart and Baxter followed suit.

Clara Cruz darted in with a series of punches to Hardy's gut. The next slash of the cleaver clipped a strand of hair from her head, blade's edge cutting the air a few centimeters from her eyes. She backpedaled.

The senior officers delivered a coordinated blow to Hardy's head with the batons, and he staggered, swinging the cleaver

THE DEATHLESS by VINCENT WOLFRAM

wildly at them. Ramirez rushed in to kick Hardy, dodging the blade. Doocy continued to wail, crawling away from the kitchen, leaving bloody handprints on the floor. All six descended on Hardy, punching, kicking, jabbing, and beating the hulk of a man until he curled up on the floor.

Ramirez relaxed once he'd kicked away the cleaver. "We got him. That punk can't mess with the Goliad crew."

The senior officers straightened. "You ready to come quietly?" Boulet asked.

Hardy answered by grabbing Boulet around the ankles and pulling hard. The man fell backward, smashing his head against the ground. Hardy sprang on Boulet, wresting the baton from the CPO's grip. Though Jones tried to bash in the lieutenant's skull, he couldn't stop him.

Hardy punched Boulet in the stomach. The CPO gaped, breathless. Hardy gripped the baton in both hands and drove it into Boulet's mouth, breaking through his teeth and lodging the blunt instrument in the officer's throat.

SR Ramirez flew on Hardy with balled fists and received an uppercut to the jaw, sending him crashing over the island, sweeping the chicken, chopped vegetables, and an assortment of knives, forks, and ladles to the ground.

Officer Jones aimed at Hardy's head again. With a sound like a baseball bat hitting leather, the lieutenant caught it in his hand and jerked it forward, bringing himself eye to eye with Jones.

"Why'd you interrupt me? I was eating," Hardy growled. "You can't save him. You can't even save yourself."

Jones let go of the baton and backed away. Hardy lifted the baton and pointed at the officer.

"You couldn't save me from the KGB. You couldn't..."

Cruz threw a kitchen knife at the SEAL. The blade flashed and buried itself in his broad chest. Hardy flinched and looked down at the knife in distaste. Boulet heaved, choking to death on the baton lodged in his throat.

Baxter fled, jumping over Doocy, who continued to scream

and drag his legs. Stuart might have considered this cowardly, if he wasn't also backing up step by step with Jones, Ramirez, and Cruz.

Hardy slid the knife out of his chest and raised his arm to throw it. The squad bolted from the kitchen. Stuart dropped to his knee to help Doocy up. The kitchen knife sliced the air by Stuart's ear and stabbed through Doocy's neck. The recruit flailed. Hardy's shadow fell upon them, and Stuart ducked from a swing of the SEAL's fist. Hardy planted his foot on Doocy's neck and pressed until his heel touched the floor, vertebrae popping under the black boot.

Stuart bounded into the hallway. Baxter was going door to door, waking sailors. Some men were still in their underwear, yawning and rubbing half-lidded, red eyes. Jones waded among them, ordering men up the ladder.

Hardy leaned into the hall. "Stop running. Stop prolonging the inevitable." His voice was deep, coming from a cavern in his chest.

"Is that the lieutenant?"

Stuart shoved men towards the ladder. "Go. Go!"

The press tightened. Stuart was trapped between the men exiting the rooms behind him and the men streaming towards the ladder.

"What's the ruckus?" a submariner yawned.

Hardy grabbed the interlocutor by the face and smashed his head against the walls, brains blossoming against steel. Stuart was crushed between the men, fighting for air.

"Hey, what the fuck's going on?"

The men in the rear fought back, trying to overwhelm the lieutenant. Hardy stood above them, his bony fists swinging down on them. His knuckles were red, pale yellow gleams of bone showing through torn flesh.

Stuart was smashed against the ladder, teeth clinking on the metal rung. He scrambled up. The man above him stepped on his hands every other rung, but he didn't care. A handful of men fought Hardy, but it still wasn't a fair fight. They could

THE DEATHLESS by VINCENT WOLFRAM

only fight two abreast. Jones hauled Stuart up at the top of the ladder, trying to speed up the process.

"Hurry up! Move it, damn you."

Hardy shoved through the crowd to the ladder and looked up into Stuart's face. When the Navy SEAL smiled, the skin cracked along the sides of his mouth.

"Give me your hand." Hardy reached up, oblivious to the surrounding men striking him. "I would be *so glad* to shake your hand."

Jones's eyes were wide. His lips trembled. "Seal the bulkhead," he whispered.

"Do what?" Stuart couldn't believe what he'd heard.

"I said seal the bulkhead. Do it!"

"But the rest of the men."

"That's an order, dammit," the XO shrilled, his hands shaking.

Several men jumped in to seal it. Hardy was peeling men off the ladder and throwing them to the side. Before Hardy could get his hand through the opening, the men closed the hatch and spun the wheel until it was sealed shut. The hatch was meant to close in the event of a leak, protecting the men below. Now, it had trapped them.

Stuart felt shameful relief, until a bang came from the other side of the hatch. Bang. Bang. *Bang.* Hardy didn't have anything in his hands when he ascended the ladder. Was he punching the steel door with his bare fist?

There was a collective gasp when the banging stopped. The men had been holding their breath.

Nothing could be heard beyond the bulkhead.

"Alright, men, back to your stations. Baxter, Ramirez, Stuart, you're dismissed. Cruz, back to the wardroom," Jones said.

"Shouldn't we tell the captain what we just saw?" Stuart asked.

Baxter joined in. "Yeah, what about our report?"

"Not necessary, gentlemen. I said you're dismissed. Joseph and Xavier, get over here and guard the hatch. No one opens it." Jones walked away.

Clara's shoulders slumped. "I thought there'd be time. That there'd be something left of him. I don't know what I'm going to tell Yelena. I just..." She left, hanging her head in defeat.

Stuart gazed down at the sealed hatch at his feet. Joseph and Xavier watched Stuart until he sidled off with Baxter and Ramirez.

Once he was out of earshot of the newly deputized guards, he asked. "Think the XO's going to tell the captain we just sealed forty men in with a monster?"

"Hey, he was a SEAL, man. Show some respect, Stuart," Baxter snapped. "Besides, it's not Hardy's fault. It's the Russian's. She was experimenting on him, altering his pituitition..."

"Pituitary."

"Whatever. And giving him roid rage. He wasn't the same man who was talking to us in the cafeteria, you know, before he freaked out on Burt."

"Are you sure?" Ramirez asked quietly.

"Sure, I'm sure! He was a United States Navy SEAL. Just a normal guy. But that evil doctor, and that Cuban bitch..."

"Hey, watch it," Stuart warned.

"...are getting the soft treatment from Captain Hopkins. I gotta let him know he's letting the Reds run loose on this ship. Hell, he might be in danger with them in the wardroom."

"What about the XO, though?" Stuart was doubtful. "You march in there; he'll say you were breaking orders. C'mon, try the captain after your watch." After you've had time to rethink things, Stuart thought.

Baxter snorted. "Good little sailor, aren't you Stuart? Always do what you're told." He walked away, shaking his head. Ramirez stayed silent through the exchange, offering a shrug to Stuart as a sign of parting. He was a recruit. He was at the bottom of the chain of command. He could only walk away.

THE DEATHLESS by VINCENT WOLFRAM

Stuart relieved the sonar tech who'd covered part of his shift, but he had to explain why the man couldn't go below decks to get lunch. The sonar room buzzed with conversation, and Stuart could barely do his work with all the questions he was being asked. Each time someone diverted his attention with a new question, Stuart checked the monitors over his shoulder. The situation was dire enough without the risk of a Russian sub sneaking up on the Goliad.

The crew was unsettled. What was the USSR capable of doing? Who else could be brainwashed into a killing machine? The sailors imagined soldiers like slavering Russian bears. They whispered of cannibalism and treachery.

Stuart heard echoes of Baxter from his fellow techs. He wondered whether the machinist's mate had left his station to talk to more of the crew. Some questioned the captain's decision to bring Dr. Tereshkova and Clara Cruz aboard. Others suggested countermanding the executive officer's order and mounting a rescue mission to save the mariners below decks.

Stuart was conflicted, mind and heart wrenched in two directions. He feared that his crewmates didn't appreciate the danger, that they would unleash hell on the whole ship if they opened the hatch. He also felt guilt, shame. How can I leave those men to die, he thought? The USS Goliad had been enlisted to save a single sailor, Lt. Max Hardy. Would it sacrifice a third of its own crew now?

When Stuart's watch ended, he got up to leave the sonar room, but he didn't know where to go. Most recreational activities happened down in the mess hall or the bunk rooms. Only officers were served food on the top deck. Nothing to do but mill about the cramped halls, stare at the metal walls, and think.

Submarines are staffed by volunteers, only those willing and able to brave months in the lightless depths of the ocean, crammed inside a metal tube. But even those with mettle for it need to keep active. With work, with play, the metal walls don't close in on a submariner. The creak of the hull and the endless hum of air scrubbers are nothing but soothing noise. Give a mariner too much time to think about the enormity of water above and below him, of the crushing darkness that surrounds him...

Stuart wandered out into the halls to join the other men, off their shifts with nowhere to go. The halls were warm, and the air was thin from the crowd of shuffling bodies. He drifted down the hall towards the sound of a growing congregation.

"We need to talk to the captain."

"The captain isn't to be bothered at this moment."

Three senior officers, Jones at the front, faced Baxter, who was backed by a crowd. The officers stirred but didn't break rank.

"Our brothers are down with that *thing*. We need to go down there," Baxter demanded. "Just let us reason with him. Captain knows best in these matters."

"You want me to bust you down to recruit," Jones threatened. "Captain Hopkins is aft, checking in on the maneuvering room. But I'm ordering you stay right here. You've got nerve to try and jump the chain of command on us."

"Go get the cap," Baxter murmured to Ramirez, who slipped out of the crowd and jogged down the hall.

"Hey!"

"Shut up, sir," Baxter spat. "Bring out the Russian and the Cuban. We need to talk to them."

"Hold on," Stuart said, threading through the crowd. "Baxter, we don't need to do this."

"Stu, buddy, we can't trust those girls, okay? We're not going to hurt them... as long as they cooperate. Don't look like that. Listen, we're just going to force the mad scientist to fess up and tell us the cure."

"And what if she can't cure him? What if she doesn't have the tools to do it?" Stuart snarled.

"Then we feed her to Hardy," he replied coldly. "If she can't come up with a cure after a minute with the monster, what do I care? One fewer Communist. Lt. Cdr. Jones, sir, hand over the scientist."

THE DEATHLESS by VINCENT WOLFRAM

"No."

The crowd took a step forward. The XO and his fellow officers took a step back.

"Do we really want to let another commie in our country?" Baxter opened his arms wide, addressing the crowd.

"No!" they shouted.

"Gorbachev wants to talk to President Reagan in Iceland. Wants to talk about ditching ballistic missiles. Maybe he's for real. Or maybe he's afraid he can't beat us in space. He's thinking he can turn our brothers in arms into some kind of mutants. Turn them against us. Yeah, real peaceful, Gorby, you rat. But we're not going to let that happen, are we?"

The crew cheered. Stuart didn't give a damn for the USSR, but he didn't like Baxter's aim. The officers were exchanging looks. Stuart was hoping they'd have cooler heads, but even Jones was nodding to the Gorbachev bashing. It was all too easy.

"What the hell is all this?" the captain asked calmly. Captain Hopkins didn't have to shout. The crowd parted as he walked toward it, isolating Baxter.

"You have something to say, Seaman?"

"I'm Petty Officer First–oh," Baxter said.

"Back to work, gentlemen," the captain said, strolling past the machinist's mate.

"No, sir," Baxter said. "We have something more important to do."

Captain Hopkins had kept his cool thus far, but he turned red here. "Are you disobeying an order?"

"The girl knows how to cure Hardy. She's been lying to you."

Hopkins squinted. "How's that?"

There was a metallic click, and the crowd turned to see Clara Cruz leveling a pistol at Baxter.

"No one is taking Dr. Tereshkova. I'm under strict orders to protect her until she's stateside. Nothing can interfere with that directive."

CAMP SLASHER LAKE: VOLUME ONE

Stuart swallowed a lump in his throat. He realized what her mission really was. He only hoped the rest of the crew didn't come to the same conclusion.

Baxter appeared to sweat, but Hopkins laughed. "Miss, you can't shoot that in here. The bullet will ricochet around the interior of the ship, destroying vital equipment, if it doesn't bounce back at you. How do you intend to complete your mission if you take out the Goliad?"

Clara turned crimson but didn't answer. The captain sent Jones to retrieve the gun. "Don't know how you managed to sneak that past us. Arms are supposed to be locked up when we're submerged."

The tension in the room dissipated. The captain put a fatherly hand on Clara's shoulder and ushered her back towards the wardroom.

Unfortunately, Baxter reached the same conclusion Stuart had.

"Wait a minute. Wait just one damn minute. Captain Hopkins, sir, relinquish the girl."

"Beg pardon."

"C'mon men. Don't you see? The plan wasn't to bring Hardy back," Baxter accused. "The plan was to steal the Russians' new secret weapon. And they're going to risk our lives to get it to the US."

"You don't know what you're saying, Baxter," the captain replied. "The US Navy wouldn't do that."

Stuart winced. Baxter did figure it out.

Baxter replied, "No, the Navy wouldn't do that. But a Cuban double agent? You're not just going to let that happen to us. Are you?" The crowd pressed in closer.

Hopkin's eyes darted, scanning the faces of the crowd, scanning the probabilities. If Hopkins allowed the men to kill Hardy, the Navy could easily discharge the captain for refusing to do his duty. On the other hand, if the crew led a mutiny–the only mutiny to ever occur on a United States submarine, a mutiny during a time when the country couldn't afford the least bit of weakness–the admiral would have his head. Perhaps literally.

Hopkins held up his hands. "Gentlemen, I feel your pain. You're worried about your fellow crew trapped below decks. Rest assured, there was no plan to leave them down there indefinitely. It is true that I knew there was a risk with Lt. Hardy, but the best intelligence gathered suggested he wouldn't feel the full effects of... his affliction... until the end of the voyage. Hardy is a SEAL and an American. He's one of us. But we won't let him hurt any more of this crew. Dr. Tereshkova!" He yelled over his shoulder.

The scientist inched out of the wardroom. "Y-yes, sir."

"We need to stop, Lt. Hardy–"

"You will kill him?!"

"Don't interrupt, miss. No, I said we need to *stop* Hardy. You and I and our medical staff are going to have a chat about how best to sedate the lieutenant, then these men are jumping into the breach."

The crew clapped each other on the back and smiled. Hopkins beamed at the crowd and locked eyes with Baxter for a moment. The petty officer stopped grinning. No words needed to be said. Baxter was in trouble. Only a hell of a lot of ass kissing could save him.

Hopkins, Tereshkova, and Cruz left to confer with the hospital corpsman.

Much of the crew was dismissed, but twenty were selected to open the hatch and descend to the lower deck. The plan was to dogpile Hardy and deliver the sedative via hypodermic needle. Five of the men carried the needles, enough to put Hardy down for good, if worse came to worst. Stuart suspected they would kill Hardy if they got the chance. The captain had orders to return Hardy alive. They did not.

Neither Stuart nor Baxter were sent below. The officers clearly wanted to keep an eye on Baxter. Fomenting this level of unrest, even for a good cause, was bad for morale. The machinist mate's career was in jeopardy.

Stuart expected to hear back soon from the group of twenty

men. He couldn't lose himself in his work. His head was full of nightmarish daydreams. The sonar spread through the silent deep and echoed off the sea floor below.

He imagined what the twenty men saw. They found men barricaded in their rooms, holding the door against the Russian-made beast. More were dead on the floor, faceless in Stuart's limited imagination, wallowing in their own blood. Despite the constant hum of the ship, it was quiet. There was nowhere for the giant to hide. Hardy could be waiting to ambush the squad, but Yelena said he would need to feed. The lieutenant stood before a refrigerator door, cramming food into his gaping maw. The squad circled behind his back; guns raised and...

Stuart took a break. He couldn't focus. He paced the hall, hoping to rid himself of the hideous imaginings. He couldn't. He had to know, had to check. The daydreams followed him down the hall.

The hatch lay open, unguarded. At the bottom of the ladder, fresh blood splattered across the deck. He hated to think whose it was.

He felt a hand on his shoulder and flinched.

"Hey, where did the guards go, Stu?"

"Baxter, you scared the bejeezus out of me. What guards? Haven't they already captured Hardy?"

Baxter shook his head. "I passed by here a few minutes ago. Was gonna go to the wardroom and talk to the skipper, but Lt. Cdr. Jones wouldn't let me in."

"But if no one's guarding the hatch..."

There was a loud clang and shouts coming from the reactor room down the hall.

Hardy was loose.

Stuart and Baxter ran, shoving past men in the control room to get to the wardroom. They both pounded on the door.

"I thought I told you to get lost," Jones protested as they moved past him. Dr. Tereshkova was crestfallen. She knew what happened as soon as she saw them.

So did Captain Hopkins. "What are you two doing here?"

THE DEATHLESS by VINCENT WOLFRAM

They told him. Hopkins blanched.

"Have you gone down there? We sent twenty men..." They were silent. "Dr. Tereshkova. Ms. Cruz. We are going to need your expertise. Assist Baxter and Stuart in finding and eliminating Lt. Hardy."

"Eliminating?!" Yelena yelped.

"If all twenty volunteers were incapacitated... This mission has become a complete disaster. The only way to salvage it is to kill Lt. Hardy and save the rest of the crew. Yelena, you said it yourself. You can't cure him with the tools at your disposal. We're still a day away from Pearl Harbor. You know what must be done."

Dr. Tereshkova looked like she was on the verge of tears, but she nodded in assent. Clara Cruz put a hand on the scientist's shoulder. Baxter sneered at the women but didn't speak.

"If he's loose, he could be almost anywhere in the sub," Hopkins said, scratching his chin.

"I've got a pretty good idea of where to look next," Stuart said. "We heard yelling from the reactor room."

There was a knock at the door. Jones groaned, "That better be Ramirez bringing me a coffee."

He opened the door, and Hardy drove the dive knife into his chest. The XO's ribs cracked, and he spat a stream of blood down his shirt.

"Shit." Jones crumpled.

Hardy had to duck to enter the room. He looked primeval, a Neanderthal nightmare. He was now seven feet tall. Ridges of bone peered through deep gaps in the flesh of his face. His boots had split, toenails like clamshells poking through the flaps. His fists were gore-soaked knots of bone.

Hardy spoke in a voice so deep it was barely intelligible. "Captain, I would like a word with you." The giant grinned and the skin split, revealing teeth all the way back to his molars.

Hopkins backed behind his desk and rifled through his drawers.

"Lt. Hardy." Dr. Tereshkova stepped in front of the SEAL.

"I know this is not you. Please listen to me."

"Yelena!" Clara cried and stretched out her hand to stop the scientist.

"It's alright. He knows me. Please, lieutenant. I did not just assist in your rescue because I had a guilty conscience. I know you have... feelings for me. Max. Please. I love you."

Hardy regarded the woman. For a moment, it looked like he would raise the knife, but his hand wavered. He got down on one knee and held out a massive hand to her.

"You were always kind to me. The KGB agent stubbed out his cigar in my gunshot wound. But you bandaged my arm. You know how I felt then. Please, forgive me..."

He pulled her forward gently and pursed his lips. She leaned forward, kissing his bulging face.

Clara let her arm fall.

Hardy pulled back a few inches to say, "You are so sweet," and resumed kissing her. Then his lips drew back, and he bit into the front of her face. There was a crunch as he bit through her teeth and a snap as he wrenched his head backward, the ragged stump of her tongue lolling down his face.

Dr. Tereshkova screamed, her hands shaking in front of the ruin that was her mouth.

"*So* very sweet," he said, savoring the tongue. "Except that you made me like this."

With a flick of his wrist, Hardy cut through her neck, severing the spine. Her head dropped, and her body fell after.

Cruz rushed up to deliver a flying kick to Hardy's gut, but he backhanded her, sending her crashing to the wall.

"She tried to save you, Hardy," Clara grunted, wobbling back to her feet.

"Too little too late. I'm already gone."

Captain Hopkins pulled a Beretta from his desk. Apparently, the rules for firearms didn't apply to him. He fired fourteen shots into Hardy.

Most of the shots hit the lieutenant's chest, but one got ricocheted off the dome of his head. A bright slash of bone and welling blood appeared.

Hardy did not fall.

Baxter fled the room, ducking under a swipe of Hardy's large hand.

"You can' kill me Cap'n," the SEAL slurred. "I can' die."

He slapped Stuart out of the way and brandished the dive knife. "I'm Cap'n ow. I'm goin' back, and I'll shove this righ' up the PREZDEN'S ASS!"

Hardy raised the knife, and the captain fired. The bullet caught the SEAL in the hand, and he dropped the knife.

"Run," Hopkins shouted at Stuart. "Don't waste ti–"

Hardy clapped his hands on both sides of the captain's head and squeezed. "Ma'e me drop m' knife."

Blood ran from the captain's eyes and nose.

Stuart slung his arm around Cruz and hurried her out the door. Behind him, Stuart heard the crack and wet gush of a skull imploding.

III

Hawaiian Ridge – 300 km from Pearl Harbor
October 14, 1986

STUART AND CRUZ FLED THE wardroom, running past bodies slumped over the controls. Stuart thought he could hear men hiding in the bridge above, but he didn't want to bring Hardy's attention to them.

The SEAL didn't give immediate chase. Stuart was revolted by the idea that Hardy was toying with them... or feasting on the captain.

"Hold on, I need to check if..." Stuart didn't finish the thought before sprinting to the sonar room. Cruz limped after. Empty. The men must have fled. He tried the weapons room further forward, but the door was locked.

"Hey. Hey!" Stuart rapped loudly.

There were curses from behind the door. "Go away!"

"But I'm with Ms. Cruz. We need somewhere to hide from Hardy. He's loose."

"Don't you think we know that? Baxter hasn't even come back. Now get the fuck away before Hardy gets here."

Stuart turned to Cruz. "Sonar's out. Weapons shut tight. Without the control room, we're blind and..." Stuart trailed off.

They could hear Hardy's footsteps before they could see him.

Stuart grabbed Clara's hand and pulled her into the nearby bathroom. There was room enough for them to stand shoulder to shoulder.

Hardy's footfalls clanked along the steel hallway. They

stopped before the door. Stuart found his hand entwined in Clara's. Neither breathed.

The footsteps wandered on, moving towards the weapons room. There was a loud knock and faint voices.

"I told you, man, you can't come in."

"Oh Nooooo?" These might have been words or just moans. The voice was wet and deep and inhuman, the speech of an ancient cave system.

There was an awful clangor, and Stuart knew this might be their only chance. They opened the bathroom door and peered into the hallway.

"Lemme in. Leh mee iiiin."

Stuart only took long enough to see the bony back of the SEAL's head before trotting down the hall to the hatch. They could hide in a bunk room below decks. Maybe the men sent to subdue Hardy were still down there. Maybe the night watchmen were sealed in their rooms.

"Dios mio," Cruz uttered.

A sailor was crawling up the ladder, hands slipping on each rung. His fingers were slick with blood.

Tap. Tap. One rung at a time. Tap. Tap.

His breaths were shallow. His arms quivered. Stuart and Cruz peered down but couldn't speak.

Hypodermic needles pierced through both eyes. Vitreous humor ran down his cheeks like gelatinous tears.

Shrieks rang from the fore of the ship. Hardy must have caught someone. Stuart and Cruz weren't safe. They had to run.

"I'm, I'm sorry," Cruz spoke down the hatch, running to catch up with Stuart.

"Who's there? Wait, don't leave me down here," the climbing man cried. "You have to help me. I don't know where he is. I-I don't know where to hide."

Stuart was ill. No one guarded the reactor room door. No one was there to give him a radiation badge. As he crossed the threshold, cancer was the least of his concerns.

"Please!" the man shouted down the hall.

CAMP SLASHER LAKE: VOLUME ONE

Clara and Stuart closed the door on his last desperate words. "I CAN'T SEE!"

The reactor room was louder than the others: the whine of steam and shush of water pumping through pipes. Stuart hoped they would be able to hear the creature coming.

The reactor dominated the center of the room, a two-story, copper-colored drum radiating tentacles of piping. Stuart and Cruz stood on a metal grating walkway that circled the room. Computers and instruments lined the walls, but there wasn't anyone to monitor them. Stuart hoped they were hiding in the maneuvering room aft.

Bang.

Hardy was on the other side of the door.

"Lemmeinnn!" He must have been bellowing like an elephant, but his voice sounded thin through the steel door.

"How could this have turned to shit so suddenly?" Cruz sunk down to the grated floor, leaning back against the railing. Stuart sat beside her and aired out his shirt. The room was stifling and warm. Water condensed along the pipes carrying cool water to the reactor. "I mean, you guys are supposed to be soldiers. Best of the best. Why the hell didn't you all get together and... I don't know, shoot him?" She put her head in her hands.

"And guarantee everyone would die?" Stuart glared at her, but her lip was quivering. It occurred to him that she had just lost a friend. "Sorry. We just... the crew needed to plan more to take down a threat like Hardy. We rushed into things. And when we can only stand in rows, two men shoulder to shoulder, I don't know that guns would have helped much."

"They didn't."

Stuart and Cruz jumped, hearts hammering in their chests. Baxter spoke from the walkway below, cradling a shotgun. They hadn't heard him walking around under the hiss of the pipes.

"When'd you grab that?"

"And from where?" Cruz asked, leaning over the railing.

"Why you want to know, Cuban?" Baxter said, raising the 12-gauge.

"Point that goddamned thing elsewhere before you blow my head off!" Stuart shouted.

Baxter hesitated but lowered the weapon. He paced the metal walkway, clicking up the steps to the top level to meet them. His gaze never left Clara as he circled the room.

"Baxter, we saw Hardy take a full clip. You think we can take him with a shotgun?"

Baxter tightened the grip on his gun. "Maybe. Maybe not. The squad took pistols and rifles below decks, not just the hypodermics. They meant to end things. To end Lt. Hardy. But I don't see any of those guys walking around, do you?"

"No. We only saw Hardy," Stuart admitted.

"So, it's hopeless," Clara groaned, running her hands through her hair.

Baxter shrugged. "Not necessarily. I mean, I only have two shots, but I'm prepared. I'm the best shot on board." His eyes flicked to the door. "Not that I'm going to open the door to take a shot."

"Are there any more guns left in the maneuvering room?" Cruz asked.

Baxter narrowed his eyes. "No. Crew took them for the turkey shoot below decks. Only gun left is this one. So, we're not going to open this door..." A loud bang on the door made him flinch. The shotgun rattled in his hands. "...where was I? I said, we're not going to open this door, unless we have to. Cause I don't exactly trust you to help us hunt down the lieutenant."

"Why the fuck not?" Cruz asked through gritted teeth. Stuart tried to come between them, but the spy wasn't having it. She pushed Stuart aside and stood in front of Baxter, who raised the gun barrel reflexively.

"I know your kind."
"*My* kind?"
"I know a Cuban when I see one."
"I'm American."
"Don't look like one."
"Fuck you. My parents are from Cuba. I'm from Florida."

The mouth of the barrel pressed into Clara's sternum. Baxter shook his head. "I knew it. All along I knew it. Stuart, you didn't believe me, but you were wrong, you stupid son of a... whatever. Water under the bridge. Let's just ice the spy, and you and I can hunker down in the maneuvering room where it's a little cooler. I'm starting to sweat here."

Clang. Clang. Clang.

Hardy was beating the door again, but now there was the harsh clang of metal striking metal. The door squealed and bent inward several centimeters.

"Jesus," Baxter murmured, then said, "That door's two inches thick. Nobody can just punch it in... what even is Hardy?"

Stuart started to pace. "We need to come up with a plan."

"What plan?" Baxter shrilled. "He took a pistol round to the head. He's breaking through the door with what? His hands? A hammer maybe? No man could do that." Baxter's eye twitched.

Cruz stepped neatly past the barrel and slapped him.

He was so taken aback that he didn't respond with anger. He was too shocked.

"Is there anything we can use to barricade the door? Anything we could use as a weapon, no matter how unconventional?" Clara stared him in the eye.

Baxter gibbered for a moment, fingers drumming on the forearm of the shotgun. He had already chosen his weapon of last resort.

"I got it!" Stuart snapped his fingers. "Clara, follow me. Baxter, stand guard and shoot him if he comes through the door before we're back."

"Stand guard?" They left without answering him. Baxter stood in front of the door, looking less than confident with the

THE DEATHLESS by VINCENT WOLFRAM

12-gauge.

They couldn't fight him in hand-to-hand combat. Hardy was as big as a Kodiak by this point. They also couldn't guarantee the SEAL would go down if they hit him with the shotgun. If Baxter shot even a little wide of the mark, Hardy might tear them apart before he bleeds out. *If* he would bleed out.

No supplies were to be found in the reactor room. Every centimeter of space was dedicated to harnessing nuclear power and preventing it from irradiating the ship. Stuart and Cruz moved further aft to the maneuvering room.

The door was open a crack. Rivulets of blood streaked down the front, and a broken fingernail lay at the threshold. Inside, the maneuvering room was filled with gauges and instruments but no sailors. Without a helmsman at the wheel in the control room, without sonar and radar techs scoping the area, the submarine was driving blind. They needed to kill Hardy quick if they wanted to save the sub and themselves.

As they searched, Stuart quizzed Clara on the lieutenant's biology, but she had only gleaned pieces of information from Dr. Tereshkova. Most of it was too technical for her understanding, but she knew that Hardy had reached a kind of developmental critical mass. There was no stopping the process at this point.

Cruz found a utility closet set before the turbine generator room in the rear. The closet was filled with cleaning supplies and repair tools. Stuart grabbed a mop, a bucket, and a bottle of condensed liquid soap. Cruz grabbed rubber gloves, bleach, and a coil of wire.

"What are you two doing out here?"

Stuart raised the mop in self-defense, but it was only Ramirez, speaking from the doorway of the turbine room. The generator roared and rattled.

"Thank goodness. Recruit, do you have more survivors back there?"

"Oh yeah. I got chased through the reactor room to maneuvering. We sealed up before Hardy got to us, but he grabbed Lou and dragged him away. I nearly–pardon the language, ma'am–I nearly shit my pants."

Stuart was grave. "Get them up here. We're going to have to fight Hardy to get to the control room. If we don't have someone helming the ship, we're all dead."

Ramirez went back to coax out the men but returned shaking his head. "A senior officer told them to stay put until he gave the orders to come out. They aren't moving. I think they're in denial. They still can't believe what happened."

Stuart's shoulders slumped, but Ramirez quickly added, "I'll join you, though. If I'm going down, I'm going down fighting."

"You're a tribute to the US Navy, kid."

When they returned, the banging had ceased, but Baxter still looked nervous. "What do you think he's doing out there?" He barely gave Ramirez a glance.

Stuart filled the bucket with soap and started mopping the floor in front of the door. Clara strung the wire between railings at the level of her knees. The seaman recruit helped her tie the wire off.

Baxter continued, "No, I mean it. He could be out there planning something, while we're in here planning to, to, what are we doing here?"

"We can't outfight him, but we can outrun him. We're getting the floor slick, so we can slip him up on the walkway before he can get traction. Maybe trip him with the wire."

"What about the bleach?"

"He can't get us if he can't see us," Cruz said, pouring bleach into a powdery white nitrile glove. "If we can knock him to the ground, I'll dump the whole can of bleach on his face. If we have to run, I'll whip one of these at his head." She tied the wrist of the glove and waved the fluid-filled hand. The nitrile held for a while, but after fifteen minutes, dribbles of bleach bled from the fingers of the glove.

Clara tossed the disintegrating glove in the bucket, pulled a new one from the box, and filled it with bleach. She had to do this thirteen times.

THE DEATHLESS by VINCENT WOLFRAM

The wait was excruciating. Each minute was tense. Stretching those minutes over nearly three hours was a nerve-wracking eternity. Baxter visited the head several times, giving an ostentatious dirty look to Cruz each time. Stuart was also feeling itchy with anxiety and boredom. He swept the sweat from his brow compulsively, fearful that if one stinging drop fell into his eye, that would be the instant Hardy burst through the door. He would be blind, and the beast would charge him down.

Stuart had time to count the rivets around the door. He had time to consider using the bathroom and then talk himself into it and then talk himself out of it. Time to imagine Hardy gorging himself on the ship's pantry and on the dead. Time to wonder whether his family would ever know how he died. A covert mission can be disavowed. A man can disappear.

When the pounding resumed, Stuart felt sick relief. Each *clang* on the door, each impossible dent in thick steel, raised the bile in his gut. He was nauseated with adrenaline. This was the last stand of the USS Goliad.

A small sliver of light peered through a gap between the door and wall. The gap filled with the tip of a pipe, and the door wrenched open after five hard yanks. Hardy must have seen himself in the mirror because his head was bandaged. The once handsome face was now a mummified mask. His staring eyes were rimmed with skinless red. His split lips oozed onto yellowed teeth. Streaks of red soaked the loose bandages. His fatigues were torn by bullet holes.

Hardy spoke in an ursine groan. His voice was now so deep that he was unintelligible, speech robbed of meaning. His throat was a tree trunk. He looked like he could swallow a man's head.

Hardy had to crawl to enter the reactor room, a bent pipe in his fist. His bulk spanned the door, and he had to squeeze in his gut to worm through. When he got to his feet in the reactor room, he was able to extend to his full height, over seven feet tall.

"Baxter, shoot!" Stuart cried.

Hardy took a step forward and Baxter, screaming for

courage, met him with a blast to the chest. The force of the shot sent Hardy onto his back, his feet sliding out from under him.

Baxter marveled. "We did it. We did it! One shot and this monster goes down. How come nobody else could..."

Hardy jerked upright. Ragged flesh peeled away in a blast radius at the center of his chest. The 12-gauge slug was embedded in a fused set of ribs. Hardy had a set of mail armor under his skin.

The four backed up, prepared to run. Hardy lunged forward and skidded on the suds. He lunged again and tripped over the wire, snapping it, falling to his knees.

Instead of giving chase again, he straightened the kink in the pipe and threw it like a javelin, impaling Baxter. There was a sound like a rotten watermelon splitting. The man tumbled, and the shotgun fell from his hands to the lower deck. Baxter scrabbled at the pipe driven through his stomach, and then his blood-soaked fingers slipped away. He was dead.

"Shit!" Cruz shouted. "Grab the gun."

Stuart made for the stairs. Hardy tried to follow, but he couldn't get traction. Cruz tossed a glove full of bleach, but it bounced off the giant's head without splitting open.

Stuart leaped down the last five steps, landing hard on the lower platform. He staggered toward the shotgun.

Hardy got to his knee and looked up in time for another glove to hit his face. This time, the glove burst, scalding his eyes with bleach. Hardy bellowed, frantically tearing at his face to wipe away chemicals. The bandages fell.

His face was ragged, strips of flesh stretched too thin across ridges of bone. His skull had grown faster than his skin, and now the stretch marks had torn apart. His brow was heavy, his chin a slab of stone, his mouth too long for a human, too full of teeth. He had the mouth of a skinned bear, jaws crowded with teeth.

As the lieutenant writhed, Stuart snatched the shotgun and bolted back up the stairs, trying not to stumble as he sprinted up two at a time.

THE DEATHLESS by VINCENT WOLFRAM

Hardy wasn't completely blind. He reached forward to grab Cruz, who had to leap back. Ramirez was just behind her. Stuart rushed to the top of the stairs to stand between Hardy and the others.

"That's it, Hardy. Follow the sound of my voice. You took the crew, but you can't take the Goliad."

Stuart aimed at the giant's head and fired. Acrid gun smoke bloomed.

He expected to see an explosion of teeth and bone fragments. He expected to be coated in a gout of blood and brains.

Hardy was too quick.

He threw his arm before his face and the slug broke through the radius and ulna. Hardy's forearm split in half, dangling from a rope of muscle. Hardy lifted the broken limb to his face and howled. His pain gave the three time to escape into the maneuvering room. They locked the door, knowing full well it would only hold Hardy for so long. Unless he bled out soon, he could bash his way through this door too. There was nowhere to run.

"What's next?" Cruz asked.

Stuart looked away.

"No. No, no, no, this can't be happening. We've tried everything. Everything! I've got to get back home. I have family. My mother. What will she think? What are they going to tell her?" Cruz stifled tears.

"We can't let Lt. Hardy, that thing, get back to the United States. I don't know if anything human is left in Hardy, but if he's smart enough to work the controls, he could make it to Hawaii."

"So, what do we do?" Clara asked.

Stuart sighed heavily. "Are you two ready to do something really selfless?"

"Yes. Uh, maybe. W-what's up?" Ramirez stammered.

"No," Cruz admitted, "but I love my home. I love America. And I'd do anything to save it. Does that count?"

"Hell yes, it does," Stuart said. "Here's what we have to do. We're going to dump the ballast, dump the water in the trim tank, and the Goliad is going to pitch forward as the rear rises. Since we're maintaining speed, the sub is going to dive. And dive. And dive. Until we hit bottom, or we surpass the operational depth limit. At crush depth the sub implodes. End of Project Koshei."

"And the end of us." Cruz said.

"Last chance to back out of this."

"No. No, if I go out tonight, I'd better damn well go out saving America." Cruz smiled.

"Yeah, boss, what do we do?" Ramirez asked.

Stuart breathed deeply. "We're going to have to open the door... and let Hardy in."

The other two exchanged glances and nodded.

Ramirez shut off the main, fluorescent lights for the aft compartments, switching to the red lights used for nighttime operations. Under the dim crimson glow, Ramirez and Clara crept into the turbine room. Stuart volunteered to open the door to the reactor room.

He laid his hands on the wheel-lock, cool steel under his fingertips. His heartbeat in his chest, his lungs constricted. He turned the wheel slowly until the bolt retracted, and he stepped back.

Step. Step. Step.

Stuart eased backward, keeping an eye on the growing rectangle of darkness as the door swung open. The grated walkway was empty, save for the still body of PO Baxter.

Stuart backed up until the turbine room door was just behind him. He looked back to make sure he didn't trip. When he looked forward again, he saw Hardy leaning through the doorway.

"Suuuuuuuuuaaah..."

THE DEATHLESS by VINCENT WOLFRAM

The sonar tech bolted into the turbine room, rounding the central generator to hide. Stuart could see the shadow of the door on the ceiling. It slammed open, but Stuart couldn't hear it. The generator was deafening.

There was no way out of the turbine room except to circle the generator. There was nowhere to hide. The engine room lay past the generator, a dead end; here the remaining crew hid, desperately hoping Hardy wouldn't stray any further aft.

Stuart slunk up to the others, giving the signal. He couldn't make out their expressions in the red light, but he could see them nodding. Clara and Ramirez would circle around the generator on the starboard side. Stuart would take the port side.

Here was the gamble: who would meet Hardy on the way out?

Stuart gazed at Clara. He wished he could offer last words. He wished he could see her face. There was no time.

He rounded the port side, and for a terrible moment he thought he would make it through. For a moment, he was afraid Clara would have to face the beast.

Hardy didn't immediately spot him. Even in the dim light, Stuart could tell his eyes were glazed with chemical burns. Hardy wandered to the port side. One broad hand, glittering with blood and pus, stretched forth, searching. The ruined arm hung limp at his side.

Stuart thought he might be able to sink back into the shadows. Hardy stiffened. His head turned to Stuart. He opened his great jaws and spoke into the roar of the generator. Stuart knew he couldn't hear it, but he thought he saw his name on the lieutenant's swollen lips.

It was what he wanted. It was what he feared. Stuart turned and fled around the generator. Hardy wouldn't chase Clara or Ramirez. They would survive to complete the mission. They would...

Stuart jerked backward. Pain burned like a blue star in his shoulder. He knew it was broken. He struggled to his feet, trying to sprint forward again. Stuart's legs swept under him, and his head struck the generator. His brain rattled in his skull.

Clara and Ramirez were already down the hall. They sprinted for the control room. Ramirez knew what to do. He would empty the rear ballast. He would empty the trim tanks.

Hardy's foot came down on Stuart's chest. He could hear the ribs break in his head. He couldn't breathe. One of his lungs had deflated, pierced by a shard of bone. Hardy grabbed the sonar tech's arm and pulled; one foot planted on the man's chest. Stuart stretched forward and snapped back.

The deck tilted underneath him. The hull creaked and popped.

Stuart watched Hardy lift his severed arm raise to his mouth and said, "We won. We won, you stupid son of a bitch." Petty Officer Second Class Franklin Stuart closed his eyes and bled out.

Two hours later, the sub's hull creaked and cracked and broke through.

The USS Goliad was no more. It sunk into the frigid lightless depths, never to be recovered.

Parts of the sub floated to the surface. Life preservers. Styrofoam packing material. And an emergency life raft.

The sub sank 30 kilometers away from Pearl Harbor. It was night, and the moon was full. Pale light glittered on the surface of the waves, and on a thick, bony hand that clung to the life raft.

The night was quiet. Hawaii was warm and calm and unsuspecting.

A Love to Die For

by J.D. Kellner

I WORKED A GOOD JOB, not a great job, but it paid the bills and served as a buffer between poverty and socio-economic annihilation. An auto-pilot lifestyle culminating in beers and self-loathing at the corner bar with my friends, who also suffered terribly dull lifestyles. I blamed social media at first. The instant accessibility of those more fortunate than myself flouting their charismatic yet strangely drivel experiences. Yet, I hungered for such a life. Spending my nine to five working inside a cube, puking out data forms to bosses I barely knew, was not the existence I wanted. College taught me that life could be fun and enjoyable. The caveat was needing alcohol and coeds. Now, ten years on, I had the alcohol, but gone were the coeds. It wasn't their fault. It was because of a lack of trying on my part.

I received a letter in anticipation of changing the game.

It wasn't entirely unexpected. During a conversation with my best friend Larissa, a dare was placed, saying I would not apply for the position. Under normal circumstances, she'd be correct. However, the odds of selection, coupled with my assumed average appearance, meant that I'd win the dare with relatively limited repercussions.

"You've been selected," Larissa said as she opened the

A LOVE TO DIE FOR by J.D. KELLNER

envelope on my behalf without haste. "I can't believe it, but you're going to be on TV!"

The show was called *Millionaire Mansion,* and as the name suggests, it was a mansion inhabited by a millionaire. More specifically, the estate was the home of an heiress named Adelita Agosti. The raven-haired beauty had graced the cover of many magazines since the death of her father. She was impossible to miss. Buxom, I believe was an apt description, and since she could have any man in the world, the idea of finding love via a reality show seemed beneath her.

"I suppose Adelita and I have something in common," I joked.

"Oh yeah? What might that be?" Larissa asked.

"We're both doing a show that is beneath us."

A few weeks, and one tortuous airplane trip later, I stood at the bottom of the stairs staring up at the Agosti complex, with a mixture of unbridled awe, and a sliver of resentment or perhaps jealously. You see these types of homes in magazines and on television, but you never expect to find yourself ogling from the stoop.

"Mr. Dillon. If you are ready, we can all enter the home and go over the rules of the show." A voice asked behind me. I turned to see a gaggle of other bachelors standing with the presumed host of the show. A man of short stature, but an ego bestowed upon him from the gods of media. Another of the *'why was he famous entourage'* that poisoned the well of the visual arts. Famous for nothing, but good looks, and made for reality television toxicity. Although, I had to admit, I admired his confidence, and the manner with which he carried himself. You don't get that doing data entry gigs.

"Of course, sir, I'm ready," I responded, and was quickly rebuked.

"Call me Daniel, Mr. Dillion."

"Call me Ezekiel," I retorted. Ezekiel, of course, was not my real name.

Daniel stopped in his tracks, and looked me square in the eye, responding. "I'll call you whatever the hell I want to, Zeke. You don't get to call the shots here. I run a tight ship as a host, and just because you view me as nothing more than a vapid host of a shallow-themed program, doesn't mean you have the opportunity to belittle me, got that?"

I froze, surprised by the tenacity of Daniel, and a glimpse of what it took to remain famous with no discernible talent or skills. I managed a nod and followed the rest of the group into the entryway. A dual grand staircase greeted us. In front, another smaller marble staircase descended into a great room. All of it was illuminated by the largest crystal chandelier I'd ever laid eyes on. Each section was a prism of luminescence, only found in the purest of genuine crystal. Ahead, the great room housed a large, round, glass table with enough chairs for each contestant.

"Gentleman, take a seat," Daniel ordered and gestured to the immense table. Each of us received a bottle of mineral water and a meal bar. Realizing that since departing the airport, food eluded me, the food disappeared in a wash of water. "The producers selected each of you for your charisma and appearance. I know a few of you are reality show regulars, and you'll be the drivers of the show. Those of you new to the game, follow their lead, and try not to swear too much on camera. Lastly, we'll need you to turn over your phones, so nothing gets leaked to social media. Daniel passed around a basket and each of the contestants placed their phones inside.

"You'll get your phones back at the conclusion of the show. A few days without a phone never killed anyone. Now, any questions?"

One of the bachelors, I assumed, raised his hand. "Trevor here. When I was on Love Island, we were given access to the bar whenever the cameras were off. I assume that will be the case here?"

Without hesitation, the next piece of television meat spoke up. "You guys may recognize me from 'Free to Love' and 'This Time for Real'," he waited for recognition, but the crippling silence mercifully pushed the conversation. "Tyler—never mind. Do we get a test drive before we pull it off the lot?"

A series of high fives startled me back to the moment and Daniel's exasperation with the brofest.

"The name of the game is simple. No one can leave the mansion under any circumstances unless there is an approved medical emergency. All food and drinks will be provided without limitation. I caution that excessive drunkenness is frowned upon by Adelita and the producers. She'll present herself in a moment as an introduction."

"Then the party is on!" barked out Trevor. He raised his shirt and revealed an impressive set of abs. Core strength be damned, but never before has a set of abdominals frightened me.

"Are you just here to party?" I asked, realizing my mistake in engaging with him.

Without dropping his shirt back over his washboard abs, he stepped towards me. "What of it, bro?" He challenged.

"Easy—bro," I responded. "Some of us are here for love."

The room burst out into laughter, and despite my preconceived notions of these men, I found myself embarrassed. Before I could respond, a woman's voice interrupted from the top of the balcony.

"Take it down a notch, boys," she said. Looking up, I realized that I had embarrassed myself in front of Adelita. A woman of means glared down at me in disdain. I wondered if she picked the lucky men, or if producers, huddled away in a backroom, sat through a hastily made presentation of our applications. Maybe she was the ringleader of the project. Picture this—Adelita sips on a glass of expensive Romanee-Conti yanked carelessly from her late father's wine cellar while she swipes left or right. "Now that we've all settled," she continued. "We can get down to business." The men whooped and cheered. Adelita moved on from the frat-like behavior without batting an eye.

She proceeded down the staircase and took her position at the head of the table. Up close, her striking beauty paralyzed the room. Her hair looked like midnight wrapped into a neat bun atop her head. She wore a blue evening dress and black pumps. A thin, black belt, with a gold buckle, completed the ensemble save for the ridiculously oversized diamond necklace plunging into her cleavage. If she had any work down, I was blind to the craftsmanship — Bravo to the surgeon.

"The rules are simple. Dates will occur each night in a separate wing of the mansion. You will not return to the others but will be sequestered to guest quarters on the other side of the compound. This is so you cannot start unnecessary drama, but it is mostly done to maintain our personal intimacy."

Murmurs spread like a growing rain through the room. None of the so-called veterans of the love show circuit knew precisely what to say, and neither did I. When Larissa brought the advertisement requesting applications, I barely took the time even to consider how this might all play out. I thought of the other shows she'd mentioned, and the surface-level nature of each seemed easily navigated, but this — this intrigued me.

The producer stepped up next to Adelita. "The cameras are hidden throughout the mansion, and unlike some of the other love shows, no interviews are required. Just enjoy the downtime and think of ways you can impress Adelita when you get the chance." He added.

"Yes, each evening, one of you lovely candidates will join me for dinner and other — activities, while the rest of you can just lay back and relax," she said, gesturing to the whole of the house. "Now, which one of you is Raj?"

A tall, dark, and devilishly handsome Indian man stood up. Dressed to the nines would be a fitting expression. His hair was slicked back, revealing high-bone cheeks, and a perfectly trimmed beard — a stark contrast to the rabble of hairs that decorated my face. The designer suit and shoes further separated him from the others.

He strode towards Adelita, gave a brief introduction, and his intentions of loving her forever—some other shit I failed to care about, and without another word, the two disappeared into the west wing of the mansion, leaving us befuddled as to the actual rules of the game.

"So—so are the cameras on?" Trevor asked.

Daniel grinned but not just any grin. A wide, slanted grin that was so cartoonishly evil I found myself questioning its very existence. I found myself staring at the producer even as the other contestants found their way to the nearby lounge. An entirely stocked bar and televisions greeted them, mirroring a hotel lobby rather than a home. While the others helped themselves to top-shelf booze, I stared down the dark hallway into the west wing. *Where were the cameras?*

"Zeke, are you hitting up the liquor?" Trevor asked, snapping me back to the moment. "Oh, my name isn't Zeke. I was just being a dick," I answered. "Call me Brock."

"I'd rather call you Zeke," Trevor quipped. "You're new to the circuit. That's obvious, bro. Take a seat, and I'll let you know how to make the best of the show." And so it went, forced into listening about how to score gigs and tv show deals afterward, and tips on advancing through the elimination phases of any dating show. Surprisingly, his advice made sense in every way except the conventional one. Maintain a strong personality but keep it under control, work out three times a day, and build a tolerance to all manner of boozy drinks. Entirely impractical for a day-to-day existence, but I admit, Trevor made a living I never thought possible.

The following morning, I awoke with a headache which wasn't wholly unexpected, but I could not recall drinking more than a few cocktails. I wondered if the bartender made the concoctions stronger than expected. After brushing my teeth and getting sorted, I walked out onto the balcony for the first time. The backyard, if it could be called that, was immaculate. A large kidney-shaped pool glistened in the California morning sun. A few of the others exercised nearby, and one of them sat poolside with a bloody Mary.

I got dressed and made my way out to the rest of the group. Daniel mingled among the others, and as I entered the patio, he turned to greet me. "Zeke. Adelita likes an early riser," he said, gesturing to the others who eagerly took it upon themselves to stand out, while ironically conforming.

"I get up early for work, not play," I countered. "She'll just have to get used to it if she wants me."

Daniel grimaced and brought everyone together under a large wooden pergola. String lights lit up the patio, but a shadow prevailed over Daniel's face, masking a devilish grin as he made the announcement of the previous night's date.

"Raj's date went well, and he's anxiously awaiting word from Adelita about what comes next. For you, the decision has been made for you," he said, pausing before turning his attention to Brad, a financier from New York City. "Brad, Adelita has summoned you for a daytime date. Make us all proud."

Brad raced off to the west wing of the mansion while, once again, we found a need to waste more time. I choose a stroll around the grounds rather than get into the pool or get drunk. I hadn't eaten, but the headache drove away pangs of hunger and replaced them with a nerve-wrenching pounding. The mansion grounds stretched for hundreds of acres, but a considerably high brick wall fenced in the inhabitants, and the contestants of the show. One of the rules we received in the handbook was the insistence of not leaving the area, or forfeit the show, and payment of all travel expenses. I didn't plan on leaving. I could hardly afford paying back the production company for the flight, rental cars, or food. A row of balconies connected the various rooms in the west wing. I scanned the roof and was surprised when I did not see a single camera. One thing did catch my eye. A red-stained window. Not a stained-glass window but *paint?* I wondered. I decided to take a closer look at it when night fell. I returned to the group and laid low until the sun dipped behind the sierras. However, my novice spy escapades would have to wait until after Daniel picked the next date.

After a few hours of swimming, drinking, and general boredom, Daniel returned to the group, and as with Raj from the night before, Brad did not return to the group. This was not entirely unexpected as that was the rule of the show after all, but never seeing either again just felt—wrong. It was like each man fell off the face of the earth. The third man chosen went by the name of Raphael, and the first thought that ran through my mind was, if she didn't select him, then she had poor taste. Raphael was the epitome of tall, dark, and handsome. I won't lie. Even I had a man-crush.

"Good luck to Raphael!" Daniel chirped. "The rest of you can grab dinner, and drinks are available at your leisure, in the dining area."

I followed the group to the dining area before turning off towards my room.

"Aren't you hungry?" Daniel asked, stopping me in my tracks.

"Just want to lay down for a bit," I responded, hoping that would be enough, but he persisted.

"Zeke, the cameras need you in the public eye as much as possible. You have remained aloof and withdrawn, which is against the contract—"

I held up my hand. "About those cameras. Where the hell are they? I haven't seen them, or any other crew member, for that matter. It's like we're alone out here."

Daniel paused and tilted his head as one might with a toddler learning to use a fork. "That's part of the fun," he grinned. "I promise the wait will be worth it."

A chill ran up my spine, eliciting an unusual amount of goosebumps. Daniel rubbed me the wrong way and not in a corporate office type of way. No, instead this was in a possible serial killer manner. Like, if I fell asleep near him, I wouldn't be surprised to wake up with him staring at me from a corner stroking a butcher's blade.

CAMP SLASHER LAKE: VOLUME ONE

When the sun disappeared behind the mountains, I made my move. The closest thing I had to a set of spy clothes was a charcoal heather soft t-shirt and dark blue denim jeans. I looked ready to raid the fridge for beer but not prepared for a covert operation. I reasoned that if I got caught, I'd just play dumb. Daniel must think I'm a moron anyway. I proceeded to the ground level of the east wing down via a back stairwell. I noted the lack of cameras and pushed open a double glass door into the night air. I could hear the others laughing in the lounge with the occasional cheer as a game played out on television. I followed the hedges and tried keeping beneath the view of the balcony. Reaching the end of the hedge line, I pushed through the sharpened limbs, tearing my shirt.

"Son of a bitch. I liked this shirt," I swore and pressed to the lower patio. A large red paver patio was all that stood between me and the walk-in entrance to the west wing, and insight into what was really going on around here.

I found the lower doors locked from the patio. I pressed my face up against the glass and peered into the blackened room. The first thing I noticed was the distinct lack of furniture—no couch, no desk—hell, not even a folding chair. For a multi-million dollar spread, it came as a surprise seeing a room completely empty. Each door I encountered was the same. It was locked and empty. To the right of the last entry was a two-story lattice.

"My greatest 1980s fantasy comes true," I quipped before beginning my climb, thanking the rebirth of hacienda-style homes in California in real estate. Ascending the wooden slats, I lifted myself up over the railing. I'm not what I used to be, that's for sure, I realized after a few minutes of catching my breath and beginning a weight-loss mantra. I wondered if Trevor would need a moment to catch a breather after the climb. I jiggled the handle, and the door pushed open. Inside, the room was the definition of minimalist. A single leather dining chair and a lamp hung from the ceiling. It was almost like—suddenly, the door swung open. I ducked back out on the balcony and peered into the room. Adelita walked in, dressed in something akin to a dominatrix outfit. Black leather bustier, a latex skirt, and knee-high, jet-black, leather boots. It was hot, and completely unexpected, but not as much as the next part.

Raphael stumbled into the room. His shirt torn, and his feet bloodied. Each step he took appeared painful; he wore an empty look in his eyes. It was as if he was drugged. He stumbled until reaching the chair. Forced into the seat, he stared blankly ahead. The light flickered above him. Adelita circled the chair, her hand stroking the back of Raphael's head before whispering in his ear. A hazy nod followed, and Raphael struggled to put his arms behind the chair to be bound. Resisting the urge to burst into the room, I began shaking as Adelita disappeared into the shadowed corner, returning with a leather roll, the kind used in carrying tools or other equipment. As she unfurled the wrap, it became clear what it carried…knives.

"What the hell is she into?" I asked myself as I watched her pull out a fixed tanto blade from the wrap. The steel reflected off the small bulb as she casually strolled towards Raphael, straddling the bound man. She raised the knife and plunged it deep into his shoulder. A gloved hand muzzled the cries of pain as Adelita slashed down again and again. Blood gushed, spilling to the floor. It was the first time that I noticed the blood stains covering the hardwood. This wasn't the first time Adelita performed such monstrous acts. I looked up, and saw she disappeared into the shadows and was returning with a sword, a goddamn samurai sword. In one motion, she reached the blade high into the air and slashed down, severing Raphael's head.

"Jesus Christ!" I cried instinctively and stumbled backward before crashing over the railing. I landed with a thud on the landscaping below. My vision faded momentarily as I tried pushing myself to my feet. I stumbled and fell again, passing out. I awoke with Trevor's face staring down at me. I was poolside and a cocktail was placed in my hand.

"Bro? What the fuck were you thinking?" Trevor asked as I regained my bearings. "The west wing is off-limits, and you're up there trolling?"

The awareness of what happened rushed back. I shot up and looked around. The others mulled around the poolside. The lights were on, and the bar televisions blared. A headache found its way into my skull around the same time.

"Where's Daniel?" I asked.

Trevor shrugged. "No idea, bro. He left with Peter like twenty minutes ago. You've been out for like an hour. I said you needed a doctor, but Daniel said you'd be fine."

"If being gutted like a fish counts as fine," I retorted.

"What are you talking about?"

I pushed myself up and stretched. Pain radiated down my back, and my head swam, but I needed Trevor to see what I saw up on that balcony.

"Follow me, and I'll show you."

Trevor and I took the same path to the lattice and climbed to the balcony. As anticipated, he shot up to the top in no time and confidently leaped over the railing. As I pulled myself over the railing, Trevor opened the door and stepped into the room. The chair remained, and the bulb flickered, but the blood and Adelita were gone.

"This is what you saw?" Trevor questioned, poking at the light bulb. "You're not from LA, man, but these sex dungeons are everywhere. Just need to know where to look."

"She stabbed Raphael right here, man. I saw it, and blood was everywhere."

Trevor looked around and shrugged. "Not now, man, but let's see what else is going on in the west wing."

To my surprise, Trevor pushed the door into the main hallway. The lights flickered from the ceiling. The carpeted floor snuffed out the sounds of our footsteps as we stepped out into the west wing. A musty odor hung heavy as we approached another room. Trevor pushed open the door and shut it again.

"Well? What did you see?" I asked anxiously.

He shrugged. "Nothing."

"Nothing?" I pressed.

"No chairs, TV, or anything. Just a room with a walkout

onto the balcony."

Millionaires, especially multi-millionaires like Adelita Agosti, didn't buy a house without finding a way to decorate it. That was half the fun of being super wealthy—presumably.

We continued further into the west wing when we heard a groan from a nearby room. I opened the door and spotted Peter leaning against a wall. He was shirtless, and his stomach covered in slash marks. He stumbled towards us, Trevor catching him before Peter fell to his knees.

"What happened, bro?" Trevor asked, studying his wounds. "Zeke, look at these cuts. Fucking deep, man."

I knelt next to Peter. The cuts were indeed *fucking deep*. A serrated edge tore at his flesh. The blood-soaked giblets of Peter's abdomen hung from the wounds. Each gash was nearly a half-inch wide. Without immediate medical attention, he'd surely die from blood loss. Before we could put pressure on any of the wounds, the sound of a door opening scattered us, leaving Peter in his own blood. Trevor went out onto the balcony. This time, however, I left the door slightly ajar, and in walked Adelita with Daniel behind. Both seemed surprised as they approached Peter, who, from my vantage point, slipped into unconsciousness from blood loss.

"Dear Peter, I fear you won't make it to the end of the show," Adelita mused. "These cuts look—" she paused, looking up at Daniel. "Did you touch him?"

Daniel's eyes furrowed in confusion. "No, of course not. I wait until you are done. That I can assure you."

Adelita pulled a blade from her blouse. This time she did not wear the trappings of a leather-clad dominatrix but a pleasant sundress. A bloodstained, yellow, floral sundress with a hidden sheath. She pressed the blade against Daniel's throat. Fear overtook his visage. I looked over at Trevor, who could do nothing but mouth obscenities at the horrors before us. She returned her blade to her sheath and knelt next to Peter's lifeless body. Revulsion forced its way to me as she reached into the wounds and licked away the blood.

"Daniel, I think the time has come for the finale of the show. I grow bored of this game. Bring the others into the west wing. Place it into lockdown. I'll be waiting for your go-ahead for the fun to begin. I'll be in my office. Once everything is prepped, just leave the rest to me." Adelita stepped over Peter's body before turning back to him. Without another thought, she reached down and slit Peter's throat. I looked at Trevor, who, for the first time in the brief few days I've known him, looked self-aware.

Adelita cleaned the blade, and they left the room. I leaned against the wall and put my hands over my knees. *What kind of nightmare did I get myself into?* I came here for the free food and pool, and if I just so happened to find love, then all the better. Now, I was trapped in a growing terror.

"Dude, we need to get the hell out of here," he said, heading for the lattice to descend back to the patio below. I placed a hand on his shoulder.

"And what? Leave the rest of the guys to the slaughter? No, we need to find our phones and call for help."

Trevor nodded and entered the room. I checked for a pulse on Paul, but I could not locate one. In the hallway, the lights still flickered, but none of the doors remained open, and there was no sign of either Adelita or Daniel. Trevor and I crept slowly down the hall towards the far end of the mansion. Another large opening was up ahead. In the fading light, I could make out a chandelier, like the main entrance, but the crystals seemed scattered or broken. Approaching the west wing door, the devastation was evident. Smashed chairs, vases, and cracked walls greeted us as we entered. A stark contrast from the pristine setting pushed to the contestants a few days earlier. Three sets of double doors lined the far wall of the circular atrium.

"Which door?" I asked, realizing that Trevor had about as much insight into this place as I did. Yet, he moved quickly towards the door on the right.

"What if she's in there?" I cowered.

"Then, we run like hell, bro," he joked.

A LOVE TO DIE FOR by J.D. KELLNER

He pushed the door open, and our jaws hit the floor. Hung from meat hooks were the bloodless corpses of Raj and Brad. Like butchered cows drying in a shop. Slabs of meat waiting for the market. I vomited into my mouth, swallowing it back down, and looked around the room. Weapon racks filled with sharpened blades surrounded us. A large metal desk stood out as the only furniture in the room. I searched the desk and found a single drawer, and inside was a single keycard. I snatched it and headed to the door when we heard a voice.

"Why the hell is this door open?" A voice called out, immediately recognizable as Daniel's. He dragged Peter's body into the room.

"Daniel? What are you doing?" I demanded.

Daniel froze for only a moment, before pulling out a 9mm from his waistband, pointing it intently at my head.

"You should not be back here, Mr. Dillon."

"Are you going to kill me? Do Adelita's bidding?" I demanded. I watched Trevor creep along the far wall. Daniel did not see him and hadn't noticed his presence. "Can't you see this is wrong, Daniel?"

The unsuspecting host took another step, never lowering his aim. "This is bigger than you, Mr. Dillon, and I can't let you live." He pulled the hammer back.

If you are going to make a move, Trevor, you need to act now. I prayed and was immediately answered.

Trevor brought his elbow down hard on Daniel's right arm, dislodging the gun. The firearm slid across the floor, and Trevor wrestled Daniel. Trevor gripped Daniel by his arms forcing him down. Daniel struggled against Trevor's strength, but he was no match for the powerful frat guy, and he passed out.

"Where did you learn to do that?" I asked Trevor as he took possession of the gun.

He checked the chamber and tucked the gun into his waistband. "I worked as a bouncer for a few years. You learn all the moves needed to handle drunk assholes."

We made our way to the door and walked into the atrium,

only to be greeted by Adelita's blade. The tanto blade sunk deep into Trevor's chest, dropping him to the floor. Adelita reached down, pulled the gun from his waist, and pointed it at me. Trevor groaned and gripped at his stomach.

"You're coming with me," she said, gesturing with the gun towards the far left door. "Daniel, get up and help me with dear Trevor."

Daniel recovered from Trevor's choke-out effort and stumbled past me. He socked Trevor in the face with a quick jab before dragging him into the room where Raj, Brett, Peter, and now Trevor lay. "I'll get Peter hung up to dry, and Trevor shouldn't be far behind," he gasped, still catching his breath.

"Don't bother. Get the others into the west wing. I grow tired of waiting for my prize," Adelita chortled before turning her attention back to me. "Your date starts now."

She jammed the gun in my back and pushed me towards the door before plucking the keycard from my back pocket and holding it to the lock. The door popped open, and in we strode, unlike the horror show meat plants that made up the other room, I faced a much more standard room — if there was such a thing in this place. Two couches faced a gigantic screen, and in the middle of a coffee table sat a VR headset. To the right of the couches was a high-backed chair with restraining straps. *There's the messed-up part of the room.* I thought.

"Take a seat," she ordered.

I went for the couch closest to me.

"Not the time to get cute with me. Get in the restraining chair."

Reluctantly, I found my way into the restraining chair. Still pointing the gun, she strapped down my hands, my head, and my legs. Nothing budged, no matter how hard I tried. It dawned on me that I should have at least tried getting the gun off her. Now — well, now I was completely and utterly screwed.

"Why are you doing this? Why kill these innocent men?"

Adelita scoffed. "No man is innocent. None of these animals, including yourself, responded to the advertisement looking for love. None of them ever do."

"What do you mean, ever?"

"Daddy brought me to all kinds of high society events in my life. He never realized the torture I faced being an attractive young woman in a sea of ego-driven, entitled creeps. Every function was the same. Daddy would be pulled away by an investor, an actor, or one of the countless American oligarchs like himself, leaving me fending for myself."

"What does that have to do with me? With guys like Trevor?"

Adelita rolled her eyes and sat on the couch next to me. "I can't very well go on a murderous rampage against Americans foremost capitalists, can I? I needed an outlet, and with the money Daddy left, I found it through these fake finding love shows."

In the presence of a madwoman. There was no other way of describing it. A psychopath, with an unlimited bank account, and an unchecked penchant for the blood of innocents. Her beauty hid it all away beneath a veil of lace and silk. She was the genuine article, a true femme fatale.

"Once the world realizes we've gone missing, I—"

She held up her hand. "I've done five of these since Daddy died, and not once have the police ever even questioned me, and do you know why that is?"

I shook my head.

"Because you were targeted for this show. All of you lacked family or friends that would have any influence in finding where you disappeared to. Did you even look at the envelopes? The address for the show is not the address you saw on the application. We emailed your closest friends and waited for them to bring you to us."

I thought nothing of the address discrepancy, and when I took the car from the airport to this mansion, I paid no mind to the location. Larissa never mentioned where she found the show, and I never bothered checking. I had nothing to lose and only saw gain. Never in my wildest nightmares could I have anticipated the disaster that followed.

She rose from the chair and lifted the VR headset over my head. "I've been waiting for this moment. One of Daddy's friends developed drone technology in Silicon Valley and gave this to me as a gift." She placed the device over my eyes. The screen remained black for a moment until it fired to life. I saw the far wall of the room until hands reached down, revealing Adelita's face. She grinned before turning the image, and I could see myself sitting pathetically in the chair. A mirror image of depression and failure. A portrait of the final moments of my demise. Poetic, if not for the gruesome death I would surely suffer.

"With these remote image transmission glasses—"

"It's called a camera," I interrupted

"Remote image transmission glasses," she retorted. "You can watch all the fun. When I am finished with those fools, I'll come back, and put you out of your misery. The headset will record all the action, and with a few modifications, you'll be forced to watch," she said, and with a click, what felt like two hook-like appendages pulled my eyelids up. I winced in pain as she continued. "You should be grateful that the footage you'll get will satiate my desires for months. You'll be saving lives."

"You're insane. A murderer. Nothing more than a deranged psychopath with Daddy's bank account. A whore for violence that, like your victims, will face the ages without purpose, until you die and rot in hell."

Her grin widened. "I like when you talk dirty."

Suddenly, the mansion's comprehensive speaker system cracked to life with Daniel's voice.

"All contestants come to the west wing. Adelita has a surprise for each of you which will make your chances with her even better. Please leave your drinks in the lounge. You'll get a fresh one once you arrive."

I could see Adelita pull a roll of duct tape from a nearby drawer. This wasn't her first rodeo of pain. That much was evident. She bent over, and I watched as she ripped a length of tape before placing it over my mouth. As a doting mother might to her child, she kissed the front of the headset. "My time to shine, baby."

Without another word, she headed towards the door. My vision was now relegated only to the images she saw. She closed the door behind her but not entirely. She turned and glanced but made no motion towards it. If there ever was a gift from God, that might be it, but I remained incapacitated. I watched as she proceeded to the previous room where Raj, Brett, and now Peter hung from meat hooks. She selected a variety of blades from the racks and held them up for me.

"This looks like the winner tonight. A karambit." She added. "Daddy took me to weapons self-defense courses as a little girl. Learned a lot about the power of a good knife. If you want to field dress game or gut an enemy, the karambit works like a charm."

I watched in agony as she took her place at the side of the long-dead Peter. "Like a hot knife through butter, as they say."

A moment later, she turned and walked to Daniel. "Everything all set?"

He nodded. "Just need the drinks. A few seem rather suspicious since Trevor and Zeke disappeared. I would start with them," he said, reaching down for his phone. "Lance, Liam, and Chad are the three I would start with. Chad asked for his phone on numerous occasions."

These guys aren't so dense after all, I thought. It might not be enough to save me, but perhaps they could still come out of this alive and in one piece.

She handed Daniel the gun. "Take this barbaric device. Use it if you need to but keep it hidden. No one must suspect a thing when this starts."

Daniel nodded and tucked the gun into his coat for safekeeping.

Adelita reached behind the weapons rack and pulled out a nondescript bottle with a clear liquid inside. Daniel held a serving tray, and Adelita poured a shot glass for each of the contestants. The last glass, she filled with what looked like water, but I couldn't tell from the bottle type. The two left the chamber and walked down the long, west wing hallway. Each of the men seemed confused by the nature of the west wing as they awaited her arrival. She entered the great hall, greeted with cheers and clapping. As she approached, I watched as Daniel locked the door behind them.

"Calm down, boys. There's plenty of me to go around, but first, we must toast to the next step in the show. Raj, Brett, and Peter all left empty-handed, so I decided to step it up a notch. We're going to play a bit of a game. We've made this wing of the mansion a haunted house, and somewhere is a key that unlocks the pleasure suite. Whoever finds it gets a night with me to do *whatever* your heart desires. The rooms are designed to tug at your fears and force you to think critically. You may bear witness to things you've never hoped to lay eyes on.

"It's not my heart's desires," one of the guys whooped. The others laughed except for Chad. Adelita stared daggers in his eyes. I wanted to call out to him. To tell him to run, but I was nothing more than an impotent specter watching the doomed face of eternity.

There were five guys left out of the original group. Four were dead. I was strapped to a chair

"To us!" She cried, lifting her glass. The others followed suit. Some grimaced, and others winced at the strength of the liquid. Recovering, they started their mythical quest for the key to her bedroom. The lights dimmed, and each of the contestants went a different way, entering separate rooms. A few began their search in tandem.

Adelita followed Chad from a distance as he entered one of the spare bedrooms. Inside, turned-over chairs and tables greeted Adelita. Chad stumbled through the dim room, randomly checking end tables, but it was clear his cognition failed him. Whatever was in those shot glasses slowed him down. Adelita pulled the karambit from her blouse and approached Chad. He fell into the wall barely managing to keep his feet beneath him.

A LOVE TO DIE FOR by J.D. KELLNER

I called out into my taped mouth as she placed the blade against his waist. Before he could turn, she slid the blade across his belly, spilling his guts. I tried in vain to close my eyes from the vile act. Chad collapsed in a heap near the far window.

"One down and four to go," Adelita cooed. I watched as she wiped the blade on her dress and headed back out into the hallway. Daniel approached her. "Take Chad's body to the rest of them but be careful not to be spotted."

Daniel nodded and hurried into the room. Adelita continued looking for the others in silence. It did not take long, as she entered a lounge area where two more men stumbled, looking in vain for the key. As she approached, I recognized the one as a former minor league baseball player named Tre. Early on in this horror show, I overheard him talking about his days in Europe, playing for a team in Italy, before tearing his ACL to shreds. As with Chad, Adelita slashed across his gut, but the blade must not have been deep enough. Instead of the disembowelment, Tre fell forward, gripping his stomach.

"What the fffff—fuck?" He cried out, slurring his words. The drug in the shot had the desired effect. He crawled towards a bookshelf near the window and pulled himself up to his knees. Adelita stood over him, but as she slashed down, the other man acted, crashing into her. His movements, slowed by the drug, exposed him to her blade. Adelita grunted as she shoved him aside. Her attacker swayed as he stood before her. He threw a dull jab, easily dodged by the nimble Adelita. In one swift motion, she swiped the blade across his throat. Blood fountained from the fatal wound as he crashed to the floor. She turned to face Tre, who had disappeared from the room. For a moment, she appeared panicked. Her head was on a swivel, looking for the former ballplayer. Movement caught her eye near the window. She raced over and saw that Tre had plunged from the open window to the patio below.

"Fuck," she murmured. She pulled out her phone and lifted it to her ears. I could hear it ring and ring without response. "Damnit, Daniel, now is not the time to ignore my calls."

Suddenly, I heard a phone ringer. The ring got louder and louder as the user approached before a mysterious hand ripped the tape from my mouth.

"Zeke, you, okay?" A voice asked. I recognized it as Trevor.

"Trevor? I thought you were dead."

He let out a gargled laugh. "Almost. Let's get you out of this thing."

Trevor gently removed the headset and eye hooks. Blood trickled down my face, but awash in relief, I felt no pain. Free, I rose from the chair.

"Where's Daniel?" I asked, gesturing to the phone.

"Dead in the other room," Trevor managed. "I'm in a great deal of pain, Zeke. We need help, but I can't get into Daniel's phone."

I took the phone from Daniel, and while the lock screen was up, the emergency button hadn't been disabled.

"Call using the emergency button. Hopefully, they can track the call. Tell them what's happening."

"What are you going to do?"

"I'm going to kill that bitch."

Leaving Trevor, I entered the torture chamber, chose a lengthy, curved blade from the rack, and stormed towards the west wing entrance. I stepped carefully through the darkened hall listening for Adelita. The eerie silence hung heavy as I trekked from one room to the next. The final room next to the entrance of the west wing only had a single occupant—the corpse of the last contestant. Whirling out of the room, I left the west wing, and walked into the beautiful atrium that served as the center of the mansion. There, no more than a few yards from me, sat Adelita stroking the edge of her hooked blade.

"I don't know how you did it, Mr. Dillon, but here we are. You're the last one standing. The last one that must fall before my blade," she warned.

I thought about telling her about Trevor and that the authorities were on their way. That her murderous spree ended now. I thought about the shamshir I carried and if I genuinely had a chance against Adelita in a one-on-one knife fight. A woman whose privilege allowed her the luxury of taking blade fighting courses. A woman with no remorse and no soul.

She stood up and faced me in her blood-spattered dress and confidently stepped to me with the blade in hand—her slip dress swung with every step.

"You chose the shamshir, but something tells me you don't know how to use it."

I took a step back, trying to create space between us, but she closed quickly, swinging her knife. I dodged the strikes, lifting the shamshir to counter her blows. My amateur status clear against her talents. A few deflections later and she connected with my thigh. I winced in pain and danced away from a thrust at my midsection. Her movements were fluid from years of training, never slowed. I rushed her, slashing with the shamshir, throwing her off guard. She parried every blow, but I pressed, driven by rage. Trying to sidestep, her attire betrayed her as the pump snapped, sending her to the floor. I leapt down and squared the blade firmly against her throat. She dropped the karambit in submission.

"That is quite enough, Mr. Dillon," a voice bellowed.

Turning, I saw Daniel with a gun pressed against Trevor's skull.

"Drop the blade, or Trevor gets another hole in his pretty head," he demanded. I dropped the shamshir and stood up.

"Daniel, you don't need to do this. She's using you. You're a tool, nothing more," I tried reasoning. "Just put the gun down, and this nightmare can be over for everyone."

Adelita scooped up the shamshir. "You almost had me, Mr. Dillon. Damn, Gucci shoes broke on me. I'll be sending a complaint to them after you die." She pressed the tip of the sword against my throat. "Should I cut your throat?" She moved the blade to my chest, pushing in against where my heart would be. "Skewer your heart?"

"Daniel, you know what's going to happen after she's done. She's going to kill you for failing her. She's going to drain you of blood and hang you like the others."

He lowered his gaze. "She—she wouldn't do that. She knows I love her."

Still pressing the blade against my chest, she rolled her eyes. "Love is a myth, Daniel. Stop pretending it's love. Just shoot Trevor while I gut Mr. Dillon like a fish."

"No," he said bluntly. "Not until you say you love me."

Adelita lowered the sword. "I can love no man. I'm sorry, Daniel."

Daniel sighed and pointed the gun at Adelita. "No, I'm sorry." He pulled the trigger, striking Adelita just above her sternum. She slumped to the floor—her words muffled from the blood pooling in her throat.

Then, Daniel turned the gun on himself.

Trevor and I sat outside the lavish mansion. The sounds of sirens called in the distance. Both of us came seeking separate things but were united against an evil neither could imagine. Bloodlust knows not a particular face, but we must endure for those who came looking for love and left only their life behind.

Work Retreat

by D.W. Hitz

Chapter One

TEN-YEAR-OLD HAL WHIMPERED under his cot. Blood pooled across the cabin floor, dripping through cracks and patting against the earth below. It crawled toward him. The edges of crimson lakes on each side of the cot closed in on him, as unrelenting as the man-thing so few feet away.

Dismembered parts of his friends eclipsed his view of the door as well as the killer. He could see Billy's entrails and the cavity where his lungs once resided, but not his friend's face. He saw Carl's legs on top of Wes's abdomen. The torn edges of skin, fat, and muscle locked their images into his brain. They were no longer people, just pieces of organic matter that had been shredded by blade and muscle.

Boots stomped on wood. The man-thing moved. Clangs and thumps. He was tossing the cots.

Hal thought he was the last one, but maybe not. His chest pounded. Maybe someone else had the same idea? Or the killer was just being thorough? His fingers shook. He tried to clasp one hand in the other to still them, but then both hands shook together.

A scream pierced Hal's ears. The sound of wetness and the crack of bone. A gurgle, blood babbling over the mouth of another friend.

He had to stop moving. He had to be still, be quieter. It was his only hope.

Again, Hal heard the unforgettable sound of steel slicing air, then meat, then bone, followed by the thump of Benny Winter's face on the floor in front of his own.

Benny's eyes were wide. Tears still fresh, they glistened on his lids and cheeks.

Thump. Clang. Another cot tossed. *Thump. Clang.* Closer. A gray boot, leather, black-soled, set foot beside his cot. Blood ran down his dark jeans, flowing over the leather.

Hal's gaze became glued to the vision as a single bead hit the monster's lace and rolled down it. The red, glistening in the low light of the cabin, a single lantern Hal remembered the counselor lighting when everyone was running in. The drop rolled down the lace until it found the tip. It hesitated. Hal wondered if it was Benny's. Did it belong inside the head now staring at him just inches away? It released, diving toward the lake below, becoming one with the rest of his friends' blood. He thought maybe that was good. Maybe that meant his friends would be together in the afterlife. Camping in Heaven, running, canoeing, throwing water balloons.

The intruder grabbed the bottom of his cot. Dirt, as black as night, coated each finger, and blood sealed the nails. His fingers were massive. It was like the hand of a giant. No wonder he was able to rip the arm off a counselor.

It was then that Hal noticed the stench. It had been there since the killer came in, but now Hal realized it had been hidden below the scents of fear and his friends' piss and bowels. It was rotten. It was long sleeping death that had been somehow disturbed and now demanded company. It made the thought of what was to come next even more terrifying. Would he even see the afterlife, or would this thing hold onto him like some decaying plaything?

The cot began to lift, and Hal bolstered his resolve. It was now or never. If he didn't want to become like Benny, Hal had to move. He knew he had to, but how? Go where? He saw Benny's eyes. If he mis-stepped, the blade would take his head as well.

Hal pressed his hands against the floor. His fingers tensed, ready to thrust him up.

The cot flew, tumbling through the air, and crashing into the far side of the cabin. The stench of death grew from a trickle to a wall, slamming into Hal and freezing him in place.

Hal locked eyes with the killer. They were almost completely white, clouded over with a milky haze. He was possibly the largest human being Hal had ever seen, bulging with muscle, his limbs as thick as logs. His skin was gray and cracked, and Hal saw muscle, tendon, and maggots beneath. Yet, the corner of his mouth lifted ever so slightly at the sight of Hal, and Hal knew the madness below the rot was such an evil, the rotting thing before him was more of a vessel than a man.

The thing reached for Hal.

Hal was immobile. His brain had forgotten how to move. Piss puddled between his feet, and he trembled from his chin to his toes.

It seized his arm below the shoulder and lifted him into the air.

Hal hung, suspended above the ground with tears streaming from his eyes. Only groans escaped his lips, squeals of subconscious anxiety and primal terror at the pain soon to come.

He saw what could only be considered joy in the thing's dead eyes. There was no visual change, but Hal saw it. Maybe it was a psychic phenomenon or pure inference, but Hal observed escalating glee as the thing dropped the machete to the floor and grabbed Hal's other arm with his free hand.

Torment tore through Hal's body, yanking him from his daze. He screamed as the monster pulled on both arms as if to rip them free from Hal's ten-year-old frame.

WORK RETREAT by D.W. HITZ

The absolute terror gave way to pain and anger, and Hal finally felt his body responding. He raised both feet and stomped as hard as his ungrounded being could manage. The soles of his piss-drenched sneakers crashed into the monster's nose and left eye. He felt each collapse under his kicks.

The killer roared. He jerked and threw Hal into the clutter of upturned cots, dismembered campers, and blood.

Hal felt a snap and soared. He landed with the leg of a cot in his back and howled; there was crunching behind his lungs. Regardless of the pain, now he knew he had a chance. He sprang to his feet and ran toward the door. His left arm hung limp. He couldn't move it. It swung from his shoulder but also from a joint in the middle of his bicep that hadn't been there before.

Thunder from behind him. Stomping, booming like bomb after bomb as the killer's feet hit the floor. And getting closer by the second.

Hal ran through the door, glancing back and wishing he hadn't. He saw the thing's face and knew it would not stop until it had another chance to rip him into pieces. Its nose swung from a strand of gray flesh under a hole in the center of its face. Its left eye was a seeping depression of black and dark green ooze. Thin strips of eye tissue flapped in the oncoming air as each stomp sounded.

Hal jumped from the small wooden porch, over the stairs, and ran toward the woods. It was dark, and the woods were deep. It was the only hiding place he could think of. But somehow, he knew it wouldn't be enough.

He was twenty feet away, and the stomping mellowed to heavy thumps. The killer was on the grass now. Its strides, although swift, had no sense of urgency. They were confident. They were of a thing who knew it had inevitability on its side.

Chills ran through Hal as he crossed the threshold into the forest. He looked back, and his knees numbed. The thing was closer. It wasn't even running, but it was closer. How, other than pure evil?

A boom shook the campground. Black ooze, bits of fabric,

and gray meat flung from the monster's side.

Hal had to stop and see.

The killer turned and walked to his right, away from Hal.

Hal's gaze followed the monster's direction. Thirty feet from the thing stood Mac Jacobs, the camp's head guy. He held an old double-barrel shotgun in one hand and shook as he fumbled with shells in the other.

The killer closed in.

Mac slid one shell into its chamber. He pushed on the second, and it slipped from his unsteady fingers. His eyes shot from the red projectile on the ground to his pocket, judging which to target. He decided on his pocket and fished another out.

The killer raised his arm, only feet from Mac.

Mac screamed in terror and dropped the second shell. It hit the ground and rolled as he snapped his weapon shut and cocked back the hammers.

Hal's every muscle clenched as he stared at the confrontation. This was it. This was his life, as well as Mac's, on the line.

Mac raised the shotgun and fired.

Lead shot ripped through the monster's left shoulder. Huge chunks of gray and white flesh soared backward. Black blood sprayed and ran down his chest. And without a sound, his right hand snatched the shotgun's barrel.

Mac stared with wide, white eyes and a gaped mouth. The killer swung the long gun like a club. A crack echoed across the camp as it shattered into a newly formed grove across the top of Mac's skull.

Mac dropped to his knees. His expression was changeless, his brain all but mush inside his mangled skull. The monster spun the shotgun around and fed the barrel end to the camp leader.

Gags, cracks, and wet suction traveled to Hal across the night. He backed further into the woods as the killer crammed blue steel into the man's gullet all the way to the stock.

Chapter Two

FORTY-YEAR-OLD HAL FELT his eye twitch as he read the email. He'd heard rumors that the execs were going to pull something like this—he thought it was BS then and had to clench his teeth together to stop himself from shouting "Bullshit!" right now.

> *It is with pleasure and excitement that we announce this year's retreat will be at the Sun Beach Summer Camp.*
> *We know what you're thinking. Summer Camp is for kids! That's exactly why we're doing it, to bring the fun and excitement of youth into this year's office retreat.*
> *So, pack your bags for this weekend, bring the sunscreen and bug spray, and be ready to relive the best times of your life!*

Hal could hear his heart throbbing. He wanted to pick up his monitor and toss it from his cubical into the walkway. He wanted to take his keyboard into Dan White's office and smash the man's face into the keys until he could read QWERTY on the man's forehead in blood. He imagined it so clearly that he barely heard John's voice from behind.

"Hal?" It must have been the fourth time he said it—that tone, Hal was sure it was the one John used with his kids when he was pissed.

Hal spun. His face was red; he could feel it. He put on a happier mask for John—not quite the *you light up my life* face,

CAMP SLASHER LAKE: VOLUME ONE

but one that didn't say *this is all going to end in death.*

"So," John paused, judging Hal's expression. As the blood eased from Hal's blushing capillaries, he found the courage to continue. "Did you get the email? Sounds like fun, right?"

"I got it." Hal bit his tongue. It was bad enough he was going to have to revisit his past, but now it seemed he'd have to have his face rubbed in it as well. "Of course, a real beach might be better."

"No." John's smile grew even wider. "Canoes, archery, team games. It's going to be a blast."

Hal withheld the urge to punch his friend in the face. It wasn't John's fault he didn't know. The old sheriff of Custer Falls County had done an amazing job of keeping the tragedy out of the media. The camp was no longer called Camp Custer Falls, and it had been thirty years since he'd lost every friend he'd had at the hands of that monster.

"Yeah," Hal said. "I'm not so sure I'm going to go, though."

"No way, hombre. You got to. Didn't you read to the end? Mandatory for the Project Management Team and the Implementation Team. I bet they have games to put us head-to-head with those PMT bastards."

"Mandatory?"

"Yeah. And we're going to wipe the floor with them."

As much as Hal liked the idea of whooping those arrogant bastards in PMT, his stomach was rolling around and ready to launch his lunch in John's face. Sure, the Camp Custer Killer — or just Custer as he'd been nicknamed by those that knew about the incident — hadn't been seen in thirty years, but he was also never caught.

Hal's mind raced with reasons he could use to get out of this. Sick mother, sick cat, dying uncle. He could quit. The image of the late notice sitting on his counter at home from his mortgage holder flashed in his mind. Lose his job *and* his house? At least he'd be alive...

He pushed the thought aside. He was being stupid. Sure, this would force him to relive the most horrific experience of his life, but the chances that anything would really happen... Was that worth losing everything he had?

John held up his hand, inviting a high five. "We are going to kick ass."

Hal obliged the man, hoping it would expedite the end of the conversation. "Kick their asses."

"Hell yeah." John nodded enthusiastically and turned away; humming what Hal thought was Queen's, *We Will Rock You*, he headed back toward his desk.

Hal had gotten almost nothing done the rest of the day. His mind spun with blood and gore; memories that he thought had long passed stabbed his thoughts like a jackhammer. Doing application installs on customers' servers was like trudging through a swamp. Server administration steps buzzed through his brain as he forgot the proper sequence and nearly crashed a customer's cluster.

By the time he had made it home, Hal was ready to get drunk. There was the better part of a twelve-pack in his fridge, and he planned on drinking from the moment he opened the door to the moment he closed his eyes. And that was just what he did.

Red blood and gray skin flooded through Hal's dreams. Nightmares repeated. Custer's white eyes stared, then the monster ripped Hal's arms off over and over again, not just breaking and dislocating one as had happened that night.

He saw Jen, his fellow app installer, screaming, her eyes gouged out by Custer's disgusting sausage fingers and her head ripped from her shoulders. The blood—there was so much; he could taste it like a thousand grimy pennies swirling inside his mouth. It cramped his stomach, clenching his waist and making him want to puke.

His eyes opened, the drunk gone, and the night half spent. He found himself staring at the ceiling in his room. His heart pounded in his chest, and he was covered in sweat.

"It's going to be okay." It was becoming a mantra now, one he didn't believe but told himself over and over again, hoping it would take hold.

By the time his alarm sounded, his eyes were bloodshot, and his skin paled from sleep deprivation. He dragged himself from his covers and lowered his feet to the floor. It was Friday, time for eight hours of work followed by a bus trip to his death.

Server after server, install, diagnose, repair, update; the day dragged. Hal wanted to blame the lack of sleep or the monotony of the work. The fact was, it was neither of those. Below the surface of each thought lay the incoming inevitability. Custer was coming.

It didn't matter that no one had seen the thing in years. It didn't matter that the camp had been running safely and successfully for summer after summer with no problems. His gut was a tight, burning mess the entire day, and regardless of how much he forced his thoughts in another direction, they returned to the blood. To the chunks of human flesh that were once his friends. To the eyes of death that had looked into his own and promised he would meet his maker. Somewhere in the depths of his mind, he knew that was a promise unfulfilled, and there was only a matter of time before Custer kept his word.

A little after lunch, Jen peeked over Hal's cubicle wall. "You ready for the weekend?" She was making that smile where her dimples made her cheeks perk around the corners of her perfect lips. It always caught Hal off guard and forced him to smile back with a stupid schoolboy gaze. He wondered if she did that on purpose since it was becoming more frequent over the past few weeks. He hoped so.

"Bags are packed and, in the car, as instructed. How about you?"

She rolled her eyes and glanced at the ceiling. "I still need to sneak out during my afternoon break and pick up a few travel-sized toiletries. Did you hear they're making us sleep in cabins like kids—four altogether—boys of each team split up, girls of each team too? I mean, I like Martha and everything, but I'm not sure I want to sleep alone with her in the cabin all weekend. I'd rather sleep with the guys. I'm sure we're all grown up enough to behave..." Martha and Jen, the only women in the Implementation Team, were at a bit of a disadvantage compared to the PMT, who were evenly split.

"I don't know if you'd want that. I've slept in the same room with John before—at that Microsoft convention last year. He is not a quiet sleeper." He shielded his mouth from the rest of the office. "From either end, if you know what I mean."

"Gross!" She protested, but her smile brightened.

She whispered, "Well, maybe you could sneak out and bunk with us? At least I know I'd have more fun. Martha said she packed like four books. I don't expect to see her eyes all weekend."

Hal felt his face warm and hoped he wasn't blushing. Nothing would make him happier than spending his nights around Jen's bright smile, even if it was in one of his most dreaded places on the planet.

"Let's try." He spoke dryly, trying to mask his excitement. He watched the gleam in her eyes, the brightness, and wondered what had taken him so long. He'd been dying to ask her out but kept putting it off, kept worrying that if she said no, it would make their work life awkward. He knew the chemistry was there; he could feel his heart throb every time she stepped near. Why couldn't he be the confident person he needed to be to make this happen?

She leaned away from the cubicle, eyes locked on his. She pointed at him and smirked. "I'm going to hold you to it."

Hal chuckled. It was forced, nervous. He hoped it looked genuine because inside, he was screaming in anxious anticipation.

She turned and left. He watched her go, watched her hips perfectly fitted inside her jeans. He had to force himself to take a breath.

From then until four-thirty, Hal tried his hardest to concentrate. He did two more installs and tweaked a few settings on a customer's server where an ongoing issue continued to elude the team. He set up some extra logging to check back on next week. As he signed out, he hoped that he would be back next week.

Dan White, head of the operations division, walked into the cubicle farm at 4:35 and cleared his throat. "That's it for the week, everyone. Grab your bags. There's a bus in the parking lot ready to go." He smiled as if he were blessing his teams with a trip to Hawaii, his chest puffed out and his business casual Polo too tight for his growing gut.

A cold flutter grabbed Hal's heart. It was time. And he couldn't escape. He tried to think about Jen, about seeing her face and hanging out with her. It worked for a moment, until his dreams from the previous night returned. The blood running down her cheeks as Custer's meaty fingers crushed her eyeballs and forced their way into her eye sockets.

"Let's go, man." John stood at the entrance to his cube.

Hal realized his fingers were cramping. He was holding onto his desk with every inch of his strength. He took a deep breath and pushed away from the cube. All he could do now was hope.

Chapter Three

JUST AS DAN WHITE HAD promised, a bus was waiting. A full-sized, yellow school bus he had contracted held all six members of IT and six members of PMT, plus Dan and the driver. When Hal first examined the old thing, he felt it could have been the same bus he rode in thirty years ago. Had it been stored in a time capsule all this time?

The PMT sat near the front, IT in the middle, and the bags piled in back. Hal stared out the window, ignoring the heavy smell of disinfectant. He lowered the sliding window as they plunged deeper into Custer Falls National Forest, and both rejoiced and tensed at the incoming smell of pine.

The trees grew denser as they moved into older growth, and ponderosas and white pines clouded the canopy. Creeping juniper and thick corpses of cedar cluttered the ground and lined the side of the roadway.

Hal felt himself traveling back in time, thinking about Benny Winter. The kid had sat across the bus from him on this same road. He had flipped through comics and rattled off the names and powers of the Fantastic Four to Carl Johnson, who rolled his eyes at the information every boy on the bus already knew. He remembered Wes Stevens sitting in front of him, practicing knots with a length of rope he'd brought with him. He later explained it was for a merit badge he wanted to get when he came home, when he went to his next scout meeting. A meeting he would never get to attend.

The bus thumped, the seat rattled, and Hal felt himself pulled toward the aisle.

"Almost there," it was Paul, a new hire right out of MSU

with a Computer Science degree. He was the kind of kid the company hired at barely minimum wage with the promise of "real-world experience with upward mobility." It usually took about six months for the newbies to realize there was zero mobility and another two to three weeks to find a different job where their CS degree would be worth more than the paper it was printed on.

"Yeah, we are." Hal agreed.

"I hope they have something good for dinner. Man, I am starving." There was an eager optimism on the guy's face. Hal had chalked it up to youthful ignorance in the past, but more and more, he was coming around to the belief that Paul was just a good guy. Kind of rare, but they were out there.

"I hope so too." Hal didn't think he could eat if he tried. If he made it through the weekend without losing ten pounds, he would be surprised.

"I heard there's going to be some cool games. I want to try the archery. Have you ever shot archery?"

"A few times." The last time Hal had held a bow was at this camp, and he'd avoided every occasion to be around one since. "So, I'm guessing you never did this as a kid?"

"No. Always wanted to, though." He had a bright look in his eyes. Just for a second, Hal thought, *Maybe, just maybe, this is going to turn out okay.*

A half-hour later, the bus pulled up in front of the Sun Beach Summer Camp's main lodge. Other than new windows filling the holes of those Custer had smashed, it looked exactly the same as when he'd last seen it. Thick and long, stacked old growth logs made its walls. A cathedral ceiling lifted almost into the canopy, where the roof blended into evergreen boughs with dark green metal sheeting. A single man, balding with a fluffy beard, waited in front of the door to greet the bus.

As soon as it stopped, Dan White got off and shook hands with the man. They chatted and smiled while Hal and his fellow employees gathered their bags and climbed down.

"Ops, this is Mike Jacobs. He's happy to have us here and is allowing us this unique experience. Let's all offer him a thank you."

A whispered round of applause passed from the IT and PMT before Dan spoke again. "We're all going to do our best to treat the place respectfully and leave it as good as we found it."

"Thank you, everyone," Mike Jacobs addressed the group. Hal couldn't help but notice the family resemblance to what must have been his father. Thin lips, bushy eyebrows, dark eyes. He pictured a ravine across the man's skull, shattered bone and brain pulsing with his heartbeat, the same way his father had looked after Custer cracked him over the head with his own weapon. He continued, "I hope you all enjoy your weekend as much as our youths do every summer. You'll find one set of boys' and girls' cabins to the east and another to the west." He glanced at Dan. "The Head Counselor's cabin is down the path by the lake, beside the boathouse and equipotent sheds."

"Thank you, Mike," Dan gestured for the Ops department to lend another round of applause, and they did, weakly.

Mike waved and walked toward a distant parking lot where a beige Subaru waited. "Just give me a call if you have any trouble."

Before the owner had reached his vehicle, Dan was handing out orders. "IT, you guys are in the east cabins, PMT, the west." Everyone shifted to start moving, and Dan unfolded a bag from his pocket and barked again. "Before anyone leaves, though—I need all cell phones and electronics right here."

"What?" Jaime from the PM team practically snarled.

"This is going to be an authentic experience. That means no cell phones, laptops, iPads, or smartwatches. If it has a battery, it goes in the bag. You'll get it back on Sunday when the bus comes back for us."

The rule made no sense. As Hal glanced at his iPhone and saw *No Service*, he doubted how much use anyone would have had for their phones. But either way, a wave of groans erupted, and one by one, each employee walked past Dan and placed their phones, smartwatches, and tablets into the bag.

"And, Eric, Shawn," Dan address his most attentive brown-nosers, from the PMT, of course. "Please hang back. I'll need your help with the food cooler and a few other preparations." His voice rose. "Everyone, meet back here in one hour for campfire and dinner."

The rest of the employees marched off to find their cabins.

Hal walked behind John and Paul. After him were Jen and Martha, then Keith, the most senior member of the team. Once they were clear of the bus and into the wooded trail, Jen hustled up next to Hal.

"You still down?" She gazed at him with one eye squinted in a devious expression. "You aren't going to abandon me with..." She glanced back at Martha, who seemed to be amazed at the trees—as if she were just finding out today that there was such a thing as *outside*.

"Yeah." Hal chuckled. It was a nice break for his nerves. "I'm *down*. After we're all settled in tonight, I'll slip over."

Hal wanted to share a sly smile, but he still wasn't sure exactly where this was leading. Was it to play cards and keep her company? Was it to make out in her bunk? Was it to break the rules just to break them as if they were all kids again?

Jen showed no such reservations. She nodded and gave him her own devious grin, then slowed until she and Martha were walking side by side again.

A minute later, they found the pair of cabins they had been assigned. Hal stopped cold. These used to both be for the boys, the cabins PMT was sent to, for the girls. He gazed across an expanse of grass, the last place he had seen so many friends alive now in front of him. He half-expected to see Mac on his knees, shotgun planted in his throat like a flag. Shivers ran down his spine as Paul grasped their cabin's doorknob and opened the old pine portal. It creaked in a long slow whine that stood Hal's hair on end.

He became paralyzed with a single thought: *I shouldn't be here.*

He was being an idiot. He should have quit his job and just let the whole thing go. Maybe he would have lost his house. Maybe he would have fallen on hard times. He'd been through that before when he flunked out of college with a boatload of student loans and no job to pay them back. But he was alive then. He was still alive right now—if he made the next decision a good one and turned around and left. He didn't know how he'd get back to Custer Falls, but even if walking fifty miles back home could save his life...

Jen stopped beside Hal. "You okay?"

Her voice cut through his panic as she rested a hand on his shoulder. He turned and saw the gentle curve of her smile. Her green eyes gazing into his. The view was like a drug, like someone had slipped him a Xanax. He let out a breath—relief—then shamed himself for overreacting and forced himself forward.

"Yeah. Thanks."

He walked to the door and stepped inside before she could ask. He didn't want to talk about it. He didn't want to explain anything and look like a fool. He just wanted to get through this weekend and get on with his life.

Hal ignored the flashes of blood lakes covering the floor, overturned cots, and children's appendages. The flesh, bone, and the smell. He unwittingly crossed the room and set his duffel on the same cot he had used thirty years ago. He took a deep breath and sat.

"This is going to be fun." Paul took the cot across from Hal's. "I think I've seen every camp movie ever and still never been."

Keith smirked. "Does that include Friday the 13th? Sleep-away Camp?"

"Yeah, but I think my favorite is the one where Jason goes to space."

"That's not even in a camp."

"*So?* I also loved Meatballs, Heavyweights, Ernest Goes to Camp, Wet Hot American Summer—"

"Okay, that was a good one," John butted in.

"You guys are killing me," Keith said. His voice was as gruff as his graying beard. At the end of a day on servers and now in a cabin with three coworkers he thought were idiots, he was almost as done with this situation as Hal was. He dug through his bag and set a Jack Reacher novel on his bed, the one closest to the door.

"Either way," Paul continued, "I think I'm looking forward to the archery and the canoeing the most. What about you, John?"

"I'm just going to take it as it goes, my friend. Knowing Whitey, I'm not sure things will be that cut and dry. He has a knack for bleeding the fun out of things."

"What does that mean?"

Keith dropped onto his cot. "There was one time we did a huge install on a Saturday, the only day the customer would let us do it. Now, any good boss would order a team some pizzas or something on an occasion like that. What does Whitey do? He waits 'til we're almost finished to order them, then makes us stay to eat them after we're done, *and* had us do maintenance on our own servers as we ate. Some reward, right?"

"Really?"

"Don't forget," John piped up. "What about the time in Vegas?"

"Oh, shit." Keith shook his head. "I'd blocked that out. We were there for the convention. We set up display units—cool—that was the job. Then, when we were ready to leave and enjoy our first night in Sin City, he marches in with ten members of the sales team and tells us to do software updates on all their machines so they can demo them during the con the next day—what the fuck?"

"Those primping little sales bitches could have brought their laptops to us anytime the previous week to get updated, but no…" John's face had grown red.

"And where did Whitey and the sales boys and girls go? Out to drink and roll dice and shit, while we were stuck doing installs."

"Shit." Paul's face hand blanked.

"Yeah, shit," Keith muttered. "But maybe this will go better." He leaned back on his cot. "They did take all the electronics, after all."

Chapter Four

HAL LET PAUL AND JOHN lead the way back to the main lodge. Behind them were Keith and Martha. He managed to leave last, and more slowly, and it appeared Jen had the same plan. They walked together at the rear of the group, both trying to appear apathetic about ending up side by side.

"So, did you get unpacked? How's the *girls'* cabin?" Hal looked at the ground and then the woods beyond the trail.

"It's a shithole." She waited for him to meet her gaze, and they both chuckled.

"I guess kids don't know any better and don't complain."

"If they do, who's going to listen?"

"I guess that's right, isn't it?" His gaze went back to the forest. He found himself verifying its emptiness. He didn't realize it at first, but his view had been going from tree to tree, from shadow to shadow. Even if he wasn't aware how strong it was, something inside him was demanding to know what was around him—especially with the sky dimming and night edging closer and closer.

"How's the *boys'* cabin?"

He answered without looking, without thinking. "Just how I remembered it."

"What do you mean? You've been here before?"

Shock ran down Hal's back. Had he really just said that? John and Keith both glanced back at him.

"No." Hal's feet were heavy. He tried to lift them carefully, to not trip and make this even worse by giving away his secrets. "Sorry, I was looking at something in the woods and misspoke. I meant it looked about how I *expected*."

The others turned back forward.

"Ah," Jen said. "That makes sense." She leaned toward him and playfully bumped his shoulder as they walked.

Hal looked her in the eyes. She gestured at Martha and mouthed *Four giant books*. She spread her hands, expressing a massive stack. As he smirked, she mouthed *Save me*. He nodded and pointed at himself, then her. *I got you*, he mouthed back.

Gloom spread within the surrounding forest, and Hal noticed the sky had been consumed with clouds. Dusk was advancing, hanging over the campground like a muddied violet umbrella and bringing with it a wind that cut through the campers.

"Anyone bring a jacket?" Martha said. She crossed her arms and rubbed her shoulders. "Isn't it still summer?"

"You know this is Montana, right?" Keith snapped, never missing a chance to belittle another teammate.

"Whitey said there'd be a fire," Paul pointed ahead. "I think we're getting close."

Scents of charring burgers and hot dogs infiltrated the woods. Flickers of yellow lit the trail ahead, and the obnoxious laughter of PMT voices broke the calm of the coming evening.

John glanced at the rest of the team, gestured a thumb ahead, and offered a gagging eye roll that took Hal back to middle school. Hal was okay with most of the PMT one-on-one, but as a team, and when it came to matters of work, the relationships between the groups couldn't have been more contentious. Almost none of them had any knowledge of how servers or applications actually worked other than their sales sheets, but they were relentless with their demands on time and output. It didn't matter when John said a job would take six hours; they would tell the client four and then insist it get done in that timeframe. If Hal was invited into a conference call for a technical consultation, he would often get railroaded by PMT members insisting his recommended specifications were over the top, and the customer could get away with less. Continuous cases of disrespect had driven a wedge across the Ops department to the point where some members of IT refused to respond to emails or calls from PMT altogether. It had evolved into PMT-scheduled jobs being worked at half-pace compared to calls for repair that had no connection to Project Management.

Martha and Jen giggled at John. Keith shook his head.

They emerged from the trail and made their way to the fire. Dan White stood behind a grill with a red and green plaid chef's apron. Beside the grill was a table with all the traditional cookout foods and condiments: burgers, dogs, buns, garnishes, ketchup, mustard, chips, even an almost empty container of sliced watermelon.

"Make a plate and grab a seat." Whitey swung his spatula, pointing at the table, then swept it toward the fire.

The IT lined up at the table, fixed plates, and sat on the opposite side of the campfire from PMT. Whitey took the last round of burgers from the grill and set them on the table, then made his own plate and joined his two teams.

"Eat up, everyone." Whitey held his burger out in front. "Then, we'll talk about what's to come this weekend."

They ate. Plates were nearly empty by the time conversations grew loud enough for one team to be bothered by the other.

Eric, from the PMT, raised his voice above the din. "So, Dan, are you going to tell the story of Custer while we're out here, or should I?"

The fire had settled low, the sky darkened, and Hal could see through Eric's condescending eyes. There was a growing smirk in the corner of his mouth that begged Whitey to let him tell the story so he could hopefully frighten the uninitiated.

Whitey shifted in his seat. "I don't know how appropriate it is, but I guess... it is tradition to tell scary stories around the campfire. Go ahead."

And so, Eric went. And Hal remembered each event of that fateful evening as Eric told it wrong. The campfire, just like this one, in the same place as this one, but there was no group chant to bring it about as Eric suggested, only the misguided reading of a book by Jimmy Huber. The idiot counselor had thought it would be funny to terrify some of the younger kids with a creepy passage he found while making out with Kelly Swanson in an abandoned shack on the south side of the woods.

Eric talked about Custer, about how he slaughtered the counselors first—another lie. He killed Jimmy and Kelly first, likely for fouling his shack. Hal could still remember how he crushed Jimmy's throat while holding him in the air, then tore his penis from his pelvis and choked Kelly to death with it—a deadly replay of the events from his woodland home. Then came the kids' and counselors' bloody deaths interwoven. The order was just whoever crossed his path next.

Hal remembered fleeing into the main lodge as if it were all happening again. A counselor, Sandra Levy, locked the door. She leaned against it as if her ninety-five-pound frame could keep Custer out.

"Go!" she shouted at the dozen kids who had followed her in. They stared at her, stupefied, shaking, no idea what to do next.

The door shook. The noise was louder than a slam. She leaned her back into it, eyes huge, hands pressed against the wood. Her mouth trembled.

Hal watched, unable to think of anything rational to do. He was stuck. He saw her jaw shake as it hung from her mouth, and it reminded him of those windup novelty chattering teeth. He'd seen them in television shows and movies and wondered if they were really real. Where would he even buy a pair if he wanted one?

He watched a bead of sweat drip from her chin to her heaving chest. The counselor jolted forward and back as the killer slammed into the door, and she fought to keep it inside its frame. The bead landed on her sternum, a wide swath of tan skin, her cleavage open between the straps of her camp-issued tank top. The drop of sweat dove into the nether between her breasts, and a blood-drenched blade burst through her chest.

Red spread over the white cloth, blotting out the words

CAMP SLASHER LAKE: VOLUME ONE

Camp Custer Falls. Her mouth jittered, then stopped. Her jaw dropped as she focused on the four inches of steel extending from her chest, and she went limp. Urine streamed down her leg, and she hung like an impaled puppet. When the blade slurped back inside her and her body dropped, Custer opened the door, and Hal ran.

"And he walked back into the lake," Eric concluded, "never to be seen again." He scanned the employees and shouted. "Until now!" He lifted a machete high above the fire.

Jaime and Sherri from the PMT squealed, and Eric, Shawn, and Jason all chuckled. The IT watched them, unimpressed.

Jen shook her head and whispered to Hal, "That's not even how it happened, I bet."

Hal shrugged.

"Okay, Okay." Whitey stood, hands raised. Now that we have that out of our systems, we can talk about the rest of the weekend." He went on about games that would be played Saturday and Sunday, hinting at prizes and surprises. Hal bet the surprises would be mixing IT and PMT to make some team building happen. After his speech and being asked if there was any alcohol in the camp, he shut everyone down and sent them back to their cabins. "Remember everyone, games start early, so get your sleep!"

Both teams mumbled and headed back, and Whitey poured water on the campfire. The sizzle of water against hot embers filled the clearing and covered the sound of wet footsteps walking up the path from the boathouse.

Keith settled into his cot with his book. Paul and John discovered an old folding table in the corner and set it between their cots for a game of five-card draw. Hal dressed down to a pair of shorts and a T-shirt and grabbed his flashlight from his duffel.

He walked to the door, about to grab the handle, when Keith spoke up, "Where're you going?"

John and Paul glanced over with raised brows, half the hand on the table, Paul mid-deal.

"I'm going to check on the girls," Hal said.

"Don't you mean check on *Jen*?" John's expression had shifted to a self-righteous grin.

Hal nodded. "Yes. To check on Jen."

"Don't do anything I wouldn't do." John nodded at Paul to keep dealing.

"I don't know if that's possible."

Keith glared at Hal. Hal had gotten the feeling that Keith had a soft spot for Jen a year ago, soon after she started. He was always quick to teach her something about the software or give her a hand without her having to ask. At first, he had thought Keith was sweet on her. Then, one day he spotted a picture of Keith with his deceased daughter—she'd died of some rare cancer in her twenties. Jen was a dead ringer for the girl.

Hal spoke softly, "She invited me, man. I'm not going on a panty raid."

Keith sighed and returned to his book.

Outside, the night had grown cooler. The breeze chilled Hal's arms as he gazed over the tree line with suspicion. He saw nothing but felt something. There was something out there. Whether it was an actual entity or merely the ghosts of that night, he wasn't sure, but more than the nightmare of the past, the sense of something yet to come bloomed inside him like a growing rot. It was a sense of dread not quite actualized, the seed of something more, warning him with whispers.

He thought of Jen. Was she waiting for him? Was she asleep? Was this what he should really be doing if his senses were crying out with frightful memories? Her smile crossed his thoughts. Her lips. The curve of her waist.

He stepped into the scrubby grass between the cabins, and a boom of thunder rocked the campsite. He took a second to look up, and rain drizzled onto his face. He hurried on to the door.

CAMP SLASHER LAKE: VOLUME ONE

At first, there was no sound from inside. The silence was broken by a laugh — Jen's laughter. There was no denying who it came from. It drew a smile on Hal's face, and he knocked.

Footfalls on pine planks. "Who is it?" Jen, playful, half the laugh still in her voice.

"Hal."

"Prove it. How do we know it isn't the camp killer — Custer?"

The name drew much of the excitement from Hal's chest. A deflation. He forced it back inside and held the smile firm.

"Um... Whitey and Eric should have gotten a cabin together."

Hal heard a muffled giggle through the door, and it opened in front of him. Jen wore a shirt five sizes too large, and it looked like that was all. Martha was in her cot near the door, covers up to her chin, with her arms and a book on her belly.

Jen looked Hal over from head to toe, then swept the area behind him with her gaze. "I guess you're okay." She walked away with a swagger that looked half sexy and half drunk.

Hal followed her in, his own gaze sweeping the grounds.

Rain began pouring, and he shut the door and locked it.

Chapter Five

ERIC, SHAWN, AND JASON SAT around a card table of their own, each holding a beer in one hand and cards from a game that had long since expired from drunkenness in the other.

"They're both dogs," Shawn slurred.

"You wouldn't do either of them?" Jason was aghast.

Rain pounded on the roof, and they all glanced up for a moment.

"No, man," Eric jumped in, having to be heard. "Martha, yeah, woof, but I had Jen in my office the other month to fix the tracking software, and her ass..." He exaggerated a big, sloppy chef's kiss.

"Maybe her ass..." Shawn waved his hands in conditional surrender. "But I'd have to cover her face. Then, maybe."

"Shut the fuck up." Jason slapped the back of Shawn's head. "You'd do anyone gracious enough to let you stick it in."

Shawn raised his hand as if to object but just smiled instead. "Yeah." He guzzled his beer.

The cabin shook with a boom, and the lights flickered.

Shawn pointed at the single overhead bulb. "Uh. What happens if that goes off?"

Eric rolled his eyes, wondering how the others even dressed themselves. "There's a generator behind the main lodge. And worst-case scenario—" he pointed at the two lanterns hanging by the front door.

"Gotcha."

Another boom. The lights flickered, and this time they stayed off.

"Assholes," Eric shook his head. "This is like Karma and shit. You guys just had to talk about it."

"No worries," Shawn sang, "just go start up the generator."

Eric turned to his beer and drank. "Pfft. Whitey can do that shit."

Another boom, but this one from the front door.

Jaime spun, looking for the source of the noise. "What was that?"

"What?" Angela glanced up from her toenails and polish.

"That noise? Didn't you hear it?" With a half-squinting *oh-my-god-bitch* expression, she swirled her paper cup of wine and tossed it back.

"You mean the lightning?" Sherri asked. She sat halfway across the room, a romance novel in her hands. Reading was her way of cutting herself off from the other two caddy bitches, refusing interaction instead of accepting rejection.

"No," Jaime snarled. "It was different. It was more of a bang, not a boom."

Angela smirked. "I see someone's been boning up on her Dr. Suess."

"Fuck you, bitch." Jaime turned to the box of wine she had smuggled in inside her bag, now on the shelf by the wall. The cup wobbled under the spigot as she found the button and poured.

A scream rose above the sound of the rain pounding on the roof.

"What the fuck?" Eric shouted at the door. He stomped toward it, clenching his fist. All he could think was that somehow the IT had grown a set of balls big enough to try to screw with them. He grabbed the knob and yanked the door open.

He stared into the night. Raindrops splashed against the cabin's small porch and sprayed his legs in ricocheted droplets. He could barely see the trees in the distance, the blackness was so deep.

"What is it?" Shawn stood from the table. His face had shifted from jovial play to concern. He'd seen Eric angry before, but this was something different. This time his anger seemed like... a mask. Like there was something more Eric was expecting to see out in the darkness. Something he was challenging, but all he had to arm himself with was machismo.

Eric didn't answer at first. He didn't move, aside from the scan of his eyes against the darkened unknown. "Uh. I don't—"

Shawn had to shake his head. What happened next was so irrational, his brain didn't comprehend the pictures. It was like Eric's leg shot backward, a red pole in the blacked-out cabin. But at the same time, he was still standing in the doorway. Blood gushed from Eric's calf, and as he sank to the ground, now with no foot, Shawn realized there was a shovel on the floor in the room's center.

But how? A shovel rocketed through? Severing his leg? Was it shot from a cannon? Shawn's brain clicked away at the pieces of the puzzle, not understanding any of it. And then, there was the screaming.

Eric howled and pushed himself up, sitting. His hand went to his leg, to his stump. Blood flooded over the floorboards, over the threshold, out into the rain, where it mixed with puddling water on the porch and ran off into the soil.

"What?" Eric shouted. He was still staring at the limb when a pitchfork slammed into his mouth. The tines ran through his face, curving up around the back of his skull. Four bloody points burst from the rear of his neck, and his back locked, holding him upright.

He gagged and twitched. Blood erupted from his mouth, over the implement's pole in pulses. As his hands rose to meet the handle, a figure emerged in the doorway.

"Jesus Christ!" Shawn and Jason jumped from the card table. Their knees slammed it upward and juggled it back and forth until it crashed to the ground, taking the cards and a half-dozen bottles with it.

Shawn heard the crash and stared at the shadowed figure in the doorway. He knew who it was. He didn't have to see his face, didn't even have to see him in the light to know. It was him, Custer.

Piss ran down his leg. He trembled. Time seemed to freeze as he scanned the room around him.

Was there an exit? There was only one door, and it was blocked—God, he was so happy it was dark. He thought he may collapse, dead of a heart attack, if he could see the man. He did see windows. Maybe he could climb out through a window? How could he have time for that? He'd have to dive through like some action movie. Was that even possible? The room began to swirl, and he found himself locked back in real time with no idea what to do next.

Custer held the pitchfork in one hand. He lifted it and Eric together. Eric rose like a ragdoll, with no will of his own. When he was nearly to his knees, lightning struck in the woods, and Shawn beheld exactly what he dreaded.

The thing in the door was no man. It stood wearing the rotting mass of a corpse. Skin hung from muscle. Cracks in the flesh went clear down to the bone where slithering, crawling things moved within. It had one eye and one empty socket. Its nose was a pair of holes against its face, and it was dressed in a shredded flannel, a pair of torn jeans, and boots.

As the brightness of the lightning bolt faded, returned, and faded again, Custer raised the other hand. Rain reflected in the object in his grip. It was long and metallic, a machete.

In the last frozen moment of illumination, Custer swung. The blade sliced through Eric's neck in a single, clean swipe. His body slumped to the floor, blood pumping from the gash of meat and bone, while the head stayed above, hovering on the end of the pitchfork like a meatball on the tip of a toddler's utensil.

Shawn wanted to scream. His chest was frozen in place. He could move it no more than he could move the body of some stranger.

The thing in the doorway locked his murderous gaze on Shawn.

No, no, no, repeated in Shawn's mind. *The window? Dive through the window. It's the only way.* But his muscles refused.

Custer lowered the pitchfork, and for a moment, relief flashed in Shawn's mind. He was done. He had just come to kill Eric, and now he was going to leave them alone.

The monster of a man flicked the pitchfork back up, and a blob soared through the darkness. Lightning flashed again, and Eric's wide, bulging eyeballs were flying toward his face. The damned killer had thrown the head.

He didn't know how he did it, but Shawn's hands shot up. More than his fear of movement, there had spiked a fear of his friend's decapitated head slamming into his face.

Shawn's hand clamped around what felt more like a wet ball of flesh than a head. Several fingers had caught a nose and an eyeball, the other hand had grabbed onto the inside of Eric's neck. He felt the wetness inside the throat, the tongue, and dropped the head on the floor.

"No!" Jason screamed.

Shawn looked back across the room and saw Custer coming toward them. The way he moved was unearthly. His legs paced, but the rate of speed seemed faster than his motions should allow.

Jason turned to run. As he spun and lifted his leg, he seemed surprised to find a cot in the way. His foot hooked on the cot's metal frame, and he tumbled face first over the bedding and onto the other side, legs straight up in the air.

Shawn suddenly felt his lower half. There was barely a thought, and he was in motion. Instead of turning and running away, he went sideways to the wall, to the window.

CAMP SLASHER LAKE: VOLUME ONE

He'd never tried this in his life, but he felt it had to work. He pulled his hands together as if he were diving into water. He leaned forward, took another step, and leaped at the window.

Pain and pressure crashed into Shawn's hands. His digits jammed back into his knuckles, and he felt something snap in each hand. His wrists curled inward, and the first crack showed in the glass. His arms were pushed back, the pane tented outward, and his head and shoulders rammed through. That was where his forward momentum stopped.

Shawn hung from the window frame, rain smacking the rear of his head. Glass sliced into his chest, and blood ran down the outer wall of the cabin. Behind him, the floor thumped with inhuman footfalls.

"Shit. *Shit!*" He lifted his hanging arms and pushed outward against the sill. He felt glass shards rip across his chest, across his belly as he inched from the window. It was pain he had no idea even existed.

Thump. Thump. It was right behind him. He pushed harder and felt something's stone grip on his leg. He pushed harder and went nowhere. The glass shards below his gut dug deeper into his belly.

There was nothing he could do, nowhere to go. Hot tears ran down his face. He turned back slowly, knowing he shouldn't.

Custer held his leg in one hand and the machete high in the other. The monster didn't smile, but Shawn felt the thing smile inside its malicious head. A brief glint as metal soared through the night, the machete came down and through Shawn's free leg.

Shawn felt nothing. The pain in his gut was so overwhelming in every inch lower than his chest. He saw his foot dangling then gone, and instead of pain, he was washed with wonder. Where did it go? Was it some sort of magic trick?

Custer raised the blade, and it shot down again. This time, the other leg came off in the thing's rock-hard grip. Blood sprayed in twin fountains.

Shawn was frozen once again, the survival part of his brain

surrendered. He waited, knowing the killing blow was coming.

Custer grabbed both gushing stumps and pushed Shawn out the window.

Jason fumbled over the cot, over his boots on the floor, and worked his way back onto his feet. He turned his sights back on the thing that had crashed into their lives, his eyes crossing the carnage of Eric's body by the door. That was real. His friend was dead, leaking over the flooring of this place that was supposed to be a haven for children.

He had a glimpse of a memory, the story at the campfire. He had been listening and thinking how idiotic the whole thing was. Thinking that anyone who believed this nonsense was a fool and a coward. Who could believe a single man could kill everyone at a summer camp alone? Unless it was some bad 80s flick. But as his eyes met the real Custer, not the one in the story, he realized this wasn't a man. It was a monster.

The thing stood with half a leg in one hand, a bloody machete in the other. They both dripped to the floor in a rhythmic pattern that brought to mind a jazzy syncopated drumbeat. The monster studied Jason. He watched the human as if judging what his prey would do next.

Jason eyed the door. He'd have to sprint and leap over Eric's carcass. There was no way he could do it without stepping in the blood. There was so much blood.

Beyond that, there were only windows. Judging by the broken glass and part of what he assumed was Shawn's leg, that didn't seem like a valid option.

There were days as a youth when Jason would race his friends. It never developed into a desire to run track; his only competitions in life had been drinking more beer and laying more women than his friends. He had started to discover that after his college days, the first, and its growing reminder on his belly, was getting in the way of the second. As he studied the gap between himself and the door, he tensed his stance and prepared to launch forward. That thing couldn't be too fast, could it?

Jason sprang over the cot in front of him. He extended his leg to meet the ground and caught Custer moving in his peripheral vision. He guessed he had fifteen feet ahead and ten between himself and the thing. As long as he could keep his momentum, he was pretty sure he could make it.

The cool air from beyond the door carried a thickness of aerosolized blood. Jason took his next step, his lungs thirsty, and the smell filled his senses. It drenched his thoughts with the deeper reality of death. That blood, from his friend, now ten feet away—it would never flow through his veins again. And that monster—he couldn't see it anymore, but his senses told him it was right behind him, maybe within reach—it was a taker of souls, the same way he saw each woman as a conquest of pussies. They were both collectors in a sense, and he may be part of that collection whether he liked it or not.

Another step. He could see rain splash against the ground now. It hit and exploded back into the air. It was like the drip of the leg and machete, a beautiful horror.

Jason felt his face wrench sideways. His left ear went numb, and with his right, he heard a dull thump. His world rolled to the side. His legs lost purchase and slid from beneath him. He could feel the dank moisture from the swelling porch. It was just beyond his reach.

He hit the ground and refused to look back. He crawled to his knees, and his vision went white. He saw a trail of blood ahead, and the severed end of Shawn's leg, as his gaze fluttered in and out. Was it beating him with a leg?

When Jason opened his eyes, he was on the floor, looking up. Custer was above him. He seemed to have been waiting for Jason to open his eyes, and as soon as his gaze locked on the rancid thing in Custer's eye socket, he swung the hunk of Shawn into Jason's arm.

WORK RETREAT by D.W. HITZ

There was a wet crunch inside his forearm and an avalanche of pain. Jason screamed and tried to get up. The monster swung again, smacked him on the head, then stomped on the other forearm. Cracks and pops, and white shards pierced the skin like a rising mountain range.

Jason howled. His body convulsed under the pain. He felt his stomach clench, his dinner rising, and the monster stepped back. He leaned down, and Jason felt a cold burst of agony that removed all thoughts of vomiting. He saw the killer's machete in his gut, blade up. Custer began sawing upward.

Hot blood warmed Jason's sides as the blade reached his ribs. In the incision below, he saw his intestines peek through and the inch and a half of yellowish belly fat he'd been thinking about losing.

Blood bubbled and flooded from his mouth as Custer jammed the machete's point through his stomach, heart, and lungs.

Chapter Six

JAIME AND ANGELA CREPT TOWARD the door as another scream cut through the night. Sherri glanced through the window, but trees blocked most of the view between the girls' and the boys' cabins. And what she could see was limited; there were no lights in their windows. And weirdly, a cut cable sparked as it dangled from the side of the cabin.

"We need to help," Angela whispered.

"Did you hear that?" Jaime scolded. "I don't know what's going on over there, but none of those guys are worth it."

Angela stared at Jaime, knowing the woman had spent more lunch hours than she could count with Jason at the motel down the street from the office. And now this? She was astonished.

Angela turned and put a hand on the doorknob.

Jaime shook her head.

Knock. Someone was there. *Knock,* this time weaker. Someone spoke on the other side, muffled and low.

"What do we do?" Angela trembled where she stood.

"Go away!" Jaime shouted.

Another knock, even weaker.

Sherri walked between the two and pushed them aside. She yanked the door open.

Soaked in rain and blood, Shawn lay in front of the door. As the girls looked at his legs, they backed away. Jaime covered her mouth as if she were going to be sick.

Shawn reached out. "Help." His voice was soft. He was hoarse, and his skin was pale white.

Sherri kneeled and looked him over. Her face was frozen in horror. She glanced into the rain at the boys' cabin. And she backed away.

"What?" Angela couldn't understand how Sherri could see anything worse out there than what was on their doorstep. As Sherri passed, Angela leaned out and saw him.

"Help," Shawn croaked.

Angela's entire body ran cold. Was he a ghost? A hallucination? A man, she swore, was almost seven feet tall and as wide as a linebacker, was carrying a pitchfork and a machete. His ripped clothes and dead-looking skin were like something from a Romero movie, but this man didn't move like a zombie. He walked toward them with purpose. He had one eye and holes in his face, but he moved like something alive.

"God, no," Shawn mumbled. His eyes had followed hers. "H—" His words were cut short as the pitchfork suddenly dove into his back and swayed in the air, bobbing up and down.

Angela screamed. Sherri burst past her and out of the cabin. In seconds, she had vanished into the woods.

Angela backed away and tried to shut the door. Shawn's arm was in the way. It stuck through the doorway as if it were about to grip and pull and drag the man to safety. But it wasn't—it couldn't—her mind jumped to the lumbering, dead thing now feet from her door—maybe it could?

She turned to Jaime. "Help me!"

Jaime was the farthest away she could be, at the very rear of the cabin—opening a window.

"Jaime!"

Jaime stuck a leg through.

Angela leaned down and lifted the arm. It was cold and stiff. Her mind boggled at how it felt more like a thing than a person so soon after death. She pushed it out, and she pressed on the door. It was almost sealed, about to catch, and as if hit by a truck, it flew open, tossing her ten feet inside.

She landed on her stomach, her teeth smashing her lip into the floor, her blood gushing over her chin. She looked up in search of Jaime and only saw a flash of something disappearing through the window.

CAMP SLASHER LAKE: VOLUME ONE

"Ugggg," Angela groaned and pushed herself onto all fours. Her head jerked back, fire running across her scalp. She rose without trying. She moved her arms and legs, grabbing at anything, but found herself floating instead.

She gazed at the window. Rain fell beyond the open space. It glinted in the light, tiny streaks of whitish yellow, a movement of nature, immune and uncaring about the strange pettiness of human pain.

The cabin rotated before her, and a memory of childhood popped to life in her mind. Dad was holding her. She flew across the yard in his arms, suspended, with a cape flapping behind her. She remembered laughing and Dad saying, "Up, up, and away!" She remembered Dad's funeral, how his skin didn't look quite right, and the flowers were the wrong shade of blue. She'd see him soon, she thought.

Angela saw her cot, Sherri's, spilled wine cups on the floor. She felt cold dead breath on her cheek. She smelled rot, the skunky, molding odor of something decaying but moist. She saw his face and screamed as fingers the width of broom handles plunged into her eye sockets and scooped them empty.

She screamed louder, harder. If only someone heard her, they'd come and help. They'd save her from this thing. She had a vision of Whitey, of the IT rushing inside, one of them with a gun. They'd shoot this monster down, and she'd live.

She felt a rock-hard thing touch her neck, then wrap around it. She felt a series of pops and cracks, and everything went numb and cold. She felt nothing, and then her head hit the hardwood floor. She heard the thing's boots stomp across wood. It was leaving, and she was fading.

Jaime ran with her hands in front, guarding her face against wet branches and whipping needles. Her bare feet burned and felt like they were bleeding from step after step on rocks, twigs, and uneven ground. As she passed the edge of the woods and found the path again, she let loose an involuntary squeal of joy. She wasn't going to get lost in the woods and die. She was going to make it.

With only the glimmer of puddles on the dirt path to guide her, Jaime pushed her way through. Her legs were like rubber. Her chest burned. But she had to make it. After what that thing had done to Shawn. After it was coming after Angela. She knew it would be after her too, and any second.

She reached the main lodge and looked around. Nothing. No one was there.

"Hello?" She screamed. The sound of the fear in her voice scared her even more. "Whitey! Dan?"

She banged on the door, and then she remembered. "By the boathouse." He had said that earlier. He was by the lake.

She turned and made out the fork in the junction. One path to the PMT cabins, one to the IT cabins, and the center path to the lake. They formed a map in her head, something like a triangle, and she focused on the straight line between her cabin and Whitey. The place where that monster was and the place she had to go. Given the distance she had already run, if Custer was headed there, he had a head start on her.

"No, he wouldn't know that's where I was going. He's just a stupid maniac." She planted her feet in the mud and sprinted down the center path.

Her days in the gym were feeling helpful now, the hours of Pilates being worth more than just the promotions at work and having her pick of men at the bar. She promised herself that when she got home, she was going to work out even harder. She'd never stop. Maybe she'd take some martial arts too, so if this ever happened again, she would be ready. It was a plan for sure. She was going to be a badass bitch no matter what it took. She would never be put in this position again. *Sarah Conner, here I come.*

In minutes, she was at the boathouse and saw rippling rings of raindrops hitting the lake. And there it was, a tiny cabin on the right with a faint yellow light in the window. It was her salvation. She was sure of it. Whitey may have taken their phones, but this place had to have a landline, and he had to have access to it for emergencies.

"Dan!" She rushed to the door. "Dan!" She banged and tried the knob. It didn't turn. "Goddammit, Dan, open up! This is an emergency!"

"Hold on," it was him. He was in there. "I'm coming."

"Hurry, Dan!"

There was thumping and then footfalls from inside. He was doing something and slowly getting closer. The doorknob turned, and Dan stood in flannel pajamas. His pants were backward, his shirt was wrinkled and uneven, a button missed. Jaime saw a phone on the bed behind him, the screen glowing and what looked like two naked women in bright, LED display.

Jaime's mind flew right past the rage she would have felt on any other day. He had a phone, and they didn't, and that was utter bullshit, but right this second, the sight of that glowing screen meant the difference between life and death.

Jaime burst past him toward the phone. "We need help! Custer's here." She reached for the device and heard a wet, gagging sound from behind. She spun, her fingers brushing over the glass screen but not quite grasping the device.

Whitey's eyes were wide. He stared at her, not understanding the three inches of steel blade extruding through his nose and mouth. Blood ran like a spring down the steel and frothed and bubbled over his lower jaw. It flooded to the floor; the sound of patting lost beneath that of the rain on the cabin's tiny roof.

Jaime screamed as she saw beyond her boss. Custer filled the door frame. His face seemed even more grotesque in the amber light of the small cabin. Things below his skin squirmed, and something moved inside his empty eye socket.

She smelled his rot. She smelled grimy water and moldy meat. It made her gag and unconsciously back away.

She looked at the windows. It had worked the first time.

Why not now? She raced to the closest one.

Dan's face made a slurping noise as Custer withdrew the machete. He flopped onto the floor and seized. Stomach gases burst past the blood, creating a geyser of dark red and pale-yellow bile. It raced across the floor as Custer stepped on his back, moving toward Jaime.

Crunch. Snap. Whitey's ribs shattered, and Custer drew something from his belt.

Jaime got the window open and began climbing through headfirst. She reached an arm out, felt the rain against her cheek and drips running from the roof.

Pain, unimaginable pain. White and blinding, it ripped through her system. She jerked uncontrollably, arms and legs, head bobbing and smacking the window.

When it calmed, she saw the cabin again. She laid flat, her belly against the floor. She could tell now, the pain was in her back, her kidney.

Rock hard hands on her shoulder, she was being flipped onto her back. Lightning bolts shot through her as her wound touched the floor. He was above her, a spade in his hand. It was coated in black soil and tipped with her blood.

She howled in terror. This was it. She saw no escape now. There was only more pain and death ahead. She cursed Whitey. She cursed Eric for planning this thing. She cursed her mother for encouraging her to get this job in the first place.

Faster than she expected the monster to move, he leaned down and rammed the spade up through her lower jaw and into her skull. Her tongue was on fire and couldn't move. She saw the blade of the garden tool sticking out where her nose used to be and wondered if this was what Whitey felt. As she tried to inhale, a hot, wet wash filled her lungs. They thrust it back up, and bubbly fluids filled her sinuses but found nowhere else to go.

She jerked and convulsed. Custer stared into her eyes, absorbing it all. His head titled as if in thought.

Chapter Seven

IT TURNED OUT THAT JEN and Martha had decided to separate their spaces with some string and the sheets from the unused cots. It wasn't a wall, but it created a fragile sense of privacy that allowed Hal and Jen to lay on her bed and whisper to each other with the illusion of intimacy.

There had been banter and jest. She had shared her flasks of whiskey, and between the alcohol and their chemistry, the cool night had grown warm all around them.

She sat up and grabbed his hand, urging him up beside her. She took her shirt tails in her hands and, with a deep breath, raised the oversized nightshirt above her head, exposing her breasts, her bare belly, and her panties. She bit her lip, tossed her shirt to the floor, and gauged his expression.

He was flushed. His cheeks pulled back as he smiled a ridiculous grin, his gaze on her breasts then rising to meet her eyes. He reached for her bare side, bringing his lips toward hers.

Jen pressed a hand against his chest, holding him back. She tugged on his shirt, the unspoken implication: *Now you.*

He lifted the shirt above his head, and her hands rejoined his chest, exploring his body. The shirt hit the floor, and he wrapped her in his arms, pulling her to him. Their lips met. Their bodies pressed into each other, radiating heat and long-simmering lust.

She pushed him down. He reclined onto his back, head on her pillow. It smelled like lilac and berries. She took his shorts in her hands and worked the fly open. He was patient as she looked him over and caressed him, then pulled the shorts and boxers down his legs and dropped them to the floor. She shed her panties above his clothes as if claiming them, then climbed on top of him.

Branch after branch, and needle after needle, the trees seemed to crash into Sherri's face with cruel intent. She had tripped twice as she ran through the woods, her hands and face now smeared with mud, streaked with gaps from the falling rain. The pleasant scent of pine had lost its charm, now overridden by the smell of dirt and blood from the open gashes on her nose and cheeks.

Her bare foot crunched on a broken limb, and pain shot up her leg. She had to bite her lip to keep from screaming. That thing was who-knows-where, and... and... Sherri watched blood run from below her foot and seep into the wet soil, and she whimpered. She lifted her leg, a chunk of wood coming with it. She pried the sharpened stick three inches from the inside of her sole and clenched her teeth together.

Her tears hid between streaks of rain. She kept moving, leaving a bloody footprint with every other step.

A few more yards, and Sherri spotted a glow through the trees. She held still, wondering. She had no idea how long she had been running, how far she had come, or even what direction she had gone. Was it the home of some random neighbor to the campsite? Had she made a circle, trying to run blindly over uneven ground as she'd heard lost people do? Jesus, the last thing she wanted was to come face to face with that monster again. His horrid skin, the holes in his face, that eye. It made her tremble just thinking about the seconds she was forced to be around him.

She crept closer, limping, but watching for any more sharp sticks.

There were two cabins ahead. Fear jolted through her. She had run in a circle. She was back... No. Both cabins had light.

Both doors were shut. Was she at the IT cabins?

Sherri hobbled across the grass, slowing, listening as she reached the closer of the two, the one on the right. Voices. Talking. Not screaming, not dying, not in terror. *God.*

She grabbed the knob and turned. It opened. They hadn't even locked it. For Christ's sake, they hadn't even locked their door with that maniac out!

"Don't you know what's out there?" She cried. Three familiar faces stared at her.

The story was so ridiculous that Paul wondered if Sherri had taken something. Had those PMT assholes slipped something in her drink? Had a date rape drug backfired? Either way, he, John, and Keith wrapped her in blankets. They found a first aid kit hanging on the rear cabin wall and started bandaging her foot.

"I'll go get Whitey," Keith said, digging a jacket from his bag. "He'll need to call an ambulance for her."

"He needs to call the police," she cried. "We need help, a ride out of here, the goddamn national guard."

Paul pressed a damp cloth against her face, cleaning away dirt and blood.

John went to his bag. "I'll go with you."

Keith waited patiently by the door. Sherri shook her head, no. Paul grimaced. What had they done to her?

The door crashed inward.

Keith, a surprise to everyone, acted in an instant. He spun, and as soon as his eyes met the disgusting thing in the doorway, he charged.

Custer stumbled backward, leaving only the odor of death behind as Keith rammed his shoulder into the maniac's chest. The killer's feet caught on one of the porch's planks, and he sank—but his grip was tight on Keith's jacket. Both hit the mud,

Custer on his back, Keith above him like a drunken frat boy, wrestling with his brother.

"The fuck?" John and Paul rushed to the door. They watched, disbelieving, blank on what to do next. It was *him*, after all, Custer. The legend was real.

Keith punched his ribs. There was no reaction. He grabbed Custer by the throat and squeezed.

There was a shining arc of water on Keith's left. A hunk of steel plunged into the side of his ribs.

Thunder boomed, and Sherri screamed. Paul failed to understand what was happening; it wasn't right. A hunk of steel wasn't supposed to be moving—sawing through Keith's chest.

Keith howled.

John went into his bag and unsheathed a hunting knife. He ran through the door, raising it, looking for a place to aim.

Custer's machete moved in and out and across Keith's chest. Keith shook up and down, releasing his grip from the killer's neck. His eyes rolled in their sockets, and his blood flooded from a gaping hole until Custer hit the sternum and couldn't cut any further. He yanked the machete free, and the blood stopped, sealed by the dam of a closed wound until Custer swung again at a different angle.

A hunk of Keith's side slurped free. It slid away like the wedge of a tree, removed by a professional lumberjack. No sooner than Keith's flesh had hit the ground, his intestines and stomach followed. The man rocked to the side, gagging, uncontrolled, landing on his own viscera.

John screamed and sprinted from the cabin. His words were a blur of noise and fear. He held the knife above his head, pointing it down, and he leaped. As he landed on Custer, his blade plunged into the killer's chest.

"Die!" John shouted. "Die!"

Paul was dumbfounded. He had to back away. He couldn't imagine that what he'd been seeing was real. One man dead, in pieces? It looked like a lousy flick on Shudder, not reality.

"Come on," Sherri pulled on his arm. "We have to go."

"He's dead." Paul pointed at Keith, then the killer. "And he's dead. Look."

Hot and stinging, Sherri slapped the side of Paul's face. "Move, you idiot."

They went together. Sherri limped toward the doorway, Paul behind her.

"Die!" John screamed again. He pulled the knife free and plunged it into the thing's heart again.

Hal held Jen in his arms, their heads sharing her pillow. Her eyes were open, exposing the kindness inside, the pull of one soul toward the other. Hal didn't know what she wanted, what this would all mean come Monday. He didn't think it was just a flirt, fuck, and forget, but as of this moment, it was unclear. He thought she wanted this to go somewhere. Some might say it was a fairytale, that you couldn't tell from looking into someone's eyes, but at this second, he thought he could. He gazed into hers, and there was something real there.

Thunder shook the cabin, and another sound trailed right behind it. It was low, but Hal knew he heard it. It was a sound he'd been dreading since he climbed on that bus, and even in the arms of this woman, this, what may indeed be love—it rocked his insides and sent spikes of terror through his nerves.

"Guys?" Martha spoke through the improvised curtain. "I think something's going on outside."

"Get dressed and run," Hal answered. He said it to both of them, but his eyes were fixed on Jen. She didn't move, but her expression shifted to wonder. He pulled himself up and grabbed for his pants. "Now. Both of you. This is serious. Get dressed and run to the main lodge. If there's no help there, start running to the road."

"Hal?" Jen sat up, pulling the sheet up over her breasts.

"If you make it to the road, run toward town." He buttoned his shorts, pulled on his shirt, and looked into her eyes. She still hadn't moved. "Jen, please. I care about you, and right now, this place is going to turn to shit. You need to listen."

"Die!" a man screamed from beyond the windows. Hal thought he recognized it, but the anger clouded its tone.

"Please?"

Jen nodded and started on her shirt and underwear. Hal didn't know if she was going to follow his instructions, but this was a start.

"Die!"

Hal pulled down the curtain. Martha was in her pajamas, approaching the window. He wished she had listened.

Martha howled, "He's killing that man!" She covered her mouth. "Is that Keith?"

Hal moved to the window. His worst nightmare was here. Custer was on the ground. Keith, or parts of him, were scattered and bloody. John—Jesus, John—he was about to die and didn't know it.

Hal sprinted to the door. He paused as he grabbed the handle and looked back at Jen. She looked as confused as she had been, but she had a shirt and jeans on and was sliding on her shoes.

"For God's sake. Even if you don't trust a thing I said. Please. Run."

He turned the knob and stepped outside.

Chapter Eight

HAL RAN TOWARD HIS CABIN, screaming, "John, that won't work! You need to get away!"

John stabbed and stabbed, his blade rising and falling like the needles of a tattoo gun.

"Leave!" he tried again with no luck. He darted inside, setting his eyes on Paul and Sherri. He spent a fraction of a second looking at her bandages. "Get out of here, now. Go to the main lodge, go to the road, get out!"

Paul watched him, wondering, as Hal grabbed his duffel and unzipped it. He turned it upside-down on his bed. Others had brought books, wine, and beer. He had brought his own contraband.

Mixed with his clothes and toiletries, a can of kerosene and a Zippo tumbled onto the cot. He seized both and looked at the other two again. "This is your last chance. Move!"

Sherri seemed to understand everything at that moment. She grabbed Paul's hand and dragged him from the cabin. They gave John and Custer a wide berth and joined Martha and Jen on the path toward the camp's main building. But they still weren't going. They had been caught in the awe of John's movements. It was like watching a fire slowly move toward you. They were antsy, knowing they should move, but their fascinations held them in place.

Hal approached Custer's feet, unscrewing the lid from the kerosene can. The pungent smell of the undead thing knocked him back in time. He saw Billy. He saw Wes. He saw Benny. Their faces. Their blood. The can in his hands sloshed, and he saw the fires of Hell waiting for Custer. "John! Move!"

John paused over the thing, his blade deep in the sliced putrid meat of Custer's chest. He looked down, his lungs heaving. "I think he's dead."

If only judging by the smell, anyone would have agreed. Hal knew better. "John. Get off of there, now."

John nodded. He leaned forward, bracing himself on the blood-soaked earth, then pushing himself up. He turned to Hal as he raised a leg to step over the body. He saw the can in Hal's hand and nodded.

John's face shifted from weary satisfaction to surprise as he fell backward.

Hal watched, only having time to clench his teeth in sympathy. The shine of the metal, the slice of the machete through the air and then through John's calf, bone, and muscle.

Blood pumped from the severed end of John's leg as he drifted toward the ground. Two pumps. Two streams of crimson life, and John was on his back.

Without even getting up, Custer swung the machete down, deep into John's gut. Blood sprayed up as the machete raised and came back down on John's ribs, cracking bone and exposing his lungs to the outside air.

"No!" Hal jumped forward, spinning the can and spilling kerosene across the ground. He poured it over Custer's legs, pelvis, waist, chest.

The killer's sights moved to Hal, and his blade swung. Hal jumped back and tossed the can in Custer's face.

John hitched, unable to pull in a breath. Custer leaned forward to get up, John's blade still deep inside his rotting heart. Hal backed away slowly, opening his Zippo and flicking a flame to life.

Hal watched the rain come down, the monster rise, and his friend dying. He couldn't help John, but he hoped to God, he could avenge him. But Custer was moving slow, probably the slowest Hal had ever seen. He wanted Custer closer, hoping not to catch John in the blaze—hadn't he been through enough? But as the rain fell, Hal worried about each drop of spilled kerosene. If it washed away, this chance would be gone.

Hal had no choice. He shook his head and whispered, "I'm sorry."

He tossed the lighter into Custer as the monster rose. Flames entrenched him. A wave of hot, burning pork and decomposition hit Hal in the face. Then John screamed. It was a weak, breathless howl.

The pool of accelerant had ridden the waves of rainfall directly to John. His legs burned with bright yellow flames. He shook them but couldn't move to put himself out. No air. Losing blood. He fell silent and still in only seconds.

Custer didn't stop moving.

The undead thing finished its rise and stepped toward Hal.

"No!" Hal shouted at the monster. He backed further away, and Custer closed the gap. His clothes blackened, ashed, fell away. His skin sizzled and crisped. It cracked open further, exposing the gray network of rancid flesh, sizzling even there, under thousands of bright, yellow tendrils — but not stopping. His footfalls squished into the dirt, thumping in a heavy, wet, repetitive cadence.

"No!" Hal turned and ran.

Custer swung his machete, whipping through the air and slicing Hal's shirt and back.

Hal kept running. He went to the path and followed the trail. Ahead were the others. Why were they here? Why weren't they further away?

His back ached. He balled his fists and wished he could see and know how bad it was. He glanced behind and saw Custer, not ten paces back, steady, blazing, and smoking like a walking torch.

"Run, goddammit!" Hal scolded the others. They stood at a bend in the path — stood! Why were they just standing there? They watched him come. They had to see Custer behind him.

Paul and Sherri were in front, Jen and Martha behind. As Hal drew within a dozen feet, he watched Paul and Sherri drop to their knees, frozen looks on their faces. They teetered forward and landed face-first on the muddy trail.

Hal lost a step in horror. What the hell was happening there? Custer was behind him; what could have—

Blood soaked Sherri and Paul's backs. Jen and Martha held knives in their grips and smirks on their faces.

"What..." Hal didn't even know what to ask.

Jen raised her palm toward Hal, and the sound of Custer's feet halted.

Hal looked behind him. Custer was, in fact, still. The flames died, relenting to wetness and fuming plumes of smoke.

"Jen?" Hal inched forward, his eyes bouncing between Paul and Sherri, Jen and Martha, then Custer. He felt sorrow widen within himself as the loss of each of these lives hooked into him. "What did you do? You—you stabbed Paul?"

"That's not all." She shook her head, her sweet charm lost in a sea of snide condescension. She swung her blade up and to the side and sliced a gash into Martha's neck. Martha's hands went to her throat as if her fingers could plug the hole that Jen had opened. She dropped to her knees, and Jen went on, "We've been trying to bring Custer back for a decade with that book Jimmy Huber found in his old shack. To bring him under our control. And then we realized why it wasn't working—we needed to bring you, the one that got away—offended him. And wham-bam, the spell was complete."

Jen pointed to her friend, who was covering her throat with her shirt, desperate to stop the bleeding. "Now his power's all mine." She gestured to her belly. "And with this special gift you put inside me, I can have him do anything."

Martha had gone pale. She trembled but slowly raised herself to her knees.

"So, I don't need you anymore," Jen said. She pointed at Hal, and the beast stomped forward again.

Hal turned. He had to see if it was true. Was Custer really under her control? He shook as he rotated and saw the thing take a massive stride toward him.

Hal spun back around to run. She may have been sending

Custer after him, but goddammit, he was still going to try to get away.

Jen shrieked, and when Hal saw her, he found Martha on her knees, her blade in Jen's thigh. She clung to the handle as she slid to the ground, filleting the leg apart. Blood gushed as the cut exposed more and more muscle.

A stone grip fell on Hal's shoulder. It clamped down, and pain radiated through his entire body.

This was it. Custer had him. There was no escaping the grip of that monster. Fear froze his blood. He wondered if Jen was telling the truth. If he was why she was able to bring Custer back—because Hal was the one that got away. And now, he would die too. And maybe he deserved it. If it was his fault, the thing came back. If he'd just had balls and quit, the others would still be alive. Maybe he should just let it happen.

"Bitch!" Jen grabbed Martha's hair and swung her knife. This time it went deep, slashing into her partner's flesh and only stopping at the vertebra.

Custer rotated Hal toward him. He stared into Hal with what were now empty, smoldering eye sockets. But Hal knew there was more. He sensed it. The thing inside that monster could see just fine, and it was staring into him with savage glee.

Another wave of pain ripped through Hal as Custer squeezed his shoulder. He felt the bones creak and snap, and he howled with pain. Everything in that arm went limp and numb, and every other part of his body burned with raging heat.

A rumble came down from above, and as if by a switch, the rain stopped.

Hal looked at the monster's grasp, his mind spinning, desperately wondering how to get away. And his gaze passed the smoldering knife still in Custer's chest.

That was it. There was at least one thing he could do to end this.

Hal grabbed the knife and yanked it free. Globs of burned flesh and black goo drenched the blade. Hal tightened his grip and rocketed the steep tip up into the monster's chin. It crunched as it cut through burnt flesh and cracked as it pierced the thing's skull.

Custer went limp. He dropped forward, giving Hal only a second to get out of the way.

"You think that'll kill him?" Jen shouted, panting. She had wrapped her belt around her leg and was tightening it into a tourniquet. "You just slowed him down, is all."

"Yeah." Hal nodded. "But that may be enough." He reached under the monster's chin, grabbed the handle, and yanked the knife free. With a large step and a downward swing, he plunged it into Jen's chest.

She hitched. Blood flooded from the wound and gurgled in her throat. She grabbed her own knife to swing, but Hal was already gone.

He ran up the path. He ran past the main lodge. He ran to the road. He didn't stop running until dawn, until he saw the sun rise over the mountain ridge and looked down over Custer Falls. Then, he dropped to his knees and cried. Because he knew this wasn't the end.

Acknowledgements

Thank you to everyone who helped spread the word about this anthology from day one.

Thank you to the indie horror community, the readers, reviewers, and authors who hold it all together.

Thank you, Candace Nola, Mort Stone, and Darcy Rose, for your superb job editing these stories.

Thank you, Don Noble, for creating the amazing cover art.

Thank you, Patrick C. Harrison III, Brian McNatt, Gerri R. Gray, John Adam Gosham, Nicholas Stella, Carlton Herzog, Derek Austin Johnson, Vincent Wolfram, and J.D. Kellner for allowing your words to make this book what it is.

Thank you to the families and friends of each author for your support. Without you, none of us would be able to do any of this.

About the Authors

Patrick C. Harrison III

Patrick C. Harrison III (PC3, if you prefer) is an author of horror, splatterpunk, and all forms of speculative fiction, and his works include *Grandpappy*, *A Savage Breed*, *5 Tales That Will Land You in Hell*, and *Cerberus Rising* (with Chris Miller and M. Ennenbach), along with other books; and his short stories can be found in numerous anthologies.

PC3 is also the Splatterpunk Award-winning editor (with Jarod Barbee) of *And Hell Followed* and the editor of several other highly-praised anthologies. Follow PC3's website/blog pc3horror.com for frequent horror movie reviews and updates on forthcoming fiction. Reach out to PC3 regarding writing and editing at pc3@pc3horror.com.

Brian McNatt

Brian McNatt is a longtime author living in the small town of Chickasha, Oklahoma. A Master of Fine Arts from Lindenwood University, he has spent the last decade writing the fantasy adventure series *Legends of Heraldale*, 5 books so far and two more nearing completion. He also wrote the superhero novella *American Kitsune* and has a story in *Books of Horror Vol. 3*.

When not walking the streets of his hometown for inspiration on his next short story, he is keeping an eye on a truly egregious number of Pembroke Corgis, not that he'd have it any other way.

Find out more about Brian McNatt on Twitter, or his website.

Gerri R. Gray

Gerri R. Gray is an American novelist, editor, poet, and short story writer in the horror and dark humor genres. She is the author of ten published books, including her popular debut novel, The Amnesia Girl! (HellBound Books). Her work has appeared in numerous anthologies and literary journals. A part-time antique dealer and former B&B proprietor, Gerri lives in upstate New York in an historic and decidedly haunted nineteenth-century house with her husband and a bevy of spirits.

When she isn't busy creating strange worlds filled with even stranger characters, she can often be found rummaging through antique shops, exploring haunted places, dabbling in the occult or traipsing through old cemeteries with her camera in hand.

Find out more about Gerri R. Gray on Twitter or on Facebook.

John Adam Gosham

John Adam Gosham's fiction has appeared in anthologies such as Hellbound Press's Schlock! Horror!, DBND Publishing's Hookman and Friends, and Colp's Suplex. His comedic collaborations with Charles Norwood can be found in Econoclash Review's Trump Fiction anthology and on the Robot Butt website. He blogs at goshamcity.blogspot.com and Tweets @AdamGosham.

Find out more about John Adam Gosham on Twitter or his blog.

Derek Austin Johnson

Derek Austin Johnson has lived most of his life in the Lone Star State. His work has appeared in *The Horror Zine*, *Rayguns Over Texas!*, *Horror U.S.A.: Texas*, *Campfire Macabre*, *The Dread Machine*, *Generation X-ed*, and *Nightmare Tales*. He lives in Central Texas.

Find out more about Derek Austin Johnson on Twitter, Instagram, Facebook, or his website.

Carlton Herzog

Carlton Herzog is a USAF veteran with a B.A., and J.D. from Rutgers, magna cum laude. He is the former articles editor of the Rutgers Law Review. He sculpts, paints, and antagonizes the extreme right.

Find out more about Carlton Herzog on his Amazon, sciphijournal.org, or Audible.

Nicholas Stella

Nicholas can often be seen scribbling away on scraps of paper at the oddest of hours and in the most random of locations, as inspiration has no respect for time or place.

Vincent Wolfram

Vincent Wolfram is a programmer and writer from north Dallas. He used to write smart reviews about dumb movies for the blog, *The Abyssal Vault*, before he disappeared into obscurity for ten years. His work has been featured in *Bleed Error*. Don't worry, his work hasn't opened a portal to a dark dimension yet.

Find out more about Vincent Wolfram on Twitter or his movie reviews.

J.D. Kellner

J.D. Kellner's affinity for science fiction and fantasy attracted him to the writing world. When not working on his next novel, J.D. writes musings and short stories for his website, jdkellner.com.

Outside of the literary world, J.D. spends his free time with his family and friends enjoying life to the fullest. J.D. Kellner lives with his family in Pittsburgh, Pennsylvania.

Find out more about J.D. on Twitter or his website.

D.W. Hitz

D.W. Hitz lives in Montana, where the inspiring scenery functions as a background character in his work. He is a lover of stories in all mediums. He enjoys writing in the genres of Horror, Supernatural/Paranormal Thriller, and Science Fiction/Fantasy.

Originally from Norfolk, VA, D.W. has degrees in Recording Arts and Web Design and Interactive Media. He has been a creative his entire life. This creativity has driven him in writing, music, and web design and development. He aspires to tell stories that thrill the heart and stimulate the imagination.

When not writing, D.W. enjoys spending time with his family, hiking, camping, and playing with the dogs.

Find out more about D.W. Hitz on his website, Facebook, or Twitter.

What's Next?

Camp Slasher Lake: Volume Two is right around the corner. Make sure to check out another tribute to the glorious slasher movies of the 1980s.

Featuring:
Evisceration Liberation by Jay Bower
Disassembler 3: The Revenge Of Billy Burns by Justin Cawthorne
Fat Fran by Kay Hanifen
Custer's Last Stand by D.W. Hitz
He Hunts at Night in the Boneyard Bog by Brett Mitchell Kent
Borrowed Symbols by Aaron E. Lee
Father's Day by Kevin McHugh
Skulls on the Shelf by Carl R. Moore
Dirty Little Family Secrets by Daniel R. Robichaud
The Gospel According to Teddy by Darren Todd
Ash Wednesday by Mark Wheaton

Still want more slasher fun?

Take a look at **Uncanny Valley Days** by C.J. Sampera, also from Fedowar Press.

Stay in touch

There's always something cooking at Fedowar Press. Sign up for our newsletter at **www.fedowarpress.com** to stay informed or follow us on Facebook or Twitter.

Thank you for reading!

Made in United States
North Haven, CT
25 March 2023